Yakuza Pride

H.J. BRUES

Dreamspinner Press

Published by
Dreamspinner Press
4760 Preston Road
Suite 244-149
Frisco, TX 75034
http://www.dreamspinnerpress.com/

Yakuza Pride

Cover Art by Reese Dante   http://www.reesedante.com

ISBN: 978-1-61581-952-2

Printed in the United States of America
First Edition
June 2011

eBook edition available
eBook ISBN: 978-1-61581-953-9

To Ana, loyal keeper of secrets.

CHAPTER 1

SHIGURE MATSUNAGA stood in front of the large mirror. He felt like an imposter, a street thug posing for a respectable picture in a borrowed tuxedo. Yet the tuxedo fit his broad frame too well to be anything but tailor-made, and the party he was getting ready for was so respectable that even a few police hierarchs would be there to hobnob with successful businessmen, actors, and politicians.

Shigure sighed. He couldn't avoid the oyabun's daughter's wedding party, no matter how hard it'd be to pretend he felt at ease among all those classy people. His friend Oyone had taught him basic table manners a long time ago, but so far, she hadn't managed to instill in him the penchant for chitchat that seemed to keep these parties going.

"Matsunaga-sama," his assistant, Atsushi, called from the door in his usual formal manner. "The car is ready."

He nodded and moved away from the mirror without another look. No point in contemplating the obvious. He was exactly what the rough planes of his face said he was, and the expensive clothes wouldn't fool anyone. There was no need to hide it, anyway, because he had the suspicion his boss wanted him there to remind all those fancy ladder climbers who was behind the money that financed their careers, just in case they forgot for even a second.

Before he reached the *genkan*, the lobby where his dress shoes would be waiting for him, he took a peek into the room where his latest acquisition hung. As always, the simple beauty of the watercolor soothed his nerves, the lonely seascape doing more for his self-confidence than any word could have. It was a mystery, how in spite of his upbringing, he was able to appreciate the subtle nuances of a masterwork. But he could, and that—as Oyone was so fond of repeating—distanced him from the underworld he so rarely left behind.

And she should know, since her establishment catered for the rich and powerful, those who had been swimming in money and beauty all their lives and yet had to trust their art dealers to choose the pieces in their collections, just as they trusted the appearance of their own houses to the tastes of renowned interior decorators.

Shigure shook his head. Nobody dictated how his house was to look, what clothes he had to wear, or which paintings he hung on his walls. The oyabun's guests could look down their noses at him all they liked. He knew where he stood, and it wasn't a bad place to be for someone born in the gutter.

KENNETH HARRIS wandered over to the buffet table. He shouldn't have come. His friend, Ryū, had insisted that he wanted Ken here, that he enjoyed showing off his personal gaijin. But, as Ken had expected, Ryū's personal foreigner was all but invisible in this group of powerful Japanese. Only a few artsy types had tried to appear polite, and just because being able to keep up a conversation in English gave them an aura of fashionable cosmopolitanism. The rest, though, didn't even feel the need to pretend they cared.

Ken sighed. He was used to it. Growing up in Japan hadn't been easy, not with his blond hair, round eyes, and big nose. He'd always been the ugly gaijin kid, the perfect target for bullies. Ironically enough, when his family returned home, he found himself on the outside of things anyway, at odds with a new set of rules no one bothered to spell out for him, his weird eyes still making him different where his looks should have been average. In time, he would discover he was weird in other, less acceptable areas of his private life, those that, if he'd remained in Japan, wouldn't even have been frowned upon. Just his luck to be in the wrong country no matter what he did.

And here he was now, back in Japan, once again standing alone in the middle of a crowded room, a very expensive and yet very ugly room. He couldn't for the life of him understand why the Japanese were so fond of shucking off the traditional beauty of their simple decoration to favor any kind of plastic eyesore. They must think modernity is in the materials, that you can just sprinkle metal and cement about and produce Western art.

He studied the flower arrangements for a while. They were fine in a too-rigid sense of harmony that he bet was very far from the original free spirit of ikebana. He could almost see the textbook diagrams they'd come from, but, hey, he was a gaijin, he sure didn't get the convolutions of Japanese culture.

What Ken really wanted to do right now was look at all those beautiful faces around him, the only natural things the Japanese couldn't alter so easily in spite of that dreadful fad of plastic surgery spreading among the young. Yet he knew here, more than anywhere else, watching people was considered rude, and he contented himself with furtive glances every now and then.

Even as discreet as Ken thought he was being, the last time his eyes had met another man's, he'd received a frown. He guessed he'd been staring, but he couldn't help it; the guy really stood out. Every man at the reception wore an expensive tuxedo, but the stranger who'd caught Ken's eye had the perfect body to fill the suit in all the right places, his broad shoulders and powerful legs giving him a solid physical presence that most of the other guests lacked.

Ken had watched the man move about with a grace that belied his burly constitution, and he'd been sure it was the practice of some martial art that gave the stranger's movements that kind of elegant self-containment. He looked dangerous, too, his face an incongruous war mask in a wedding reception, his eyes sending a clearly hostile message, almost a challenge to anyone foolhardy enough to meet them. Not that Ken was foolhardy, but he had a keen eye for improbable beauty, and he couldn't help getting lost in its contemplation wherever he found it; it was what Ryū called his "artistic trances." Not everybody was as patient with his eccentricities as his childhood friend, though, and the frown that had creased the stranger's forehead was testimony to it.

As soon as Ken realized he'd been staring, he turned quickly away, fixing his gaze on the first innocuous thing he could find, his heart galloping as he pretended to study the already melting ice sculpture on a nearby table.

Christ. How could he be so stupid? It was no secret that the party's host was the leader of a powerful yakuza *kumi*, one of the local gangs of mobsters, and looking a yakuza in the eye was a definite no-no, however stunning the man was. Ken should know, too, for many of

Ryū's family business associates came from the shadier sides of Japanese economy.

But even then, anxious as he was about the possible consequences of his breach of etiquette, he couldn't help really watching the ice sculpture in all its melting ugliness, his mind already finding ways to include its nightmarish quality in a visual composition that he might use later in one of his illustrations. He was a lost case.

SHIGURE looked around, trying to hide his boredom behind a severe look. It worked in its own way, most people steering clear of him, save those who dealt with him on a regular basis, like that kid Nishimura Ryū, who was so bold anyway, Shigure had the impression he'd talk an axe murderer into borrowing his weapon of choice. Now that Ryū had moved away, though, Shigure was left on his own to study the crowd.

There were all kinds of people milling about, with even a few gaijin thrown in the lot, their mostly blond heads sticking out over the sea of black-haired short humanity. Yet Shigure's eye had been following a particular blond head that didn't stand out, its owner as short and light-framed as the Japanese around him. Or maybe he was Japanese, one of those trendy youths who bleached their hair to death. Shigure couldn't tell, since the man was facing away from him.

The youngster seemed to be alone, and Shigure was amused to see that he was watching the crowd just as Shigure was, one hand curled around a tumbler he wasn't really drinking from. Something in the way those fingers held the glass spoke of an inner strength that caught Shigure's attention. He was used to judging an opponent by his grip on the *bokken*, the wooden sword that had taken the place of the lethal katana in trainings, and the foreigner's long fingers seemed to exert just the right amount of pressure to hold the weight and yet be loose enough for the hand to move with ease. If the tumbler had been a sword, the blond man would have wielded it like a master.

The foreigner was now studying one of the lifeless flower arrangements that decorated the place. As his profile came into view, Shigure could tell he was indeed a foreigner, his nose betraying his Western origin. Not that it was an ugly nose, for it was rather delicate by gaijin standards, and Shigure always took his time observing things before dismissing them as ugly. That was an advantage when it came to judging art. Because he didn't know the names of the famous artists, he could simply focus on the painting in front of him and decide whether he liked it or not on his own terms.

When the foreigner turned to look around, Shigure decided he definitely liked the face that came into full view. In fact, he liked it so much that he felt the tingle of anticipation that always came to him when he discovered a piece he wanted to own, or rather, needed to own, since beautiful things seemed to wake a hunger in him that left him restless till the object was in his possession.

He drank in the alien features of the young man, the tall forehead framed by soft curls, the straight lines of his brows, the big eyes, the full, sensual lips. Then those eyes met his, and Shigure frowned, catching something slightly disquieting about them. Could they be of two different colors? Was that even possible? Maybe he'd wanted to create a shocking effect by wearing contacts of contrasting shades, but he didn't give off that kind of vibe. He looked to be more on the shy side, the way he quickly looked down and turned around when he saw Shigure watching him.

The yakuza debated what to do. He wanted to get closer and take a good look at those eyes, but it was a gaijin he was thinking about. Even if he approached him, what was he going to say? Shigure couldn't speak a word of English, and in his experience, most foreigners didn't go further than "hai" and "arigatō" in their knowledge of Japanese.

The gaijin stood in front of the ice sculpture of something that might have resembled a swan some hours before, but now it just looked like a pudgy ball of melting slime with wings. Shigure's frown deepened. It wasn't like him to step down from a challenge. He knew it was more than the other man being a foreigner. If he was here, he had to be one of those rich kids with a high position in the local branch of a foreign company, granted by a degree from a prestigious university and powerful family connections. If it were so, he'd be way out of Shigure's league.

He almost groaned aloud. He wouldn't be in the ballroom of one of the most expensive hotels in Japan if he'd kept up that attitude. Since he was a kid, he'd always known what he wanted, and fought for it with all his might, no matter how out of reach his goals had appeared at the time. What did he have to lose now? The gaijin would probably take one look at Shigure's face and run for his life, anyway.

His mind made up, Shigure nodded to himself. He didn't even notice the way people opened a path for him as if they sensed a predator moving among them. He was just focused on the slim figure in front of him, his eyes undressing the slender body as he got closer. When they stood side by side, he saw that the foreigner was slightly shorter than him, his hair a fine halo of bright curls, and he almost hummed in appreciation.

As the seconds ticked by, Shigure raked his brain for something to say, his eyes fixed on the melting ice bird as if waiting for inspiration. But just then the foreigner spoke, his voice low enough that only Shigure could hear him.

"Niwatori mitai, aitsu."

Shigure blinked at the young man's perfect Japanese, and then his words sank in—*Looks like a hen, that guy*—and Shigure laughed in surprise. He turned to find the foreigner looking at him with a shy smile on those kissable lips.

Shigure bowed and introduced himself in Japanese. "My name is Matsunaga Shigure."

To his delight, the gaijin bowed back to the same exact degree and answered with the proper formula, even adding the extra U to his family name to pronounce it the Japanese way. "I am Harisu Ken. Pleased to meet you, Matsunaga-san."

"Your Japanese is very good, Harisu-san."

"You're too kind. I grew up in Japan, so I manage a little. But please call me Ken."

"Ken as in Kenji?" Shigure asked.

"It's Kenneth, actually, but my friends call me Kenshin."

Shigure noticed that Ken avoided starting his sentences with a negative, in a very Japanese way. He nodded his approval before asking, "After Uesugi Kenshin?"

Ken hesitated, and Shigure could see a slight blush darkening his cheeks at the mention of the great leader of ancient times.

"After Himura Kenshin," the gaijin finally said. Shigure schooled his face into a blank expression that prompted Ken to explain. "You know, red hair, ugly scar on his cheek—"

Shigure had to stifle a chuckle. "You mean the manga character." He didn't make it a question. He could understand why they'd given Ken the name of the fiery assassin with a noble heart: where Kenshin had his red hair to speak of his demonic ability with a sword, Kenneth had big, mismatched eyes that gave him a similarly alien look.

They were truly different, those eyes, one brown and the other green, but Shigure found that odd trait made Ken's beauty exceptional, unique. Perfect symmetry only dulled aesthetic pleasure; contrasts enhanced any feature dramatically, allowing the eye to explore every rich nuance, and Ken's face was an irregular landscape Shigure'd never tire of contemplating.

The yakuza knew he wasn't going to stop until that beauty belonged to him, no matter what it took. And as always, the decision made all his previous anxiety slip away. He knew exactly what he wanted, and he would fight for it. It was that simple.

CHAPTER 2

KEN looked up into Shigure's dark eyes. There was amusement in them, but also something that Ken couldn't put a name to, something both attractive and dangerous, a hunger that Ken found difficult to relate to himself. And yet Shigure was looking at him as if he were trying to decide what parts of Ken's body would be especially tender to sink his teeth into.

He tried to focus back on the conversation. "My friend Ryū and I used to love those Edo stories, and we would swing our *shinai* at each other yelling dialogues from the manga. Somehow I ended up being Kenshin. Don't ask me why."

Shigure smiled. "Maybe because your friend always lost against you?"

Ken blinked at the big man. How could he possibly have guessed that? No, Shigure was just being polite or, most likely, joking at the improbable picture of a gaijin besting a native at a sword match. Before he could answer, Shigure asked, "Do you still swing a sword?"

"Yeah. I love it. Keeps me focused when my mind strays."

Shigure tilted his head to study him, and Ken felt anxious under the sharp gaze. He wasn't used to people looking at him that way. Sure, his mismatched eyes got some stares, but everybody tended to look quickly away, as they would with a disability that they felt both curious and disgusted about.

"Where does your mind stray to, Kenshin-san?"

Oh God. Ken couldn't help shuddering at the way Shigure said it, the way Ken's nickname rolled on his tongue like a very tasty morsel. It was the name only a few close friends gave him, too, and it made the whole sentence feel like an intimate brush of fingers over naked skin.

Shigure had noticed Ken's shudder, and for a moment his eyes grew darker, just before a hint of worry crossed them. "Are you cold, Kenshin-san?"

Christ. If he kept that up, Ken was going to burst into flames. As it was, the heat on his cheeks would soon be enough to melt what was left of the ice sculpture. He just hoped his tuxedo would hide another, less acceptable reaction, because the fact that the Japanese didn't regard homosexuality as an unnatural perversion did not mean that particular Japanese would be pleased to be the object of his lust.

"It's that bird thing," he tried to joke, though his voice sounded strange even to his own ears. "It's giving me the chills."

Shigure chuckled, but something in his eyes told Ken he hadn't bought it for even a second. "Yeah, it doesn't look like a bird anymore. It gets scarier by the minute."

Ken was relieved that the Japanese had followed the joke, and he found himself admiring the gentle consideration underlying Shigure's every move. He wasn't just being polite to a foreigner, but outright delicate, as if Ken were made of some faulty foreign material that would break in his hands if he weren't careful handling it. And damn if Ken didn't want to be handled by those strong hands.

He turned to the ice sculpture to hide the emotions bubbling inside him, and saw that the bird seemed to have grown talons, the wings the only trait identifying the awkward creature as one with the ability to fly.

"It looks like a Harpy right now," he said.

"A what?"

Shit. He'd done it again. Shigure would think he was trying to sound clever. Ken wasn't, really, but he couldn't help the way his mind searched about in his own personal image bank to pick something from the most obscure source. And he kept blurting those things out, even though the best he usually got in return were blank looks.

"It's a mythical creature." Ken tried to wave the whole thing away. "Just an ugly-looking beast."

Seemingly unfazed, Shigure kept asking. "What's it like?"

"Like a…," Ken stammered. He was no good with words. "Like a woman with wings."

Shigure raised a brow, obviously getting the wrong angelic picture. Ken hurried to add, "I mean, like a beast with claws and all, but with a woman's head and breast."

Now the Japanese frowned, and Ken made a frustrated sound, wishing he could just draw the damn thing and show it to Shigure. As soon as the thought crossed his mind, he remembered the tiny notebook he always carried with him, just in case an idea bloomed in the most unexpected place.

He reached into the inner pocket of his jacket and pulled out the notebook with the small pencil attached. In a few quick strokes, he drew a rough sketch of a Harpy as they appeared in the most terrifying pictures he could remember, and then offered the notebook to Shigure.

The Japanese took it in his hands as he would a card with Ken's name on it, carefully studying every single line as if they represented Ken's distilled essence and should be treated with due respect. When he finally looked up at Ken, the American saw something different in the other man's eyes, something Ken would have called admiration if he didn't know how absurd it'd be.

"You're an artist, Kenshin-san." Shigure said it as if he were stating a fact of life, but with a touch of pleased recognition, just like someone who'd pulled the curtains open to a winter morning and exclaimed in quiet awe, "It's snowing."

Ken felt a different kind of heat at Shigure's words, not anymore the scorching proximity of flames, but the soft warmth of a blanket wrapped around his shoulders. He fought the urge to close his eyes and savor the moment.

"It's just an outline," Ken mumbled to break the embarrassing spell, but Shigure went on to up the ante.

"May I keep it?"

Ken stared at the Japanese. Was he serious? He wanted to keep a poor sketch of a hideous creature? Shigure held his eyes, serious as a heart attack, and Ken gave up trying to figure out his intentions.

"Of course," Ken said, barely hiding his befuddlement.

Shigure's expression brightened as he gave the notebook back for Ken to tear the drawing from it. When Ken did, the Japanese bowed his thanks. "Arigatō gozaimasu."

"You're welcome, Matsunaga-san," the American replied with an answering bow.

"Please call me Shigure."

Ken was about to say something when a familiar voice called, "Hey, Kenshin, you've met my good friend Matsunaga-san!"

Ken had to smile at Ryū's expansive charm. His friend always appeared to be in his element, no matter the circumstances, and Ken really envied his easy way with people.

Shigure bowed in greeting, his expression only faintly amused, but as he straightened, something seemed to dawn on him, and he turned to look at Ken.

"Nishimura-san is the friend you used to beat at kendo?" he asked candidly.

Oh shit. Of course Ryū pouted. "You didn't have to tell him how clumsy I am, Kenshin."

"I—" Ken fumbled for something to appease his friend, but Shigure cut his efforts short.

"He didn't tell me, Nishimura-san, but you know Battōsai Kenshin would never lose to the likes of us."

Ryū smiled and threw his arm around Ken's shoulders. "Not against me, anyway. I'm a klutz. But I bet he'd have a hard time beating you, Matsunaga-san. The rumor is you're a modern Musashi."

Shigure laughed. "Rumors are just that, and you shouldn't believe all that you hear. But I'd certainly be honored to cross swords with Kenshin-san."

Ken smiled until he saw the two Japanese looking expectantly at him. Weren't they talking about the fictional character anymore? He turned to his friend Ryū for help.

"He's challenging you to a match, you *baka*." Ryū didn't even bother to call him dork in a language Shigure wouldn't understand, and he just went on as if Ken weren't there beside him. "He accepts your kind invitation, Matsunaga-san. He's staying with me, so feel free to call me to arrange the match. And now if you don't mind, I must borrow my friend for a moment. There's a certain lady I want to impress with my knowledge of the gaijin tongue."

"I'll be sure to call," Matsunaga said with a parting bow, and Ken barely had time to bow back before Ryū dragged him away. His friend wouldn't stop till they'd crossed the French doors to the garden outside.

"You're an airhead, Kenshin," Ryū finally said, switching to English. "Have you any idea who you were just chatting so amiably with?"

Ken blinked his confusion. "Matsunaga Shigure?"

"Yeah, that's his name all right," Ryū said with a huff. "But do you know who he is, or rather, what he does?"

Ken shook his head, embarrassed, and his friend answered his own question for him. "Matsunaga is a captain in the Shinagawa-gumi, one of the most powerful gangs in Tokyo, with branches all over the country and on the continent."

Ken cursed aloud, and Ryū smiled at his contrite expression. "Damn, Kenshin, I let you out of my sight for a minute, and you manage to engage in conversation with a yakuza." Ryū chuckled, patting Ken's back. "And you even made the stony-faced bastard laugh. I wish you'd seen the way his men stared. I bet they'd never heard their boss laugh before."

"His men are here?" Ken asked in surprise.

"Of course. Yakuza like to show off some of their entourage, just as feudal lords would, though I'm sure Matsunaga doesn't need their protection. It's rumored that he uses his *bokken* for more than practice, and you know how deadly those wooden swords can be."

"Then why on earth did you accept his challenge on my behalf?" Ken almost squeaked. "Or were you both just being polite?"

Ryū gave him a mischievous smile. "Have I already told you what an airhead you are?"

Ken rolled his eyes, a little peeved. "Yeah, I know I'm a dumb gaijin, so just explain it to me in simple words."

"Don't get mad, Kenshin. I enjoy teasing you, that's all."

Ken relented, as he always did. It was impossible to be angry with Ryū for more than two heartbeats. "You expect Matsunaga to forget about the match?"

"Definitely not," Ryū answered. "But you can't back down from such a challenge."

Ken gave him an uncomprehending stare, and his friend tried to explain it further. "It doesn't matter whether you're defeated or not in the end, but if a yakuza challenges you, you must accept. It's like one of those old Western duels—even though you know the other is faster than you, you must face him if you don't want to lose everybody's respect."

"Even if the other kills you."

Ryū shrugged. "Japanese value honor over life, and yakuza hold a tight grip on tradition, even though most of them have adapted to the changing times, in appearance at least."

"Uh-huh."

Ryū laughed openly now. "Don't worry. Matsunaga wouldn't hurt any friend of mine. It'd be bad for business."

"That's some real comfort, thank you."

Ryū turned suddenly serious. "You know I wouldn't do anything to hurt you, don't you?"

Ken met his friend's eyes, studying that gorgeous face he'd always admired: the high cheek bones, the slightly upturned nose, the almond-shaped eyes with their long lashes, the smooth skin. Ryū was as pretty as a girl, something Ken took care not to mention, even though his friend didn't have any masculinity issues. Ryū's success with women kept him well reassured in that area.

"I know," Ken finally said.

Ryū gave him a bright smile and shoved him playfully. "Good. Now go mingle with guests who don't belong to any gang, okay?"

"Okay, I'll avoid baseball fans from now on," he offered with his best innocent expression.

"Dork."

"Baka," Ken countered, knowing that the trade of insults in two languages was one of their favorite pastimes since childhood. Sure enough, Ryū was about to answer in kind when feminine giggles made him turn his head. Ken followed his friend's gaze to a group of young women gossiping nearby, and fought the urge to roll his eyes.

"Go to them, Don Juan-san," Ken said. His friend laughed and shook a warning finger at Ken as he moved away. Ken only nodded, no words needed to convey Ryū's concern for his well-being. It had always been that way, his friend probably the only one in Ken's life who really cared what happened to him, gaijin or no.

SHIGURE sighed when he saw one of his men smoking in the hallway. He hated the smell of tobacco, for it brought back memories he didn't want to revisit, especially the recurring image of his father pilfering money from his wife's purse to buy the cigarettes that would kill him in the end. Maybe because of that, because his father had been a sorry excuse for a man, Shigure always associated tobacco with weakness, no matter how tough kids thought it made them look.

His man's eyes went wide when he saw Shigure approaching him, and he quickly crushed the cigarette under his shoe.

"Shit, I'm sorry, boss."

It was Kinosuke, the youngest of his deputies, a quick-witted guy who Shigure knew would get far in the organization. He had a foul mouth, but was very responsible, a rare trait to be found among Kinosuke's generation of over-spoiled, computer-game-fed, despondent kids.

Shigure smiled. Being surrounded by men barely past their teenage years made him feel ancient at thirty-seven. He wondered how old Kenshin was. He couldn't tell with gaijin, but his guess was Kenshin must be in his early twenties. The American could be older, but the curiosity in his eyes made him look quite young, almost a child, gaping in amazement at the strange world around him. That was probably the reason he drew so well, his strokes bold and compelling in spite of his obvious shyness, everything in him speaking of a hidden passionate nature that screamed to be unearthed. And Shigure was just dying to dig deeper under those protective layers to get to the true Kenshin underneath.

"Boss?"

He saw Kinosuke's concerned look. Yeah, the gaijin was turning into a full-blown obsession, even though he'd met him barely an hour before.

"Are you enjoying the party, Kinosuke?"

"I'd enjoy it better if they weren't looking down their fucking noses at us."

Shigure nodded. "They have to pretend to despise what we are, but they wouldn't be here in the first place if they didn't need us. Just keep in mind who's hosting this party, and it'll make you see things quite differently."

"You're damn right, boss," Kinosuke said with a smirk, and Shigure patted his shoulder as he moved past him.

When he was a few steps away, Shigure said without turning, "And don't stand smoking in the hallway like some boorish yakuza." He could hear Kinosuke's laughter as he pushed the door to the restroom.

Shigure's eyes went straight to the slender figure bent over one of the sinks. He would have recognized that body anywhere, even if he hadn't been able to see the blond hair falling forward as far as its short length allowed. He went to the paper towel dispenser and pulled one to bring back to Kenshin, who seemed oblivious to his presence.

The American finally lifted his head, water droplets shining on his white skin, full lips parted to let out the breath he'd been holding, round eyes meeting Shigure's in the wall mirror and going wide in surprise. It was the sexiest thing the Japanese had seen in quite a while, and he decided to go for bold, sensing that Kenshin needed to be pushed.

Shigure took a step forward, effectively crowding Kenshin against the sink, and reached out to grab the American's chin and force him to turn his face. When those weird eyes looked up at him, the yakuza searched them, finding a more than reasonable fear but also—as he'd expected—big doses of curiosity and excitement mixed together to create a deep need, a craving that called loudly to Shigure's instincts.

Having seen what he needed to see, the Japanese used the paper towel to softly draw every contour of the upturned face, watching avidly as the pupils fixed on him dilated into big black pools of desire. Yes. The gaijin was beautiful, even more beautiful when he let go, though Shigure suspected he'd barely scratched the surface of the mask Kenshin wore. It didn't matter. He had all the time in the world.

Right now he needed a taste, though, an appetizer to keep his hunger in check for all the assaults he knew it would take to conquer Kenshin's elusive beauty.

Shigure dropped the paper towel and used his free hand to take hold of Kenshin's hip and guide the slender body toward the stalls behind them. The American turned without resistance, letting the bigger man lead him into one of the stalls where the yakuza shoved him against the door as soon as he locked it.

Shigure's mouth closed on Kenshin's hungrily, his whole body pressing hard against the gaijin, reveling in the telltale arousal he could feel against his thigh. Kenshin's lips parted for him, a sexy little noise escaping his throat when Shigure's tongue plunged in, making the yakuza grunt and push his hands down Kenshin's back to grab his ass and press the slim body even closer to him.

Kenshin's arms snaked around Shigure's neck, and he all but crawled on top of the yakuza, his tongue battling Shigure's for all he was worth, desperate noises pouring out of him as if he couldn't get enough, as if his hunger would kill him if he didn't take what he needed.

Shigure broke the kiss to study Kenshin's face, the frustrated noise the American let out making him smile wildly. Yeah. This was more like it. The creature in his arms was starting to show teeth, big bright eyes of impossible shades drinking him in, swollen lips moving closer to recapture Shigure's, strong fingers pulling him down to get to him and eat him alive.

The yakuza shifted to make his stance more stable and lifted Kenshin off the floor. The sexy gaijin immediately wrapped his long legs around Shigure, moaning low as their erections pressed together, driving Shigure so crazy that he slammed the slender back against the door and bent forward to bite Kenshin's neck even as he ground hard against him. Kenshin let out a choked cry of pain, belied by the way his hips rolled to meet Shigure's thrusts, blood pooling under the soft skin to leave a proprietary mark, the first one of many the yakuza intended to tattoo all over Kenshin's body.

Just imagining that sweet body exposed before his eyes pushed Shigure so close to the edge that he had to bite his lip to stop from coming. It was useless, though, because right then Kenshin surged forward to sink white teeth in the yakuza's tender earlobe, and the sharp sting of the bite, the full pressure of the body against his, the way it made their erections collide with the most delicious ache, brought Shigure to climax in long shudders that rocked Kenshin against the door again and again, those amazing eyes completely focused on Shigure, taking in every change in his expression as pleasure roared out of him.

Kenshin seemed to wait for him to come down completely before abandoning himself to his own climax, as if watching Shigure in the throes of pleasure were more important to him than reaching his own orgasm. That confirmed in the yakuza the notion that he'd found something truly special in the gaijin who now shook beautifully against him, his white throat exposed as he threw back his head, his body arching in pleasure, his eyes closed as he bit his lip to prevent the cry that fought to come out.

When Kenshin finally slumped against his chest, Shigure held him close, softly nuzzling his neck, soaking in his warmth, sniffing at his skin to catch his scent. The American wasn't wearing cologne, and Shigure strongly approved. He could really smell Kenshin, the mix of salty wet sand, clean sweat, and passionate sex that made him feel as if they'd been making love on an empty beach instead of humping away in the men's room of a posh hotel.

Kenshin's legs slid to the floor, and his arms disentangled from Shigure's neck rather reluctantly. To the yakuza's surprise, the American tugged at the pristine white handkerchief peeking out of his jacket front pocket, and with his eyes down, offered it to Shigure. God. That was so sweet that Shigure couldn't help himself from crushing Kenshin against him one more time, the smaller American clinging to him fiercely, both their cocks obviously interested in another round as they sprang back to life against each other.

Shigure took a deep breath and broke the embrace gently. Kenshin's eyes searched his like those of an anxious puppy. "Kenshin-san," he whispered as he stroked the soft blond hair. "If I stay with you one more second, I won't be able to hold back, and this is not the place for what I intend to do to you."

Kenshin closed his eyes and whimpered softly, his reaction making it really hard for Shigure to control himself. He groaned and moved away from Kenshin.

"Here," he said as he offered his own handkerchief to the American and chuckled. "Now we have another excuse to see each other. This handkerchief is a family heirloom, and I definitely need to have it back."

Kenshin beamed brightly at him. "Of course, Matsunaga-san. I'll be sure to give it back as soon as possible."

"Excellent. And please call me Shigure."

Kenshin moved in the constricted space to make room for the yakuza to leave, and as the Japanese walked out the door, the American bowed. "Shigure-san."

Shigure fought the urge to walk back in and scoop Kenshin into his arms, but they'd been lucky enough that no one else had entered the restroom. He couldn't risk exposing himself at the oyabun's party.

He bowed briskly and walked away as fast as he could, not even stopping to clean the mess in his underwear. He'd find another restroom. He just couldn't stay another minute beside Kenshin without touching him.

CHAPTER 3

KEN studied the man he'd just drawn. It was supposed to be a thief from the story he was illustrating, but he looked suspiciously close to a certain yakuza for Ken's comfort.

He chuckled. Maybe he should keep it that way, make the thief look dark and menacing and yet so attractive the kid in the story would find it difficult to stay away from him. Wasn't that the point of the tale, to show that sometimes appearances can be deceitful, that a thief might turn out to be a good person while your nice next-door neighbor wouldn't move a finger to help you? Yeah, well, that was the problem with children's books—they were great because they had nothing to do with reality.

Ken sighed. He couldn't get Shigure out of his mind. Every time he remembered what they'd done in that hotel restroom, Ken would go from embarrassed to horny in the blink of an eye. God, the way that man kissed, the way those big hands had felt on him. It had been the best sex Ken had had in a while, and they had been fully dressed, just rubbing away at each other in a toilet stall.

Ken sighed. It didn't really matter. He'd enjoyed himself, and Ryū had left the party with two pretty girls, so Ken hadn't even had to hide the obvious signs of what had transpired between Shigure and him from his friend. The bite mark on his neck had later given him the chance to go for a little cosplay and dress up in gothic style—with a most convenient choker over the bruised skin—so everything was perfect, save for the way his ears kept perking up every time Ryū's phone rang, as if Shigure would call any moment to arrange the promised sword match.

It'd been a whole week since the party, and the yakuza had probably forgotten, or, most likely, he'd never even considered the challenge anything but a joke. Well, it'd be his loss, then.

"That's one scary face you're making."

Ken almost jumped off his stool at the sound of Ryū's voice. "Jesus, don't creep up on me like that."

His friend chuckled and came closer to touch the spikes on Ken's hair. He'd kept on the gothic look even though the mark on his neck was fading. It was his own act of defiance, and he kept telling himself Shigure wouldn't even look at him if he saw Ken as he was now, in skinny black pants and a ragged T-shirt, black lace choker circling his neck, studded jewelry all over his thin arms, and black eyeliner making his eyes look even weirder than usual.

"I love the way you look like this, Kenshin. And you don't even need makeup or contacts."

Ken snorted. "Yeah, I have the complexion of a geisha and the eyes of Marilyn Manson."

Ryū ignored him and pulled out his cell phone. Like a good Japanese, his friend always carried the latest model, and he hadn't any reservations when it came to using the camera in it.

"Make a spooky face like before," Ryū ordered as he aimed the phone at Ken.

"No problem," Ken answered. All he had to do was think about Shigure not calling and he would get pissed enough to look gothic-scary.

"Great, Kenshin, keep it up," his friend said, as he clicked away in delight.

"Come on, Ryū, stop already. You're blinding me with that flash."

Right then the cell launched the first notes of a J-pop song, and his friend switched to Japanese to take the call.

"Moshi moshi."

Ken shook his head and turned to study the outline on his desk. It was nice, having his friend's voice as background noise, the string of Japanese words comforting in its childhood reminiscences. He understood everything that Ryū said, but it was easier for him to disconnect from actual meanings and just let the flow of familiar sounds lull him into a cozy state of mind that lasted up to the moment a certain name left Ryū's lips.

"Of course, Matsunaga-san." His friend smiled impishly at Ken's startled look. "Though you might change your mind if you could see him right now."

Ken waved a warning finger at his friend, but he realized too late it only served to encourage Ryū.

"Wait. You *can* see him."

Ken sprang from his stool and reached for Ryū's cell, but his friend's fingers went on pressing buttons furiously even as he ducked.

"Don't you dare," Ken whispered, but his alleged friend showed him the display window on the phone as it slowly blinked with the word "sending."

Ken hid his face in his hands, surprised at the intensity of shame he felt. He loved radically changing the way he looked, letting his disguised selves last for only one day or two, as if he were a shape-shifter with identity problems, but somehow, he didn't want Shigure to know that about him. It made him feel like a phony.

"Yeah, I'll pass the phone to him."

Ken looked up to see Ryū handing him the cell phone with a smirk. He sighed and took it from him. As soon as he put it to his ear, Shigure's grave voice came from the other end.

"Kenshin-san?"

It seemed he couldn't help shuddering every time that man pronounced his nickname.

"I'm here, Matsunaga-san."

"It's Shigure, remember?" He didn't wait for Ken's answer. "I'm sorry I marked you where everybody can see. I'll be more careful from now on."

Ken blinked. Shigure had guessed the reason for his spooky clothes? And had he just said he'd be careful "from now on"?

"It's all right, Shigure-san," he managed to say in a hoarse voice.

"Your friend has agreed to drive you here on Friday. Is that okay?"

"Yeah. Perfect."

"Good. Just don't wear what you're wearing right now." Ken felt his cheeks heat. Of course a conservative yakuza would hate seeing a

guy in jewelry and eyeliner. He felt so ashamed he almost didn't catch
Shigure's next words when they came as a throaty whisper. "You look
good enough to eat, and I don't want to have to scold my men for
ogling. See you, Kenshin-san."

He would have kept the phone plastered to his ear if Ryū hadn't
taken it from him, chuckling. "Don't be so surprised. I told you a
yakuza would always follow through on his words."

"What did he mean you'll drive me there?"

"He meant to his place in Setagaya." Ryū's smile widened.
"You're gonna love it. He lives in one of those old clan houses with an
incredible garden, all walled up and closed by an ancient gate."

Ken couldn't hide his astonishment. "How has he managed that in
this cramped city? Was it his family's house?"

Ryū snorted at the improbable picture of a yakuza having that
kind of family to inherit from. Yeah. Ken knew most yakuza came
from the lower ranks of Japanese society, but still, the way land prices
kept rising, if you got hold of that kind of acreage, you'd be sure to tear
down any ancient structure surviving to build tall—and profitable—
apartment buildings.

"It seems Matsunaga convinced his oyabun—the don of the
Shinagawa gang—to keep the house as a training place for new
recruits," Ryū explained, "so there's always a number of the
organization's men living there, doing all kind of housekeeping chores
while they learn the ropes, just as they say it was in the old times."

"Wow." Ken was already imagining a traditional Japanese house
with its beautiful garden, hard-faced men walking about in the casual,
cotton *yukata* garments, hand-polishing wooden floors, carrying lumber
to heat the collective bath, or training in the dojo.

"Don't get any ideas, Kenshin." His friend's voice brought him
back to earth. "They won't be keen on you sketching away as soon as
you cross their door."

Ken blushed. Ryū knew him too well. He tried to change the
subject. "Have you been there often?"

"Just the one time. Yakuza don't trust easily, so you must be
grateful for being allowed inside the premises without so much as a
background check. I don't expect any other gaijin to have set foot there
before you, either."

"It's because I'm your friend, Ryū. Matsunaga seems to trust you."

Ryū shook his head. "It's more than that. He trusts *you* for some reason. The fact that you're my friend only warrants that you won't be in danger while you're in their hands."

"That doesn't sound too comforting, you know."

Ryū gave him a serious look. "I wouldn't let you go there if I thought you'd be in any danger, but I want you to tread carefully around those men. Just watch your step, Kenshin, that's all I'm saying."

Ken reached out to squeeze his friend's arm. "Thank you for worrying, Ryū. I promise I'll be careful."

"That doesn't sound too comforting, you know," Ryū mimicked him with a smirk.

"Oh thank you very much for placing so much confidence in me." Ken pouted at his friend, who now laughed openly.

"What can I say? You have your head in the clouds half the time, and the other half, you're too busy drawing what you just saw up there."

Ken shoved his friend playfully. "Come on. It's not that bad."

"No? Have you forgotten that time we left together for school and ended up in two different schools—with you of course in the wrong one?"

Ken tried hard not to laugh. "It wasn't my fault if the girl next door made you forget we were walking to school together."

"Yeah, well, but I still managed to get there. You got to Shiouran High instead." Ryū chuckled. "And even went into a classroom and sat at a desk. Damn, Kenshin, didn't you notice there were no girls around?"

Ken shrugged. "I just thought my class felt especially right that morning."

Ryū shook his head. "You're crazy."

"No. I'm gay."

His friend cracked up, his arm going around Ken's shoulder and pulling him close. "That's right—you're my *gay-jin*."

Ken chuckled, leaning against his friend. It was true Ryū had taken him under his wing from the very first moment. For some unfathomable reason, he'd always wanted Ken to be his personal gaijin. Ken looked into those smiling, tilted black eyes and wondered how he'd never developed a crush on that gorgeous Japanese male. He supposed Ryū was too close to a brother for him to see his friend in any other way, and he guessed he was lucky for the heartbreak it'd saved him.

"What are you thinking?" Ryū asked, squeezing his shoulder.

He just shrugged, blushing so obviously that he couldn't help the laughter that escaped him.

Ryū's brows went up. "Are you trying to pull the hermetic Japanese on me? Because I'm sorry to tell you, dude, but you're not even Asian."

"Well, I was born on the East Coast—that's the Far East for you, you know."

Ryū rolled his eyes, but then he fixed those black coals on him and studied Ken for a long moment. "Are you worried about the match?"

Ken sobered and thought about it. Crossing swords with Shigure didn't bother him too much, even if he lost—which was the most probable outcome. What made Ken anxious was seeing the big man again, but he didn't want to tell Ryū that, at least not yet, not until he was sure of what was really happening between the yakuza and him— or not happening, which, again, was the most probable outcome.

"I don't think I am," he finally answered.

"It'll be okay, Kenshin. You're very good with a sword, incredible as it may seem."

"I kind of like you better when you stick to polite lies."

Ryū laughed. "You know what I mean. As absentminded as you are, it's a true wonder you can be so focused when it comes to kendo."

"I'm also focused when I draw."

"Yeah. The problem is you're still drawing even when you don't have an actual pencil in your hand."

Ken shrugged, trying to make light of it, but he knew his friend was right. The extent to which he could get lost in his mental imagery was appalling, so much so that he'd taken to using his bad sight as an excuse when he bumped up against utility poles or—even more embarrassing—people; of course his eyes were perfectly all right, but nobody had to know that.

"It's a cute trait you have there," Ryū said, hugging him tighter. "I wouldn't change you for any other gaijin."

He smiled mischievously. "Any other gaijin wouldn't fit in that child-sized futon you keep for guests."

"Hey! Have you seen the size of this condo? I can't possibly afford bigger futons."

Ken stifled a laugh. Ryū's place was a sensitive matter. It always irked his friend that he had to live in a rather small condo when his family owned a construction company, but his father was adamant that his son start from the bottom and get to know the company from every point of view before he took over the reins. So for now, he was just another salaryman, though the condo he complained so much about was much better—and slightly bigger—than any other company man in his current position would have access to.

"It's all right. I sleep curled up all the same."

Ryū whacked his head, but there was a smile tugging at the corners of his lips. "Come on, you big gaijin, let's go for a walk."

"Good. These walls were closing in on me, this place is so tiny."

Ken didn't wait for an answer before he started for the front door. He had to laugh as a loud "kuso gaijin" resonated down the hallway.

CHAPTER 4

SHIGURE stepped out of the car as Kinosuke held the door for him. Standing on the curb, Kotarō was making a show of checking the street for possible threats. The young apprentice looked so earnest—and so obvious—that Shigure had to fight the urge to roll his eyes.

This part of the red-light district of Kabukichō was dangerously close to the Daitō-kai territory, but so far, relations with the Korean gang had been smooth, so Shigure had deemed it safe to bring Kotarō and let the kid start getting involved in their day-to-day business operations. Yet they could not afford to be slack, and that was why Kinosuke was there as well, just in case Shigure happened to need some serious backup.

Kinosuke was well on his way to become a young leader, and as such, he had to assume responsibility over the younger brothers, the shatei that would be in his charge. Keeping an eye on Kotarō was good training for that end, especially since the kid could try the patience of a saint. It wasn't Kotarō's fault that he'd just landed in Tokyo from a rural town, but sometimes it was hard not to put him on the first train back to his cows. He had good intentions, though, and an eagerness to learn that was rewarding—most of the time.

Shigure patted the car roof, and the driver pulled into the heavy traffic. Parking on these busy streets was impossible, especially at night, when the whole city seemed ready to leave their air-conditioned refuges and risk a walk on the wild side. The funny thing was that, for many, the wild side turned out to be a twisted reproduction of their morning lives, and the tiny clubs were full of offices, classrooms, and even train cars, meticulously reproduced down to the last detail, save that the office ladies, schoolgirls, and women commuters in those live postcards didn't mind at all being groped.

He moved purposely through the sea of young men handing out flyers and trying to lure passersby into the garishly lit clubs all around. In spite of the lingering heat, only a few men wore casual clothes, and none of them worked in the establishments that lined the street and imposed a certain dress code on their staff. Most clients wore suits, too, many coming straight from work, and others still working in a way, since many company decisions were made at the business parties that took place in exclusive hostess and cabaret clubs. Shigure could only imagine the expression on some accountants' faces when they checked the establishment names on some business-expenses receipts.

"Which one, boss?" Kotarō asked in a loud voice. So much for walking by unannounced. Their suits would have made them more or less invisible in the crowd, but Kotarō had to use a word for boss that no company man would ever hear himself called—*wakagashira*, the word that marked Shigure's position in the gang's chain of command.

He almost laughed aloud when Kinosuke's hand shot out to deliver a slap to Kotarō's head. "Lower your voice, you damn hick," Kinosuke hissed through clenched teeth.

The poor kid's eyes widened in realization. "Oh, I'm so sorry, boss," he whispered, his cheeks deeply flushed as he bowed his apologies. He looked like the healthy, rosy-cheeked country boy in every folktale, the one who inevitably brings disgrace to his village by sheer foolishness. Shigure could only hope he'd also grow into something better after all the suffering—or at least end up eaten by the fairy-tale monster and save them a lot of trouble.

Kinosuke shoved the contrite apprentice forward. "Just keep your eyes open. Don't go asking silly questions."

In spite of the harsh tone, Kinosuke didn't raise his voice, and even after he'd pushed Kotarō, his hand came briefly back to squeeze the kid's shoulder. Yeah, Kinosuke would be a good leader, strict but affectionate, like a father should be, something that many among their ranks had only found after joining the yakuza.

They finally reached Haihīru, the silhouette of the high-heel shoe that gave the establishment its name blinking in pink neon curves over the door. It was one of the soaplands—basically bathhouse brothels— that paid the Shinagawa-gumi for protection, though this one had a particular importance due to its location. That close to the Daitō-kai territory, every minor disturbance had to be checked and smoothed to prevent a turf war. That was why Shigure himself would answer the call of a minor establishment owner like the Haihīru manager, though he had to admit even a minor soapland like that moved quite a lot of money, enough so that they could provide their girls with an "alibi service"—a receptionist to pick up the calls of the girls' families when they phoned the "company" they were supposed to be working for.

The doorman bowed as they passed, and Shigure went straight to the front desk while his men spread seamlessly to cover his flanks.

"Please tell Harada-san that Matsunaga is here."

The man behind the desk scrambled to his feet, almost toppling all the sex toys, figurines, and pamphlets that covered the Formica surface in his haste to bow to Shigure. "Please go ahead, Matsunaga-san. The owner is waiting for you."

Shigure nodded and moved away from the desk, glad to leave behind the cluttered space. It wasn't the sheer amount of useless gadgets that made him sort of claustrophobic, but the proliferation of signs brimming with instructions for the customers, the ugly lists of forbidden conducts with their glaring red signs, and all the garishly decorated menus of services offered. It was almost impossible to spot a blank area on any wall, as if the reception had been built out of scraps of printed paper.

The hallway was a little better, in spite of the gilded frames on the wall mirrors, but it was definitely a relief to walk into Harada's office, with its brightly lit, bare white walls. The man even dressed in light colors himself, his three-piece linen suit making the place feel cooler than it really was.

"Thank you for honoring my humble establishment, Matsunaga-san," the owner said as he bowed profusely. Shigure bet he was glad to see him, since said establishment couldn't well afford to have the police sniffing around. Of course every soapland skirted the laws against full intercourse taking place on the premises, but the owner could be the unlucky one who got busted for it if he wasn't careful, so whenever there was a problem, he resorted to the yakuza, like most citizens in Japan did. The yakuza was the only well-oiled machine within a system rife with bureaucratic hurdles of unbelievable proportions.

Harada gestured for them to sit and made a call to have drinks brought to them. Shigure suppressed a sigh at all the time wasted on formalities. It seemed he grew more impatient as the years went by, maybe because his responsibilities kept growing, too, or simply because he was more acutely aware of the relative importance of things. He wished he was a gaijin and could cut to the chase without appearing rude. As soon as the thought crossed his mind, he had a very vivid recollection of a certain blond gaijin with mismatched eyes wrapping his legs around Shigure and kissing him as if his life depended on it.

The yakuza suppressed the urge to shift in his seat and tried to change his train of thought, but he only managed to bring forth yet another image, the picture that Nishimura had sent him of a young man glaring at the camera. Kenshin looked even sexier in those ragged clothes and studiously disheveled hair, the eyeliner making his eyes look fiercely odd, more in accordance with the impression the gaijin had left on Shigure. The man could be shy, but it was easy to see the extraordinary amount of energy tightly coiled inside him, an energy that only those slender fingers could tame and mold into art.

Shigure had studied many times the brisk sketch Kenshin had drawn for him, and his well-trained eye kept telling him the American was far past the point of simply good technique. Kenshin's bold strokes left a personal signature behind. Art was a language the gaijin spoke as fluently as he spoke Japanese, and Shigure couldn't wait to discover all the nuances that colored the young man's voice in both languages.

"Scotch?"

He looked up to meet Harada's questioning look and cursed inwardly. He just hoped meeting Kenshin on Friday would somehow quench his thirst for the gaijin, because it was proving a major distraction, one he couldn't afford in his line of work.

"Just tea, thank you."

Harada ignored Shigure's men. They were too low in rank to receive any attention, as shown by the fact that Shigure hadn't properly introduced them. Business was business anywhere it happened, and it always had the same rules of etiquette.

"So, what can I do for you, Harada-san?"

"We had a problem with a client a few hours ago," Harada began.

"A regular?"

"The front desk clerk said he'd never seen him before, and he has a good memory for faces. His name didn't ring a bell, either."

"I take it he used his credit card, then," Shigure said.

"Yeah. Save for the regulars, everybody else pays that way."

Shigure nodded. Credit card use was not as spread in Japan as in other countries, but in this kind of establishment it was the only insurance they got if the customers caused any trouble.

"We offered him the full service," Harada went on, which Shigure understood to include a seated massage, oral sex in the bathtub, full-body massage on an air mattress, and intercourse on a regular bed. "But the guy said he'd only go for oral sex. Our man tried to sell him the full package anyway, but the customer was adamant, so our girl— Kei's her name—was instructed accordingly."

Shigure imagined where the tale was going. "I guess he changed his mind in the middle of it."

Harada nodded. "It's not unheard of, you know, and we sometimes go through the bother of arranging it, but this man didn't want to wait for his credit card to be taken to the front desk and a new receipt brought back for him to sign. When Kei refused to have full sex with him if he didn't, he became violent, and Kei is not strong enough to stand up to a man."

Shigure took a deep breath. He hated that kind of men, those who wouldn't raise their voices in front of a superior at work, or a wife at home, but would invariably get nasty with rent girls, as if paying for sex was the only way they had to feel superior to someone and give back all the hassle they got.

"She didn't cry for help?"

Harada shrugged. "We tend to ignore the noises coming from the rooms. There's no telling what a guy is going to ask for in that area. We could have done something later, since there's only one way out of here, but the bastard knocked Kei out so that she wouldn't alert anyone."

"Is she all right now?"

"Yeah, bruised and scared, but all right."

Something in Harada's tone told Shigure there was more to the story. Having the name of the troublesome customer would have sufficed to take some measures—making sure the client was banned from the establishment, to begin with—but the owner had thought it necessary to call the Shinagawa, so there must be something else. As he expected, Harada went on.

"You know, we have many girls who aren't professionals. They're good for our business, bring fresh air to it, but of course they really don't need this to survive, so if the whole thing turns risky, they'll just curb their cravings for Prada handbags and won't come back to 'sell it'—as they say."

"You want us to pay a visit to this guy and make sure he doesn't come around here anymore. Is that it?"

The owner bowed his head. "I'm sorry to inconvenience you, Matsunaga-san, but the man has Kei really scared. I bet she wouldn't have told me anything if we hadn't found her passed out in her room. Even now she insists it was her fault and she'll pay for the damages."

Shigure frowned. Threatening these girls with exposure was the easiest thing to do. Even though none of them used their real names, a photo posted on the right website would do the trick nicely. But maybe the bastard had threatened her with something simpler and equally frightening, like pure physical violence.

"I'd like to talk to Kei-san, if you don't mind."

Harada shifted nervously. "I told her to stay, just in case you had any questions, but I couldn't possibly stop her when she said she wanted to leave." He lifted both his palms in a helpless gesture. "I don't think anything I might have offered would have made her stay."

Shigure considered that for a second and then asked, "The room is being used now?"

"You mean Kei's room?"

Shigure just nodded, and Harada blinked his confusion. "Well, the cleaning staff has been very busy tonight, and I don't think they'd have been able to straighten it yet."

"It's okay. I just want to take a look at it, see if I might get some idea of what happened in there."

"Oh, I see," Harada said, looking like he didn't really see a thing but wanted to humor the yakuza anyway. "I'll show you the way."

CHAPTER 5

THE room Harada left them inspecting was the usual tiled affair, with the bathtub—in bubble-gum pink—as the outstanding fixture, and the air mattress following close in bulk and garishness, the towel-covered bed pressed into a corner as an afterthought.

Shigure imagined it might look slightly better in its normal tidy state, though there wasn't much to be done when you had to keep a huge pink air mattress in the middle of a room. He supposed it wasn't the decoration that brought customers in, anyway.

"What a mess," Kinosuke said, nudging a pink plastic bottle lying on the floor with the tip of his shoe. It rolled halfheartedly, leaving a trail of pink gel in its wake until it collided against another bottle, smaller and filled with a clear liquid. Lube, Shigure guessed.

The rest of the usual toiletries were strewn all over the floor, as well as a pair of towels, and a small plastic shelf—needless to say, pink—had been thrown against the only mirror in the room, cracking it in a beautiful, spiderweb pattern.

"What's this?" Kotarō asked, toying with a seemingly broken piece of pink, plastic furniture. "A towel holder?"

Shigure tried not to laugh. "I wouldn't touch it too much if I were you."

"It's a fancy chair, Kotarō," Kinosuke said, obviously trying to hold back laughter himself.

"A chair?" Kotarō tilted his head. "Is it upside down, then?"

"Nope."

"Oh, it's broken."

"It ain't broken."

Kotarō looked up at Kinosuke. "But you can't sit on that crack! Your ass would be in the air!"

"That's the whole point, Kotarō."

The kid blinked in confusion, and Kinosuke threw his arm around Kotarō's shoulders as he patiently explained.

"You see the part under the seat is like a small plastic tunnel?"

Kotarō nodded and Kinosuke went on in lecture mode. "And you can tell there's enough room for someone—say a girl—to crawl in and end up with her head right under the seat."

Kotarō was frowning now. "Why would someone want to have her face right under some dude's ass?"

Shigure had to turn away to avoid cracking up. In the brief silence that followed, he could almost hear the kid's mind working.

"Oh," he finally said when Shigure had almost despaired of him ever getting to some conclusion. The disgusted expression on the kid's face was priceless, and the way he quickly jerked his hand away from the plastic stool got Kinosuke laughing so hard that Shigure couldn't help chuckling himself.

"That's gross," Kotarō protested, his cheeks a fiery red. Kinosuke just patted the kid's back between bouts of hilarity.

"Let's get some work done, boys," Shigure chided, though he was pretty sure they both could hear the smile in his voice. Soon enough they were going methodically through the room's contents in companionable silence.

For a room that small, it was filled to the brim with knickknacks of every size and color, but with an obvious prevalence of pink. That was why the small round piece of metal caught Shigure's attention, because it was outstandingly silver and black in the ocean of pink.

Even before he picked it up, Shigure knew what it was. He'd seen enough lapel badges to recognize one when he saw it, and the girl's fear started to make a lot of sense to him now.

"What did you find, boss?"

Shigure turned the badge in his hand so that the geometric design of the crest was facing Kinosuke. The young man blanched when he recognized the twin blades that symbolized the long sword in the rival Korean gang's name, the Daitō-kai.

"No wonder the girl was scared shitless," Kinosuke said. Even if people couldn't tell the gang a particular badge belonged to, everybody recognized yakuza badges.

"Yeah, and the guy probably put more pressure to his threats knowing he was out of his turf."

A loud thump made them both turn in time to see Kotarō emerge from under the bed rubbing the top of his head.

"*Itai*," he groused.

"It wouldn't hurt if you paid attention," Kinosuke scolded. "What the hell were you doing under that bed, anyway? Looking for peepholes?"

Kotarō blushed and waved the object in his hand at Kinosuke with an offended glare.

"And why are you waving a charm at me? I'm not one of those evil spirits, you know."

Shigure had to laugh at Kotarō's frustrated grunt. He took pity on the kid and approached him to fake interest in his finding. "Was it under the bed?"

"Yes, boss," he answered, throwing a sideways glance at Kinosuke. "I thought it might be important."

He made a noncommittal sound as he studied the flowery pattern on the charm. It looked vaguely familiar to Shigure, which wasn't a surprise. Every shrine in the city sold them by the dozen to protect their bearers against every conceivable evil, but that made the little sachets quite indistinct, and they might belong to anyone. With any luck, all you could tell was in which shrine a particular charm had been purchased—not that it mattered much if you didn't know to whom the thing actually belonged.

Shigure placed the charm on the bed. "Let's leave it here in case it's Kei-san's. She might want it back." Kotarō's face fell. He had yet to learn not to show his emotions so clearly, but Shigure understood he was just a kid and couldn't help wanting to soothe his disappointment. "Try to memorize the pattern, though, we can't be sure it isn't that man's."

"Yes, boss," Kotarō peeped, obviously happy to be useful. Shigure caught Kinosuke looking at him in an odd way, but the young man quickly averted his gaze. He probably thought his boss was a softy. As long as the Daitō-kai didn't think along the same lines, Shigure could live with that notion.

CHAPTER 6

SHIGURE rolled his eyes at the sight of the brand-new red Cadillac parked in front of the entrance to Silvano's, the restaurant they'd established long ago as a neutral meeting place for the two rival gangs.

That they'd gone for Italian cuisine was as casual as Shinji Onga's choice of car brand, and Shigure wondered—not for the first time—what it was about American mafiosi that attracted Japanese yakuza so much. It wouldn't be the glamour, for sure, though he had to admit that the Cadillac CTS looked pretty sleek, much better than the hideous limousines the don of the Daitō-kai favored.

Shigure didn't care much for Coppola's movies, fettuccini, or American sedans, but he understood that displaying luxury items was another, more or less subtle, way to assert power. That was why his driver was parking a Mercedes E350 right behind the Cadillac, its sedate black lines making the red car appear garish, almost toylike in comparison.

Kinosuke and Shinya checked the street before opening the car door for him, but they all knew Onga wouldn't try anything in plain daylight. The days of open war were over. The rules for this kind of encounter were another safety net, too, establishing that each captain would only bring two of his men, plus the driver, to a public place like the one Onga and he had chosen. No guns were allowed, though nobody checked the other party—it would be a serious breach of etiquette to imply that the other gang members weren't honorable enough to keep their word. Times might have changed, but most yakuza still placed *giri* over any other value or personal ambition, at least the old guard did, and Shigure wanted to believe that he was training his men to follow that code of honor that seemed so alien to Japanese kids these days.

Shinya walked before him like a massive bulwark, his scarred face and crew cut letting the world know where he was coming from. No need to wear badges when the big man was near. His image was catching, almost like an infectious disease, making Shigure look like an overdressed hoodlum and Kinosuke like a juvenile delinquent in a bōsōzoku biker gang. And since that was mostly what they were, Shigure didn't have a problem with it, especially not when they were meeting one of the worst dressed yakuza in the country. The moment they sat at Onga's table, nobody would have a doubt which side of the jail bars they should be watching the world from.

The heady scent of garlic and tomato enveloped them as soon as they crossed the threshold. Silvano's was that kind of quaint little place that the Japanese were so fond of, each one a theme park on its own, too full of perfectly lifelike details to be the real thing.

Shigure spotted Onga at once—he'd have to be blind not to, since the Korean wore a Hawaiian print shirt under a white jacket—and walked over to his table, strategically placed by the far wall of the restaurant, with a clear view of the door and easy access to the kitchen and the rear exit. Onga's two men were dressed down in comparison, almost looking like a pair of salarymen if it weren't for the tieless, open shirts, longish hair, and overly cocky attitude.

"Hey, the men in black have finally arrived," Onga teased. Shigure knew they were right on time, so he didn't bother checking his watch. He nodded to the Korean underboss and pointedly ignored his men.

"We just wanted to give you time to check the place for land mines," he teased back. His conversations with Onga were always full of this kind of banter, and they were both more than happy to keep their hostility to that level. They even got some honest laughs out of it, so it was a kind of win-win situation.

The Korean smirked and pointed to the chair in front of him. "Take a seat, Matsunaga-san, you're giving me a neck ache." He made a show of checking the tables around them before adding, "And the other patrons a heart attack."

Shigure sat, his men taking the seats at either side of him. A harried-looking waitress approached their table, handing out menus and bowing convulsively at them. She was a pretty little thing, and of course Onga wouldn't miss the chance to flirt.

"What do you recommend, onē-chan? We're all big guys, as you can see." Then he leaned forward and whispered, "We're also big where you can't see—if you get my meaning—so we need a lot to be satisfied."

Geez. How subtle. The girl did her best to smile, and Shigure guessed she was used to greasy compliments, though obviously not from a yakuza, the way she stammered.

"The pi... pizza napoletana is very good, sir."

Onga hit the table with his open palm, making the girl flinch. "Pizza it is, then. For six, with the best wine you have."

Shigure arched an eyebrow at him, but the Korean dismissed him with a wave of his hand. "This one's on me, Matsunaga-san, so let me do the choosing."

He shrugged and collected the menus on his side of the table to hand them back to the waitress. She gave him a real smile before picking up the rest of the menus and scurrying away into the kitchen.

Onga shook his head. "Man, I don't know how you do it. No matter how charming I am, they always smile at you."

"Must be the suit."

The Korean laughed. "Yeah. They must think you're in mourning and pity you."

"Women are a compassionate lot," Shigure agreed, thinking it was about time to steer the conversation in the proper direction. "Fragile too."

Onga was smart enough to notice the change and follow in the same register. "That they are, in need of protection more often than not."

Shigure nodded. "They should always be out of harm's way. No man worthy of that name should expose them to any kind of violence."

The Korean's eyes narrowed significantly. "That's what I teach my men, Matsunaga-san, and nobody will ever see me treating women with anything but respect."

He guessed many women would object to Onga's notion of respect, but Shigure knew they understood each other. They kept silent while the waitress retired the water glasses and uncorked a wine bottle, pouring for Onga first and waiting for his approval.

"Hmm. Really good, onē-chan. Go ahead and pour these nice gentlemen some."

He almost snorted at being called a nice gentleman, but he imagined Onga was trying to show him how respectful he could be. The Korean didn't seem to get that, even though Shigure'd been joking about the suit earlier, it was true that as long as Onga dressed and acted like a low-life gangster, no decent girl would look at him twice. He might as well have had "Korean good-for-nothing" branded on his forehead for all the good being respectful would do him. Shigure had had ample experience in that area, but he'd also been lucky enough to have a lady friend like Oyone, someone who would point out to him every style, manner, or speech mistake he made with the persistence of a Doberman.

They finally had their glasses filled with pinkish wine and their plates overflowing with thick pizza slices, a combination that was trying to make Shigure's stomach turn. He wasn't overly fond of Western food, either too salty or too sweet for his taste, but pizza was at the top of his hate list. How could anyone enjoy a slice of gummy bread dripping greasy cheese and even greasier, sugary, fried tomato? Obviously Onga did, maybe because of the great doses of garlic that might remind him of Korean traditional dishes.

The only advantage of pizza, though, was the fact that you were allowed to eat it with your fingers. He couldn't begin to imagine what Onga's goons would have done with silverware in those meaty hands.

"Dig in, Matsunaga-san, there's nothing worse than cold pizza."

He almost shuddered at the thought of all that congealed grease. His men were waiting for him to start eating, too, so he inhaled deeply and picked up the slice on his plate. What an underboss had to go through for the sake of his clan.

Fortunately, the Koreans didn't extend their Italian enthusiasm to dessert, and they finally settled for good ol' sake. Time to put the cards on the table, or rather, time to go through fire and see if he could manage to avoid the flames.

"Onga-san, are you familiar with a soapland called Haihīru?" he asked tentatively.

The Korean nodded. "I know where it is," he replied, meaning he knew whose territory it belonged in and why Onga shouldn't be familiar enough with it to know anything else but its name and location. Yeah. They understood each other perfectly.

"We've had a little incident there," Shigure went on. "Nothing we can't handle, mind you, but I thought I might pass it through you first, the way it stinks of foul play."

The Korean was fully alert now. Shigure was treading on dangerous ground, and they both knew it. He couldn't make direct accusations if he didn't want to start a war, but he had to make sure the infraction was noted and punished. So Shigure pretended to believe someone was trying to frame the Daitō-kai.

"A customer beat up one of the girls and fled, but we found this in the room," Shigure explained as he placed the badge he'd retrieved on the table. Onga's men looked like startled owls, two pairs of eyes going wide in surprise and then narrowing in outrage, but they were disciplined enough to look at their boss for guidance before opening their big mouths. And their boss showed you didn't get to be a captain in a powerful gang if you hadn't what it took.

"Hmm. They went for a lieutenant badge too. Neat," he said pensively. He didn't show the slightest intention to touch the pin, though his men were obviously dying to. "Stolen credit card?"

"Yeah. Belongs to a Toyama Makoto, married salaryman with two kids. His picture didn't make an impression on the Haihīru receptionist, either," Shigure answered, his eyes fixed on the Korean, waiting.

His eyes rising to meet Shigure's, Onga finally said, "It might be just a prank—you know those damn bōsōzoku kids—but I'll look into it anyway."

That was all Shigure needed, so he stood to signal the end of the meeting.

"Thank you for the delicious lunch, Onga-san," he said, with a slight emphasis on the delicious part.

"You're welcome," the Korean answered with a wry grin. "It's always worth it to see the face you make when you swallow your pizza."

The bastard. Onga's men were snickering like hyenas, and Shigure could almost hear his own men's teeth gritting. That wouldn't do.

"You don't fool me, man," he said amicably. "I know you choose Silvano's every time because their tablecloths match that little car of yours."

Onga chuckled, almost puffing up at the mention of his pride and joy, and Shigure took a few steps toward the exit before adding, "I hear they're assembling that model in Shanghai now. We should all follow your example and stick to Asian products."

He didn't turn back to watch the smile freeze on Onga's face, and his men waited until they were inside their own car to crack up. Yep, the Shinagawa knew how to score one in style.

CHAPTER 7

"DO I look presentable?" Ken asked his friend as he closed the car door, only to see Ryū roll his eyes at him.

"Yakuza aren't especially renowned for their sense of fashion, Kenshin."

Ken huffed. "So you say, but Matsunaga doesn't strike me as a sloppy dresser, either."

Ryū thrust the beautifully wrapped gift into Ken's hands. "Stop worrying. You'll be out of those clothes in no time, anyway."

Ken blinked. Was he that obvious? He thought he'd been careful hiding what had happened between Shigure and him, but maybe he'd underestimated his friend's perceptiveness.

"Or don't you intend to wear the uniform in that bag?" Ryū asked.

He stifled a relieved sigh. Ryū was talking about the traditional practice uniform in the bag hanging from his sword carrier. Yeah. He was supposed to be here for a match, no matter what secret hopes he harbored. Shigure wouldn't lay a hand on him in a house full of his men; most probably, he wouldn't do it ever again. It was the best outcome Ken could expect, given the man's profession, but the irrational part of him wasn't happy about it, and considering he illustrated fairy tales for a living, his irrational part had to be rather big.

Ryū squeezed his arm, mistaking his thoughts for worry about the sword match. "Come on, it's been a long time since you had a worthy opponent. You know you'll enjoy it." He moved away from Ken and back to the driver's side of the car before he added, "Even when he beats you."

Ken's hands were too busy to give his friend the finger, so he contented himself with sticking his tongue out at him. Ryū chuckled.

"Be careful with your body language, Kenshin. Yakuza are very fond of severing body parts."

"Oh, thank you for the reminder. I feel much better now."

"You're welcome," his friend said as he got into the car and shut the door. Ken stood on the sidewalk watching the small blue car pull away and disappear round a corner. He was still smiling at their bantering, but the prospect of spending the afternoon in a yakuza compound was making him more than a little nervous.

He took a deep breath and walked over to the impressive wooden gate set in the tall white fence. If anything, he'd have the rare chance to see a traditional Japanese home—supposing they hadn't just kept the fence for show and refurbished the whole interior into some modern, barrack-style monstrosity.

Ken studied the dark wooden planks and noticed the lines of iron reinforcements—sharp-pointed spikes that told the story of a turbulent past, confirmed by the presence of a guard tower directly overlooking the gateway. He tilted his head to look up at the simple wooden structure with its narrow window slits and its beautiful sloping roof, imagining for a second how it would be to approach the gate in those times when a guard would be looking down at him, ready to inquire about his business in visiting the house.

"Harisu-san?"

He almost jumped out of his skin at the disembodied voice barking his name. There must have been a camera somewhere near, but it was so well hidden that Ken didn't know where to look as he answered.

"Yes. I'm here to—" His polite phrase was cut short by the overriding noise of the gate swinging back on its hinges to show a paved driveway ample enough for a truck. As soon as he crossed the gate, it started swinging closed with an ominous sound, and his eyes came level with another solid structure, though this one looked more along the lines of the gigantic Niō statues that guarded temple entrances—the closemouthed one of the pair.

Ken found himself staring at the guy blocking his path, his eye immediately drawn to the nasty scar on his left cheek before he remembered to lower his head and bow in greeting. Christ. One of these days his staring was going to get him into trouble—he just hoped it wasn't this particular day, with this particular knife-scarred goon.

When he lifted his eyes, Ken saw the man blink and give him a narrow-eyed glower, though he wasn't sure he could have told the difference between a glower and any other expression on that fierce guardian mask. Then the guy just turned and started walking, and Ken guessed it was all the invitation he'd get, so he followed at a prudent distance, fighting his natural tendency to stop and look around.

They marched across a gravel esplanade with just the occasional tree breaking the open view to the group of one- and two-storied buildings ahead. Ken couldn't help noticing the beautiful black tiles on the roof of the nearest house. He loved traditional Japanese tiles, loved the round ornaments that decorated their ridges, the Buddhist symbols that flowed like waves on the slick black surface.

The sound of a door sliding open made him look back down from the roof just in time to see the wide back of his guide disappear inside the house. He followed into a wooden-floored entryway with a shoe rack to the left and a pair of slippers resting on the step in front of him. They looked brand new, so Ken guessed they'd been left there for him, but he didn't want to take any chances, so he just took off his sneakers and climbed the step in his stocking feet.

Scar-face was nowhere to be seen, and Ken wondered whether he was supposed to go on inside or wait. He didn't mind waiting. He could stand there all day just watching the delicately latticed paper shoji doors separating him from what had to be a hallway. If the entrance was any indication of what lay ahead, Ken knew he was in for a treat. The house had clearly been kept in its ancient splendor, its clean simplicity displaying what had to be the most unattainable luxury these days: open, empty space.

The door slid to let out a young man in a suit. He raked a quick look over Ken and made the sketchiest approximation to a bow Ken had ever seen. And yes, that was a glower on his face—no possible confusion this time.

"Please follow me, Mr. Harris," the man said in English, his accent as stiff and curt as the guy himself. Ken didn't bother to answer or even bow to the retreating back. He'd had a lot of practice with that kind of haughty attitude, though he didn't quite expect to find it here.

He'd been prepared to be despised as a gaijin, not to face the Japanese version of one of those sneering British butlers that always found your manners lacking.

"Please wait here," the man said with a rigid wave of his hand that looked more like a dismissal than the invitation it was supposed to be.

"Wakarimashita. Domo arigatō gozaimasu," Ken answered in formal Japanese just to spite the guy. He had the satisfaction of seeing the man waver at Ken's perfect accent, and didn't hesitate to offer the yakuza his most innocent smile. Of course that only got him a glare before the man turned to leave without another word.

"What a jerk," Ken muttered under his breath.

"Excuse me?" a grave voice asked in Japanese right behind him. Ken felt his cheeks go all shades of red before he remembered Shigure didn't understand English. He turned to meet serious dark eyes.

"Did Atsushi say something wrong?" Shigure asked.

Shit. Matsunaga looked ready to rip his man a new hole if Ken said the word, and damn if it didn't make him feel like grabbing that rough, frowning face and kissing Shigure out of breath.

"He was very…." Ken fumbled for something to say that wasn't an outright lie and only came up with, "Polite."

Matsunaga raised an eyebrow. "Well, next time he's very polite to you just tell me."

Ken made a dismissive gesture. "It's easy to sound brusque when you're using a foreign language. I'm sure he didn't mean anything by it."

The yakuza studied him for a moment before a small smile lifted the corners of his mouth.

"What?" Ken asked, frowning. He hated it when people got all smug on him.

Shigure smiled openly now. "With all those bundles you're carrying, you look like a temple offering." He made a visible and quite unsuccessful effort to curb the smile before adding, "If you don't mind my saying."

So the big guy had a sense of humor. Great.

"Well, since this particular offering is for you, I'll be more than glad to get rid of it," Ken retorted, lifting Ryū's gift pointedly. "And if your assistant hadn't been so intent on showing the gaijin his proper place, he should've noticed and taken it from me."

As soon as he'd blurted it out, Ken froze. What on earth was he doing antagonizing a yakuza? Had he gone out of his mind? Shigure looked menacing enough, but Ken found there was something about the man that made him feel at ease. He couldn't help saying what was on his mind any more than he could help wanting to drop everything he carried to crawl all over that hard, stunning body.

Ken watched in fascination as Shigure's eyes narrowed. The yakuza looked like a powerful god deciding whether he should be angry with the insignificant human or let it run for the time being, and Ken couldn't take his eyes from him. Then Shigure just shook his head and chuckled.

"You're something else, Kenshin-san."

He'd heard that many times, but the appreciative note in Shigure's voice made him look away in embarrassment, and that second was all it took the yakuza to cross the distance between them and lift Ken's chin gently with his strong fingers.

"Look at me," Shigure ordered in the tone of someone used to being obeyed, the kind of tone that usually made Ken do the opposite of what he was told. Not this time, though. There was something about Shigure that made his words, his actions, feel right, and Ken found himself obeying without a second thought.

The yakuza searched his eyes with such intensity that Ken felt his whole body respond to the scrutiny, his heart rate speeding up, blood flowing down to make his belly heavy, a long shudder shaking his frame from head to toes. Shigure's gaze registered every reaction, pupils dilating as if to swallow Ken into their black-hole gravitational pull.

"Why aren't you afraid?" Shigure finally asked in a hoarse whisper.

Ken tried to think of a single logical reason as he watched the sharp-boned structure of Shigure's face, but there was nothing logical about the way his fingers itched to touch all those hard planes. He shook his head minutely, wanting to say *I don't know* or, most probably, *I don't care*, even though he did feel a little fear in the pit of his stomach. He was afraid Shigure might break the contact and leave him standing there with his hands full of things he didn't need.

Shigure sighed. "You should fear me, Kenshin-san. I can't seem to find my control around you." His fingers slid down Ken's chin to his neck, as if reluctant to let go.

"Control is overrated," Ken said under his breath, his head coming down to get more of Shigure's elusive touch. He hadn't noticed he'd closed his eyes until the sound of Matsunaga's soft laughter startled him out of his reverie.

"I should keep you around," the yakuza said. "I don't usually have many reasons to laugh."

Ken found himself frowning at the implications those words might have, but Shigure only smiled at him, and Ken forgot what he was thinking. Smiles were his weak spot, and he couldn't imagine anything else so powerfully transforming.

Shigure's smile was a small, almost furtive gesture, a little lopsided grin that made his eyes crinkle with laugh lines. It didn't exactly soften the air of solid power surrounding the yakuza, but it did break the stony immobility of his features. When he smiled, he looked capable of mischief.

"I wonder what you see when you look at me that way," Shigure said, still smiling, and Ken realized he'd been staring. Again.

"I'm sorry, Matsunaga-san. You must think I'm very rude."

Shigure's fingers kept him from looking away, dark eyes growing serious as the yakuza spoke. "You're an artist, and artists aren't rude, just curious." He paused, his eyes fixed on Ken. "But I'm definitely going to feel insulted if you don't call me by my given name."

"Okay."

The Japanese raised an eyebrow at him, and Ken had to smile at the subtle hint.

"Okay, Shigure-san," he said obediently.

The yakuza nodded. "Much better. Now, I believe we have a challenge to meet."

"Uh-huh."

Neither of them moved, Shigure's fingers still resting under Ken's chin, their eyes meeting once again as if they were seeing each other for the first time.

Ken groaned at all the useless weight he was carrying. He needed his hands free now, needed to move closer to the source of heat that was Shigure's body, needed it as badly as if he were in the throes of hypothermia. And Shigure seemed to know Ken would die if he didn't get closer to him, the yakuza's big hands grabbing Ryū's present to shove it away none too delicately. Of course, right then, the gift made an awful, creaking noise, and they both looked down in time to see a wet spot growing steadily on the beautiful cloth wrapping.

"Kuso," Shigure swore, looking so vexed with his hands still squeezing the mauled gift that Ken had to bite his lip to stop from cracking up. But he wasn't doing a great job of it, given the way Shigure narrowed his eyes at him and asked, "What's so funny?"

"Sorry," Ken answered, a snort belying his repentance. "You looked just like King Kong after smothering a puppy."

Oh shit. He was a dead man.

Shigure blinked twice, his expression frozen between astonishment and something else that Ken didn't even want to figure out. As seconds ticked away with nothing but a loud heartbeat ringing in his ears, Ken raked his brain for something to say that could soften the insult, some excuse about his poor knowledge of the Japanese language or, more accurately, his mental retardation. But then Shigure's lips twitched, and—to Ken's utter amazement—he started laughing so hard his whole body shook, his laughter so infectious that Ken had to chuckle himself, especially when Ryū's gift started dripping in Shigure's hand.

Ken couldn't help himself. "Now look what you've done," he teased. "You've scared the poor thing into wetting itself."

The look in Shigure's eyes as he doubled over with laughter was priceless, and Ken had to think that the yakuza wasn't lying when he said he didn't have many reasons to laugh. Just being a high-ranking executive in any Japanese company would have been stressful enough without having to deal with the extracurricular risks of illegality that Matsunaga's position had to imply.

What had driven Shigure to get there? Ken wondered. Joining the yakuza was not just an easy way to make money. Japanese gangs had a tightly regimented organization that forced you to accept a heavy weight of duties and obligations that might outbalance the rewards in the end. In truth, something like the yakuza couldn't exist in a society less imbued of giri—that cross between honor and debt that soaked Japan from the emperor down to the lowest blue-collar worker. For the same reasons, it attracted a lot of people nostalgic for some honorable past forever gone, or in desperate need of the kind of leveling justice Japan's legal system would never provide. So maybe Shigure was not so much ambitious as vengeful, but then again, he might just like power or even need the army-like discipline to feel at home.

The yakuza sighed loudly, shaking his head. "I think my jaw will be sore tomorrow," he said wistfully, and Ken just wished he could be there every day to make the big man keep laughing. Shigure's face looked softer now, relaxed, almost happy.

"It's a good look on you," Ken said without thinking, his eyes widening in surprise at the same time as Shigure's did. "I'm sorry, I didn't—"

"Don't apologize," Shigure cut him off short. "I really appreciate that you can be honest with me. It's a rare thing to find someone who dares say what he thinks."

Yeah, the way Shigure looked, Ken guessed not many people would speak up to him. He himself wouldn't, if he was less of an airhead and thought about the consequences more often. But Ken didn't want Matsunaga to read his forwardness the wrong way.

"I hope you know I mean no disrespect, Shigure-san. It just feels as if we've known each other for a long time."

Shigure gazed into his eyes with an intensity that made Ken feel utterly exposed. "I'm honored that you would think so, Kenshin-san," the yakuza said with a bow. And somehow the formality only added weight to the sentiment, Shigure's dark, serious eyes conveying a kind of respect Ken had never felt addressed to him that way.

He nodded to Matsunaga, unable to find the right words to answer him. Shigure held his gaze for a moment and then lowered the present to the floor carefully. "Please follow me, and I'll show you the way to the dojo," he said as he straightened up, the play of hard muscle unmistakable in spite of the suit he was wearing.

Ken licked his lips unconsciously, and Shigure's eyes followed the movement of his tongue until the yakuza seemed to realize what he was doing and jerked his head away as he started for the shoji doors.

Ken forced himself to follow Shigure with his eyes focused on the big man's shoulder blades and not significantly lower down the broad back. It wouldn't do to reach the changing room with an erection to hide. Then again, when Matsunaga slid open the back doors, every thought went out the window.

CHAPTER 8

SHIGURE smiled at the face Kenshin was making. He was proud of his garden, of the subtle way trees and bushes were trimmed to allow the light through and yet appear almost wild in their deceivingly spontaneous growth.

"It's...." Kenshin faltered, his eyes wide.

Shigure had to chuckle at the childish awe the American showed, but he couldn't deny the way it made his pride swell. It wasn't often that he found someone who appreciated his efforts in that area, especially since most of the time he had to hide his interests from his comrades. A penchant for gardening wouldn't be considered befitting a yakuza, no matter how Japanese it was. So he hired the monks from a nearby sanctuary to keep his garden beautifully natural—and their shrine lavishly financed, a satisfactory agreement for all the parties involved.

"Come, let me show you," Shigure offered, placing his hand on Kenshin's shoulder and steering him forward. The gaijin nodded without even looking at Shigure, too busy trying to absorb every little detail around him. He shook his head, smiling, and guided Kenshin down the wooden steps to the pond.

"Put these on," Shigure said, pointing to the sturdy wooden geta sandals they used to march across the garden to the other buildings. Kenshin looked down briefly enough to see what he was doing and then looked up and met Shigure's eyes with a smile so full of praise that the yakuza felt warm all over. He didn't even remember the last time someone had looked at him that way for something other than the place of power he occupied. And here was this American kid, showing so much of himself in his open admiration, without minding what Shigure could do with that knowledge. Surprising as it might seem, he appeared to trust the yakuza.

He must have been looking at Kenshin in an odd way, because the bright smile in those full lips faltered a little, and two-colored eyes searched his with concern. Shigure tried to smile reassuringly, though he knew his face wasn't very well suited for that purpose.

"Watch your step now," he said to save the awkward moment. "You wouldn't want to end up down there with the koi."

"You actually have fish in the pond?" Kenshin asked, and Shigure almost laughed at the way his mood had immediately lifted. The American was really a kid, all enthusiasm and cuteness.

"Of course I do, who do you take me for?" he joked.

"A big fish in a small pond?" Kenshin said before darting across the pond and away from him, moving with surprising deftness for someone not used to the cumbersome wooden sandals. But then again, he could be used to them for all Shigure knew. All bets were off where Kenshin was concerned, and the yakuza found he liked the prospect of discovering all there was to know about the man. It would be a thrilling experience, something like bungee jumping in his dining room.

Shigure followed Kenshin into the trees and found him soon enough near a moss-covered stone lantern, predictably lost in its contemplation.

"What do you do for a living?" Shigure asked in amusement, wondering what kind of job could keep that mind focused for more than two seconds at a time.

"I illustrate children's books," Kenshin answered distractedly while his hand traced the faded bas-relief on the lantern.

Of course. It made perfect sense. Shigure found himself trying to imagine the kind of illustrations those delicate fingers would produce. Surely nothing like pastel princesses or frog princes, but Shigure couldn't quite predict what Kenshin's style would be. He would have to see for himself.

"Shall we go ahead, then?" he said.

"Hmm."

Kenshin started walking without tearing his gaze from the lantern until Shigure startled him by chuckling. Then the American had the good grace to blush and smile ruefully at him.

"Sorry. I know I'm a little—"

Shigure didn't have time to react as a white projectile made its hissing way toward them. He instinctively lifted a hand to protect his eyes when he heard a loud thump beside him.

He couldn't believe what he was seeing—Kenshin's left hand holding a white ball, the white ball Shigure hadn't even been able to recognize as such at the speed it had traveled in their direction. Then Shigure had another reason to wonder. "Are you left-handed?" he asked.

"Not exactly," Kenshin answered, seemingly embarrassed. "But I've learned to protect my drawing hand."

He must have worked pretty hard at that, since the kind of reflex he'd just displayed was difficult to come by spontaneously. Kenshin was showing him the back of his left hand now.

"You see?" the American asked. "This hand has taken the brunt of my clumsiness."

Shigure reached out to take the hand in his and studied it carefully. There was a thin, white scar almost parallel to the line of the knuckles, and an oddly shaped ridge marring the smoothness of the nail on the little finger. He traced the scars with his own fingers, fascinated by the rough texture, imagining what it would feel like if he licked them, wondering if they would taste different from the rest of Kenshin's skin. Just when he was about to lift the hand to his mouth there was a rustle of branches and a flustered Kotarō came trundling through, barely managing to stop before he collided with them.

"Sorry, boss. I sent the ball flying in this—" The apprentice's eyes widened as he took in the way Shigure was holding Kenshin's ball-seizing hand, and it was almost comical to see his gaze travel from their hands up to Kenshin's face and from there to Shigure's, only to jerk back to Kenshin as Kotarō did a double take, his eyes as big as saucers now. Shigure guessed the kid had never been this close to a gaijin before, much less one with Kenshin's eyes. The way he was acting, he might as well have stumbled into an alien in the middle of the garden.

"Kotarō! Don't—"

Shigure almost groaned. Did all his men need to converge in that particular spot? He felt Kenshin try to shake his hand free, but he held on, even lifting their joined hands higher so that Kinosuke wouldn't miss them. As he expected, the young man stopped staring at Kenshin to focus on the hand holding the ball.

"I'm sorry, boss," Kinosuke finally said, bowing deeply. "I hit the ball too hard. I could have caused an accident."

Shigure frowned. Hadn't Kotarō admitted that *he* had sent the ball flying in their direction? The way the kid fidgeted told him he was right, even though Kinosuke kept his face blank.

He didn't like it. To assume responsibility for your charges' mistakes was one thing, but to lie for them was definitely not the way to go about it. He'd have to talk to Kinosuke once Kenshin left. He wouldn't embarrass one of his men in front of a stranger. Maybe inviting Kenshin over had been a mistake after all.

He took the ball from Kenshin and tossed it to Kotarō. Even at that short distance, the kid didn't manage to catch it, and Shigure had to stifle another frustrated groan. It irked him that a gaijin—and an absentminded gaijin at that—would prove to be faster and more alert than the men he trained.

"Let's go, Kenshin-san," he said, more sharply than he intended, only to see the American flinch at his aggressive tone. Shit. He definitely needed to break something, or even more practical, to swing his *bokken* in someone's face. He just hoped Kenshin was proficient enough not to take the brunt of Shigure's anger on his body—that gorgeous body he just wished he'd never touched.

"Try not to send the ball out of the field next time," he told Kotarō, letting Kinosuke know that he was well aware of his little lie. It wasn't of much use, though, since he found Kinosuke too focused on glaring at Kenshin to listen.

Shigure almost cursed aloud. First Atsushi and then Kinosuke. It seemed his most trusted men were intent on disappointing him. Hell, he didn't like foreigners, either, but couldn't they see Kenshin was different? And even if he wasn't, did they have to embarrass their boss in front of a guest?

He started striding in the dojo's direction, not once turning to see if Kenshin followed him. It didn't really matter. He guessed he wouldn't be seeing much of that blond head after the day was over. It seemed he couldn't afford the distraction after all.

KEN gave his obi an angry tug. It wasn't the belt's fault that Shigure had gone from obsequiously polite to growly in two minutes, but it was either jerking his belt around or telling the yakuza to go fuck himself. Jesus. If he didn't want a gaijin in his house, he should have thought twice before challenging him.

He stomped into the dojo after Shigure, his bare feet slapping hard against the wooden floor. Yeah, well, let the world know he was there. He wasn't going to back down now, and as pissed as he was, he would surely prove a challenge for the damn yakuza.

He didn't wait for Shigure to say anything. He assumed the seated position to formally bow to the dojo, to the altar honoring past masters, and to Shigure. He rose then, holding his wooden sword at the ready. If the man thought choosing the *bokken* over the *shinai* would work to his advantage, Ken would be glad to point out his mistake to him. Most people practiced kendo—the modern sword discipline—because it was flashier, more fitted to competition and showing-off, bamboo swords striking like lightning against the handsome protective armor. He still preferred to practice *suburi*, the traditional training method, using a wooden sword. The *bokken* was heavier, more solid, almost a real cutting sword in its balanced weight and slender form. It centered his usually flittering attention better, maybe because, free of the burden of masks and armors, he could enjoy the beautiful flow of movements, the traditional uniforms enhancing the impression of having walked out of time into an era in which sword training was a way of acquiring wisdom.

He didn't feel very wise now, though. He was watching Shigure's posture with a critical, narrowed eye, searching for an opening in his defensive stance and cursing the yakuza for looking so damn impressive in his *hakama* pants, wooden sword poised without apparent effort in the perfect, initial position. Then again, maybe Shigure was fool enough to believe Ken would just adopt *kumitachi* positions—the exercises designed to train with a partner—one after the other in a soft, innocuous dance. And it seemed he really believed it, since the yakuza stepped in, lifting his sword over his head and moving on toward Ken while he brought the *bokken* down in a perfect line that reversed exactly its previous upward path.

Shigure's deft movements were beautiful to watch, his hold on the *bokken* that of an expert: left little finger curled beneath the weapon while the rest of the fingers wrapped around the handle, right hand tilted slightly upward as the right forefinger extended along the shaft. Ken could just tell the yakuza was holding back, though, and he almost smirked. He would show no mercy.

Before Shigure's sword completed its descent, Ken moved in to counterstrike, cutting down against the yakuza's *bokken* with a sharp blow. Shigure looked startled as Ken pivoted to his right, sliding his sword along Shigure's and then continuing his fast rotation with the *bokken* flowing with him until he was just positioned to step back and strike a blow that would have been lethal if he had been holding a live sword.

Ken controlled the downward strike so that his *bokken* stopped inches away from Shigure's shoulder, the movement fast and energetic enough that the yakuza could feel Ken wasn't going for light and playful. He was demanding the basic right granted to an opponent, the chance to prove himself without being disregarded before the combat even started.

Shigure turned his head to look at him, and in his intent, dark eyes, Ken saw something new. So far, there'd been appreciation and desire in those eyes, but now he could see—for the first time—respect. Until that very moment, Ken was sure he'd just been a gaijin Shigure found attractive for some reason, and maybe even someone whose ability to draw he admired to a certain extent. Only now Ken was seen as a man, an equal, someone who counted for reasons other than his exotic appearance.

As if to confirm his thoughts, Shigure nodded, acknowledging him. Ken nodded back, feeling warmth spread over his limbs in soft waves that took away his anger, his fears. They had drawn a new starting line on the sand, and nobody could tell what would happen next, because there were no more expectations attached to their names. Now he could say that his name was Kenshin, and Shigure would believe him.

CHAPTER 9

IT HAD been a long time since Shigure had enjoyed bokken training so much, probably since the time his sensei had been there to teach him.

To say that Kenshin was good would have been an understatement. The American had that easy way about him that meant much more than a rigorous daily practice. It meant the sword was a part of him, and not an object he picked up and brandished on occasion.

Kenshin looked like a different person as he faced Shigure, the cute, awkward kid replaced by a sure-footed, graceful warrior. He was dangerous, too—his movements so fast and to the point that Shigure had to struggle to keep thwarting the deadly blows. And damn if the yakuza didn't love it. He was sure his teeth were showing in a wolfish grin as his vision took on that enhanced quality that only came when he was in the middle of a good fight.

The dojo was now crowded with the men who had come to watch, attracted by the sharp noise of two *bokken* clashing together, but Shigure's mind didn't quite register their presence save as a background, innocuous element. He was too focused on Kenshin as the only danger in the room.

They moved about in a frantic dance, the floor squeaking under their combined weight, bare feet slapping hard as they lunged, Kenshin's eyes gleaming with the hunger of an animal on the prowl. Shigure was sure neither of them wanted the combat to end, or even thought in terms of winning or losing anymore. This wasn't about results. What really mattered was the game in itself, the satisfaction of letting the *bokken* strike with all its might because it would always be stopped before it reached flesh or bones. That was something beginners had a hard time understanding, that you didn't expect your opponent to fail when you wanted a good match. It was the trust you placed on his ability to cope that made the experience unforgettable.

Kenshin pressed forward as he raised his *bokken* for a side strike. Shigure mimicked him as if they were in either side of the same mirror, almost shuddering in anticipation as he watched the American move effortlessly through the paces of one of the most difficult attacks, the one that would cut an enemy in half if you had the right blade. It was not a question of strength, but speed and, most of all, precision. You had to break the balance of your opponent and land a flat blow to cut across his midsection. When reaching this point, all of Shigure's trainees would inevitably swing the *bokken* like an ax and try to shove their way across their teacher's abdomen, frustrated when Shigure's *bokken* stood firmly in their way. Not Kenshin, though. As light framed as he was, it would have been useless to go for a pushing match against Shigure, so instead he moved slightly to his right when their *bokken* connected and pressed the yakuza's sword from that position. Shigure almost laughed in delight when his attempt at defense from the awkward angle he'd been cornered into was easily countered by Kenshin's perfect horizontal cut.

When the wooden sword touched his belly, Shigure smiled openly and nodded. Kenshin blinked, as if unable to assimilate that he'd bested his opponent, and Shigure could tell that the shy kid he'd first met was back in full force. But it was too late now. The yakuza had seen the kind of strength that hid behind the boyish façade, and he wouldn't be fooled anymore. Neither would his men, if the silence filling the dojo was any indication. Yeah, the small gaijin had suddenly grown teeth.

Obviously uneasy at all the attention, Kenshin ducked his head and busied himself with the precise ritual of the final formal bows. But even that was a telltale sign of his expertise, his movements fluid and elegant, showing the proper respect of someone who understood what sword training was really about.

When they both got up from the formal sitting position, the heavy silence in the room had an uncertain quality to it, the men obviously gauging Shigure's mood before saying anything. After all, they'd seen their boss lose to a gaijin, and it was only reasonable to wait for Shigure to make the first move, but there was someone among them who didn't even know what reasonable meant.

"Wow, boss. That was one hell of a side cut. I bet none of us would stand a chance against him," Kotarō said, as loud and clear as if he'd been trying to be heard over the rumble of an incoming train. Then the dojo seemed to suddenly turn into a tennis court, all heads turning at the same time to stare at Kotarō first and then back to watch Shigure's reaction. And Shigure couldn't hold back his laughter when he saw a hand shoot out to hit Kotarō's head.

"That hurt, aniki!"

"I hope it did, you dumbass," Kinosuke mumbled, but the men were chuckling and teasing Kotarō now, relieved that the tension had been broken.

Shigure chanced a look at Kenshin and saw that his cheeks were red from more than the strenuous activity. The yakuza could have laughed at his embarrassment, but he was too busy trying to keep his breath from hitching at the way Kenshin looked.

The American's pale skin was flushed now, full lips parted, eyes bright in the outrageous contrast between their irises, his beauty enhanced by the simple elegance of the black and white uniform. For the first time, he appeared focused and relaxed, and Shigure understood what he had seen so far was the wound-up side of his personality, the kid that couldn't stop hopping from one foot to the other as his eyes darted right and left trying to take it all in. If it had been physically possible, Shigure knew Kenshin would have been looking in both directions at the same time, much like chameleons did. Those traits were endearing, even his shyness was, but the yakuza was not one to linger over cute things. If he had been attracted to Kenshin from the start, it was because he'd caught a glimpse of something else beyond the charming surface. He just hadn't known what it was until they'd crossed swords.

"Kenshin-san," he said, feeling the new weight the name carried, as if only now he *meant* the honorific attached to the name. "Thank you for the great practice. I haven't enjoyed myself that much in a while."

"What you mean is you haven't lost in a while, boss," one of his men said, the others only too happy to join in the teasing.

"He just beats the crap out of us on a daily basis."

"And that's no fun at all, dude."

"You bet. Once you've seen Kotarō's *bokken* hit the floor for the seventh time, you don't even want to hoot anymore."

"Hey! I don't drop it that often!"

"No, man, you just send it flying across the dojo for fun."

They were all laughing now, and Shigure was amused to see most of his men had moved closer as they spoke, obviously curious about the gaijin who had beaten their boss, no matter how lightly they seemed to have taken it. He guessed the next time he trained with them he was going to see some bold moves, and of course he would be glad to disabuse them of the notion that they were even close to Kenshin's level. At least it might give them a reason to practice harder.

He took the chance to introduce the men in the dojo to Kenshin, making it clear that he intended the American's presence to be a more or less—preferably more—permanent fixture in their house. Even as he did, he realized this wasn't what he'd planned, though it didn't exactly come as a shock. He'd been trying to ignore his first impressions of the man, pride blinding him to what he had in front of his eyes. Ironic that a social outcast would come so easily to resent another outcast and forget his first rule of survival. It never paid to ignore your instincts when you lived on the tip of a sword.

KEN followed Shigure back to the changing room, still smiling at the good-natured teasing the men had submitted their boss to. All those scary-looking goons had acted like a bunch of schoolboys, joking and patting their captain's back while they commiserated with him over losing to a gaijin.

Except for that kid, Kotarō, no one had openly praised Ken—it would have been offensive to their boss if they had—but he could see appreciation in their eyes. And Shigure had gone as far as introducing him around, something that might not have meant anything back in America, but here, it was a huge step for Ken. It prevented him from being invisible.

Shigure left his *bokken* on a sword rack and started undressing. Ken turned to do the same, feeling suddenly anxious. When they'd changed before, he'd been too angry to realize they were naked for the first time in each other's presence, and he hadn't even glanced in Shigure's general direction. Now he was too aware of the body moving close to him, so close that the rustle of clothes as the yakuza disrobed sounded overly loud, raking on Ken's nerves as he did his best to ignore the impulse to turn and risk a look at what he knew would be an amazing view.

He fumbled with his uniform like a beginner wearing Japanese garments for the first time. Shit. He'd been so mad when he did all those knots that now he might need a fishhook to pry the strings apart.

"Need help?" Shigure asked, not quite chuckling, but obviously amused.

Ken raised his head to glare at him, and his jaw dropped open.

"Holy shit," he swore, reverting to English in his dazzle, his eyes not knowing where to settle on the incredible scenery of Shigure's tattooed body.

The yakuza laughed openly now. "What? You don't have tattoos in America?"

Ken would have rolled his eyes if he'd been able to tear his gaze from the sea of colored ink. "Of course we do. All solid colors and nice single lines drawing hearts, names, and even a dragon or two, but that...." He waved his hand as if to cover the whole intricacy of blue waves crashing against Shigure's thighs, white foam pushing the stormy ocean up his torso, red peonies floating here and there, one of them blossoming right around a rosy nipple that seemed part of the luscious flower. "That should be framed and hung in a museum."

Shigure grinned, obviously flattered. "I'm not ready to be skinned just yet."

Ken made a disgusted face. "That's gross. Shut up and let me look."

The yakuza let out a hearty laugh and opened his arms wide. "Here. Look your fill."

Damn. It was the most beautiful thing Ken had ever seen on a living body. It looked as if someone had lent the yakuza a silk robe ten sizes smaller than his own, the sleeves ending right under his elbows, the sides never managing to overlap at the front, leaving a clean strip of naked skin down the chest and along the inner thighs, the collar never reaching Shigure's strong neck, the lower rim cascading across the front thighs to stop a few inches short of the knees.

It was cleverly designed to go under everyday clothes, but Ken thought it was a pity to keep all that beauty hidden away. He couldn't begin to imagine how many hours of torture it had taken to create that bubbling ocean, or the vivid peonies, or—

"Oh shit. That's a dragon up your arm!" Ken almost squeaked at the sight of the slender, scaly beast, red tongues of painted fire licking at Shigure's shoulder.

"Yep. Want to see my back?" The yakuza asked, seemingly caught up in Ken's excitement. Ken could only nod, too dazzled to find his voice.

When Shigure turned, Ken gasped loudly. He'd never been too interested in fish, but the giant carp leaping up the broad back was breathtaking, its bright red scales making it stand out over the white and blue waves it'd sprung from, the fins delicately traced in shades of orange and light red as if they were almost translucent, the whole picture giving a sharp impression of movement, the carp as fully alive as the troubled waters beneath it.

"You know why I chose a carp?" Shigure asked, looking at Ken over his shoulder.

"Because of that legend of the waterfall?" Ken ventured. He remembered something about a carp leaping a huge waterfall and transforming into a dragon. He also remembered the fish being used to suggest going up in the world, but it might sound a bit too crude if Ken were to say so.

"Yeah," Shigure said, nodding. "That's what inspired the artist, anyway, but for me, it's mostly about pulling a carp out of the water."

Ken frowned and met Shigure's eyes briefly. "It would die if you pulled it out," he said.

"Exactly," the yakuza went on. "It would put on a brisk fight till you laid it on the chopping board, and then it'd keep perfectly still, knowing there's nothing more to do but to die honorably."

Ken fought the urge to roll his eyes. An honorable death was no laughing matter for the Japanese, and he bet it was even less so for the yakuza who brushed death on a daily basis.

Shigure was still looking at him, as if waiting for a reaction, and Ken understood it was important. Shigure had chosen that tattoo for reasons that went deeper than a trite conception of what was proper for a man's man to adhere to, and somehow he was offering them for Ken to see.

He met the intense black gaze as the image of the carp filled his mind's eye, and the idea came unbridled to him, the quite subversive notion that, in spite of all the talk about the carp being a powerfully muscled fish, strong enough to leap a waterfall, it was, in the end, no more than a fish, a rather fragile animal, with no outer shell to protect itself, its inner skeleton easy to crush, a weak creature that would not survive if you brought it out of its murky waters.

Shigure's carp had always longed to be a dragon, the mighty beast that lived without fear in any element. Being a fish out of water took on a new meaning here, not so much one that included all that babble about dying honorably, but more about being always out of place, always trying to reach higher, to leap out of safety even if nothing but death was to be expected.

Ken felt recognition constricting his chest. All his life he'd been fighting to escape what he was supposed to mold into: his parents' aspirations for him, peer pressure leading him into certain folds, social values pushing him to conform. And if he'd experienced that urge to escape, he could only begin to imagine what it'd been like for Shigure, who most probably came from a family without means, in a place like Japan where you weren't worth a dime if you hadn't the proper labels attached from birth. Ken had found the kind of job that made being eccentric permissible, even chic, and Shigure had found the yakuza.

"I guess your carp didn't become a dragon as a reward for leaping the waterfall," he said slowly, almost whispering. Shigure turned to face him, his eyes serious, eager, as Ken continued. "It leapt the waterfall *because* it wanted to be a dragon."

Shigure's eyes glowed, and for a terrifying moment, Ken thought he'd said something so wrong the yakuza was going to strike him, the way he strode across the room to invade Ken's personal space, never mind the fact that he was only wearing a loincloth—it only made him look even more intimidating, more like a warrior in his war paint, ready to rip off some heads with his bare hands.

Ken forced himself to stand still and lock eyes with the yakuza. Shigure looked down at him with fire in those sharp eyes, his body sending waves of heat that threatened to scorch the smaller American who stood in his way.

Whatever Shigure had been meant to be, he was definitely a dragon now, the tattoo covering his body with the scales that made his skin his armor. Even terrified as he was, Ken's hand moved on its own, hesitantly reaching out to touch the ink, just like a kid fascinated by the flames about to swallow him. Shigure caught his wrist in midair, holding so tight Ken felt his bones might snap, though he didn't have time to feel any pain before hard lips closed over his in a punishing kiss. Ken couldn't do anything but open himself for the invading tongue to take what it wanted, his body starting to shake as the mix of fear and excitement came crashing down on him like a landslide.

As if sensing Ken's knees might give way under him, Shigure's free hand grabbed Ken's bony hip and pulled fiercely without ever stopping the kiss, groaning when their bodies bumped hard against each other. Ken moaned, his own free hand moving to find skin before the yakuza caught his other wrist to stop him. He might have whimpered in frustration, his fully clothed body in desperate need of access to that skin that pressed heavily against him.

"Kenshin-san," Shigure breathed into his lips, the name coming out in such awe that it made Ken shudder. He tilted his head to catch those burning lips again, hungry for more of Shigure's taste, but the yakuza kept the maddening distance, as if he needed it to admire Ken properly.

He couldn't help the pained sound that left his throat, wanting Shigure so much that his whole body ached for him. But the sound had quite the opposite effect, making the yakuza realize with a start that he was still holding Ken's wrists in a strangling hold.

"I'm sorry, Kenshin-san," he apologized, immediately letting go of Ken and stepping away from him. "I didn't mean to—"

"I know you didn't," Ken said and waved impatiently, trying to close the distance between them, but Shigure took his hands and kept him at arm's length to inspect the red marks with obvious concern.

Ken surprised himself by growling. "Will you stop it? I'm not that fucking fragile."

The corners of Shigure's mouth lifted. "I sort of learned that the hard way, you know. I just didn't want to mark you so visibly."

"Oh." That was all he could manage, heat spreading over his face in a blush that was far more visible than any mark Shigure might have left on him. God. He hated being so transparent. And the damn yakuza was obviously fighting laughter as he dropped Ken's hands gently and went for the strings in his uniform instead.

"Here, let me help you out of this," he said, deftly undoing the knots Ken hadn't even managed to loosen. "It's too hot to be wearing so many clothes."

Ken pouted and mumbled, "Tease," making Shigure finally crack up. As much as he'd wanted to keep pouting, Ken couldn't help smiling. He liked hearing Shigure laugh, liked it especially because he was sure the yakuza didn't let himself be so open in front of many people. It made him feel special, part of something Shigure kept zealously guarded.

Big hands pushed Ken's clothes down, and they slid easily to puddle around his ankles. He looked away, feeling slightly ridiculous in his boxer shorts, though he knew he'd have felt even more self-conscious if he'd worn the typical Japanese loincloth. There was a limit to what a foreigner could wear with grace, especially if he had to compete with the real McCoy.

"Your skin is so beautiful," Shigure said, no trace of humor left in his voice.

"My skin?" Ken repeated dumbly, looking up to meet hungry black eyes.

The yakuza nodded, the pads of his fingers brushing Ken's throat, tracing the lines of his collarbone and farther down to ghost over his nipples. Goose bumps broke out all over Ken's body, and he reached out to grab Shigure's biceps as if he needed to steady himself. And he probably did, the way blood was leaving his brain to travel south, his shorts suddenly too tight to bear.

The yakuza's fingers continued their excruciating exploration, feather touches moving over Ken's abdomen, circling his navel, dipping under the waistband of his underwear to splay over his ass cheeks and rest there, Shigure's eyes searching his, asking for permission.

"Your men?" he croaked, not really caring if the full gang were to cross the door to find them like that, but knowing Shigure might. And wasn't it crazy, that he could forget himself for this stranger while he couldn't stop looking out for him?

Shigure groaned and rested his forehead against Ken's. "You're right."

Ken let his eyes close, the hands on his ass keeping him warm, the scent of Shigure's clean sweat somehow as comforting as his touch. "They could come any minute now," he whispered.

"Kotarō might, that's for sure."

Ken snickered. "Yeah. He'll probably come searching for his milk teeth."

Shigure laughed at that, the vibrations shaking them both as they stood grabbing each other like a pair of drunks.

"He's not much younger than you, Kenshin-san," Shigure said, and Ken felt his stare on him, as if the yakuza was trying to gauge his age.

"Said the ancient one."

Shigure snorted as he pulled away from Ken. "I'm old enough to be needing my soak right now." Their eyes met, and Ken tried hard not to reach out again for the solid body in front of him. He could see Shigure was fighting his own desire to touch him, the strong features tensing into a mask of stubborn restraint.

Ken sighed. As much as he admired Japanese single-minded determination, sometimes it made him feel inadequate, as if he lacked enough self-control to be deemed presentable in Japanese society.

Shigure turned to walk away, and Ken silently admired the tight ass so beautifully framed by the simple, stark white lines of the loincloth. Maybe without the tattoo that piece of rolled cloth might have looked slightly incongruous, but against the dark ink, it appeared perfectly dignified, possibly the only thing that could match the timeless beauty of the design.

"Are you checking out my ass?"

Ken looked up to meet amused black eyes, and managed not to blush too much as he grabbed the towel and washcloth Shigure offered. "Nah, just checking if those peonies needed watering."

Shigure grinned. "Sure. Now get rid of those boxers, and let's get some watering of our own."

Ken nodded and waited in vain for the yakuza to turn around. It was silly to be shy now after what they'd already done, but still Ken's fingers trembled as he pushed his underwear down under Shigure's unwavering stare. Shit. The man could drill holes with his eyes, and Ken didn't dare imagine what it would be like to face those eyes when they were angry.

"Don't cover yourself." Shigure's voice stopped Ken's unconscious movement to place the towel in front of him, and he looked up to see the yakuza rake hungry eyes over his body. Ken felt almost too naked, too skinny, too plain, but the obvious appreciation in Shigure's gaze made him also feel too excited, his freed cock rising as if to meet the expectation in those eyes.

"Hmm. Never seen hair so blond," Shigure said after an agonizingly long silence, and it took Ken's addled brain a few more seconds to figure out which hair the yakuza was talking about. "May I...?"

Before he could answer, Shigure was right in front of him, thick fingers reaching out to comb through Ken's pubes. God. It felt so intimate, that gesture, even more than touching his straining shaft would have been. The way those fingers caressed him carried a world of emotions, an interest in his body that went further than immediate stimulation or even pleasure. He was being learned, like a landscape that needed to be recorded to memory, like a picture chosen to be examined again and again over time.

He had to close his eyes to fight a shudder, his chest suddenly as tight as his balls were. If Shigure kept at that, he was going to embarrass himself by either coming or whimpering like a lost pup.

Suddenly the hand was gone, and Ken opened his eyes to see the yakuza's retreating back, his movements brusque as he tugged at his loincloth and yanked it off his body. Ken swallowed, his erection dwindling in spite of the magnificent view of Shigure's naked form as he walked away and disappeared through a door.

Ken took in a ragged breath, his hand raking nervously through his hair. The problem with Japanese people was not that they didn't show any emotion. The problem was they did, in the most maddening, closemouthed, confusing way they possibly could. And Ken was not sure he was up to trying to cope with it anymore.

CHAPTER 10

SHIGURE rubbed his skin so hard it stung. Cool water had helped with his problem, but he was still a little irked at himself for acting like a sullen kid.

If Kenshin had been a woman or, more to the point, a Japanese man, he wouldn't have had a problem with the chance of his men walking in on them. He never had in the past, and the truth was his men kept mostly away, either because they guessed what he might be up to or because they chose to offer him some respect and left him alone with his guests whenever he had them.

And here he was now, walking away in panic when all he'd wanted was to devour that pale beauty so trustingly exposed to him for the first time. Kenshin was so different from every man he'd ever laid eyes on, so close to the light-framed body structure of the Japanese and yet so stunningly different, his skin so pale, the light dusting of hair on his arms and legs so blond it was almost transparent, the curls above his shaft so soft he'd almost given in to the need of rubbing his cheek against them. "Almost" being the key word here. Just imagining himself going down on his knees in front of a gaijin had filled him with anger.

The carp tattooed on his back stood for pride—as Kenshin had so smartly guessed—and the pride that had carried him so far was going to be the worst obstacle to getting what he wanted now.

Shigure turned to look at Kenshin's stiff back as he washed himself, two stools away from where the yakuza sat in front of the taps. He was sure the American would leave as soon as he rinsed the lather off, going directly back to the changing room to get dressed without taking the time to relax in the hot bath with him. And why would he, after Shigure's display of rudeness?

He took a deep breath and stood. It was time to be a man about it and do what was right. Not many things in life were worth begging for, but this was.

Kenshin's back tensed even more as Shigure approached and sat on the stool behind him, but the American never turned to look. Shigure rinsed his own washcloth and pressed it gently against the pale back that went ramrod straight as soon as he grazed it, though Kenshin didn't quite pull away, probably because he thought it would be impolite.

Shigure kept still, waiting for the strained muscles to give a little under his touch, and then he started moving the cloth in small circles, slowly covering more and more skin in a soft caress that he hoped would carry his message for him. After a while, Kenshin's head fell forward, exposing his nape to Shigure, that minute gesture of trust making the yakuza finally relax the tension in his own muscles.

He kept washing Kenshin's back, enjoying the now-comfortable quality of the silence between them. Then he moved to the arms, taking his time to caress every inch of exposed skin with the lathered washcloth. His touch lacked the impatience of sexual gratification, but it wasn't the neutral contact of strangers sharing a bath because he couldn't touch Kenshin without feeling something stir inside, something that urged him to both enjoy and claim what was silently offered.

He stood and rested his left hand on Kenshin's shoulder for balance as he bent forward to run the cloth over the pale, hairless chest. The bones under his fingers were sharp. Kenshin didn't have an ounce of fat on him. He was all lean muscle and sinews, his skin soft as it stretched over clearly marked ribs.

Shigure pressed down to lather a flat stomach that went taut at his touch. He liked to see how sensitive the American was, how he would squirm when Shigure grazed certain spots, while pressure on others would bring an instant, glorious, full-body shudder.

He crouched to one side of Kenshin's sitting form and ran the washcloth down a slender thigh, past the knee to the slim ankle. Then he lifted a fine-boned foot and took his time over each toe, admiring the soft skin, the perfectly trimmed, small nails, and the way Kenshin shivered when he ran the cloth over the sole.

Touching the American like this was like having an intimate conversation with him, so different from sex and yet so personal that Shigure felt as if he were opening all the drawers in the young man's bedroom to see what he kept inside.

He reached out to Kenshin's other leg and pulled gently until the lean body slid to the edge of the stool, facing Shigure now. That way he had perfect access to all that gleaming skin he intended to cover.

When he finished his journey down the other leg, Shigure pushed the bony knees apart, spreading Kenshin's legs to get to his groin. He took his time to appreciate the blond curls nestling a rosy cock that was, like the rest of the pale body in front of him, beautifully long and slender, a funny feeling growing in the pit of Shigure's stomach as he saw the shaft widen and rise without being touched.

He looked up to meet Kenshin's unique eyes, the brown one almost black now, the green one glowing like a reservoir of ancient magic. The American was looking at him like old ghosts might, with a hunger for life that only long deprivation could bring forth, desire melting every boundary between this solid world and the world of the supernatural from where Kenshin seemed to have crossed over just to get a look at the mortal now crouching in front of him, wanting him as if he were ready to forfeit whatever power he might have accrued in his long banishment from this Earth.

Unable to tear his eyes from the strange eyes watching him, Shigure reached out blindly to wash Kenshin's genitals, the cloth running along the shaft with a firm caress that brought out a gasp from the already parted lips, and then moving on to clean the heavy sac and reach behind it to graze the sensitive skin there, pressing along Kenshin's cleft to make the slender body tighten when the ridged fabric touched his hole.

Shigure felt his own cock filling, but he ignored it. He wanted Kenshin, but this was far more important, this connection he was sealing with every slow touch, with every look they exchanged. Kenshin had to be assured that he had a place in his life now, and Shigure himself needed to understand where that place was exactly—if it was a guest room he was getting ready for Kenshin to visit or if it was rather the main bedroom, which had to be refurbished for him to stay.

He discarded the washcloth and took a gob of soap in his hands, rubbing them together to lather them up. Kenshin's eyes followed his every move, and Shigure couldn't resist the tug of those strangely colored orbs, his fingers reaching up to trace soap circles on the skin around them, and then follow the straight line of the nose down and to the sides to caress the flushed cheeks. His fingers sank next into the wet strands of fine hair, gently massaging Kenshin's scalp until the young man closed his eyes and sighed.

Shigure stood and moved to stand behind Kenshin, pressing his legs against the American's back to offer him support while he kept lathering his hair. When Kenshin leaned against him, Shigure felt he was recovering his trust, all the more so because the young man was abandoning the weight of his head to Shigure's hands, and it was a surprisingly exhilarating sensation to hold him with his fingers, to trace the solid contours of the bone underneath and feel it both strong and extremely fragile at the same time, just like Kenshin himself seemed to be—his beauty delicate in its china smoothness, and his character as strong as the wiry build of his body.

Without moving his legs from where they stood supporting Kenshin, Shigure bent to pick up a wooden bucket and fill it with water under the tap. Still Kenshin didn't open his eyes, and Shigure studied the handsome face for a moment, knowing that was exactly the kind of view he wanted when he opened his eyes every morning. It didn't surprise him anymore, how quickly this shy man had burrowed his way under his tattooed skin, but it made him a little anxious in a way he wasn't sure he understood completely. It had something to do with Kenshin's being a foreigner, but Shigure guessed Kenshin's condition had two different kinds of drawbacks for him. He might be both ashamed of wanting a gaijin and resentful of the unreachable status that very condition granted Kenshin over someone like Shigure, who lived in the shadows of society.

Rare eyes met his, and Shigure realized he had kept still for a while, one hand holding Kenshin's head, the other keeping the now overflowing bucket under the faucet. He let his expression soften into an almost smile. He wasn't dumping his confusion on Kenshin anymore; he deserved better, probably better than Shigure could offer, but he wouldn't go there right now.

He straightened and poured the water in the bucket over Kenshin's hair, carefully bending Kenshin's head back to keep the descending rivulets from his face. He then proceeded to rinse Kenshin's body thoroughly, refilling the bucket and emptying it over the white skin until there was no trace of soap left, picking up a fresh cloth to finally rinse Kenshin's face.

Before Kenshin stood, Shigure cupped the upturned face in his hands. "Will you have dinner with me tomorrow?" He didn't even know if he'd be free the next evening, but he had to let Kenshin know he wanted to see him again, in a place where they wouldn't feel constricted by what they were, the gaijin and the yakuza.

Kenshin blinked once, and his expression remained serious. "Okay," he just said, sounding so young and uncertain that Shigure couldn't help brushing his lips against the young man's in the sort of tender kiss he wasn't used to giving, but then again, there were so many unusual things he kept doing around this beautiful gaijin that he might not recognize himself anymore. Yeah. Maybe the carp tattooed on his back was turning into something else, and he wasn't at all sure it'd be a dragon he saw in its place the next time he looked in the mirror.

CHAPTER 11

IT WASN'T right. A wakagashira should not open the doors to the clan house for anyone, much less a gaijin. This was the house where they grew up to be what they were expected to be, and it shouldn't admit any kind of rabble.

What if the gaijin could speak some Japanese and swing a *bokken*? Trained monkeys knew how to do that and more, but you didn't introduce them as people. If Matsunaga wanted a male whore, there were lots of places he could've gone to, host clubs under the protection of the Shinagawa, where the boys were rail thin and wore their hair dyed just like the gaijin, and with a little extra tip, he might've even found a guy wearing contacts to make his eyes look like some evil *yōkai* too. Hell, he was a yakuza boss, and he could afford first-class entertainment. He didn't have to defile the communal bath with one of his flings, didn't have to train with him, didn't have to parade the little twink as he would a prospective wife.

Matsunaga could hang as many artsy pictures as he liked on his walls, but he didn't have what it took to stand proud in a long line of ancestors. He was all façade. And someone would have to show the world what lay underneath that façade. And do it soon. Before the Shinagawa-gumi wasn't worth fighting for—or against.

"SERGEANT UEHARA showed him every picture they had of Daitō-kai men," Kinosuke said.

Shigure nodded. "We'll make sure to have a more substantial gift for the sergeant when New Year comes."

"I think he would've done it anyway, boss, even if he wasn't getting anything from us."

Shigure had to agree with that. Uehara was one of the old-school cops who knew that working with the yakuza was a lesser evil that kept the neighborhoods safe and crime statistics shiny. That he received payoffs from both gangs in his jurisdiction was as normal as it was for doctors to receive gifts from their patients. It was the Japanese way, no matter how much Westerners would put their hands in the air and cry bribery in outrage.

Now Uehara was trying to prevent a turf war that might cause collateral damage to innocent citizens, as it had happened before. That he helped both gangs to police their ranks was only saving time and taxpayer resources, and far more efficient than trying to coax some closemouthed yakuza to rat out their own.

"Did the Haihīru man recognize anyone?"

"No," Kinosuke said. "The bastard probably doesn't even have a record. The Daitō-kai is too big for the cops to keep track of all of them."

Shigure shrugged. "It was worth trying. Did Harada tell you anything new about the girl? Has she come back to work?"

"No. She hasn't been back, and Harada doesn't know how to reach her. All he has is a cell number that goes right to voice mail every time he calls. I checked and it's not registered."

"Bank account?" Shigure asked.

"No. Harada-san paid her in cash."

"So, all we have is the front desk clerk and a stolen credit card."

"That's pretty much it, yeah," Kinosuke answered. "We can only hope Onga does his fucking job and gives his man what the coward deserves."

He hoped so too. Onga was as interested as they were in avoiding a war between the two gangs. They were both doing pretty well in their established territories, and the need to expand hadn't appeared yet and probably never would. Still, there was something disquieting about the whole incident, though Shigure couldn't quite put his finger on it.

"The owner of the credit card, do we know where he reported the theft?"

"You mean which police box he went to?"

Shigure nodded, but before Kinosuke could answer there was a knock at the door, and it slid open to let an excited Kotarō in.

"I found a lot of them, boss!" he said, lifting two plastic bags. Shigure tried not to laugh at Kinosuke's resigned sigh. Kotarō was the worst apprentice they'd ever had, but at least he was a good kid, and it made it very difficult to be harsh with him. Yet Shigure was only glad the responsibility of training him rested on Kinosuke's shoulders and not his own. He might not have that kind of patience anymore.

"Kotarō," Kinosuke said, his voice dangerously low. The kid gave him an uncertain look, as if he couldn't understand why his senior would interrupt him when he had such good news.

"Aniki?" God, that was cute, the way he deferred to his senior, calling him "big brother" with those puppy eyes of his. Shigure didn't envy Kinosuke's task at all.

"Did you hear the boss tell you that you could come in?"

Kotarō frowned, obviously trying to remember if he'd heard Shigure and failing miserably to come to any conclusion.

"You have to wait till the boss says it, no matter how long it takes."

"But I—"

"No matter how urgent your message is."

"But what if—"

"Your only excuse to crash through that door like an animal would be a mortal danger to the boss's life. Understood?"

Kotarō looked down in shame. "*Hai*, aniki," he said, and to Shigure's amusement, he started marching back to the door. Kinosuke looked anything but amused, though.

"Kotarō?"

The kid turned an innocent look on Kinosuke. "Aniki?"

"Where are you going now?"

"Uh, I just thought you wanted me to—" He pointed helplessly to the door and then looked back from Kinosuke to Shigure, some revelation finally dawning on him. Maybe he wasn't so clueless after all. "Oh, that's right." He walked purposely to Shigure's desk and deposited the bag on it. "You can take a look at them while you wait, boss." And then he turned his back and strode out of the door. Shigure couldn't help laughing out loud when Kinosuke rubbed a hand over his face in despair.

"He'll learn, Kinosuke. He's still too young," Shigure said over the knock on the door.

"He's a damn yakuza. He won't live long enough to learn if he doesn't shape up." Shigure sobered at Kinosuke's words, admiring once again his man's easy appraisal of reality. It was hard for him to imagine a time when Kinosuke might have acted young and foolish, and he couldn't help feeling both proud and bitter about it. Most of them had grown up too fast, with no time for innocence or playfulness in a world that threatened to step on them if they didn't bite as soon as they got some teeth to show.

"Come in, Kotarō," he said, shaking his head at Kotarō's effort to hide a proud smile at his display of good manners. It sure took a lot to dampen the kid's enthusiasm. "What is it that you wanted to show me?"

Kotarō's face lit up like a neon sign. "I went to pick up Atsushi's order at the bookstore, and they had a lot more books by Kenshin-san, like five or six more, and I bought them all!"

He saw Kinosuke scowl before he had time to ponder the implications of Kotarō's babble. Shit. What was it about Kinosuke and Kenshin? He couldn't hear the man's name without showing his disapproval one way or another, and it was starting to get on Shigure's nerves.

He focused his attention on Kotarō before he got too riled up. It was surprising for the kid to show so much initiative, especially at a bookstore, when he probably didn't have that good a hold on his kanji at all. Then again, maybe children's books were the only ones he could really read.

"What made you look for more books, Kotarō?"

"Oh, I didn't figure Atsushi was wrong, him being so smart and all, but the nice lady at the bookstore told me they had some more books by the same illustrator." Kotarō laughed sheepishly. "You know I almost didn't buy them because Kenshin-san's name wasn't there at all, but I thought if Atsushi had ordered those two, then the others had to be Kenshin-san's as well. I guess he uses his gaijin name in the books."

At least he'd come to that conclusion by himself and bested Atsushi at his task. Not a small feat for a school dropout like Kotarō. What really worried Shigure was that his secretary had failed to find not one but six more books. It wasn't like Atsushi to overlook something like that.

"Don't you wanna see them, boss? They're great."

Shigure smiled. Only Kotarō would admit to have gone through the books he'd been ordered to collect.

"You read them?" he asked in amusement.

"Nah, I don't like reading that much. I just looked at the drawings on the train. And I was very careful too. I didn't thumb the pages or anything. Those pictures are really cool."

Shigure couldn't resist anymore, and he dug his hand into the plastic bag and retrieved one of the books. It had a surprisingly dull cover for a children's book, with just big silver letters on a purple background. *How to Feed Your Pet Yōkai* it read in hiragana script, with the name of the author of the text and Kenshin's written in katakana beside the title. It was obviously a translation, and Shigure wondered what the original word for yōkai could be. It was probably monsters the story talked about, as the first picture he saw confirmed. Yet by then he was too busy keeping his mouth from hanging open to think about translations and differences between supernatural beings.

"That's one of my favorites," Kotarō said, "that and the one about this boy who has a ghost as a friend."

Shigure barely heard him. His eyes were glued to the diminutive beast sitting on a small boy's palm. The creature wasn't bigger than the kid's hand, but it was done in such detail that you could see each colorful scale on its body, each tooth in its open mouth, each delicate feather on its incredible crest. The boy was dangling an ant in front of the creature's mouth, the little insect so alive that Shigure could almost see it trying to wriggle free. He scanned the text and read, "The *lizuana* is a very shy repbirdian that feeds on ants and sleeps the afternoons away. Keep it warm and cozy, and it will keep your house ant-free." And from those two single sentences Kenshin had built a whole universe of miniature fauna. Amazing.

"Wait till you reach the big ones, boss, they're incredible."

Spurred by Kotarō's fervor, Shigure skipped some pages to go to the last pictures—where he supposed the biggest monsters would be—only to have his breath catch in his throat at the image spreading in front of his disbelieving eyes.

It was just a head, the biggest, craziest animal's head he'd ever seen, spreading over two facing pages to leave only one corner free, where a small boy stood with his tiny hand lifted toward the beast. The monster had cruel, yellow eagle eyes, but its snout was that of a four-legged animal, a wolf, or rather a lion, given the breadth of the open mouth. And what a mouth it was, with two rows of sharp teeth on each jaw, the canines so long they'd protrude when the jaws were closed, drool dripping from the corners of the outstretched lips. To complete the scary picture, the head had a fantastic mane of live snakes, each one of a different, bright color, forked tongues coming out to test the air.

The first portion of the beast's furry shoulders had been drawn, too, as if to imply the end of the page had cut the whole picture, and Shigure turned the page like a kid who couldn't help upending the cookie jar even though his hand had already touched the empty bottom.

To his delighted surprise, he found that the animal's body did continue on the next two pages, its bizarre figure making him chuckle. Its forelegs were tall and strong like those of a lion, but the hindquarters were low, with freckled fur, ending on an erect tail that the half-hyena, half-lion appeared to be wagging in excitement. The small text had been printed in a way that it seemed to rest on the steep romp of the beast.

"The *Iyena* is a mammal of the *Chocovora* order, famous for its loyalty to owners who feed him only 75 percent minimum cocoa chocolate bars."

Shigure turned the page back to where the little boy stood, and studied his raised hand carefully. Sure enough, there was something those tiny fingers were holding, though he couldn't quite tell what it was.

"Can you see the candy bar?" Kotarō asked, pointing at the picture. "It even has gaijin letters on it. I bet it says something funny."

All three of them bent over the picture to try to read the romaji words, but it was obvious Kotarō couldn't read the Roman alphabet, Kinosuke was frowning as if he couldn't quite make out the letters, and

Shigure already knew his eyesight was not that of a young man anymore.

"Don't you have one of those glasses, boss?"

He looked blankly at Kinosuke until he remembered the ugly magnifying glass someone had given him for his desk. He retrieved the thing from a drawer and placed it over the drawing.

"Valrhona... Man... Manjari," he read. It sounded familiar, something his friend Oyone had mentioned once.

"What does it mean?"

And then he remembered. "It's the name of a French chocolate brand," he answered with a smile. "It's said to be the best dark chocolate you can find."

"Wow. Kenshin-san rocks."

Shigure laughed. Yeah, Kenshin rocked—his world at least. He was dying to go through all the books, see what that feverish imagination had come up with to illustrate children's fantasies. As if Kinosuke had read his mind, he started to herd Kotarō to the door.

"Come on, let's go, kid. The boss is busy."

Shigure looked up at those words, gauging Kinosuke's expression in search of any sign of disrespect. The young man's face was a blank, his eyes meeting Shigure's straight on.

"Is there anything you want to tell me, Kinosuke?"

A muscle twitched in his subordinate's jaw, but he shook his head. "No, boss."

Shigure guessed he needed to have a serious conversation with Kinosuke, but this was not the moment, not with Kotarō present. "Find out where the credit card was reported stolen, and we'll go on from there."

"*Hai,*" Kinosuke answered as he pushed Kotarō out the door and closed it behind them.

Shigure sighed. He wasn't superstitious, but he couldn't help a growing feeling of dread as the little details added up. Maybe he'd been sitting in his comfortable position for too long and change had finally caught up with him. The world of the yakuza was only stable because it kept changing to adapt and remain, and he was just one of the lesser pawns in the game of power that went on between the gangs and the heaviest political players. And on top of everything else, there was this nagging voice reminding him that everything had been fine until Kenshin showed his gaijin face.

It was most unfair to blame Kenshin, but a part of him found it easy to do, the part of him that still looked at the world from the other side of the shop window, the part that resented everything he couldn't touch with his dirty hands.

His now perfectly manicured fingers still felt incongruous on the delicate items money could afford him, and it made him angry all over again. He was sure that if he were to wipe his skin clean of all his tattoos, a thick coat of shame would appear covering his naked flesh. He had fought his way out of the place he was supposed to fit in, but he couldn't shake the fear of being discovered and thrown back into the mud where he belonged. That fear had been imprinted in him to make sure he didn't do exactly what he had done, move up from his assigned lot.

He emptied the bookstore bags onto his desk, the colorful little books spilling like candy on the dark wood. He had a right to this, damn it. And if he chose to be lovers with a man who was everything Shigure wasn't, it was nobody's business but theirs. He had never lied to Kenshin, and if the gaijin still wanted him, he'd be a fool to throw that kind of gift out the window.

Shigure might have been born an outcast, but he'd never been a fool.

CHAPTER 12

KEN laid his head back against the headrest. The plush leather seats were making him stir-crazy, or maybe it was the hard stare of the driver that he met from time to time in the rearview mirror, or—most probably—Ryū's disapproval of tonight's escapade.

His friend had been all right with Ken's visit to the tiger's lair, and in fact it had been his idea to send him to a known yakuza house carrying a sword with him. It seemed okay to exchange blows with a yakuza boss, but to actually date him had sent Ryū into a hissy fit.

"Are you crazy?" his friend yelled when Ken asked to borrow one of his suits.

"Come on, you know any place that requires a tie can't be that dangerous. It's a public place, too, so what's gonna happen?"

"For Christ's sake, Kenshin. Matsunaga is a yakuza, and you're going to one of his joints. Anything can happen."

He gave Ryū a disbelieving stare. "Why do you have to make it sound so sleazy? It's not a *joint* I'm going to. I'm just having dinner with the man in a classy restaurant. There's nothing wrong with it."

"Yeah, host clubs can be very classy, but they're still what they are."

There was an awkward silence after that sentence, and Ken felt the color drain from his face. He'd never discussed his sex life with Ryū, but his friend knew he was gay, and all this time Ken had thought he was all right with it.

"Good to know what you consider me. But don't worry, this gaijin won't shame you anymore. I'll move to a hotel tomorrow. Just don't wait up for me. I don't expect the orgy to finish before dawn."

"Kenshin—"

He slammed the front door after him, though it didn't give him much satisfaction. Ryū was the only safe harbor he had in his life, and to find out that even he judged Ken so harshly was a hard blow. His purported friend hadn't asked for details. He'd just heard Ken was going out with a man, and he immediately assumed it was more or less a male brothel they were going to.

"Want me to stop?"

Ken opened his eyes, startled. The driver was looking at him in the mirror, waiting. Yeah, he probably didn't look much like a guy about to enjoy himself.

"It's all right, thank you," he said to the man he'd taken to think of as Scar-face, though he'd learned that his name was Shinya.

"We'll be there in a minute."

He tried to smile reassuringly, though he wanted to shake his head instead. What was it about him that made all those big badass guys treat him with such consideration? At least they'd seen what he could do with a sword, otherwise it might have prompted him to believe they considered him weak, fragile even. But no, it didn't seem to be the case. Ken supposed they were just being gentlemanly in the gentle—*yasashī*—Japanese way. Who would've thought the yakuza had such delicate manners? Not his friend Ryū, to mention one.

He groaned in exasperation. He wasn't going to think about Ryū again. Not tonight. Tonight he would enjoy Shigure's company, be with him like he would with any other man he'd gone out with—if he could remember the last time he'd dated someone, that is. He sure didn't remember any other time someone had shown so much passion and so much restraint toward him all at once. Just like the day before, Shigure washing him with such slow, sensual caresses all over his body, taking his arousal to an incredible level, and then leaving him there, both of them sitting in the hot communal pool without even touching until the yakuza reached out to take his hand under the water and hold it, the sudden contact so electric he had shivered in the scalding bath and almost came with just the touch of that strong hand.

Scar-face was gazing at him in the mirror again. He must look like an oddball gaijin, sitting alone in the back of a Mercedes making faces. He smiled and nodded, and got a nod in return. Yeah. These guys could teach manners in business schools.

The sleek black car turned into a small alley and pulled up at the curb. Big, mean-looking Scar-face opened the back door with a white-gloved hand Ken hadn't even noticed as the man drove.

"Boss'll be waiting for you inside, Kenshin-san," he said, bowing slightly.

He tried not to blink too much at the disconcerting picture of a street thug in white gloves and steward manners. "Uh, thank you."

The restaurant was indeed a classy, traditional one, its entrance covered with a black *noren*, a half-curtain with beautiful white kanji on it. As soon as he entered, a whole team of pretty girls in matching kimonos greeted him with a synced "Irasshaimase," one of them sinking to the floor to unlace his dress shoes while the others smiled and generally hovered over him like a flock of humming birds.

Once in his stocking feet and properly flustered by all the attention, Ken had to adjust his pace to keep behind the petite waitress showing him the way. Watching her move graciously in the strict confines of a long kimono made him feel gangly and awkward. He wasn't very big by gaijin standards, but he was still taller than the average Japanese, and far less graceful.

When the door to a private room slid open and Shigure stood to greet him, Ken couldn't help the relieved smile that came to his lips. Yeah. There was a man he didn't feel awkward around—hot and bothered maybe, but not uneasy in his own skin.

Shigure gave him an arch smile, black eyes twinkling as they raked over Ken's body. Ken didn't even notice it when the girl disappeared. He couldn't for the life of him take his eyes off the incredible man in front of him.

It seemed black was Shigure's color, the dark suit hugging his broad frame like an affectionate lover, a striking white shirt enhancing the elegant cut of the jacket and the unpretentious black tie. He looked tall, powerful, and altogether good enough to eat.

"Hmm. Nice suit, Kenshin-san."

Shigure made it sound as if he weren't speaking about the suit at all, and Ken tried to contain the surge of heat traveling straight to his cock. "I just bought it, since Ryū wouldn't—" He closed his mouth abruptly. What was he babbling about? Jesus. He couldn't up and tell Shigure he'd fought with Ryū because of him, could he?

Shigure covered the space between them in two strides and reached out to cup Ken's chin, lifting it so that their eyes met. He was getting very good at invading Ken's space to claim his attention. "Something wrong?"

Ken searched the dark look fixed on him and swallowed. Nothing seemed to be wrong when he was with this man, at least when there was no one else around to judge them.

He shook his head, unable to say the words, his fingers seeking the comfort of Shigure's warm skin, resting lightly on the yakuza's nape. Shigure's eyes darkened even more, his look turning heated, possessive, as he bent to take Ken's lips in an urgent kiss.

Ken opened up for him with a moan, his body leaning toward the furnace that was Shigure's body in the air-conditioned room, and strong arms immediately enveloped him, crushing him against Shigure's front.

"My my, what a nice view."

He almost jumped out of his skin at the amused female voice, but Shigure kept him close, his arm firmly seated around Ken's waist.

"Watch your manners, Oyo-chan. Private rooms are called that for a reason."

"Are they now."

Ken couldn't quite tell the age of the woman smirking at them. At first sight, she looked to be in her thirties, her delicate face expertly made up to enhance her best features without appearing to be wearing any makeup at all, her thick black hair kept out of her face in a simple bun, held tight with a carved wooden pin, her kimono in a sober gray that made her look distinguished. Her beautiful white hands were those of a young woman, while her laughing eyes told a different story, them and the deep, knowing voice, showing a kind of mature detachment that could easily put her past forty. Now those eyes were scrutinizing Ken as if he were back in first grade with the math teacher staring at him.

"So I guess this is your artist. Aren't you going to introduce us?" she finally said, and Ken couldn't help blushing at her words. That Shigure had obviously been talking about him felt as embarrassing as it was flattering, goose bumps rising all over his skin at being called Shigure's anything. It didn't seem to have escaped the yakuza, either, the big hand on Ken's hip squeezing tightly as if to confirm ownership.

"Oyone, this is Kenshin-san. He does these amazing illustrations for children's stories. You wouldn't believe the monsters this pretty head can come up with."

"Hajimemashite, Kenshin-san."

Ken was too busy answering Oyone's formal greeting to really pay attention to Shigure's words.

"Kenshin-san, this is my friend Oyone, the owner of this posh establishment. She could teach the emperor manners, but she often chooses to forget her own in favor of satisfying her curiosity, which is bottomless."

"Oh shut up, Gure-chan. I just worry about my friends, and I can't help them if I don't know all the facts. So Kenshin-san, dear, are you wearing contacts?"

Shigure laughed heartily at Ken's discomfiture. "Don't make him blush, woman."

"Why not? He looks even cuter when he blushes. And you should have told me he was a cutie-pie. Now I'm going to have a bunch of disgruntled employees when they learn he's already taken."

"Damn right he is." Shigure's arm tightened even more around Ken's waist, and Ken couldn't make himself feel annoyed at the primitive display of possessiveness. It was the first time someone had shown pride at being with him, and however unhealthy or dangerous it might be, Ken just felt his blood rush with the elation of being wanted.

"I'm not wearing contacts, Oyone-san, and I don't mind being asked," he said, knowing that, in spite of their banter, Shigure really trusted her. The affection between them was very easy to see, easy enough that Ken would have been jealous if it wasn't pretty obvious, too, that the connection between them had no sexual undertones to it. And if he hadn't already been blushing, he would have now, considering being jealous over a man he barely knew.

Shigure rolled his eyes at Ken. "Never tell Oyone that you don't mind her questions, or she'll never leave us alone."

Oyone totally ignored him. "Have you tried wearing them just to confuse people?"

Ken couldn't help smiling. It was as if she'd guessed how much he liked to disguise himself. "I've thought about it once or twice—for the fun of it—but I never did it in the end. It'd have felt too much like hiding."

"And it isn't a flaw you have there"—she nodded—"but a striking feature. Not that you wouldn't be pretty enough without it, but it makes you really special."

"Don't call him pretty, Oyone. He's a man."

Now it was Oyone's turn to roll her eyes. "You called him pretty yourself, you macho man."

Ken snorted at that and received a glare from the yakuza. "You know you did, Shigure-san," he said, holding the dark gaze steadily, seeing it burn with something intense that wasn't anger as those lips he was jonesing to feel on his own twitched slightly.

"Traitor," Shigure whispered, his eyes traveling down to Ken's parted lips as if he, too, was craving a taste.

"Well, now. Seeing that my high cuisine will just be ignored, why don't I show you to a really private room, with a bed and all?"

Ken blushed to the roots of his hair, but Shigure wrapped him in his arms as if he could hide him within the bulk of his body, and laughed, the big oaf. "That would be great, Oyo-chan, and we'd appreciate it if you could leave us some little snack, too—you know, just in case we wake up hungry in the middle of the night."

Oyone put her hands on her hips. "Don't tell me how to treat my guests, you caveman." Ken snickered a little too soon, it seemed, for Oyone wasn't done with them yet. "I wouldn't leave a growing boy without his dinner."

Now it was Shigure's turn to snicker. "He sure is growing," he said, letting his gaze drop none too subtly below Ken's waistline.

"Shigure!" both he and Oyone cried out at the same time, their eyes meeting as Ken realized he'd dropped the honorific in his outrage at Shigure's crassness. Oyone's knowing eyes smiled at him, and Ken knew exactly what they were seeing, knew that Shigure might be clueless about it, but his lady friend had Ken pegged for what he was, a silly gaijin falling hard for a yakuza.

CHAPTER 13

SHIGURE tried to school his face as he locked the door, but seeing Kenshin's flushed cheeks as soon as he turned around brought the smile back to his lips. Now Kenshin outright pouted, and it made him want to do much more than smile. Damn. He looked so young and adorable that Shigure felt like the big bad wolf about to devour a helpless kid, and just as if Oyone had seen it that way, too, she had glared at him when she handed him the key card, whispering fiercely in his ear, "Now don't you scare this one away, you hear me?"

He approached Kenshin slowly, never taking his eyes off him as he circled the king-sized bed. No. This beauty with exotic eyes could be skittish on occasion, but he wasn't easy to scare. He was stubborn, and proud, and brave, and Shigure intended to keep him.

Kenshin watched him with what appeared like apprehension until a pink tongue came out to wet his full lips. Now that was sexy, and Kenshin wasn't even doing it on purpose. The man had a sensual way about him, his slender body graceful in its every movement, inviting, oozing sex in the most natural and unselfconscious manner, every piece of clothing he wore just disguising a skin that was made to be displayed in all its naked splendor.

He stopped inches away from Kenshin, the slight difference in height between them making the shorter man tilt his head to look up into Shigure's eyes, challenging, taunting him even when that very posture exposed his white, vulnerable neck in a show of proffered submission.

He let the noise forming deep in his chest come out as a growl and reached out to grab Kenshin's head and tilt it further back so that he could sink his teeth in that tender expanse of flesh. Kenshin yelped in pain, but his hands immediately came up to latch at Shigure's neck and bring his slender body against Shigure while Shigure sucked a mark right under Kenshin's jaw, where he knew it would be very visible, even if Kenshin wore one of those sexy chokers he was so fond of.

Kenshin moaned against him, hungry lips searching Shigure's as soon as he let go of the red mark he'd just imprinted on him. He swirled his tongue around the invading one, tasting Kenshin's sweet flavor, tickling the sensitive surface of his palate, nibbling at the upper lip whenever he could catch it between his teeth, the few seconds at a time Kenshin allowed him to control the kiss.

His hands slid down to unbutton Kenshin's jacket and push it out of the way. The light brown fabric felt crispy under his fingers, and he remembered Kenshin saying something about the suit being new. His mouth was too busy to ask questions now, though, and his fingers were getting desperate to reach the soft skin under the endless layers of clothing, so he just loosened the silk tie and tried to push shirt, jacket, and tie up and over Kenshin's head, only managing to make a tangle of clothes and long limbs along the way.

Kenshin's breathless laughter came to him muffled from under the mess of shirtsleeves and jacket lining, Shigure's own laughter joining his when he saw one of those small plastic bags holding spare buttons still attached to the inner seam of Kenshin's jacket.

"You bought it on your way here?"

The bundle of clothing stopped moving. "Crap. Don't tell me—"

Shigure tried hard not to keep laughing. "Afraid so." But Kenshin cursing a blue streak in two languages proved too much for him.

"Stop laughing and help me, you baka."

Crazy enough, being called dork by a runt like Kenshin made him feel happy, as if he'd just realized he was missing the normalcy of male banter, the unfettered give and take of male friendship.

He slowly peeled every onion-like layer of fabric draping around Kenshin's head and arms. At the sight of a tousled, red-cheeked gaijin, Shigure felt a most uncharacteristic wave of tenderness and leaned forward to plant a kiss on Kenshin's nose.

Kenshin laughed, the sound so sweet to Shigure's ears that his smile grew until his lips felt about to split. God. It seemed all he could do around this man was grin like a fool.

"Shigure-san?"

"Hmm?"

"How come I'm half-naked and you're still wearing a suit?"

He chuckled, letting his arms wrap around Kenshin's trim waist. "Must be a gaijin thing."

Kenshin's laughter turned into a moan when Shigure's hands slid along the exposed back. Their lips met again, the kiss now softer, deeper, with more intention behind the simple, frenzied craving for each other that sprang to life every time they touched.

Without letting go of that delectable mouth, Shigure pushed Kenshin until the back of his knees collided with the bed. A gentle shove and Kenshin toppled onto the covers, bouncing slightly on the mattress.

Shigure took his time disrobing, his eyes glued to the long-limbed beauty sprawled on the bed as those peculiar eyes followed every move he made, the look in them charged with a hypnotic mixture of need, appreciation, and longing. Shigure's whole body rose to meet the challenge that desire posed, his tattooed skin prickling with its own need for contact, the veins on his cock pulsing in the same erratic rhythm of his heart, his fingers trembling at the sight of all that white, untouched skin still half-hidden under slim, elegant, brand-new pants.

He got rid of his underwear, seeing his nakedness reflected in the hungry eyes that traveled all over him, long hands lifting off the bed and reaching out to urge him closer. He slapped the hands away playfully, smirking at the frustrated groan coming from Kenshin. Not that he didn't want those long, expert fingers on him, but first he needed to even out their state of undress, remove those fancy pants that might be still carrying a price tag.

"What's so funny?"

He chuckled openly. "You managed to find the right size in spite of the haste."

Kenshin was trying not to smile. "Shut up. They're too tight in, uh, certain spots."

Shigure hummed, scrutinizing the spots in question. The way Kenshin lay, the rich fabric stretched deliciously over lean thighs, getting tighter the further up Shigure's eyes roamed, fitting narrow hips snugly, closing on a flat belly without any need for a belt, the zipper pressing down so hard he could perfectly draw the outline of Kenshin's cock as though he wasn't wearing any underwear. Or was he?

"Were they so tight that you had to...?" He knew his voice had gone all husky at the thought, and seeing Kenshin blush in answer made him curse, his cock twitching as if he needed the reminder to notice how turned on he was by this incredibly brazen yet shy gaijin.

"Help me take them off?" Kenshin asked, big eyes pleading, hands reaching out for Shigure one more time, needing the contact more than he needed getting free from the oppressive clothing, needing him more than anything else. And damn if that need didn't bring out Shigure's most primal instincts, his own need to claim what was offered to him, pushing his body forward and into the territory Kenshin's arms delimited.

He was immediately encircled in warm, naked flesh, the sexy gaijin trying to wrap himself around Shigure, sweet lips latching onto his left nipple and sending shock waves straight to his cock. He cursed and tried to keep focused on the simple task of getting rid of Kenshin's trousers, his fingers fumbling with the button while Kenshin sucked, licked, and nibbled on a different kind of button, again and again until Shigure thought he might go crazy with need.

The button finally gave way, but the zipper was far too new to slide down easily and Shigure groaned. He felt Kenshin smile around his nipple before white, perfect teeth sank into the sensitive nub, and he couldn't take it anymore. He grabbed Kenshin's head with his hands and forced him to look up.

Round eyes blinked at him in confusion, making Shigure's protective instincts kick right in. He bent to pepper that sweet upturned face with tender kisses, pressing Kenshin's body back onto the bed. "I need you naked now," he breathed into already swollen lips, moving out of reach when Kenshin tried to kiss him. "Now," he repeated by way of explanation, his fingers moving back down to the stubborn zipper.

The next try didn't get any better results, Kenshin's erection making the task especially difficult—no matter how much Shigure enjoyed seeing his young lover's obvious reaction to him. Then again he was a resourceful man, and he wasn't letting two strips of metal stand in the way to his goal.

He gave Kenshin a wicked grin and bunched his fingers on the fabric below the lean hips. And then he just started pulling.

"Oh fuck."

His grin got wider at Kenshin's expletive. The tight fabric was sliding down one inch at a time, scratching its way over sensitive skin, metal teeth raking over the beautifully flushed cock, making its hue go even darker with the friction. Sock-clad feet rose to the edge of the bed to help Kenshin push his hips off the mattress and allow the pants to go further down, but Shigure didn't rush. He wanted to savor every second of it, watch every desperate wiggle of those hips, absorb every expression on Kenshin's face as he labored on the thin line between pleasure and pain.

When the zipper pressed against the most sensitive area over the head of Kenshin's cock, brown-green eyes closed, and a pained moan filled the air. "Shigure-san, please," that sweet voice pleaded, almost out of breath, husky, needy, bordering on desperate.

Shigure swallowed, his own cock achingly hard and already leaking pre-come. He hadn't been kidding when he'd said he wanted Kenshin that very second, but the last thing he'd do was hurt him in his haste.

He forced one of his hands between the offending zipper and Kenshin's straining shaft, palming it down while his other hand yanked at the pants with a tearing sound.

Kenshin cried out, collapsing on the mattress, the trousers sliding now easily to his ankles, but still Shigure wouldn't let go of the pulsing heat under his fingers, stroking it lightly to feel it harden even more, the scent of Kenshin's arousal making his nostrils flare. Shigure got rid of the pants and socks without even looking at them, too busy watching Kenshin writhe, listening to his panting breaths, seeing his pupils take over bicolored irises until Kenshin's eyes appeared like weird black planets encircled by shining rings of poisonous gas.

Unable to wait, Kenshin surged up from the bed, long, naked limbs coiling around Shigure and pulling him down for avid lips to smother any resistance in ravenous kisses, hungry little noises filling Shigure's mouth along with the taste of that strange creature who seemed blind to everything Shigure was, the only creature on Earth who could look at his tattoo and see only the work of a fellow artist.

Shigure growled into the kiss. He knew what he wanted, had wanted it from the moment he'd laid eyes on this weirdly beautiful gaijin, and he wasn't waiting any longer. He made use of all his strength to disentangle the sexy boa constricting his body, his fingers squeezing at the base of Kenshin's shaft before they let go. Kenshin let out a strangled sound at the reversal of their predator-prey roles, his disgruntled surprise allowing Shigure to lift him bodily and toss him back onto the huge bed's middle.

"Stay there, you hungry yōkai," he said, watching the mesmerizing play of muscles under Kenshin's skin as he tried to recover his balance. But then he saw those same muscles tense, bright-colored eyes searching his as Shigure realized his commanding tone and the word he'd chosen might be easily misunderstood by someone used to being called names. He knew what it felt like, was very familiar with the shame, the insecurity, and the rage needed to overcome all that contempt. And he wouldn't let Kenshin imagine he'd ever direct that contempt at him as part of a power play. He didn't believe in humiliation as an aphrodisiac.

Shigure climbed into the bed, folding his legs under him to sit back on his heels at Kenshin's feet, his back as straight as if he were about to bow formally to him, but instead he reached out to grab one of Kenshin's ankles, his grip hard and unforgiving. "No one has ever made me need this badly, Kenshin-san," he said, staring straight into wide, glittering eyes. "And if I don't take you right this moment, I swear I'm going to die."

Kenshin looked at him for just a heartbeat, and then he simply folded the leg Shigure wasn't holding up and to the side, exposing himself for his lover in silent invitation. It was the sexiest thing the yakuza had ever seen, Kenshin's serious face making it more intense than playful, as if he truly believed Shigure might die if he didn't make Kenshin his.

He didn't let go of the warm ankle in his hand as he leaned to the side to open the first drawer in the nightstand and dug out condoms and lube. He worked single-handedly, tearing and uncapping, his eyes never leaving Kenshin's, watching for any change, absorbing every detail of their mineral perfection.

When his cock was properly sheathed and slicked, he pulled Kenshin closer, tugging at the bony ankle to drape the long leg over Shigure's thigh, the position spreading Kenshin wider and tilting his hips to allow Shigure better access.

The contrast between their skins had a striking effect, especially where Kenshin's white leg rested on the dark waters of Shigure's tattooed thigh, and he couldn't resist the impulse to run both his hands over that tantalizing expanse of light skin, following the contour of long legs up to the tiny waist that he almost seemed able to cover with his outstretched fingers, tanned skin tattooing its way over Kenshin's marked ribs and up to the rosy nipples that begged to be touched.

He loved the way Kenshin squirmed under his roaming hands, soft needy sounds leaving that white throat as Shigure's fingers toyed with his nipples, applying what he knew was too light pressure, leaving his lover craving much more, restraining his own need to grab those narrow hips and push all the way in with one single, savage thrust.

"Shigure-san, please," Kenshin pleaded, long fingers wrapping around Shigure's forearms as if to stop the distracting movements. He sounded breathless, and it made Shigure's stomach feel funny, being wanted that way, no pretense masking the desire he saw plainly in those extraordinary eyes.

Unable to answer, his own need too strong to let him articulate coherent words, he straightened into a kneeling position and pressed forward, letting the head of his cock rub over Kenshin's sensitive entrance. Kenshin moaned, his fingers digging deeper into Shigure's flesh as he tried to bear down on the teasing shaft. Shigure grabbed the slim hips and held them back against the mattress.

"Easy, Kenshin-san. I don't want to hurt you."

Kenshin made a dismissive sound. "Just go slowly. But go. Now," he said, his eyes blazing with impatience, his Japanese becoming less formal, the ending particles turning into the bold, pushy sounds street kids used.

Shigure smiled in spite of himself and reached out to push Kenshin's long bangs out of his flushed face.

"*Wakattaze, bozu,*" he said, enjoying the American's frown at being called a squirt. He complied anyway, his own need too desperate to linger over the foreplay, his cock pressing against the tight ring of muscle and breaching it as slowly as he could while his fingers traced soothing circles on Kenshin's belly.

White teeth sunk into Kenshin's lower lip, his eyes closing in a pained gesture that made Shigure stop, muscles rippling under his fingers as Kenshin tightened around him before the viselike grip on his cock loosened and Kenshin's body swallowed him whole, his lubed shaft sliding all the way in with a sucking sound.

Their moans came out at the same time, and when their eyes met, he saw the laughter that pushed out of his own throat reflected in Kenshin's eyes before they both chuckled breathlessly. He shook his head. It seemed this crazy gaijin would make him laugh even during sex—a completely new experience for him.

He looked down into those big, smiling eyes and finally understood the extent to which that exotic creature joined to him would alter his life if Shigure let him, how far from everything he'd ever known Kenshin would drag him if he just let himself go, let himself sink deeper into that inviting warmth, let himself forget what the ink carved into his body screamed so loudly to everyone else around him.

Kenshin's expression sobered, mirroring what he must be seeing in Shigure's eyes. Shigure held that serious gaze, his whole body poised in wait, knowing it was time to make a decision: enjoy what was left of his little foreign experiment and send Kenshin on his way, or go for broke and fight to keep him against all odds. It was as simple and as overwhelmingly difficult as that. There was no way he could really own Kenshin without giving himself whole in return. That beautiful gaijin wouldn't take less—and he certainly deserved much more than Shigure could ever offer.

Kenshin kept silent, sensitive hands holding onto Shigure's arms lightly enough that the stronger man could shake them off easily, tight enough to make a statement of their own, just like those weird eyes did, baring the deep need in them for Shigure to see, but not pleading, not pushing, just offering, waiting, accepting whatever Shigure was ready to give. And it was that silent offer that tilted the scales, the caring respect Kenshin showed him, a respect Shigure had only received grudgingly from others, and only for as long as he kept fighting tooth and nail for it. Kenshin's respect would hold up no matter what he did, strong and unconditional as nothing else Shigure had ever received in his life.

He curled his fingers around bony hips and eased almost all the way out of Kenshin's body, his eyes boring into those round, bicolored marvels as he thrust back in hard, finally unleashing the full strength of his craving, instinct taking over now that his mind had only room for one powerful word—mine.

Kenshin's back arched off the mattress in response, his hands tightening on Shigure's arms, his voice, his whole body reacting to Shigure, demanding more, offering more, giving all and wanting nothing less in return, their forces equal in a kind of match Shigure had never been in before, the kind of match where your opponent wanted you to win while you wished for nothing other than to die at his hands.

He let his grin show teeth, his joy something primal, almost brutal as his hips slapped against Kenshin's tight ass, the smaller body beneath him sliding over the sheets every time he thrust forward, sexy sounds leaving that throat Shigure wanted to lick as much as he wanted to taste the beads of pre-come dripping from the rosy tip of Kenshin's cock, hard and leaking for him and him only, his lover lost in the intensity of their coupling, his hungry gaze locked with Shigure's, the challenge in it as clear as if those swollen, red lips were mouthing the word *more* to taunt him.

He almost growled, wanting deeper, harder, everything. His hand moved of its own accord to grab Kenshin's leg and lift it to rest on his shoulder, spreading his lover wider for him, narrow hips tilting further up, Shigure's next thrust pressing his chest against the back of Kenshin's raised leg, the full contact as deeply satisfying as the way his aching cock sank into Kenshin's tight heat, going so deep he felt he was touching his lover's core, the very soul of him.

Shigure watched in awe as that slender body arched impossibly off the bed, a low keening sound filling the air, tremors shaking lean muscles as wide brown-green eyes unveiled raw feelings: pleasure, need, love.

He abandoned any pretense at control, desperately needing to possess that exciting creature and never let go, his thrusts nailing Kenshin's gland every time, craving the wild noises that poured out of his lover's mouth, the heat between them rising so high that he felt the burn traveling down his spine, squeezing his balls, making him cry out, his need for release only thwarted by the stronger need to watch his lover come as he was, deeply joined with him, completely exposed, abandoned, naked before his eyes.

He stared into those unusual eyes, chewing out the words he didn't even know he was thinking, his brain reduced to its most primary functions.

"Show me," he growled, and Kenshin's body seemed to understand better than his mind—if the way those eyes widened was any indication—every muscle tensing before the convulsions raked over the slender body, come spurting all over their joined flesh as that sweet voice cried out Shigure's name.

Hearing his name called that way, the honorific dropped at last, Kenshin's voice reaching out to him in the throes of pleasure, joy and need shared without reserve, pushed Shigure over the edge, his eyes rolling back in his head as his orgasm exploded out of him, blinding him for a second as his seed filled the condom. He would have liked that final barrier between them gone, but he felt a goofy grin tugging at his lips as a thought formed in his mind. That was another of the myriad things to look forward to that piled high on the tab he'd opened with Kenshin's name on it. And if there was something yakuza excelled at, it was debt-collecting.

CHAPTER 14

His red Nissan Micra pulled into the gated entrance easily, like a cheerful little bug approaching some dark, elegant flower. Ken waved at the camera before he could think the bright red car was distinctive enough for any of Shigure's men to recognize the crazy American who had invaded their lives.

He spent a lot of time here these days, coming and going in this rented car that looked completely incongruous next to the huge black cars that lined Shigure's garage. Not all of his soldiers drove Mercedes, though. He'd seen everything from the Porsche Atsushi owned to Kotarō's bike parked in the little esplanade in front of the dojo. And their attitudes toward Ken were as varied as their means of transport, the extremes once again marked by Atsushi's sour reception and Kotarō's enthusiasm. Most men kept their feelings to themselves, anyway, probably thinking it wasn't their business if their boss wanted to play with a gaijin this month—next month he might try his hand at golf.

Ken shut down the ignition. He'd promised himself he wouldn't do that, expect too much from this thing going on between them. He didn't even know how to call what they had, the way both of them seemed to tiptoe around the big issues until their bodies clashed together, and then there were no words left, only a hunger they couldn't sate no matter how hard they tried. And boy, did they try. He still felt pleasantly sore from their last romp, his lips still slightly swollen from having Shigure drink his every cry directly from the source, so that Ken wouldn't wake the whole hotel.

The car door was pulled open, and he looked up to meet a frowning Kinosuke. Shit. He must have been grinning like the airhead Ryū said he was. Yeah. And thinking about the friend he'd just lost was the fastest way to erase that foolish grin from his face and confirm Kinosuke in his belief that all gaijin were mentally handicapped.

"Good afternoon, Kinosuke-san," he offered as he got out of the car and bowed.

Kinosuke bowed back, the frown never quite leaving his handsome face. "Boss had to go. Said you could start warming up."

Ken bit back a sigh. It was always this way with Kinosuke. He wasn't outright hostile like dour Atsushi, but his messages were always clipped, his expression blank or marred by his signature frown, always halfway between puzzlement and annoyance. Atsushi he could understand—and ignore. His was the classic, conservative Japanese reaction to anything foreign—impersonal and altogether harmless as Ken let it slide over him like rainwater. But Kinosuke's motives were difficult to fathom in that closemouthed enmity that Ken couldn't help imagine directed straight at him and not the proverbial gaijin he embodied. Probably the man just didn't like Ken, and that was all there was to it.

He smiled as he pulled his equipment out of the trunk. Dating Shigure was like going out with a member of an extended family and trying to get along with all the in-laws, or dating a gunnery sergeant and going barhopping with the whole platoon or—

"Kenshin-san?"

Well, at least now Kinosuke had gone from outright frowning to raised-brow bewilderment. Go Ken.

"Sorry to keep you waiting. I get easily distracted." The understatement of the century, but Kinosuke seemed to take it at face value, nodding gravely as he took the sports bag from Ken's hand, leaving him only with the sword carrier, since touching another man's sword would have been a serious offense. Yakuza were probably the only people on Earth who still practiced the kind of protocol meant to appease blade-carrying guests.

He followed Kinosuke into the empty changing room and thanked him. Kinosuke stared at him for a second, looking as if he were about to say something, but then he just bowed and left without a word. Ken sighed. Japanese society might be sin-free, but it was so ridden with shame that it was extremely difficult to get a spontaneous reaction from anyone. That was why having a friend like Ryū was a true miracle—or rather, had been, seeing that two weeks had passed since they exchanged their last, angry words.

He started changing into his training uniform. He missed Ryū. The whole point of his extended vacation had been to spend time with his friend, and now he'd probably lost him forever. He'd retrieved his belongings from an empty condo, leaving the spare key with a note he hoped would prompt Ryū to call him, but he hadn't heard anything from his friend yet.

Maybe he was waiting for Ken to take the first step, but Ken felt he was the offended party this time. He understood Ryū had been concerned, but his disparaging remarks had cut deep, his friend appearing for once like the high-class, spoiled brat who would look down his well-formed nose at the scum of the Earth that loosely comprised the yakuza, the gaijin, and—of course—the queer.

He pulled the *bokken* out of its carrier and straightened his jacket. Enough. He'd made his decision, chosen a man he barely knew over his childhood friend, and whatever came out of it was nothing but his fault. Time to shut up and face the music.

There were a few men on the mat, practicing their kata on their own or crossing swords with a partner, but all of them stopped what they were doing to look at Ken. So much for discretion.

He tried to walk as unselfconsciously as he could with all those eyes on him, choosing an empty corner of the elongated room and practicing his strikes as soon as he'd got the formal bows out of the way. He focused on the cadence of his movements and was relieved to hear the others resume their activities and presumably ignore him—he wouldn't dare look their way to check.

"Kenshin-san!"

Oh shit. Here came Hurricane Kotarō, and any hope of carrying on with his practice unobtrusively had just gone out the window.

"What's up, Kotarō?"

And now the boy was giggling, of all things. That Ken was able to use informal Japanese and still handle the wide range of honorifics to give each person the proper one was something that amazed the kid to no end. Kotarō sobered soon enough, though, his eyes going wide as he realized something.

"You're training alone because the boss is meeting with our sōkaiya people?"

Shit. He most definitely didn't need to know that the Shinagawa-gumi had people to disrupt shareholders' meetings. Ken looked beyond Kotarō in time to see Kinosuke rubbing his hand over his face. Yeah. His feelings exactly.

"Don't worry, he'll be back in no time. These guys know the ropes, even if that company is trying to cut—"

"Kotarō!" Kinosuke called in outrage.

The kid had the grace to blush. "Sorry, Kenshin-san. Aniki says I go babbling all the time." And just as fast, he was grinning once again. "May I train with you until the boss gets back?"

That sure caught Ken by surprise, and it probably showed in his expression, the way Kotarō's face fell.

"Sorry. I'm only a beginner. You wouldn't want to…," the kid said, and Ken couldn't resist that brokenhearted look.

"Of course I would like to train with you, Kotarō, but maybe Kinosuke-san would prefer…."

"Oh no, aniki'd be glad to get rid of me for a while," the kid said with a bright smile, looking back at Kinosuke like a dog checking on his master—a puppy dog, that is, bouncing on his haunches in excitement while he waited for permission to go play. And of course his "big brother" gave it, Kinosuke nodding slightly, but as soon as Kotarō faced away, hard eyes met Ken's, showing him exactly what he thought of leaving his charge in the hands of a gaijin.

"Is this *suburito* all right?" Kotarō said.

Ken tore his gaze away from Kinosuke and looked at the wooden sword the kid was gripping. He had to focus, swallow his anger, and show Kotarō's senior that he could teach the boy all right. It still hurt, though, even if Ken knew there was no reason for any of these hardened men to like or even trust him in any way. He was just a foreigner their boss had thrust into their lives, and they needn't go any further than proper manners dictated.

He forced himself to really look at Kotarō's sword. It was slightly wider and heavier than a *bokken*, which made it ideal for practicing cuts, but the kid was holding on to it as if he was afraid it might start trying to wiggle free of his grip. "The sword is fine, Kotarō, as long as you don't keep trying to squeeze the juice out of it."

"Don't worry, Kenshin-san. That's not the wood he's fond of squeezing," someone said in the background.

Christ. All the men were laughing now, and if Kotarō's cheeks got any hotter, he might be able to fry bacon on them. Still the boy didn't look upset, the way his lips twitched telling Ken he probably enjoyed being teased since it made him one of the guys. Well, Americans could play that game too.

"The trick to handling any kind of wood," Ken said, ignoring the rude noises around them, "is to be firm but gentle, only two of your fingers curled tight around the shaft, while the others are loose enough to just guide the movement."

He demonstrated the proper grip on his *bokken*, the basic combat stance—with the sword tilted upward from just below his navel— looking positively obscene in the context, as the catcalls he received showed.

"Listen hard, Kotarō, that's pretty solid advice you got there."

"I think there were two pieces of advice there, dude."

"How come?"

"No, I don't think he got to that part yet."

There were snorts and chuckles at that point, all those tough men in hakama pants acting just like over-developed teenagers.

"No, seriously, Kotarō. That one about being firm but gentle? That will come in really handy when you find your chick."

"Yeah, right, and what's the other one for?"

"The one about curling your fingers around the shaft? Well, kid, that will do wonders *while* you find your chick."

"Yeah, and right after you marry her."

Raucous laughter filled the dojo, and Ken had to wonder why it was that wherever a bunch of men got together, they always ended up talking about the same old shit, be it Japan, Kansas, or Ukraine. It was good to laugh with them, anyway, and he could understand why Kotarō wanted to be a part of it. These men were street thugs all right, but they also made a disciplined, tightly knit group of armed soldiers, teamed together under a chain of command, with clear goals and rules to follow, and an obvious sense of comradeship stemming from the long time they spent training, working, and even sleeping together. They certainly took risks together, too, their job being what it was, and so they went further in their shared trust than company men ever did— even in Japan, where companies intended to function as surrogate families.

Ken and Kotarō practiced basic stances and strikes for some time, the kid eagerly drinking in every piece of advice Ken gave, following his instructions, and going through repetition drills again and again until he mimicked Ken's movements fairly well. It was a heady feeling, teaching a native one of Japan's more traditional arts, but Kotarō seemed oblivious to the fact that his improvised sensei was a gaijin, and his eagerness spurred Ken's own enthusiasm at the task, until he realized Kotarō seemed exhausted. He looked at his watch then, his eyes widening when he saw they'd been at it for almost two hours.

"It should be enough for today, Kotarō," he said, reaching out to pat the kid's shoulder. "Good job."

Kotarō beamed. "Oh, thank you, Kenshin-san. You're a great sensei."

"Nah. I'm just older than you. You'll beat me in no time."

"Yeah, like that'll ever happen. The boss is even older and still has trouble beating you."

Ken tried not to laugh. "I don't think your boss would like hearing you call him an old man, Kotarō."

"I didn't mean it that way!"

He had to laugh at the kid's disgruntled expression. "Don't worry. I won't tell him." And for good measure he added, "I'm no better than your boss, really. He just lets me win most of the time so that I don't look the clumsy gaijin."

It was worth it, seeing Kotarō's amazement. "He does?"

"Yep." He couldn't help laughing, though, so he just shoved the boy toward the exit, hoping to distract him. "Let's go get a good bath. We deserve it."

"Oh great." Kotarō gave him a taunting gaze. "Race you to the changing room?"

Shit. Hadn't he heard Ken say he was older? He was going to need some advantage, or that long-legged kid would make him eat the dust. He went for his most serious face.

"You have to remember to always leave the dojo in a dignified manner. Many generations of sword masters are looking at you from these walls," he said as he strolled discreetly toward the door, Kotarō's head bowing in shame.

"*Hai*, Kenshin-san."

"It's okay. You just have to remember," he said lightly, giving the kid an evil smile as soon as his feet crossed the threshold, "to act with dignity *until* you're out the door."

And with that, he bolted in the direction of the nearest building, vaguely hearing his name called in outrage and then the distinct sound of running footsteps. He barely had time to dart into the changing room before Kotarō caught up with him, the boy's grin two miles wide.

"I can't believe you cheated, Kenshin-san!"

He shrugged. "I'm an ill-mannered gaijin."

Kotarō shoved him playfully. "That's a load of crap." But then he realized what he'd said and covered his mouth with his hand.

Ken laughed and reached out for the kid, giving him a one-armed hug, enjoying the obvious way the boy relished it. Yeah. The other thugs might act like teenagers, but Kotarō *was* a teenager, and he needed to be reassured as often as possible. Ken knew how imperious that need could be sometimes, just as he knew what happened if it wasn't fulfilled.

They started undressing in companionable silence, Kotarō stealing glances at Ken in what he probably thought was a discreet way.

"I need more time under the sun. I look half-baked," Ken said to give him an opening.

Kotarō laughed. "Your skin is very white, and smooth. I thought all gaijin were—"

"Big hairy gorillas?" he said with a smile, watching Kotarō blush. "I'm afraid I'm not very representative of my kind. My father was very disappointed in me when he saw I wasn't going to grow any more inches—or hair. Thank God my brothers grew enough to compensate."

And dated every girl they came across until they found suitable wives to perpetuate the lineage, so now his parents could die happy.

Something flickered in Kotarō's eye before he ducked his head. "My brother is big too," he said in a low voice that told Ken he was talking about much more than his size. The fact that the kid was living in a yakuza house in Tokyo when his accent was unmistakably rural said a lot too.

"Well, your boss is bigger than him, and he thinks the world of you."

Kotarō's eyes searched his eagerly, desperate to believe. "He does?"

"Yes, he does." Shinya's rough voice startled them both. "So stop pestering Kenshin-san, and go wash yourself. You stink."

"*Hai, hai,*" Kotarō chirped, and there sure was a spring in his step as he got rid of his remaining clothes and marched into the outer room, where the taps were.

Ken turned to Shinya, smiling, and met the by-now-familiar scary gaze. It had much to do with the lack of mobility of scarred tissue, but also with the reason the scar was there in the first place, not to mention the black-eyed glare that never relented until the other party looked away first.

Fascinated by the rough landscape that face offered, Ken studied the deep line starting above Shinya's left brow and marking his prominent cheek all the way down to almost reach the jaw. It was a miracle the eye had been undamaged, or it probably wasn't, given the nature of the offending weapon. A katana would bite at the bone and slide down in a fast, straight line if the man handling it didn't have the strength or the skill to cut through flesh and bone alike, yet a knife— even if it struck downward—would inevitably tilt as the wrist bent, and scratch or gouge the eye in its trajectory. So, yeah, brawling in Japan had its benefits.

It wasn't until Shinya turned that Ken realized he'd been staring. Christ. Why did he keep doing it? Probably because he was used to being invisible to most people in this country, but Shigure's men had no problem looking him straight in the eye and holding his gaze for as long as it took to stare him down. And as soon as that thought crossed his mind, he realized Shinya had looked away first.

He blinked, watching the wide back move as Shinya untied his belt. No way. But it made sense. The big man had showed he cared about Kotarō in front of Ken, and now he probably imagined Ken considered him a softie. That's why he'd looked away first—in embarrassment. Nothing but big kids, the whole bunch of them. He almost laughed until he saw Shinya's hakama pants slide to the floor and reveal an all-encompassing tattoo that, unlike Shigure's, didn't stop above the knees. It was an incredible mixture of dark blue waters with floating reddish maple leaves, bands of red Buddhist prayers curling around both thighs.

Ken knew he should look away, but when Shinya took off his uniform jacket, Ken simply forgot about good manners. Damn. There was a giant snake covering every inch of the exposed back, its brilliant coils masterfully executed to look alive, fanged mouth open and about to strike over the man's shoulder. Probably sensing something was wrong in the absence of any noise, Shinya turned his head to look at him.

"It's, uh, incredible," Ken stammered, pointing at the tattoo and blushing for all he was worth. Shinya studied him, hard face unmoving, and then turned all the way around, showing him the tattoo's front.

Oh shit. Even though the design was simpler there, obviously so the back would stand out more, it was a beautiful composition, thin lines of white alternating between the dark blue and guiding the eye to the center of the chest, where the red script of a sutra flowed down to rest on an untattooed navel. Big asymmetric peonies graced the sides down below the nipples, and the coils of a small snake disappeared under the white line of the loincloth Shinya wore. Ken's eyes followed the snake down and then shot all the way up in shock.

"Don't tell me...."

For the first time since he'd known the scarred man, Ken thought he saw him smile. It was the tiniest movement of the thin lips, but those slanted eyes were crinkling unmistakably.

"Shit. I can't begin to imagine how it must have hurt."

The big man just shrugged, but he didn't fool Ken. Of course it had hurt like hell, and of course it made Shinya proud, so much so that he loosened the loincloth and took it off for Ken to see the rest of the tattooed snake emerging from under thick, black pubic hair.

He had no words. The scales had been painstakingly—in the most literal sense—tattooed all along the shaft, the head showing a pair of vivid eyes that made the snake look about to sprout a forked tongue. Jesus. You had to be crazy to let someone tattoo your cock. Damn crazy.

Shinya laughed at Ken's astonished expression—or at least made a rough noise that Ken took for laughter—and walked away. Only the ruckus of a group of men entering the room shook Ken out of his daze. And then he almost cracked up. All the men in the dojo had left it barely ten minutes after he and Kotarō did, none of them ready to admit they couldn't take more training than an American and a kid.

Kinosuke glared at him on his way to the farthest open rack in the room, while the others spread neatly around Ken.

"Can't untie your pants, Kenshin-san?" one of the men taunted. Of course ten minutes had gone by, and he was still half-dressed, but he couldn't just tell them he'd been busy studying a tattooed penis.

"Yeah, I learned this fancy knot and can't undo it for shit." And didn't the punks love that, a gaijin proving unable to grasp the subtleties of Japanese clothing. They laughed like first-graders, but to his amazement, one of them moved closer and undid the knot for him.

"At least you tied them the right way," the man said. "Should have seen Kotarō the first time he put on hakama pants."

"Oh man, that was rich."

There were chuckles all around, and Ken tried hard not to stare as tattooed skin was revealed everywhere. Lions, clouds, flowers, and Buddhist deities stretched over wide backs, up bulging biceps, and down muscled legs, beautifully shaded colors covering more or less skin but always there, crying "yakuza" as proudly as gang badges did, only more permanently—and much more painfully, he guessed.

"Arigatō," he thanked the man who had untied the knot.

"No problem," the guy said, watching openly as Ken stepped out of his pants. He felt more exposed than ever, his white skin appearing especially naked without any color on it. Still he went on to take off his boxers, pretending not to notice the looks he was receiving. It was probably the first time these men had seen a naked gaijin, and they were as curious as Ken was about their tattoos—only he was trying not to stare.

"You shave?"

He looked up. The guy who had asked was looking straight at him, no hint of mockery in his expression. Was he seriously asking if Ken was old enough to grow facial hair?

He touched his jaw. "Do you mean…?"

The man didn't answer, but rubbed his hand over his tattooed chest.

"Oh, you mean that." Great. Another one who thought gaijin were hairy monkeys. "No. I don't have hair there."

"Uh-huh."

So the guy didn't believe him. Typical. He wasn't going to insist, though. He knew Japanese were obstinate, especially when you tried to challenge their world view.

"Okay. See you out there, guys," he said, retrieving a washcloth and soap bar and starting to walk in the direction of the baths.

"Yeah, go ahead, Tsurutsuru-san."

Ken almost stumbled at being called "Mr. Smooth." Men's men used that name to scorn those guys who would remove any body hair to please women, but they'd usually say "Tsurutsuru," indicating they considered those guys inferior in rank. Yet now the man had added the more respectful "san" to the derogatory term, as if to show he didn't mean it as an insult. Christ. Would it kill the Japanese to be a tiny bit less complicated?

"*Hai, hai*, Irezumi-sama," Ken answered as he left the room, relieved to hear good-natured peals of laughter at his calling the man "My Lord of the Tattoos."

Still smiling, Ken walked into the bathing area. This was obviously an old house, and Shigure had had the good taste to keep as much of the ancient structures as he possibly could while allowing modern facilities to be installed. So the bath occupied the main area of the building, everything from the beams in the ceiling to the small stools and buckets in beautiful, time-darkened wood, only the steel taps looking brand new in their metal shine.

The big pool was also made of wood, round smoothed logs dividing it into deep basins and serving as headrests for the bathers. Ken approached the pool to fill a bucket with its steaming water, his smile widening at the sight of the three men already there. Kinosuke and Shinya were relaxing in silence, the perfect picture of grave serenity, with their eyes closed and their black-haired heads resting on the dividing logs. And right between them, Kotarō was babbling away, bright eyes open, his boyish energy making the older men look like patient, suffering parents.

As Ken sat on a stool in front of the taps, the rest of the men came in from the changing room, strutting away in that über-masculine gait men tend to revert to when naked.

He closed his eyes and upended the bucket over his head, letting his body begin the adjustment to the smoldering water of the pool. It was the first step of the ritual, the Japanese bath being much more than a perfunctory cleansing of the body. It was something intended to be shared, to strengthen the ties among family, friends, and even strangers, united by the temporary shedding of everyday symbols of status.

The conversations around him became subdued, even these boisterous thugs affected by the quiet atmosphere of the place, their loud tattoos covered in white lather as they scrubbed themselves clean. It was amazing to see people who usually avoided touching, wash each other's backs without a second thought, when touchy-feely Americans would throw their hands in the air at the sight of two men sharing a shower. Here, as every other social animal knew well, grooming was a sign of camaraderie—or affection, Ken thought as he remembered the tender way Shigure had washed him the first time Ken visited the house. It had been sensual because neither of them could help feeling aroused by the other's touch, but it was above all a loving way of sharing deep-seated emotions. And God, how it made him miss Shigure.

"Want some help with your back?"

Ken almost jumped out of the stool, the man who offered was standing so close. He'd probably been spacing out, as usual, the guys around him chuckling quietly at his startled expression.

"Uh, thank you," he said, ducking his head. He couldn't possibly say no without offending the man, and offending a burly yakuza who had a demon tattooed on his back wasn't very wise, to say the least. He only hoped his blush would be seen as a consequence of the vigorous scrubbing the guy was giving him. It was a pleasant sensation, anyway, like a satisfactory scratching, and Ken couldn't help being amused at the weird situation. A skinny American bathing amicably with a bunch of tattooed yakuza—any documentary writer would kill to be in his place.

When it was time to return the favor, Ken found himself studying the masterful tattoo on the man's back, smiling as he covered the demon's mouth in lather.

"What's so funny, Kenshin-san?" another man asked.

The back scrubbing had left him so relaxed that he just blurted it out. "I've given his demon the rabies."

The man closest to them took a look and hooted. "He's foaming at the mouth all right," the guy managed to say between bouts of hilarity. And then the rest of the men were getting closer to look, the demon owner trying to crane his neck to see what they were laughing at.

Ken laughed with them until his eyes met Demon-Back's narrowed stare. Oh shit. He was in deep trouble.

"I'm going to give *you* the jitters," the man threatened as he stood to his full height.

He hadn't time to make any sense of the words before the guy advanced on him and thrust his shoulder into Ken's stomach. He let out the most undignified squeak as he was lifted in a fireman carry, the other bullies laughing themselves sick when they saw the gaijin being carried like a sack of potatoes. As the man reached the edge of the pool, Ken closed his eyes in anticipation of being thrown into the smoldering heat, but the guy lifted him instead off the wide shoulder and manhandled him as if he weighed less than a miniature poodle, submerging Ken in the scalding waters in one single controlled movement that made the tiniest splashing over the pool edge.

"Fuck, fuck, fuck." He instantly reverted to English, to the goons' delight. As much as he appreciated not being thrown into a pool so shallow that he might have hurt himself, getting into the water without adjusting to it first felt like being boiled alive. And of course he understood about the jitters now, his whole body shifting restlessly in a futile effort to escape the unbearable heat.

But he wasn't giving them the pleasure of seeing him get out. He'd die a steamed gaijin first. And they finally seemed to understand that, one after the other beginning the careful dousing of their bodies with the hot water they'd gathered in their buckets before submerging themselves in the pool.

Ken started feeling better, more comfortable in the warm embrace of the water, feeling his pores opening and getting rid of every toxin in his system. He shifted to rest his head on one of the floating logs and saw Kotarō give him the thumbs up. Ken smiled as he closed his eyes. All in all, it was turning out to be a good day. He only wished the boss of all these schoolyard kids had been there to share the fun.

CHAPTER 15

SHIGURE massaged his temples. He wasn't prone to headaches, but the meeting had left him worried. It wasn't every day that a company decided to stop its regular payments to the Shinagawa, that money the only thing that could prevent the gang from turning their shareholders' meetings into pure, unadulterated hell.

He wasn't ingenuous about the motives behind the gang's activities, but in a country where a lawsuit against one of the big companies would take years to be settled—and most of the time not in the best interest of the claimant—the yakuza did their particular service to the community by exposing the firms' dirtiest secrets, even though, in the end, they were only doing it to be paid to stop being so civic.

And yet no company had stood up to them ever before, not even the huge conglomerates—or especially not them, seeing as they had loads of money to spare. It was a small price to pay to keep their reputation clean and their meetings smooth. Besides, it was the Shinagawa-gumi they were refusing, not a petty syndicate that could not follow through with their threats, as they'd be sure to prove to them soon enough. That was what Shigure and the sōkaiya had been planning all afternoon—ways to let the company realize the mistake they'd just made and help them right the wrong—but still he couldn't help feeling there was something deeply disturbing in the whole situation.

If the company's bright minds had decided this was the right moment to present battle, it meant they'd come up with some piece of information that gave them the—no matter how false—impression that the Shinagawa would be somehow weakened. Shigure couldn't begin to imagine why now, and it was driving him crazy.

His conversation with Sergeant Uehara the day before hadn't helped to improve his mood either. The stolen credit card that was their only evidence in the Haihīru incident had been reported missing at a police box that wasn't even in the Daitō-kai territory, but much farther south, where only the Terada-kai operated, a smallish group of *tekiya* yakuza, the branch of the big yakuza family that had traditionally run festival vending stalls at temples and shrines. That a member of the Daitō-kai had gone to those lengths to cover his trail spoke of a kind of premeditation that didn't sit well with the spur-of-the-moment appearance of the beating.

Why would a yakuza enter another gang's territory to steal a credit card when he could do it with impunity in his own, larger territory? And—more to the point—why would he then enter yet another rival gang's club and make a fuss? One had to be very stupid to do that expecting not to be discovered, or extremely canny—if all one wanted was to be discovered.

Uehara had hinted at other troubling developments. The streets were lately filled with rumors against the Daitō-kai and their Korean ethnicity. It wasn't a secret that yakuza syndicates comprised all sorts of society rejects, but no gang worth its salt would use that knowledge to undermine another gang's reputation, mostly because none of them could afford to do without every member whose ancestry was not squeaky clean. And Shigure more than anyone should know about that.

The source of those rumors might not be inside the yakuza underworld, and that was even more disquieting. Who would be trying to stir up the hornets' nest? The police? Japan wasn't looking good at all those international cop conferences, their statistics—even when manicured—showed incredibly low figures of organized crime arrests. Undermining one of the bigger gangs' reputation by planting evidence to convince the other gangs that it didn't respect the deals it'd cut with them might prepare the ground for a serious crackdown. But then again, there were cops like Uehara who knew that keeping relations with the yakuza smooth went a long way in showing the kind of regular crime statistics that were the envy of the developed world.

Companies, on the other hand, would save a lot of money if they didn't have to pay the yakuza for this or that, but Shigure found it difficult to envision strategic committees brainstorming ways to bring down any particular syndicate. Besides, the yakuza had its uses for the big firms too. Who else would get rid of their toxic waste cheaply and without fuss? Or prevent strikes? Or supply them with cheap labor? Or offer them classy—or less so—entertainment places to carry on their business parties? Or even lobby for them with the political figureheads whose careers had been partly financed by the gangs?

Shigure closed his eyes. There was something going on, and he couldn't put a finger on it, which was the worst kind of nightmare for someone like him, who had to control all the pieces on the board if he wanted his business to flourish and his people to survive.

He heard the gate close behind the car and opened his eyes in time to see the little red Nissan Kenshin drove parked in front of the dojo. A smile immediately pulled at his lips imagining those strange eyes that looked at him as if Shigure were the most interesting thing they'd ever seen. And he still couldn't believe that after the initial shock of meeting a yakuza had worn off, the foolish gaijin was still there, still looking at him with the same fascination that made Shigure feel ten feet tall—which wasn't a small feat for the average Japanese man.

Shigure laughed at his own bad joke and saw the startled look his driver gave him in the rearview mirror. Of course his men weren't used to seeing him laugh so often—something else he had to blame on Kenshin, that and an almost constant, physical need to lay his hands on flawless white skin many Japanese women would kill to posses.

He stepped out of the car, his worries all but forgotten as he waved to the driver and almost ran the short distance to the dojo. Finding it empty, he made his way to the nearest building, his smile widening as he recognized some of the teasing voices coming from there. He couldn't deny he'd been a little afraid of his men's reactions to Kenshin's presence, but the gaijin had proven not easy to intimidate, and his ability with a *bokken* had certainly helped them look at Kenshin in a different light. All in all, Shigure was sure most of them respected the American, the exceptions maybe more evident because of that.

He approached the half-open door with caution, wanting to hear what they were saying before his presence could change the tone of the conversations going on in the relaxed atmosphere after a bath.

"Seriously, Kotarō, a self-respecting yakuza would never wear those pants."

"Why not? They look great on Kenshin-san."

"Yeah, well, Kenshin-san is Kenshin-san."

"What's that supposed to mean?"

"It means he can pull it off because he has that look to him, but you'd just look like a hick in a borrowed costume."

"I'm not a hick."

Shigure chuckled quietly at the pout in Kotarō's voice and the chorus that immediately answered, "Yes, you are."

"Am not."

"Are too. Just ask any cow from your village."

"There are no cows in my village! You tell them, boss."

Everybody looked up from what they'd been doing to look at Shigure. He'd grown too curious about Kenshin's discussed clothes to keep eavesdropping.

"There aren't?" he asked as his eyes zeroed in on a half-dressed, slender figure. He barely heard the men's chuckles at Kotarō's huff. He was too busy suppressing a groan at the sight Kenshin offered: damp hair looking as if he'd just rubbed a towel over it, disheveled strands falling over brown-green eyes fixed on Shigure as if there was nobody else in the room anymore, full lips already curving in a smile that managed to be relaxed and hungry at the same time, all that skin from his cheeks down to his navel flushed from the hot bath, gray-black camo pants riding low on narrow hips, bare feet looking even more delicate against the military attire, making Kenshin appear cute and vulnerable by contrast—and so edible Shigure thought he might be drooling.

"See? Boss likes the pants too."

Pants? Shigure focused on the only piece of clothing Kenshin wore, following the fabric down as it covered the long legs in a simple, multi-pocketed design. Rather on the tame side for Kenshin, considering what Shigure had seen him put on, so he couldn't really see what the fuss was all about until he took a step forward and looked at the camo pattern closely.

Every patch of color had two small spots in the other predominant hue—black for the gray areas, gray for the black ones. Seen from a certain angle, those spots were in the right position to look like eyes, and once he realized that, Shigure could suddenly see the whole camo pattern was made out of gray and black ghosts of the most childlike type, the kind that wore bed sheets with two holes for the eyes.

Kenshin chose that moment to put on his T-shirt, a ragged piece of black cotton, the holes too strategically placed to have been accidentally torn, the back that Kenshin showed him now decorated with the typical ghost-buster symbol, but this time the contours had been drawn in gray instead of red, signaling the end of the prohibition as the letters below confirmed.

"Ghost booster," Shigure read as he cracked up. "Now, Kotarō, please don't go shopping with this man if you care for the Shinagawa's reputation at all."

The men laughed, Kotarō and Kenshin looking to be in the same age range as they pouted at Shigure.

"And I'm afraid you'll have to leave your car here, Kenshin-san. We definitely need tinted windows today."

"Is that so?" Kenshin answered in a tone that suggested he wasn't thinking about his clothes anymore.

"Can't be helped, I'm afraid," he answered in the same, seductive drawl.

"Well, then, if there's no other way around it...."

Sensing the conversation was turning into something they didn't quite need to understand, the men started trickling out of the changing room, bowing to them both on their way out, smiles still on their lips except for one serious face that made Shigure frown. He was tempted to stop Kinosuke and have a word with him, but Shinya chose that moment to ask if he wanted him to drive, and the moment passed.

Finally alone with Kenshin, he shoved every other thought to the back of his mind and focused on the man in front of him.

"Sorry it took me so long to come back."

Kenshin shrugged. "It's okay. I know how business meetings can go sometimes."

Shigure studied Kenshin's face, searching for any sign of mockery there. When he didn't find any, his brow arched in disbelief. "You do?"

"What tree do you think I've fallen from? Of course I do."

He couldn't help smirking. "It's difficult to tell, you know, looking at you."

"Are you implying that I don't know how to dress properly? Because I seem to remember someone saying I had a talent for choosing suits."

Kenshin had taken two steps closer to Shigure as he spoke, his index finger raised and just about to poke him in the chest to emphasize his point. Shigure moved even closer, his fingers itching to dig into the holes so brazenly exposing Kenshin's skin, their faces so close he could see every single one of the long, blond lashes lending their shade to weirdly colored eyes. He closed his hand around the pointing finger, the index finger of his free hand sliding through one of Kenshin's belt loops and pulling him forward until their bodies pressed against each other, clicking into place as if their differences in height and build had been expertly designed for them to fit.

"I said you had a talent for choosing sizes, and I can certainly vouch for that," Shigure said, wiggling his hips to illustrate what he was talking about. Kenshin hissed as their crotches rubbed together, the sound breaking into choked laughter when he tried to move his hand and couldn't dislodge his finger from Shigure's tight hold.

"Speaking of sizes, I think you're grabbing the wrong shaft, Shigure-san. I'm wider than that, you know."

"Hmm. Wider, longer, and far tastier," he said, lifting his hand to his mouth and loosening his fingers enough so that he could give a playful lick to Kenshin's captive digit.

"Shigure-san?"

"Hai?"

"If you don't stop that, I'm gonna give your man Shinya a show."

Shigure looked at those dilated pupils, his gaze traveling down flushed cheeks to deep red lips, and further down to the one hole on the black T-shirt that showed a hardened nipple, not needing to look for any other sign when he felt a telltale pressure against his thigh. Pride rushed through him in the opposite direction his blood did at the way Kenshin reacted to him, that incredible man all but self-combusting with a single touch, a lick, even a word from Shigure.

He couldn't help himself, his free hand pressing the seam of Kenshin's pants into his cleft to rub it against the nerve endings hiding under the layers of fabric.

"Shigure-san," Kenshin breathed, his slender form shuddering at the harsh contact, pressing against Shigure as if his body couldn't produce enough heat by itself to keep him from shivering in summer.

"*Kuso*," he cursed, knowing full well he had to extricate himself from the sexy gaijin if he wanted to ever leave the house. And Shinya must be waiting for them, the car sitting idly with the engine running, the longer they took, the easier for Shinya to imagine what was happening in the changing room.

A slender hand pressed against his chest and pushed. Kenshin must have felt something change in the way Shigure held him, his lover always so attuned to him, so responsive in every sense that it both aroused and scared him to death, the usual mixed signals wafting off Shigure as he could tell by Kenshin's way of moving away without looking at him, immediately getting busy with his duffel bag and sword carrier.

To the American, Shigure must always seem to be starting things and then wanting out as soon as it got heated, the house looming over them to remind them which side of the fence they stood on, who would be forever the temporary visitor. Kenshin hadn't said anything, though, never complained about Shigure only spending the night with him if they were in the tiny apartment Kenshin had finally rented, just as if he had resigned himself to the crumbs Shigure chose to throw his way.

That quiet resignation made Shigure feel so many different things at the same time that he could never decide how to react to it. He felt proud that someone would want him so much that he'd settle for anything Shigure was ready to give, but he also felt angry that Kenshin wouldn't push for more, as if he didn't care enough to demand all. And then he felt guilty because he could clearly see how much it hurt Kenshin whenever Shigure stiffened in his arms, how much it must feel like rejection every time Shigure inched apart from him, every time he appeared to be ashamed of touching a gaijin under his own roof.

He reached out to take Kenshin's bag, but the American yanked it away. "I can carry a pair of hakama pants, for Christ's sake." And with that he stormed out of the building, his jaw so tight Shigure could almost hear his teeth grinding together.

In the time it took Shigure to leave the changing room, Kenshin had already made it to the car and sat looking out the window in the opposite direction, his things parked on the seat beside him as a makeshift barrier.

Shigure sat by the opposite door and nodded at Shinya, their eyes meeting briefly in the rearview mirror. There they were again, Kenshin and him, sitting in silence like two strangers sharing a taxi, though their silence was as tinted as the glass panes that surrounded them. And Shigure couldn't stand it.

"Kenshin-san?"

The muscles in that slender neck tightened, but Kenshin wouldn't turn his head.

"Look at me, please."

"What for? You know what a gaijin looks like."

Shinya's eyes drifted to the mirror, and then the privacy shield slid shut with a quiet thump, his man sensing the storm brewing between them. It was his fault, probably, but if Kenshin kept fighting him, he'd have to do something rash.

"Kenshin-san."

Still the American wouldn't look at him, but Shigure saw his shoulders slump, his voice coming out in a resigned drone.

"Don't mind me. I'm just tired. Please tell Shinya-san to drop me anywhere."

Oh no, he wasn't having any of that. He shoved Kenshin's things to the car floor and grabbed a handful of black T-shirt, pulling with all his pent-up frustration until Kenshin's body slid over the leather upholstery. But then there was a loud ripping sound, and Shigure found himself with a black rag in his hand and a pair of bright eyes glaring fiercely at him. He glared back, and their lips curled as if they were both about to snarl at each other. And then somehow their eyes drifted down at the same time, Shigure looking at the bare skin gaping through the hole he'd just ripped, Kenshin looking at the way Shigure's fist strangled the torn fabric and back up to meet his eyes, the fierceness in those weird orbits rising up a notch, anger fueling some other primal instinct and pushing the snarl out as Kenshin lunged at him.

Shigure's back hit the door, his hands shooting out unconsciously to catch Kenshin's wrists as his full weight landed on Shigure.

"Let go, you baka," Kenshin growled as he tried to shake his arms free.

"Make me, *gaki.*" The look on Kenshin's face at being called a brat was priceless. Shigure's lips stretched into a feral smile, daring Kenshin to call him something stronger. And the gaijin didn't disappoint.

"Aho."

Yeah, asshole was more like it, but he still needed to reel Kenshin in a little more. "That's all you can manage, chibi?" Look at that. Kenshin obviously hated being reminded he wasn't that tall, and not being able to use his hands was driving him mad.

"Fuck off, ashi-fetchi!"

They both froze in place at Kenshin's outburst, silence stretching awkwardly between them until Shigure breathed. "Did you just call me *foot fetishist?*"

Kenshin groaned and hid his face in the crook of Shigure's neck, his whole body shaking on top of him when Shigure burst into uncontrollable peals of laughter.

"Shut up." Kenshin used his now free hands to pound Shigure's chest. "I can't think when I'm angry."

"I like you when you're angry," Shigure said, trying to rein in his chuckles, his hands cradling Kenshin's face and studying his flushed features. "I like you a lot."

Bright green-brown eyes searched his, pupils growing huge as Kenshin's lips parted to let out a needy sound, their bodies suddenly remembering they were touching almost from head to toes, their hips shifting on their own to rub against each other. Shigure used his hands to bring that beautiful face closer and pressed his lips against the luscious flesh of Kenshin's lips. He tasted like nothing Shigure had ever savored before, something not exactly sweet or salty, probably a whole new flavor to add to very few existing—the soon-to-be-famous Kenshin flavor.

Shigure felt his lover break the kiss to look at him. "What?"

"Nothing. I just like the way you taste."

"Just?"

He chuckled. "You want the whole list?"

Kenshin nodded so many times that Shigure felt he might get seasick watching the blond head bob. He tightened his grip on Kenshin to stop the movement, his fingers immediately moving to comb the strands of disheveled hair. "I like your hair, for one."

"Why?" Kenshin said, his eyes going half-mast at Shigure's caress.

"Because it's soft, and it makes you shine like a small sun."

Kenshin smiled enticingly. "Want to be in my orbit? I promise not to burn you."

"Hmm. I don't know." He let his hands follow the curve of Kenshin's scalp down to his long neck, his fingers sliding inside the black T-shirt. "You feel hot enough to me."

Kenshin shifted, planting his knees more comfortably on the leather seat to straddle Shigure's lap. "I might have the hots for you." The American rolled his hips, making their groins rub together. "Would you do something about it if it was so?"

"Well, I'd have to check first, you know," Shigure said, his hands traveling down until they found another large hole in Kenshin's T-shirt and slid under the ragged fabric to touch skin. "It wouldn't do to apply the remedy if you didn't have the symptoms."

Kenshin leaned into his touch, Shigure's fingers exploring every nook and cranny of that gorgeous, warm skin. He loved how the gaijin's voice came out a little breathless, a little hoarse. "And what do you think so far? Is it serious? 'Cause it sure feels as if I were running a fever."

"I'll have to look into it," he said, his own throat going dry, his cock pressing against the zipper of his slacks as Kenshin responded to his words by grabbing the hem of his T-shirt and pulling it up and over his head, throwing it on top of the heap of his things already on the floor of the car.

"Please do a thorough examination. It's getting worse by the minute."

Damn. Kenshin sounded so needy, so oblivious of their surroundings, those huge eyes fixed on Shigure as if nothing else mattered to him, that gorgeous body offered without restriction or fear, wanting every single thing Shigure wanted, their instincts so much in synch that words were only a hindrance to them, or rather, the biggest obstacle standing between them.

Watching the man straddling his hips, Shigure felt a rush of power course through him. There was no reason to explain it, but he was sure that man would do anything he asked of him. Anything. Kenshin wasn't bound by gang loyalty, he hadn't signed any contract or made any deal, and fear didn't drive his actions. Yet there he was, offering himself to a man he didn't really know anything about, just because it was him and no one else. It was something Shigure had seen the first time they'd talked in front of an ice sculpture, something that made all the pieces inside him click into place and stilled the nagging voices of Shigure's past, something he craved to turn chaos into the comforting peace of *wa*, the harmony all things naturally tended to.

He pressed the button that lowered the privacy shield, catching Kenshin's arm and holding tight to prevent him from moving away. He ignored the startled look in those amazing eyes and turned to look at Shinya.

"Take us to Oyone-san's place."

Hard eyes met his in the rearview mirror. Shinya knew what he was about to do because he understood power very well, every yakuza did, and every single one of them respected it even more than honor— or rather because of it, because honor without power was a useless decoration and power without honor was the simple flexing of muscle.

"Sure thing, boss," Shinya said, his voice neutral, his eyes returning to the traffic ahead, his fingers never moving from the steering wheel. His man wouldn't raise the partition again, Shigure knew, so he turned his full attention to Kenshin.

"Strip for me," he said, his voice serious, letting the American know this was no joke. They'd been playing hide-and-seek for too long, the two of them.

Kenshin swallowed, his eyes searching Shigure's. Shigure held the anxious gaze steadily, his hands dropping to his sides to show he didn't intend to touch the button that would give them back their privacy.

The American hesitated, his eyes darting nervously to the front, where not only Shinya could see them, but any passing car, any pedestrian crossing the street. Then those frightened eyes returned to Shigure, and for a moment, he thought Kenshin might plead his way out of his predicament. But he never did.

Shigure felt his heart rate speed up as he saw the change in Kenshin's attitude. Suddenly the scared kid disappeared, round eyes narrowing as a telltale twitch in his jaw showed how hard he was bringing his teeth together. Yes. This was the man who could outmatch Shigure anytime he wanted to, anytime he chose to unleash the power Shigure had always known he had.

When Kenshin finally moved, it was with brisk gestures, hard eyes never leaving Shigure's as his hands yanked his sandals off. And then he was standing, deft fingers immediately attacking the pants button and zipper, never mind the low roof that made him hunch his shoulders, never mind the greater exposure that position brought. His mind was set, and his whole body radiated determination, pride so strong it seemed to waft off him in scorching waves that made the air heavy and breathing almost impossible.

It was the hottest thing Shigure had ever witnessed, those long fingers pushing pants and underwear down as if they could barely restrain the urge to tear them apart, Kenshin stepping out of them and standing naked in front of him, hands raising to press against the roof to steady himself and look daringly at Shigure.

Now it was Kenshin issuing the challenge, and it made Shigure dizzy, his cock getting so hard he had to palm it to soothe the ache. Those glorious eyes followed the movement of his hand, and Shigure felt his lips stretching in a feral smile. He pulled his zipper open and reached inside to free his straining cock.

"Ride me," he growled, the ball back in Kenshin's court with a vengeance.

Kenshin's nostrils flared, his eyes blazing in two different shades of rage, white fingers pressing against the roof to propel him forward. This was a battle of wills, and his gaijin wasn't backing down, Shigure was sure.

He almost laughed out loud in joy, but Kenshin was advancing on him like a charging bull, his head lowered to avoid hitting the roof, long legs bending to straddle Shigure once again, only this time he was stark naked, all that gorgeous skin looking even whiter against the yakuza's black suit. And wasn't that incredibly erotic, the fact that he was there, slouching fully dressed on the plush leather seat as that wild creature stalked him, ready to devour him, beautiful features contracted in a fierce mask that left no doubt who the prey was in this baiting game?

Kenshin slapped his hand away and grabbed Shigure's leaking cock in a painful grip of his own fingers. Shigure didn't make a noise, though, he was too busy inhaling the incredible scent of Kenshin's heated skin, watching the bicolored simmering of that scalding gaze as Kenshin lined Shigure's cock and started lowering himself onto it, fast, too fast for it not to hurt, Shigure's hand immediately reaching out to still those hips, his fingers digging hard enough to leave bruises.

Kenshin moved so fast that Shigure didn't have the time to blink before white teeth sank into his neck, the sharp pain forcing him to momentarily loosen his grip on Kenshin's hip. That was all it took. One moment he was yelping in pain, the next he was moaning as the tight heat of Kenshin's body enveloped him to the root, unable to do anything but watch as the American raised his head, his eyes fixed on Kenshin's strained expression, on the sweat breaking out on that clear forehead, teeth sinking into a full lower lip as Kenshin waited for the burn to go away.

And then it happened. Kenshin's eyes fluttered open, meeting Shigure's head on, the challenge still there, loud and clear, until Kenshin started to pull up and froze halfway. Shigure saw the exact moment the American realized there was no barrier between them, no condom to guarantee they were still playing safe, no more time to learn just how far he could trust the man he had opened himself to.

Shigure hadn't planned it like this, but he couldn't deny the most primitive part of him was elated to have Kenshin completely cornered. It was up to him now. In the world in which Shigure lived, there was no room for the weak of heart, no halfways about anything, and nothing to hide from the members of his clan. Shigure might wear a business suit, but he was a yakuza, and Kenshin was either ready to risk it all for him or stop playing with fire, because there were no tourists in the world of shadows.

He held Kenshin's eyes, but didn't offer any reassurances, not even a nod or a comforting touch. And Kenshin seemed to understand the exact nature of the test Shigure was putting him through, because the anger in his eyes took on a different quality, something far more dangerous and hard, something that made Shigure want him more than ever, the need to posses that incredible creature so strong Shigure felt every last muscle in his body tighten, his hands clutching at the leather upholstery to stop them from shaking in deprivation.

Kenshin planted his hands on the front of Shigure's suit, not making the slightest movement to unbutton it, just pressing down hard while his eyes never left Shigure's, the slender body moving up until only the head of Shigure's cock remained inside him, time suspended in that last second when anything might still happen, when Kenshin could still pull all the way out and away from Shigure's world, when everything was still a casual game either of them could walk out of without ever looking back.

For as long as he lived, Shigure was sure he'd never forget the look in Kenshin's eyes when his hips pushed back down to take all of Shigure's length. He'd only seen something as fiercely beautiful when he watched a storm rage over the Sea of Japan on one of his smuggling trips to Pusan, lightning suddenly illuminating the menacing columns of water and giving them the strangest of colors, Shigure's hands grabbing the deck railing to hold him there, soaked to the bones and terrified by those dark waves that threatened to knock the big ship over as if it amounted to less than a floating leaf, but unable to stop watching the beauty unleashed in front of him even if it meant his death. And now he felt exactly the same, lost in the storm brewing in those foreign eyes, unable to move as every nerve ending along his shaft sent shock waves that threatened to collapse his brain functions, the heat of Kenshin's body so intense he started panting, the tightness engulfing him as uncompromising as the raw strength of the muscles he could see flexing under smooth skin, moving that slender body to rise above him and all the way down again, taking him whole, owning him, leaving him defenseless against the need to surrender his spirit to the powerful yōkai devouring him.

Suddenly Kenshin lifted his hands off Shigure's chest, and he couldn't stop the disgruntled groan escaping his throat at the loss of contact, up until the moment Kenshin straightened as far as he could go, long fingers splaying against the car roof to get leverage and push further down. Then Shigure had to cry out, his cock sliding so deep inside that tight heat Shigure felt he could touch a part of Kenshin no one had ever touched before, no one had ever been brave enough to claim before.

He looked at that beautiful man, those alien features flushed, all that exposed skin gleaming with sweat, nipples hard like armor decorations, flat belly tight, long cock standing proud as pre-come dripped from the flushed tip. He looked up into those naked eyes as emotions flowed out of them, and knew there was no way he could prevent his own fall. If this otherworldly creature demanded that he give up his soul, he would do it, whatever it took to keep the beautiful demon feeding from his very life for all eternity.

Now that it was clear to him how things stood, Shigure didn't regret the lack of privacy. Kenshin hadn't looked around once, so completely focused on Shigure, the yakuza was sure he wasn't even conscious anymore of Shinya's eyes in the rearview mirror or the other anonymous eyes that grazed his body from time to time. Shigure resented that contact, however brief it might be—it made him want to growl possessively at those strangers who gaped at the naked gaijin in the back seat of a Mercedes—but he knew he had to give Kenshin some proof of his own, and it was only fair that he should be subjected to the same exposure he'd forced on the American.

Before Kenshin could move up, Shigure let out the growl building in his chest and grabbed the narrow hips tightly, holding Kenshin flush against him even as he rolled on the seat to turn the tables and cover the naked body with his own. Kenshin cried out in surprise, but he was wrapping himself around Shigure in the next heartbeat, long legs hugging his waist and pressing him down in silent urgency.

Shigure grunted as the position tilted Kenshin's hips, allowing his cock to push so much deeper that he felt every pulse of Kenshin's heart in the veins of his own shaft and knew there was no way on earth he could last more than a few thrusts, if at all.

Ignoring the fact that he was now the one on display for anyone who happened to look through the windshield, he braced himself against the window pane in front of him, his free hand going straight for Kenshin's leaking cock and tugging roughly as he pulled out of the tight heat enveloping his shaft, only to push back all the way in with a hard shove.

Kenshin moaned loudly, his fingers closing in tight fists around the lapels of Shigure's suit. Unable to rein in his craving, Shigure set a punishing rhythm, every hard thrust dragging Kenshin along the bench, the beautiful cock pulsing as Shigure fisted it, noises pouring out of him and driving Shigure so crazy, he didn't even notice the car engine had stopped running.

All Shigure's senses were focused on the man shuddering beneath him, as the waves of orgasm shook him, seed spurting all over his flushed belly and chest, his expression going from wide-eyed to almost pained as pleasure shook him, those incandescent eyes never leaving Shigure's and sending him right over the edge as the emotions filling them hit the yakuza full in the chest.

The force of his orgasm made Shigure's teeth clack, his vision blanking as he marked Kenshin with the hot sperm pouring out of him, the notion of the risk Kenshin had taken for him enough to keep his cock from deflating completely even when he collapsed on top of his lover, unable to hold his own weight anymore.

There was a loud sound as the privacy shield went up in the exhausted silence around them. Kenshin stirred under him, and Shigure inhaled the heady scent of sweat and sex before shifting off the warm body beneath him, both of them groaning as his cock slipped out of Kenshin's hole.

He was about to open his mouth when he heard the rap on the window. Shit. He was going to have a long talk with Shinya, one that involved very few words and a lot of fist work.

"What on earth—"

"Get your ass out here, you big fucking hoodlum!"

Oh shit. No one would call him that and expect to go on breathing, no one but his very dear, very dignified lady friend Oyone. And there she was, standing right beside the car door with her hands on her hips and a glare that could burn whole cities to ashes, never mind the plush silk kimono, the intricate arrangement of her long, black hair, or the perfect makeup. She sure as hell could look like a *hina* doll while cursing like a trucker.

"It's good to see you too, Oyo-chan." He offered his best smile as he slid out of the car, trying to open the door as little as he could.

"Save your sweet talk for your bedroom. Now what kind of third-rate brothel do you think I'm running here?"

He deemed it safer not to answer that.

"What if it hadn't been one of my girls who saw you, huh? I pride myself on offering my clients discretion and elegance. You think they'd come back if they found a yakuza making out in my parking lot?"

"Sorry, Oyo-chan. I swear I didn't realize we—"

"I don't care if you want to brag about your conquest of the week. Just go fuck your whores under a streetlight, but don't bring your show to my establishment, you hear me?"

Shigure shut his eyes. His last hope that Kenshin hadn't heard that bit went out the window when the door on the other side of the car opened and the American stepped out fully dressed, grabbing his bag and sword carrier. Under other circumstances, he would have enjoyed the nonplussed expression on Oyone's face at seeing who'd been in the car with him, but right then all he cared about was stopping Kenshin from getting away.

"Kenshin-san—" He started walking in the other man's direction, but the look in those alien eyes stopped him cold.

"Go find another gaijin whore to fuck under a streetlight," he spat, turning his back on Shigure and not even looking at Oyone as he strode past her and out of the *ryokan*'s gate.

CHAPTER 16

KEN hefted the bag with his groceries. He probably shouldn't have bought so much food, all things considered, but it wasn't that easy to be exact about the amount of vegetables he might still need. Yeah, right, he could kid himself as much as he wanted, but the truth was he'd done it out of spite, the same reason he'd kept the flight date unchanged. He'd planned to stay in Japan for two months, and he wasn't leaving a second earlier.

The walk back to his apartment seemed inordinately long today, the weather too hot for even humid Japanese summers, his skin clammy and itchy—and achy. The bruises Shigure had left still a vivid purple after two days, not to mention the ones he couldn't see, the ones that made it difficult to sit without remembering the damn yakuza.

Jesus. He felt so tired he was tempted to dump the food he was carrying and lie down in the middle of the sidewalk. Was he coming down with some bug? He definitely didn't want to go there, feel all kinds of stupid at having allowed that bastard to take him bareback.

It'd be the icing on the cake, getting some STD—he didn't even want to consider HIV—on top of losing his main reason for visiting Japan. He had no more friends left here, so next time he came, it'd be just for the views, damn right, for the fucking cherry blossoms.

He climbed the steps to his apartment with his jaw set. He knew he was being his usual stubborn self, but he couldn't care less. He'd decided a long time ago that he wouldn't back down no matter what, and so far he'd stuck to his decision. The fact that he wasn't on speaking terms with his family or that he'd lost his only childhood friend or that he'd flashed his ass at a handful of Japanese drivers and pedestrians didn't really amount to anything, did it?

The bag made a weird chuffing noise as it hit the table, but that was as far as Ken could go right now. Putting the food away was beyond his ability before he took the nap he'd been dreaming about since he left the apartment, and it was just typical of his luck these days that the doorbell rang the moment he started undressing to hit the futon.

He didn't bother putting his tank top back on. He was a little fed up with the Japanese and their sense of propriety just for the sake of appearances. Maybe seeing a half-naked gaijin would drive whoever it was away and leave him alone to take his nap.

"Hi, Kenshin."

Oh. Ryū. There, on his doorstep.

They blinked at each other like a pair of owls, but then Ryū gave him a sheepish smile, and Ken couldn't take it anymore, he just stepped forward and hugged his best friend like there was no tomorrow. He only relented when he felt Ryū tense in his arms, the Japanese in him bristling at being touched so blatantly, and in the doorway, too, where anybody could see the rude, bare-chested gaijin grabbing him.

"Sorry, come on in, Ryū."

Ryū shook his head as he entered, but he waited until the door was closed to reach out and squeeze Ken's shoulder.

"No, Kenneth, it's me who should apologize. I've been a jerk."

He fought back the urge to cry. Ryū would only use his full name to show him how important something was to him, how important Ken was to him.

"Don't call me Kenneth. You sound like my father."

"Ew."

It was so good to laugh with Ryū, to have his friend back.

"I've missed you."

"Me too, Kenshin."

"You've missed yourself?"

"Shut up, you crazy gaijin. You know what I mean."

He sobered. "I do. Thank you, Ryū."

"You're welcome." His friend looked around for the first time, his trained eye quickly appraising the cheap apartment. "And you're welcome back to my house too. This is a shack."

He smirked. "Says the man who lives in the world's tiniest condo."

"Well, yeah, it might be small, but Nishimura Construction only builds first-quality living spaces."

"Just this time your firm put in all the quality and forgot about the spaces."

"Shut up." But Ryū couldn't rein in his chuckle, and they laughed like a couple of fiends for a moment, all the emotions they'd kept at bay for weeks finally pouring out in their laughter, their eyes beaming with a kind of joy that had nothing to do with the silly joke.

"Don't stand there. Come sit." Ken waved in the direction of the futon, since there was no couch to speak of. "Want some beer?"

Ryū plopped down on the futon. "Yeah, thanks. It's really hot out there."

"You don't say."

He brought two cool Asahi from his little fridge and handed one to his friend, folding his legs under him to sit on the floor facing Ryū. They drank in silence for a moment, smiling at each other when their eyes met, just as if nothing had happened between them. But they both knew it had, and his friend put on his serious face before he spoke.

"I'm sorry I said those things to you, Kenshin. I really am."

"It's all right. I know you were worried about me."

Ryū nodded. "I work with the yakuza often. I know what they can be like, and I thought... I was afraid...."

"You were afraid I'd get hurt. I understand, Ryū, but it was just as if I couldn't fend for myself, as if it was okay for you to deal with the yakuza on a daily basis, but not for the helpless gaijin."

"Shit, Kenshin, I've never seen you that way. I was there every time you kicked the shit out of those high school bullies, remember?"

"Yeah, you were always there with the Band-Aids."

"Well, you got Band-Aids, they got stitches. So I know what you're capable of. It's only that you never dated them."

"Oh, gross."

Ryū laughed. "Yeah, I know."

They drank their beers, the silence between them more comfortable now, though Ken could tell there was something his friend still wasn't saying.

"Come on, Ryū. I can hear you thinking from here."

"Sheesh. You Americans can be so rude."

"Yep. So spit it out. I'm waiting."

"Okay. Here it goes." Ryū was smirking, but the way he avoided Ken's eyes made Ken dread his next words. "Are you... I mean, you and Matsunaga are still...?"

"You don't have to worry about that anymore, Ryū." And somehow he couldn't feel any relief at saying it out loud.

"You mean you two aren't...?"

He shook his head, getting a little impatient. And damn if his friend's relieved expression didn't anger him a little bit.

"I'm so glad, Kenshin. I didn't want to tell you, but the Shinagawa don't only run night clubs and foreign construction workers. They're loan sharks and drug dealers, and I've heard they're in league with the Hong Kong triads to traffic in women from all over Southeast Asia."

The words were out of his mouth before he thought about them. "Shigure would never do any of that."

"Kenshin—"

He knew he sounded like a kid with a crush, but he couldn't help it. Shigure might be an arrogant, stubborn prick, but he wasn't that kind of man.

"He just wouldn't."

"Yeah, right. He became a yakuza boss by helping old ladies carry their groceries home."

He clenched his fists. "All right. He can be a crook, but he's also—"

"He's what, Kenshin?"

"A man of honor!"

Ryū's eyes widened in disbelief, and then he just hooted. "Matsunaga. A man of honor." It wasn't even a question, and Ken felt his cheeks burn. Jesus. He had to admit it had been absolutely lame, but somehow the man had managed to put that notion deep in Ken's subconscious. It must have been something in his manner, something in the way he treated his men, or kept that old house just as it had been in its days of glory, or fought with a *bokken*, or the way he walked when he was only wearing his pride.

Ryū was still laughing. "Shit, Kenshin. The man is a *burakumin*."

All the air rushed out of Ken's lungs. "A burakumin?" he mumbled.

"Yeah. They're the lowest of the low. Their ancestors were butchers, tanners, beggars, or executioners, and they've lived in closed communities for ages, doing nothing to work their way out of their ghettos, just complaining about their luck and joining the yakuza for the easy money. They don't know a thing about honor or respectability."

All the exhaustion of the past days fell on Ken like a wrecking ball. He didn't even have the energy to feel angry anymore. "Thanks for the explanation, Ryū. It's been a real eye-opener."

His friend must have felt something was wrong, though, the way he hesitated. "Kenshin?"

He met Ryū's concerned eyes. "Yeah, Ryū. I already knew who the burakumin were. I just never thought I'd hear you talk about them like my father talks about African Americans. I guess it's only right that they should work your luxury construction projects at the lowest wages, doing the hardest jobs and having to pay a commission to a yakuza who runs them so someone will deign to hire them. Yeah, burakumin can be useful that way, and yakuza too. I wonder what you think the use of a gaijin might be."

"Kenshin, you know I've never—"

He raised a hand. "It's okay, Ryū, I understand. I just can't deal with it right now."

"Kenshin, please, don't let some words come between us. You know me, and you know I'm your friend."

"I used to know it, yes." His eyelids felt so heavy he was tempted to let his eyes close and never open them again. His voice came out in a breathy whisper. "I'm sorry, Ryū. I just need some time, okay?"

Ryū looked like he wanted to say something else, but he was too Japanese to plead. He gave Ken a curt nod and marched to the door like a daimyo exiting a laborer's shack, so much so that Ken would've rushed to open the door for him if he hadn't felt so exhausted. It was only when he heard Ryū exchange a few words with someone in the hallway that he approached the door cautiously.

Jesus. What was this? A convention of his own personal ghosts of Christmas past?

"Kenshin-san."

He sighed, looking at the man standing in front of him, really looking at him, at the short cropped black hair, the slanted eyes staring straight at Ken, the rough-boned features, the clenched jaw, the thick neck, the wide shoulders, and the black suit that made him look taller, meaner. Yeah, there was no doubt he was looking at a yakuza. Anyone could see that. And yet, even as mad as Ken was supposed to be, he couldn't deny seeing him at his door made his belly heavy.

Shigure didn't say another word. He just stood there, looking at Ken as if watching him were his chosen profession. And damn if he couldn't feel the hot trail of those hard eyes over his body, his nipples going all tight, his cock twitching in anticipation even if his mind was trying to recite all the reasons he had to slam the door in Shigure's face.

They stood staring at each other for a long moment, until Shigure bent one knee, and to Ken's astonishment, sank to the ground to prostrate himself at Ken's feet in the kind of bow reserved for the emperor or the people you'd seriously wronged—right there, in Ken's hallway, where any neighbor could come out of his door and see a yakuza kneeling in front of a gaijin.

"Shigure-san, please, don't...." He crouched beside the yakuza, trying to pull him to a standing position, but Shigure wouldn't budge.

"Please forgive me, Kenshin-san."

"You don't have to—"

"Yes, I do. I had no right to expose you like I did."

That gave Ken pause. "Why did you do it, then? Were you trying to prove that I'd be scared enough to obey you?"

Shigure's head shot up. "That wasn't my intention!"

"Then what was it? I'm sorry if I'm a little dumb here, but I just can't see any fucking reason why you should make me put on a show for the whole city plus your man Scar-face."

"I just... I needed to be sure you were with me."

"As opposed to what? Getting you naked for tattoo espionage?"

And damn if those lips weren't twitching, the asshole trying to look contrite when he was barely reigning in his laughter. Ken let his fist land on that chest, the solid wall of muscle there making his punch feel like a halfhearted pat.

"You bastard."

"Don't get mad at me, please." Shigure's big hand closed over Ken's fist and held it against his chest. "It was a stupid thing to do, but I've never met anyone like you in my whole life. I couldn't believe you would want to be with a second-rate hoodlum like me."

"You should get out more."

And now Shigure did laugh, the big oaf. Ken tried very hard to stay angry, but it was a little difficult to focus when Shigure's free hand was stroking his face, the touch so gentle, so tentative, the look in those laughing eyes so tender that Ken only managed to pout for a second or two.

"I'm sorry to break the news to you, but you're kneeling in a hallway with a half-naked gaijin."

"Yeah. So what?"

"Someone might see you?"

"Let them. I enjoy being envied."

It suddenly hurt, that this man he barely knew, this man who was a crook, an outcast, the lowest of the low, this man would be proud of being seen with him when his childhood friend couldn't stand to graze his arm in the open. The heir to Nishimura Construction had deemed it improper to beg for Ken's friendship, while this man who lived on reputation alone hadn't hesitated to publicly humiliate himself for Ken, because Shigure—the mean yakuza, the despised burakumin—Shigure thought Ken was worth it.

"Kenshin-san?"

He tried to move away when the first tear ran down his cheek, but strong arms pulled him down and pressed him against a wide chest. Ken didn't even think of resisting then, or stopping the sobs that poured out of him. He felt safe for the first time in he didn't remember how long, and all the tension of the past weeks yanked at the thread that connected it with all the others he'd been patiently storing away for years, decades even, back to the very first moment he'd understood he wasn't very welcome in the world he'd been thrown into.

Shigure kept stroking his back gently, giving him soft words of comfort Ken didn't really pay attention to, as he just clung to the secure haven of those arms, letting the tone of that grave voice soothe him until his tears dried away and he slumped against Shigure, soaking up his warmth.

"Hmm. You smell so good," he said with a contented sigh.

"I don't wear perfume."

Ken couldn't help chuckling at Shigure's outraged tone. The Japanese and their quirks. It must be insularity that made them so persnickety—if the British were anything to go by.

"Everybody smells, Shigure. Pet dogs would be out of commission if we didn't."

Oh, that was incredible, the way Shigure's laughter resonated in his chest, Ken's whole body moving with his, joy shared directly from the source.

"You're nuts." Shigure's eyes were full of affection, though, and his usually hard features softened into an expression that made him look especially handsome and forced Ken's chest to constrict in a dangerous way. "But I like it when you say my name like that."

Shit. He hadn't even noticed he'd dropped the honorific. "Sorry. I meant no disrespect. It's just that—"

"Shhh. I said I liked it, and I mean it. It makes me feel closer to you."

"Fuck, Shigure, if you got any closer, they'd have to pull you out with a scalpel."

There it was, that shit-eating grin, six parts joy, four parts owner's pride. Possessive bastard.

"Is that so?"

"What? You thought I let any man fuck me in public on the first date?"

Shigure smiled sheepishly. "It wasn't our first date."

"Yeah, well, our first make-up sex. Whatever."

The smile on that handsome face turned mischievous, large hands sliding down Ken's back and grabbing his buttocks, pulling until Ken was right in Shigure's lap.

"That wasn't our first make-up sex. This is," the yakuza said, taking Ken's mouth roughly, his fingers squeezing Ken's ass, pressing his body against Shigure's, his suit rubbing almost painfully against Ken's exposed nipples, their cocks grinding together through too many layers of clothing.

When they came up for air, Ken shoved at Shigure's chest halfheartedly. "Stop it," he said, the way he kept his hips plastered to Shigure's not lending him much credibility. "I'm not giving a repeat performance for the whole neighborhood to see."

And damn if that wasn't amusement in the big man's eyes.

"Yeah. And 'Scar-face' isn't around either."

Ken hid his face in Shigure's neck. "I hoped you hadn't heard that."

"Oh, I heard. Just wait till Shinya hears it."

He raised his head to look at the big man. "You wouldn't dare."

"Yes, I would."

"You would?"

"Sure I would. Unless, of course, you offered an appropriate compensation for my silence."

"So it's true what they say about yakuza and bribes."

"Yeah. Same as it's true about politicians, cops, businessmen, doctors, and civil servants. It's the Japanese way."

He searched Shigure's eyes for a moment and saw the truth behind the joke. This man didn't need to give things a different name to feel better, to feel less guilty. He'd chosen a path in life, and, whatever the reasons for doing so, he didn't try to pretend he was something other. And Ken couldn't help admiring him for it, the damn romantic that he was.

"What?"

"Nothing," he lied. "Was just trying to appraise the value of my assets."

"And have you found something valuable enough to pay for my silence?"

"Hmm. Would you accept payment in kind?"

The yakuza's dark eyes roamed appreciatively over Ken's body, his hands sliding on Ken's pants and making him shudder from head to toes. It seemed Shigure wreaked havoc with his sensitivity threshold every time he put his hands on him. That, or Ken was just going through deprivation after two whole days without the man's touch, even his aches changing when those fingers—those eyes, even—grazed him, the small pain going from uncomfortable to pleasant as the rest of his body felt electrified, ready to send sparks flying at the slightest contact.

"Are you offering yourself to me?" Shigure asked.

Christ, the way that sounded. Ken felt it first in the tightening of his balls, a glob of pre-come pulsing out of him as his cock throbbed, but he felt it mostly in the pit of his stomach, in that squeezing sensation so close to vertigo, fear and apprehension so tightly knit with excitement that he knew he had reached the point of no return, as Shigure's next words confirmed.

"Think it through, Kenshin, because if you are, I'm not giving you back."

It might have been the way Shigure said his name, or the way those eyes bore into his, or the words the yakuza had chosen, or the way those fingers dug into his flesh to leave fresh marks of ownership, but Ken had no doubt Shigure meant exactly what he said, and for the first time in Ken's life, his whole being answered for him, his "Yes" coming out like a cry as his muscles shook, his eyes rolling back in his head as his seed gushed out of him, his hips jerking against Shigure, his hands clutching at the strong biceps to stop from keeling over, noises pouring out of him without his control.

Then, just before everything in him melted, he had a clear notion of what he had done, and a wave of panic washed over him. His eyes shot open to the crude reality of his surroundings, to the fact that he had creamed his pants right in his hallway, straddling the lap of a suited yakuza, noisily crying out his pleasure without really being touched at all, just because this one man had said he wanted to keep him.

Ken feared meeting Shigure's wide-eyed stare, but it was impossible to avoid, especially since the yakuza's hands moved up to frame Ken's face and stop him from looking around. He braced himself for the shame he might find in those black eyes and looked right into them, right into the shock reflected there and past the surprise to the other unmistakable emotions written all over that rough, handsome face.

But Shigure didn't allow him to linger there. Something close to a growl left his throat, and Ken almost yelped as the yakuza stood, lifting the smaller man with him, as if he weighed less than a paper fan, and carrying him inside the apartment.

Shigure kicked the door closed and strode to the futon with Ken in his arms, carefully depositing him on it, sure hands immediately undoing Ken's pants and yanking them down with his underwear. When he was naked, Shigure straightened, his gaze never leaving Ken as he took off his suit and tossed every discarded piece on the floor without caring where or how it landed.

Ken's throat went dry at the sight of that stunning tattooed body, his cock starting to come back to life in reaction to the hunger in those eyes that touched him avidly even before hands followed, Ken's body arching off the mattress at first contact, his skin so sensitive after his release that Shigure's fingers seemed to be digging painful furrows to get to the heart of him, that hard, flushed cock wanting to drill inside him in search of those places no other man had reached before. And Ken needed it desperately, his own fingers reaching up to touch Shigure's lips, to beg for something he didn't exactly understand until the yakuza opened his mouth and took two of Ken's fingers inside, a wet tongue circling and coating them with saliva.

Ken whimpered at the sight of his fingers in Shigure's mouth, licked and tasted like some salty delicacy, Shigure's hand closing around them next and guiding the wet digits from his lips to Ken's body, to the part of him that quivered with the need to be filled, taken, marked. Ken's knees folded of their own accord, and he lifted and spread them as far as they could go, exposing himself to his lover, silently offering what was already his.

Shigure watched him avidly, his eyes going so dark Ken couldn't tell where the pupils ended, a low, animal grunt leaving his chest as if it was growing more and more impossible for him to restrain himself from ripping Ken apart to eat at the most tender flesh in the center of his body. And yet this time it was exactly what Ken wanted. Before, he'd just experienced the strong attraction of opposites, the pull of the challenge Shigure posed for him, always daring him to go further, deeper, harder, but now he wasn't even looking for the pleasure of completion or the adrenaline rush of victory. Now he simply needed this man to break through the carefully constructed defenses of his self and take the most hidden part of him, the part that only showed in his crazy drawings, the part that was wild and scary, and brittle like an origami tiger.

He pulled his own wet fingers out of Shigure's grip and shoved them inside the tight ring of muscle at his entrance, the instant pain making him bite back a scream. He was still tender from their romp in the back seat of Shigure's Mercedes, but he didn't care. He wanted this, and he could barely wait for the burn to subside. He tried to start moving his fingers, but Shigure groaned and pulled them harshly out of Ken's body.

Ken's eyes shot open in distress, only to see Shigure bend to close his mouth over Ken's aching opening. This time he couldn't contain the scream that tore out of him, his hips bucking even before a wet tongue thrust inside him, soothing the burn while it ignited all his nerve endings, pushing in and out, again and again, slicking and opening him, driving him so crazy with need that he had to beg Shigure to stop.

The yakuza finally lifted his head, his hungry gaze traveling all over Ken's flushed body, from the tip of his hardened nipples to his already erect cock, and Ken had to shut his eyes before he came for the second time that day without a single touch to his cock.

He felt the futon dip as Shigure moved even closer, felt gentle fingers on his lower lip and realized he was biting it to fight the urge to come.

"Are you all right?" Shigure asked hoarsely.

Ken almost laughed at the thought that the yakuza was as far gone as he was, but then he remembered he had already come once and opened his eyes to look at Shigure. And then he just wished he hadn't, the bare emotions in those dark eyes threatening to push him over the edge.

"Shigure, please," he panted. "In me, now."

When Shigure didn't move, he glared at the yakuza. "What?"

"I want you to know that I'm clean."

Christ Almighty. It would have been funny if Ken hadn't been dying with need. He planted his hands on the mattress and raised his torso until he was level with the yakuza. He tried his best not to yell, but wasn't really sure he succeeded.

"Do you think I give a rat's ass about your STD status after I rode you bareback on the fucking leather seat of your damn car? I swear to God, if you don't put your fucking cock in me right this minute, I'm gonna have to rape you."

If Shigure had dared laugh at him, he was sure he would have hit him, but the yakuza didn't even answer. He just grabbed Ken's legs and raised them to his wide shoulders, the posture tilting Ken's hips and leaving him completely spread, wide open for the blunt head of the shaft that immediately pushed inside him, one powerful thrust of Shigure's hips driving him in to the hilt in the first try.

They both cried out at the same time, Ken's back hitting the futon as the sensations exploded inside him, not so much pain as the overwhelming intensity of being completely filled, no barriers left between him and the pulsing heat of another life, the throb of Shigure's cock inside him echoing in ripples all along his passage, his hole contracting with the need to touch, hold, keep.

Their eyes met for a moment, language deserting both of them at the same time, when no word could have said what they both knew, that there was no turning back from here. They might go up or down, rise to high heaven or crash down to hell, but never back to where they had been, back to the time when Ken was just another gaijin to Shigure's yakuza.

When Shigure pulled out of him, Ken stopped pretending to be strong and reached out to grab Shigure's arms, letting the needy whimpers push out of him, begging with his whole body until his lover sank back into him, a harsh mouth closing over his to feed from his desperate noises.

Shigure set a hard rhythm in and out of him, and Ken could only see the waves of that tattooed sea crashing against him, threatening to drown him in their liquid strength, the ebb tide pulling him back with it, deeper and deeper into the unknown, the dragon that crawled up Shigure's arm snarling at him as it rippled with every flex of the powerful muscles that held Ken under the water, panting for air, desperate for those lips that forced air into his lungs, that kept him alive and aching, keening like a dying soul until heat pulsed deep inside him, the waves finally touching his heart and making it turn into flotsam that the powerful currents carried away for someone else to pick up.

When their bodies stopped convulsing, Shigure found the strength to lift Ken's legs off his shoulders and deposit them on the futon before collapsing on the mattress beside him. Ken couldn't possibly move, but he needed something, needed everything, and Shigure must have read it in his eyes, because he grunted and reached out for him, strong arms wrapping around him, muscled legs trapping his in a sweaty embrace.

Ken sighed as his head found the crook of Shigure's neck, feeling that he was, finally, where he belonged.

CHAPTER 17

SHIGURE rushed along the hallway, carefully ducking nurses and people in striped pajamas until he reached the waiting room with Shinya at his heel. Kinosuke jumped out of the plastic chair, as wrought up as if he was high on *shabu*. Crystal meth wouldn't have made him look so worried, though, concern wafting from the young man and mixing with the smell of disinfectant to create a solid cloud of dread.

"How is Kotarō?" Shigure asked before he noticed the quiet figure who stood next to Kinosuke, and greeted him. "Uehara-junsa-buchō."

Uehara nodded, waiting for Kinosuke to report the latest developments. The presence of the sergeant didn't bode too well for the reasons Kotarō had ended up in a hospital bed.

"The doctor said the broken ribs wouldn't be too bad if the bone hadn't—" Kinosuke gestured impatiently, but it was Uehara who finished his sentence.

"Punctured his lung."

Shigure huffed. It was serious, then. He had hoped for a pair of broken bones and a lot of bruises, but this meant Kotarō might die. And he couldn't stop the anger from surfacing. "What on earth was he doing there?"

"I was hoping you could explain that to me, Matsunaga-san."

He looked at Uehara as if he was raving mad. "And how the hell should I know?"

"He's one of the Shinagawa."

"He isn't yet, but even if he was, it's not a jail I run. My men don't have to account for every move they make."

"Well, I suppose entering a rival Korean gang's territory carrying a trophy from the Korean wars is an important enough move to be accounted for."

He ignored the sergeant and turned to Kinosuke.

"Kiriyama-sensei's sword," his man explained.

He heard Shinya gasp behind him. No one ever touched that sword, not even to dust it. The old Korean blade was the single most valuable object in the whole house, because it was the only thing Shigure had received from someone he admired, the only heirloom he could speak of, the rest of his belongings—no matter how expensive—having been purchased with his own, hard-earned money, or gifted by people he just had a working relationship with.

"I need to know if it is a turf war I'm facing here, Matsunaga-san."

Of course he did. If the two biggest gangs in the city started battling away, there'd be civilian casualties as well, no matter how hard they tried to keep it inside their ranks.

"I can't speak for the Daitō-kai, but I can assure you the Shinagawa aren't planning to break the truce any time soon."

Uehara's eyes held his for a moment. The sergeant was a wisp of a man, short and rail thin, his gray hair and quiet composure making him appear harmless, but Shigure knew better than to underestimate the old cop. Those unwavering eyes had seen too much to let fear cloud his judgment, and he would do exactly what was needed, even if it meant skirting a few laws along the way. It'd be stupid—and dangerous—to lie to him.

"I trust you'll look into this incident yourself, then?" Uehara finally asked.

"Yes. I'll take responsibility for anything my man might have done."

Uehara bowed to him. "Please keep me informed."

Shigure returned the bow and waited until the sergeant was well out of earshot to turn to Kinosuke. "Sit down and tell me what happened."

Kinosuke didn't meet his eyes as he sat. He knew it wasn't a polite request, knew that if they'd been back at the Shinagawa house, he'd be on his knees right now, his forehead touching the ground as he answered for the apprentice under his supervision, the apprentice who might have just started a war.

"Kotarō dropped the sword accidentally, and the scabbard got damaged."

Shigure clenched his teeth. The black lacquered scabbard was more beautiful than the sword itself, the blade a piece of average craftsmanship, while the protective cover had been designed by his sensei himself, the golden serpent curling around its polished surface intended as a symbol of the strength tightly coiled in the hands of the wielder.

"He learned of a place where they still do lacquer work in the traditional way, and he took the scabbard there, or was going to when a group of Onga's men found him."

"Where's the scabbard now?"

Of course he got no answer to that. Onga was probably pawing at it with his chubby fingers and imagining ways to make Shigure's humiliation worse.

"The sword?"

"It's safe. Kotarō just took the scabbard with him."

Shigure paced up and down the narrow waiting room. Kinosuke made it all sound so simple and unavoidable, and yet it felt deeply wrong in many little, upsetting details.

"Did you tell Uehara about the blade?"

"Yeah. I had to explain everything to him."

Since his boss wasn't there to do the talking, Kinosuke seemed to be implying, even though he still wouldn't look up to meet Shigure's eyes. Better this way, because his boss was definitely not in the mood to tolerate accusations.

"Did you tell him where it came from?"

"I told him it was Kiriyama-sensei's sword."

"And?"

Kinosuke gave him a blank stare.

"Did you tell him how the sensei got it?"

"Uh... I suppose I did."

"You suppose or you did?"

"I don't fucking remember what I said, all right? Kotarō'd been in surgery for two hours, I didn't think it mattered where the sensei had bought the damn sword."

He heard Shinya moving to watch the door even before Shigure realized his own hands were grabbing a handful of Kinosuke's clothes. His voice came out as a snarl, delivered inches away from his man's face as if to respect the silence due in a hospital.

"You don't fucking remember because you were too scared to pay attention, you stupid piece of shit. You think Uehara works for us? He's a damn cop. You have to be very careful about the information you share with him if you don't want it used against the Shinagawa."

"And how the hell should I know! It's you who deal with Uehara all the time, and you weren't here. How was I supposed to fence a cop for more than two hours?"

"What are you, a first-grader? You can't expect me to solve every little problem for you. You have men who rely on you to act in time, to make the right decision. Damn, Kinosuke, we're not salarymen here. If you hesitate, people will get hurt or killed, and I won't always be around to help you."

"No, I guess you won't."

The silence in the room became tense, charged. Even Shinya had stopped looking out into the hallway to focus on the two men facing each other, Shigure's hands still fisting the younger man's shirt, their narrowed eyes meeting in a challenge that was impossible to ignore.

"What are you implying, Kinosuke?"

Kinosuke swallowed, Shigure's voice so deceptively soft that their aggressive posturing seemed totally incongruous, as if they were playing a part neither of them could quite believe. Shigure held the young man's eyes, waiting, giving him a chance to back off.

"You should've been here," Kinosuke finally mumbled, looking down.

"Be a man and say that to my face."

Kinosuke lifted his head, burning eyes meeting Shigure's, words spat in Shigure's face with a rage that made his whole body shake. "You know how many times I tried to reach you? Kotarō was calling your name as they took him into surgery covered in blood, the Daitō-kai might be preparing a full-out attack, Uehara wouldn't stop asking questions I didn't know how to answer, but your phone was off because you were busy fucking a gaijin whore!"

The force of the blow made Kinosuke reel back. He looked at Shigure in surprise for a moment, the skin on his face beginning to darken just as his eyes filled with something very close to hurt, disappointment and defeat tugging at each other and losing to pain as Kinosuke stormed out of the waiting room.

Shigure stood there, breathing hard. He tried to convince himself that he couldn't watch over his men twenty four/seven as if they hadn't yet lost their milk teeth, but he knew the time he spent with Kenshin wasn't even the problem. The problem was Shigure had never acknowledged the American as an equal, and so his men felt no need to respect him.

If he hadn't been a coward, he would have asked Kenshin to move in with him so they would have both been there to keep Kotarō from harm.

"You never told Uehara about the sword?"

Shinya's question startled him out of his thoughts. "Never, and I don't think Kinosuke did either."

"Nah. He was probably smoking on the school rooftop the day they explained the Korean wars."

He had to chuckle at the image, which was probably accurate, since Kinosuke had dropped out of school to join a bōsōzoku gang of teenage bikers.

"You think the sergeant's got the scabbard?" Shinya asked.

"No. He would have told us even if they kept it as evidence, and I'm not sure he'd have noticed anything peculiar about its shape. Truth is, I'm not sure Onga would have noticed either."

"He's Korean."

"His father is Korean. And Onga is more into firearms. He probably couldn't tell the difference between a sword and a carving knife."

Shinya frowned. "If it wasn't him, who told Uehara the sword is Korean?"

"The sergeant would have spoken with both sides if he suspected there's going to be trouble with the Daitō-kai, so I'm sure it was Onga who told him. The question is, how did a Daitō-kai underboss find out about a sword that's never been displayed, that nobody outside my household has ever heard of, not even our oyabun?"

Shinya's face fell. "The same way he found out someone from the Shinagawa would be bringing its scabbard into his territory."

"Exactly."

CHAPTER 18

"I SUPPOSE I don't need to explain how humiliating it was?"

"I'm sorry, oyabun." Shigure bowed his head. Of course he knew what it might have been like, the leader of the Shinagawa having to listen to an angry rival yelling about a sword he didn't even know existed.

Silence stretched between them, only the soft purr of the engine reminding Shigure that they were moving, the sleek black limo gliding along mostly empty streets. The oyabun was an early riser—as old men tend to be—though a call from the Daitō-kai might have contributed to his light sleep.

Shigure didn't raise his eyes, but he could imagine the face their supreme leader was making. He'd seen those thick black brows knit together in a deep frown many times over the years, and he knew the corners of the oyabun's mouth tended to drop down in a gesture of disgust more often than not. Now that he was in his sixties, the old boss didn't look any less imposing than he always had, his bald head accentuating the sharpness of his features, the alert look in his narrowed eyes letting the world know he was a force to be reckoned with, nothing to do with one of those grandfatherly figures you went to for guidance. No, this man didn't impart the wisdom his years had earned him. The Shinagawa oyabun was a ruler, and as such, he didn't give advice but orders.

"I expect you to fix this blunder, Matsunaga. I don't care what it takes."

"Hai."

There was no need to waste any more words, and they both knew it. When the car stopped by the curb, Shigure bowed and climbed out, standing there with his head down until the limo pulled away and disappeared from view. Then he found himself inhaling deeply, trying to keep down the rage threatening to take over.

It might have been the way the oyabun dismissed him, as if he were no more than a rank-and-file soldier, a junior aspirant to the lower tiers of the organization. Of course that was the oyabun speaking, and everybody was the oyabun's inferior, but still he resented it, resented that, no matter how many men he led, no matter how many years he'd struggled to build his reputation, to earn the respect of the people he worked with, it just took one misstep to throw him back to the starting line, where all he could do was accept orders without question. Even when those orders meant giving up his most cherished possession to a man who was not only his enemy, but utterly unable to appreciate— much less honor—what he was given.

Just imagining what Shinji Onga—who thought Hawaiian print shirts were the summit of elegance—would do with Kiriyama-sensei's sword made bile rise in Shigure's throat.

He stood on the curb with his eyes tightly shut until the increasing number of passersby told him it was getting close to the peak hour, salarymen striding purposefully around him to start their long working day, ignoring the conspicuous yakuza stranded on the concrete beach.

This was his life, and he hadn't really chosen it. The truth was he'd never had a chance to become one of those office workers who now surrounded him, with no more responsibilities than a bunch of paperwork piling up on a desk. His parents didn't have the money to pay for the cram school he would have needed to keep up with his studies, to prepare for the tough exams to access university. Then again, what was the use in going to university when no company would hire a burakumin for anything that wasn't cleaning its offices?

Of course he could have chosen to go for the low-paying jobs, but then he would have been working under a yakuza boss anyway, so he'd taken the shortcut and joined the yakuza straight away, working for the only business in Japan that actually had a minority hiring policy.

All these years he'd been fiercely loyal to his company, made every sacrifice requested of him. He didn't have the luxury of free time, never went on vacation, didn't have a family of his own, and even his house had been turned into a place of training for other members of the organization. He'd dirtied his hands when necessary, kept secrets safe, never complained when his salary was under the minimum-wage line or took too long to arrive. He would have given up everything he possessed, sold the art collection that was his pride and joy, rented out the big house, driven a Honda Civic, whatever the organization needed of him. Anything but give away that old piece of worthless junk. And of course, that was exactly what they were asking of him, because the yakuza—like every other company—was all about profit, and it would always take away more than it gave back.

When the crowd around him became almost solid, Shigure stepped off of the curb and flagged down a cab. He just told the driver to head north, his eyes following the deft movements of white-gloved hands on the wheel without really seeing them, his own fingers toying with the key ring in his pocket.

It was only when he saw the building through the car window that he understood where he wanted to be, where he'd meant to go all along. He paid the fare and got out, his legs moving faster than his brain and taking him up the stairs and in front of the door before he had time to think about alternatives.

The key went into the lock, and the door opened and closed without a sound, shutting out everything Shigure wanted to forget, the low hum of the air conditioner muting the noise from the street, making him feel as if he'd stepped into another dimension, a small, peaceful bubble of time out of time.

He inhaled deeply, letting the quiet atmosphere soothe him. His shoes went off, then his tie, and finally his suit jacket, making his step incredibly lighter, as if he'd been carrying a ton of bricks in his pockets. Then he crossed the room without a sound, stopping to stand beside the seated figure he'd kept in sight from the moment he'd entered the small apartment.

Kenshin sat cross-legged on the floor, working on a low table beneath the window, blond hair looking almost white under the sunlight that filtered through the glass pane. He was so focused he hadn't yet noticed Shigure's presence, and the yakuza took the chance to soak in the view, his eyes roaming over foreign features, circling round eyes, following the straight line of the nose to lips pushed slightly forward in concentration, the soft curve of the neck guiding Shigure's gaze down along the back to the patch of skin left uncovered by the crazy bright purple, sleeveless T-shirt Kenshin was wearing. As the American bent forward to draw, the purple shirt went up just a little, but his trousers slid so low down his hips that Shigure could see the beginning of his cleft, showing him there was no underwear between the smooth skin and the rough, black fabric of the pants.

Shigure's mouth went dry, his fingers itching to touch that beautiful skin, his cock starting to demand room inside his clothes. He let his knees bend till they hit the floor, not even the low thump managing to startle Kenshin out of focus until Shigure's hands pressed against the small of his back. Then the American yelped, and only Shigure's quick reaction prevented his long legs from bumping against the table and overturning it, his arms pulling the slim body against him to still his movements.

"Shhh, baby, it's me."

"Jesus, have you gone all ninja on me now?"

Shigure let the chuckle pour out of him. "Sorry, same old yakuza here."

"Old, my ass."

"This ass, you mean?"

His hands slid between their bodies to cup Kenshin's firm buttocks, the sexy American arching into his touch, a soft moan escaping his throat. Kenshin's trousers were so loose that Shigure's fingers had room to stroke and squeeze freely, and he wondered what would hold them in place if Kenshin stood. Not that he wanted the man to stand anytime soon, the pressure against his chest too delicious to let go.

"Don't distract me when I'm trying to chide you."

He didn't stop his fingers, though, enjoying the way Kenshin's voice had gone all husky and breathless.

"Chide me for what?" he asked.

"For stalking me."

"Stalking?"

"Yeah, you know, approaching stealthily your intended... uh... prey."

"Oh, that. I thought you meant...." He chose that moment to try and slide one of his hands under Kenshin's zipper while leaving the other splayed over the sweet curve of his ass, and Kenshin's immediate reaction tore a loud moan out of him, the slender body wiggling between his hands as Kenshin cried out, pushing a throbbing shaft into his fingers and then rocking back to press his ass against Shigure's other hand, the movement effectively trapping the invading fingers between smooth, heated flesh and rough fabric.

"Hmmm. You're so responsive."

"Can't help myself around you."

Shigure felt his hands tighten their hold, something deep inside pushing forward at Kenshin's words, making the American whimper, the bruising pressure too close to pain where it squeezed his cock. It wasn't something he was used to feeling, this anger, so different from the one that had led his steps to Kenshin in the first place, and yet anger all the same, drinking from the same cup, filled to the brim with the frustration he'd been forced to swallow down earlier.

"I hope you're not like this around anyone else," he almost growled in Kenshin's ear, his mouth immediately closing over the delicate skin of a bared throat and sucking hard, pulling blood to the surface to leave his signature where everybody could see it and know what it meant.

Kenshin moved his head from side to side. "Just you," he breathed, his hands desperately trying to reach Shigure. "No one has ever—"

His words were lost in a sharp cry when Shigure sank his teeth into the tender flesh, a violent shudder raking Kenshin's frame, his shaft in Shigure's fingers jerking as it let out a glob of pre-come, as the message Shigure was trying to deliver came through—*and no one ever will.*

He held on to his prey until he was sure he'd left an imprint as unmistakable as a dental record, the words he hadn't said still ringing loudly in his brain. He didn't want to let go of this man, this treasure he'd found. Let others despise Kenshin for being a gaijin. If it was up to him, Shigure would make his lover invisible to everyone else, would lock him up in that tiny apartment and keep him there forever, just waiting for him, safe from the predators that might want Kenshin only because he belonged to someone else.

"Shigure."

He licked a trail along the smooth jaw to the sweet lips calling his name, closing his hungry mouth over them to taste the need he could feel in the hand that fisted Kenshin's cock, the American making small noises that Shigure swallowed avidly, his own need growing so urgent that he feared he might hurt Kenshin in his eagerness to possess him. His lover didn't complain, though, he just kept trying to turn to face Shigure, the slender hands finding it difficult to get purchase in this position, the nimble body trying to both push into Shigure's hands and do some exploring of his own with their lips fused together, tongues pressing against each other, teeth clicking with the urge to close around flesh.

Finally Shigure couldn't take it anymore, the restraint of Kenshin's clothing, and he pulled his hands out of Kenshin's pants long enough to undo the button and zipper. But as soon as he was free to move, the American shifted to straddle Shigure's lap, legs and arms wrapping around the yakuza, lips latching onto Shigure's with a vengeance, feeding from the breathy chuckles Shigure let out. There was no way to get to skin with Kenshin plastered to him like a limpet, though he had to admit the new position had its advantages, especially when Kenshin rocked his hips to bring their erections together.

Any other day he might have contented himself with rubbing against Kenshin in the most simple, urgent mating, but today he needed more, needed to be acknowledged, to be shown there was something completely and exclusively his.

It seemed all he did was test Kenshin, the extent of his loyalty to him, but he knew he was going to do it once again when he pushed forward until he was on his knees, and then kept pushing to bring the body wrapped around him down under the weight of his own heavier body.

Kenshin cried out as his back slammed against the floor, but he didn't let go for even a moment, long limbs roping around Shigure and holding tight. Shigure let out a frustrated groan, barely forming coherent words as his hands fought purple cotton.

"Need you naked. Now."

Bicolored eyes studied his, and Kenshin must have seen the urgency in them, because he was disentangling himself from Shigure and chucking his clothes as fast as if any fire in the world could be extinguished by throwing extravagant garments at it.

Shigure didn't pull away any farther than was strictly necessary for Kenshin to wiggle beneath him, his hands not hindering but neither helping, just reaching out to cover any expanse of bare skin that presented itself, the need to mark so strong that he was stamping his palms on every available surface, wishing his digits were inked to leave behind the recognizable pattern of his fingerprints.

He didn't move to get rid of his own clothes, he was too busy craving the man exposed under his gaze, his hands intent on their task to press against the smooth skin as if they were really sculpting every ridge, rounding every curve, tugging until soft buttons became erect mounds, sharpening hip bones, curling the shock of blond hair that crowned the long shaft Shigure's fingers were molding into a beautiful, weeping rod.

Kenshin kept anticipating his needs even as he moaned and writhed under Shigure's harsh exploration, long fingers pulling open Shigure's pants and freeing his cock. Shigure didn't follow those fingers when they left him, didn't take his eyes from the firm curves his hands were kneading now, lifting them off the floor and pulling roughly as he rocked back to sit on his heels, forcing Kenshin's buttocks to rest on his own thighs, long legs bracketing Shigure, flushed cock slapping against a flat belly with the sudden movement, hairless sack hanging heavy, pointing the way to the rosy, puckered hole that was Shigure's target.

Suddenly cool fingers wrapped around his burning shaft, spreading a sticky gel from root to tip, and Shigure had to wonder where Kenshin had left the lube the last time they went at each other— probably a little tube on every flat, near surface, which was almost everywhere since the apartment was so small.

Shigure wrapped his hand around a delicate wrist to stop Kenshin's movements when the massage became too much.

"Are you—"

"Yes," Kenshin panted, tilting his hips further up, offering himself. And Shigure couldn't resist it, that offer. He pressed forward, his cock pushing into Kenshin's warmth, tight muscles closing like a fist around his shaft.

Kenshin's head banged against the floor as he cried out, the slender body arching closer to Shigure, meeting him halfway, two magnetic fields pulling at each other with the need to absorb and be absorbed, to collapse into each other and melt into raw energy.

Shigure moaned loudly when his cock was completely sheathed in tight, pulsing heat, and he felt the urge to resume his self-imposed task of mapping the gorgeous body lying before him—his hands itched to knead, maul, and bruise all that naked skin that was showing a deep flush now, blood moving to the surface to help Shigure turn white marble into something living, irregular, messier, and more beautiful than ever.

He realized he was still clutching Kenshin's wrist and bent forward to stretch the arm over the American's head, the movement pressing his cock impossibly deeper into Kenshin, pulling the white skin taut over the thin torso, Shigure's mouth so close now to the full, swollen lips that he could feel Kenshin's rapid breath moving against his own lips.

"Kenshin." He murmured the word reverently, wanting to stay forever like this, covering Kenshin's exquisite, naked body with his, in and around him like a rough armor that was slowly melting and mixing with his flesh to turn the delicate bones into something indestructible. But then his sweet lover pushed against him, peaked nipples grazing Shigure's chest through the shirt he was still wearing, hard cock pressing against the waistband of his boxers, wetting his belly, hungry lips closing on his as one hand latched onto his neck to pull him down.

The need he tasted on those lips was sharp, mirroring his own and giving it back magnified, making his muscles tense with the urge to move and take more. Unable to wait, he broke the kiss and straightened his back, his hands going to Kenshin's hips and digging his fingers into them, shoving the slender body away from him as he pulled out of the heated passage. A soft whimper called to him, urging his movements as he thrust back in while he pulled the slim hips flush against his own body once again.

Kenshin's cry was so loud, Shigure thought the neighbors might call the cops, but there was so much pleasure in the sound, so much need, that he wouldn't mind going to jail if that was what it took to hear Kenshin scream for him again. He repeated the sequence of movements one more time, in and out of the tight sheath, dragging Kenshin's whole body with him, falling into a rhythm that kept his sexy gaijin keening, long legs shifting until Kenshin had his feet firmly planted on the floor to push up against Shigure, slender fingers ignoring his neglected cock to close around Shigure's forearms and pull the yakuza to him every time, as if he didn't care about pleasure but proximity, the need to have Shigure deeper inside him outweighing everything else and making Shigure wild.

He hadn't known a lover like Kenshin before. Whenever he'd had great sex in the past, it all came down to both partners focusing on one another's pleasure, giving back as much as they took, so that in the end it was no more—and no less—than a highly enjoyable exchange of abilities, just like a good match between two practiced opponents.

But Shigure had never seen anyone bare his needs so completely, never had a lover appear so naked and vulnerable before him, wanting only to be taken, not caring about the returns, his whole pleasure coming from his lover's own pleasure. It made him feel so powerful, Kenshin's hunger for him, his total abandon accentuated by his more submissive position, by the contrast between the American's naked flesh against Shigure's fully clothed body. It made him feel desperate to go further, deeper, harder, right to the center of that beating heart to snatch it and keep it in a safe place no one else had access to.

An animal growl pushed out of his chest, and he reached back to grab Kenshin's bony ankles and bring his legs to the front, forcing more of Kenshin's buttocks to leave the floor as Shigure pushed the long legs toward Kenshin's chest and let his body follow the movement, let his full weight lean on Kenshin's upturned ass.

His hands pushed his lover's legs forward, almost bending the lithe body double, and the new angle forced Shigure's cock even deeper into Kenshin and over his gland. The reaction was immediate, striking. Kenshin's cry rang in the small apartment, his back arched off the floor in a perfect curve, his flushed cock jerked just as if Kenshin had touched a live wire, but even then, it wasn't his shaft Kenshin's fingers were instantly reaching for, but Shigure, holding on to the back of his thighs and pulling the yakuza to him as if he could never get enough of him.

Shigure groaned, sensing his control slip completely. Instinct took over, and his movements became harsh, almost brutal as his hips thrust in a fast rhythm, shoving his cock deep into Kenshin every time, nailing his gland every time, his incredible lover screaming at the top of his lungs as his body was forced to its limits, the muscles on his legs pulled taut, sweat beading his flushed skin, beautiful features contracted in the agony of intense pleasure.

Kenshin's eyes were so dark now that they looked identical for the first time as the huge pupils chased away any trace of color. It made Kenshin look drugged, high on the rush of pheromones their aggressive coupling was releasing amid the scent of sweat and sex. Their bodies were producing heat, too, if the sweat that trickled down Shigure's back was any indication, or the never-stopping buzz of the air conditioner.

The pressure on his balls was growing so much that Shigure felt about to burst. His whole body was pulsing as his cock did, but the desire to stay forever buried in his lover was almost as strong as the urgency to claim him, and so he tried to make the moment last, tried to look away from Kenshin's face, but only managed to direct his gaze to something even sexier. He looked down to the point where their bodies joined and saw his shaft pull out of Kenshin's body, heavy with blood, its surface shinning wet, going only as far out as Kenshin's hands on the back of his thighs gave him room to, and only to thrust back inside with such force that Kenshin's body slid over the floor a few inches, a sweet new cry filling the air as Shigure's length sank back completely into him and come spurted all over the flat belly and chest.

The vision was too much for Shigure. He froze for a moment and then just let go, anger, frustration, and need exploding in flashes of white behind his lids, Kenshin's body rippling around him, moving with him, his lover's sexy voice calling his name in something so close to a sob that Shigure felt his heart swelling painfully, as if it, too, were about to burst.

They both collapsed at the same time, Kenshin's legs and arms sliding to the floor as Shigure slumped against him. Kenshin didn't seem to mind having his full weight on him, and Shigure's addled brain knew that even if he was smothering him, his sweet lover still craved the connection, so much so that he was even trying to wrap his long limbs around the ungainly body slouched against him. When those slender legs shifted, though, it was with the uncoordinated movements of after-sex exhaustion, and there was a loud bump and a cry when a bare shin connected with the low table Kenshin usually worked on.

Shigure rolled off Kenshin, grunting as his cock popped free of its comfortable nest, his lover immediately turning to one side and curling into a ball as he grabbed his injured shin. It was only then that Shigure noticed how hard their lovemaking had been on the American.

Naked against the floor, with Shigure's weight dragging his back over the hard surface with each shove and pull, the skin from his delicate nape to his buttocks had turned an angry red, his neck and shoulders showing all kinds of marks, a trickle of semen running down the back of one slender thigh, deep finger-shaped marks decorating his hip and rounding his ankles as if he'd been shackled.

Shigure felt like a jerk. There he was, all dressed up, not moving a finger to make things easier for his lover, just waiting for the other man to satisfy his every need. He wondered—not for the first time— what Kenshin was doing with a brute like him.

His fingers pressed gently on his gaijin's thigh, forcing the slender body to turn.

"Let me see."

"Shit," Kenshin cursed while his hand kept rubbing at the sore spot. "That's IKEA for you."

Shigure took one look at the stout wooden table and burst out laughing. "You should have chosen Muji instead. Their furniture is more… harmonious."

"Yeah, right. What you mean is they're flimsier."

Shigure let his hand slide down Kenshin's leg in a slow massage. "What I mean is they'll break before you do."

Kenshin snorted. "And that should be taken as a symbol of the impermanence of all things?"

"Nah. Only as a symbol of a limited budget."

Kenshin looked at him and laughed, the sound happy and relaxed. He couldn't help wanting to taste that happiness, and he bent to take those smiling lips in his, chuckling into the sloppy, openmouthed kiss.

"Feeling better now?" Shigure asked, pulling the naked body to rest against him, his hand drawing lazy caresses on the battered leg.

"Yeah. What about you?"

He had to smile. Damn gaijin. Of course he had noticed Shigure wasn't having the best of days. But he didn't want to talk about it, not now that Kenshin had almost made him forget what had been eating at him. So he just put his hand on the American's jaw and turned the blond head till those swollen lips were close enough to kiss.

Kenshin immediately opened for him, and they took their time breathing each other in like chain smokers on the twentieth cigarette of the day, their kisses slow and thorough now that the urgency was over. When he let his lips follow the line of Kenshin's jaw, something on the floor caught his eye, and he raised his head to check it out.

There was a sketching pad lying spread open—it had probably fallen when Kenshin hit the table—and Shigure blinked at the carbon likeness drawn on the white page.

"Is that…?"

They both reached out to pick it up, but Shigure was faster, and his eyes widened when he took a closer look.

"You've drawn me." He had to say the words aloud to start believing it, in spite of the evidence in his hands. And it wasn't that the man in the drawing was difficult to recognize—Kenshin had nailed every feature, every single detail of his face and body, including the intricacies of his tattoo—but there was something about the way Shigure appeared on that page that wasn't quite right, or rather, was too right to be true. The tattooed figure in the sketch stood so confident, so proud, so much in control, that he looked taller, dangerous, handsome even.

Kenshin turned to look at him, uncertainty in his eyes. "You don't like it."

"Of course I like it."

"But—"

"But that's not me in there."

Kenshin pulled a little away to better look at him. "You mean it doesn't look like you?"

"Yeah, it looks like me—like an upgraded version of myself, that is."

They kept silent for a moment, both of them looking at the drawing as if it were about to give them its own view on the matter.

"I've only drawn what I see," Kenshin finally said, frowning at him, not quite understanding what Shigure was talking about. And

Shigure had to swallow hard, his throat had gone so dry all of a sudden. That was what Kenshin saw every time he looked at him, that strong man even Shigure found difficult not to like. It wasn't what he saw in the mirror every day, or reflected in the eyes of others when they looked at him. But it was what that beautiful foreigner had seen from the start, and Shigure couldn't stop the funny feeling rising in his chest—the urge to both laugh and cry—that he hid by pulling the slim body to him in a bone-crushing hug.

"Does this mean the artist's not dismissed?"

"It means I'm keeping him."

And Shigure knew he wasn't even trying to joke.

CHAPTER 19

KEN pushed the door open with his hip, hands busy with an elaborate fruit basket and a bag full of presents. It wasn't exactly visiting hours, but nobody had said a word to him. He loved that about Japanese hospitals, the way it was less like the nurses trying to keep everyone from disturbing the patients and more like giving families and friends leeway to make the sick feel at home.

There wasn't anybody in the room with Kotarō. Probably one of Shigure's men was in the cafeteria right now, or had just left because there was someone else on his way here. They were like a bunch of fussy uncles, those tough guys, taking turns to look after Kotarō, Shigure himself spending hours by the kid's bedside.

It wasn't an exaggeration when people said the more traditional gangs were like close-knit families—much more like family than Kotarō's blood relatives, anyway. The poor kid was still waiting for them to at least make a phone call or send a get-well card.

Ken left his presents on the windowsill and sat on the chair that the nurses had stopped trying to get out of the way, since there was always someone dragging it back to the bedside.

Kotarō was sleeping, his technicolor face looking a little less swollen, his mouth open to compensate for his broken nose, the scraped knuckles on his hands making them look small as they rested on the sheets, just like the hands of a little boy gone to bed without supper after some mischief. The problem was this boy's mischief had cost him a severe concussion, two broken ribs, and a free, get-to-look-like-a-crook beauty treatment. Maybe now that he looked meaner his enemies would steer away from him. Something good might come of it after all. Yeah, that or a war, if Kotarō kept treading enemy territory as if it were the floor of a shopping mall.

"You can't be here," Kinosuke's whisper sounded so close to his ear that Ken almost jumped out of the chair. He turned to meet the usual murderous glare. "Only family can stay after visiting hours."

"Oh, I get it. Only close relatives like you, aniki." He poured as much acid into the word "big brother" as he could, too tired of excusing Kinosuke's hostility. Kotarō was his friend, too, and worry had taken its toll on him as well, but Ken wasn't barking at anyone for stress relief.

"Haven't you done enough harm already?"

"What?"

Ken must have raised his voice, because Kotarō shifted in his bed, letting out a small, pained moan. Before he could do or say anything else, Kinosuke grabbed his arm and dragged him out into the hallway.

"What the hell—"

"Shut up, you stupid gaijin."

It'd been so long since he'd last heard those words spoken right to his face that Ken didn't react, didn't even shake the painful grip of Kinosuke's fingers on his arm. He just stood there, stunned into silence by the coldness in the other man's voice, by all the venom he'd been storing up for Ken.

"You're just the boss's plaything. You have no right to be here. And what is it that you want, anyway? Kotarō is in that bed because of you, the boss is humiliating himself in front of our enemy because of you, what else could you possibly ask for?"

"It wasn't me who beat Kotarō, and I sure as hell haven't…. Wait. What do you mean, 'humiliating himself'? Where is Matsunaga-san?"

"No, you didn't actually beat Kotarō. You wouldn't dirty your hands like that. You just went at it the coward's way, putting stupid ideas in the boy's head, making him think he'd be invincible with a sword. And Kotarō's just too naïve to understand the boss lets you win so that you let him fuck you."

"You bastard—" Ken tried to shove Kinosuke off, but the young man didn't budge, his fingers digging even harder into Ken's arm, pulling him so much closer that their noses were almost touching when he started speaking again, his voice low, his tone cold enough to make the air conditioner stop working.

"You fight like a girl when you can't hide behind a *bokken*. And what are you gonna do now that the boss isn't here to protect you? Call the cops? Maybe you should, 'cause I don't expect your sugar daddy'll be in a good mood after giving up a sword that's ten times more valuable than your skinny ass."

"The sword? What's happened? What do you mean he's had to give it up?"

"Oh, he didn't tell you? Guess he thought a gaijin slut wouldn't know the first thing about honor and obligation."

"You stupid fucker! Where on earth is he? Tell me!"

"You wanna know where he is right now?" Kinosuke smirked, taking his time to answer. "Right now our boss is kneeling in front of Shinji Onga, a Daitō-kai captain, and he's giving that Korean bastard the thing he values most in this world, because that's what it takes to avoid a war. Now you may enjoy going down on your knees to suck cock, but I can assure you the boss is hating every second of it. He's just man enough to do his duty and pay for the mistakes of those who answer to him."

"Yeah? And what are you doing to pay for the mistakes of the one *you* were responsible for?"

That seemed to throw Kinosuke off-kilter, and Ken took the chance to shake himself free and take a step back, being very careful not to rub the painful marks of fingers on his arm. He wouldn't give the asshole the satisfaction of seeing how much it hurt him. He went for his most indifferent tone.

"You know, Kinosuke-kun, you can pretend that everything that's happened is the gaijin's fault, but that's all I am—a foreigner, a visitor—while you've been here all the time, so busy hating me that you abandoned your charge, left him alone when he most needed the guidance of an older, wiser brother. But if blaming me will help you feel less guilty, go ahead. Either way is fine with me because, believe it or not, I don't give a shit about the half-assed taunts of a lowlife like you, someone who knows as much about honor and duty as a sewer rat."

He didn't wait for Kinosuke's reaction, he just turned and walked back to Kotarō's room, praying that his steps looked steady, that Kinosuke wouldn't see how his hands shook. As soon as he closed the door behind him, though, he let his body slump against the wood, gulping for air like a carp pulled out of the water. And he couldn't quite decide which tied his guts in tighter knots, rage or fear.

He wasn't afraid of what Kinosuke might do, but what he'd said had brought Ken back down from the clouds to the harsh reality of the yakuza underworld. It wasn't a sports club he'd been visiting. This was the Mob, plain and simple, where the careless behavior of a kid might bring about a turf war. And it wasn't exactly wooden swords these men would wield against each other, but big, automatic, American guns. And Shigure would be there, right in the middle of it all.

What frightened Ken the most was that he didn't really care about a gang war as long as the Shinagawa won it—as long as Shigure came out of it unscathed.

HE'D thought it'd be the worst day of his life, having to go to Onga's headquarters to present him with Kiriyama-sensei's sword as a formal apology for Kotarō's breach of the agreement established between the two gangs. Of course he hadn't exactly enjoyed it, but at least he'd felt detached from all that happened around him, as if he were just enacting a traditional yakuza ritual that had nothing personal to do with him.

Maybe that was the key, the way their steps had been choreographed to the last detail, both of them trying to make it go as smoothly as possible because they both knew who the winner had been in that particular confrontation, and there was no need to rub it in any further. He had to acknowledge that about Onga. The Korean might have bad taste in everything from clothes to women, but he was still an old-school yakuza, someone you could trust to show due respect at funerals, weddings, and peace talks.

Or maybe Shigure was finally old enough to understand his sensei's words when he said that one should act as if the things he cherished the most were already lost or broken. Detachment. Maybe he was already there, and his confidence didn't need any props to sustain itself, his past as a destitute burakumin finally dead and buried.

As he made his way through the hospital hallways, Shigure contemplated still another reason for his oddly good mood. All those years the sword had been so important because it was the first time someone had cared enough to offer him something invested with sentimental value, something he was not so much given as entrusted with. Lately, though, there was someone who offered him a much higher level of trust and appreciation, someone who wouldn't just gift him with a valued possession, but who offered Shigure his very self every single time, with no restrictions, without holding back, however far he might push, just because Shigure was Shigure, no more, no less.

And damn if that feeling wasn't the most intoxicating he'd ever experienced.

"Evening, boss."

Kotarō sounded so contrite, Shigure had to bite down a chuckle. It wouldn't do to laugh at the kid after all he'd been through—no matter that he'd brought it on himself, it was still too harsh a punishment. Especially today, though, Shigure had to keep the severe face on, because the sooner his apprentice learned there were consequences to every action, the better. The yakuza world was moving too fast, and when Kotarō's generation reached the top, traditions might have been completely shunned in favor of a ruthless, self-serving policy of instant profit, and no enemy would be appeased by a symbolic gift anymore.

"Evening, Kotarō. How are you feeling today?"

"Fine, thank you, boss."

So well-mannered. He sat on the chair by the bed, wondering how long it would take for Kotarō to go back to his old, babbling self. He just waited, almost smiling when he saw the outrageous silk pajamas the kid was wearing, a sure sign that Kenshin had been there, that and the pile of manga on the nightstand, the tastefully arranged fruit basket on the windowsill, and the sketch pad Kotarō was holding. The kid loved Kenshin's drawings—small wonder, that—and he would stare at them for hours on end with a stunned expression on his bruised face.

"Uh, boss…."

Here we go, Shigure thought, nodding to encourage Kotarō.

"I… I'm really sorry."

Shigure nodded gravely. There wasn't anything to say to that, and Kotarō knew it. The silence only lasted two more seconds, curiosity too strong for the kid to rein it in.

"Was it bad?" Shigure raised a brow, and Kotarō hurried to correct himself. "I mean... did Onga... uh... you know... laugh or something?"

Laugh? Shigure could quite envision the scene in Kotarō's eyes, with Onga as the proverbial manga villain, teeth shining with an evil spark as he smirked at a frustrated Shigure.

"He didn't laugh. He was very correct about the whole thing, carried it out the proper way."

"But it was his fault! I mean, it was wrong to ask you for the sword. How could he be correct about it?"

"He could have asked for anything. It was the Shinagawa who broke the truce. He was within his right to ask for any compensation, and that included your little finger, Kotarō."

The kid paled, his bruises appearing lurid by contrast. Of course Shigure knew Onga would never have asked for Kotarō's pinkie after his men had almost beat him to death, but the kid didn't need to know that. He'd do better next time with a healthy dose of fear in him. He also didn't need to know that, hadn't Onga contented himself with a paltry sword, it might have been their own oyabun who requested a little finger as atonement, and not exactly Kotarō's.

"What I mean when I say he was correct is that he showed me respect in spite of all. He could have gathered all his men to watch the Shinagawa underboss humiliate himself in the Daitō-kai training hall, but he received me in the tatami room instead, with only two men and Sergeant Uehara as witnesses, and he made a show of handling the sword carefully and put it in a place of honor."

"And there won't be a war, then?"

"No. We drank sake to seal the pact once again. As long as we both keep to our territories, the truce will stand."

"I'm sorry, boss."

Shigure finally let a smile show. "It's all right, kid. I bet you've learned your lesson. Just be sure to ask for advice next time you feel daring."

"Yeah, for all the good advice does me. I just get more confused than before I asked."

He had to laugh at Kotarō's words until a terrifying notion crossed his mind. "You didn't ask anyone before you went there, did you?"

"Uh, well, not exactly. I just threw some hints around, tried to see what people thought."

Damn. The way Kotarō "hinted," he might as well have spelled it out straight to Onga. "And what did they say?"

"Atsushi-san told me not to do anything dangerous. But then aniki said I should stand on my own two feet and solve the problems I created. So I just had the same doubts all over again and I...."

Shigure stopped listening. Had Kinosuke known what Kotarō intended to do and actually encouraged him? Maybe Kotarō had managed to be subtle about it, but Shigure very much doubted it. If all had gone as he imagined, at least two people in his household knew about Kotarō's plans and had the chance to alert Onga.

It seemed Atsushi had acted in his usual line, mostly dismissing the kid with some inane advice about danger. But it wasn't like Kinosuke at all to push Kotarō into doing something that might have gotten him killed. The problem was that lately Kinosuke wasn't acting at all like the responsible young man Shigure had come to rely on, not since Kenshin entered their lives.

"Where's Kinosuke now? Wasn't he supposed to be here with you?"

By the way Kotarō blushed, Shigure knew he'd guessed right. No matter that it was Kinosuke's turn to watch over the kid, he must have made a bolt for the door as soon as Kenshin showed his face.

"He... he went to fetch something. But I wasn't alone. Kenshin-san left just a minute before you came, boss."

"And I bet he brought you those elegant pajamas you're wearing."

His question got the effect he intended, the kid's face brightening as he started going on about all the presents Kenshin had brought and the things he'd drawn for him. Shigure pretended to pay attention while his mind drifted back to Kinosuke. He should have confronted him earlier about his behavior toward Kenshin, but he knew he'd ignored it because of his own guilty feelings about the American. And maybe now it was too late. If Kinosuke had risked Kotarō's life and a war with the Daitō-kai just because of some petty grudge against Kenshin, he had no place in the Shinagawa. Their business didn't allow for hurt feelings or personal vendettas. The truth was it didn't allow for personal dalliances, either, not if they interfered with their company's personnel management. Maybe it was Shigure who didn't have a place in the Shinagawa anymore.

CHAPTER 20

KINOSUKE crouched lower behind the car hood for a few seconds, and then raised his head to check on the small playground. He didn't know why he bothered to stay hidden. The gaijin was so lost in his fucking drawings that Kinosuke could have banged his fists on a taiko drum and still Kenshin wouldn't have noticed.

And why did they call him Kenshin, anyway? If the guy had any quality resembling the manga assassin, Kinosuke was a Buddhist monk. He'd been following the damn gaijin for three whole days, and he'd never seen anyone less alert than Kenneth Harris. He paid attention to his surroundings all right, but just the wrong kind of attention—the weirdest kind, really, like that time when the American stood for exactly ten minutes watching water drip from the awning of a storefront, in the rain, without taking refuge under the very awning he was watching.

He kept the weirdest hours too. There he was, sitting on a swing and scratching away on a notebook at three in the morning. Could he even see what he was drawing? Not that Kinosuke should complain much, since it suited his plans to perfection, but he couldn't help the way the gaijin's every move grated on his nerves, even now that he was about to end it all.

He let his hand stroke the tantō's handle while he watched the American. In this light, sitting as he was with his back to Kinosuke, the gaijin almost looked like a Japanese youngster: thin, short, long-legged, hair dyed blond, and in the latest fancy outfit there was to be found. If he'd been carrying a PSP instead of pencil and paper, it wouldn't have been so shocking to find him out there at that time of night. He might have been just another drunk teen who'd missed the last train home. But Kinosuke knew better. He'd seen those freakish eyes go dark with rage, had felt hard muscle on that skinny arm, and knew how dangerous the man was.

Very slowly, like the worm he really was, Kenneth Harris was eating away at the foundations of everything Kinosuke cared about. His past as a bōsōzoku biker had made it difficult for Kinosuke to win the respect of his seniors in the Shinagawa family, but he'd strived to prove to Matsunaga that he was worth the chance the underboss had offered him, and he'd finally made it. His seniors listened to him now, the boss had started to give him responsibilities, and the apprentices, like Kotarō, were looking up to him. For the first time in his life, he felt proud of who he was.

Until a damn gaijin whore had wiggled his tight little ass in front of Matsunaga, that is. Of course Kinosuke understood the boss had his urges like every other guy, and it was all right by him if he chose to fuck a man this time, but the boss was completely besotted with the little slut, and he was beginning to take one false step after another, the strong leader Kinosuke admired so much acting as if he didn't care about his reputation, letting a gaijin beat him in front of his men, treating the American as if he was an honored guest in the clan house, and worse still, ignoring all the signs around them that something big was on the move, something that might mean serious trouble for the Shinagawa.

And wasn't it a beautiful coincidence that all the trouble had started right after the boss had met the gaijin, who was, by pure chance, a close friend to none other than Ryū Nishimura, the heir to Nishimura Construction? It didn't take a genius to figure out how that powerful company would increase its profits if the Shinagawa didn't hold a tight rein on the foreign workers' market. Cut out the middleman, that's what they'd manage if they offed the gang. And what better way to do it than through a turf war with the other most powerful gang in Tokyo?

Kenshin was doing a perfect job, appearing harmless enough that the men thought nothing of him being about places no outsider had ever been before—much less a gaijin. They found him cute, the useless bunch of thugs. Didn't they see the way he moved with a sword in his hands? Hadn't they caught the lethal focus in those *oni* eyes when he attacked? It wasn't only his eyes that belonged in a demon. The gaijin might act like an absentminded whackadoodle most of the time, but Kinosuke had seen his lightning-fast reflexes, and the things that came out of that pretty head when Kenshin drew were surely not of this world, and not in the angelic sense, either.

Kinosuke took a deep breath. It was time. He checked that the Daitō-kai badge was still in his pocket. If he were lucky, he'd manage to leave no trace but that badge, and the cops might believe it'd been the Koreans getting back at the Shinagawa for Kotarō's stunt.

He was prepared to go to jail if it didn't work. No matter that Matsunaga would feel betrayed when they found the body, someday he'd understand it had been for the best, and even if he never did, Kinosuke would always know that he'd done the right thing for all of them. He owed it to the man who'd offered him a chance when nobody else would.

Leaving all caution behind, Kinosuke stood, fingers tightly curled around the knife's handle. He started to walk around the nose of the car when his eyes caught a flicker of movement to his left. He crouched back down in the space between the two cars and peeked carefully over the hood of the nearest one.

There was someone there, inching his way into the playground, the light too dim for Kinosuke to see anything under the ball cap the guy was wearing. Was Kenshin about to get mugged? Any other day it might have been funny, but tonight Kinosuke had plans, and that dumb fuck was going to spoil them. Yet there wasn't much he could do without alerting Kenshin of his presence, without letting him know he'd been followed.

The man didn't make any sound as he approached the gaijin, and Kinosuke had to wonder what a thief was doing in a deserted suburban area when he could be picking drunks' pockets in busier streets. Maybe he was just going home, and Kenshin looked like an easy job to end the day's work on a good note. Yeah, the stupid American was still drawing even as the man stood right behind him.

Kinosuke couldn't help smirking. Kenshin was in for a nasty little surprise. But then the guy put a hand in his pocket and pulled out something that looked like a piece of cloth, and Kinosuke felt the smile slip. *What the hell?*

It all happened so fast that Kinosuke only had time to curse under his breath before the man pressed the cloth to Kenshin's face and held it for the seconds it took the gaijin to stop struggling, his limp body sliding to the ground without more noise than the crinkle of paper from Kenshin's sketch pad.

Shit. This was no random mugging. If someone was after the American it could only mean one of two things. Either he was being simply targeted as a rich foreigner they could get a decent ransom for, or someone knew about Kenshin's connection with Matsunaga, and it was through him that they intended to hit the Shinagawa.

Kinosuke cursed inwardly as the man carefully put the cloth away inside a sealed plastic bag that went back into his pocket and crouched near Kenshin. Now that the gaijin was out of it, the fucker was taking his sweet time going through Kenshin's wallet as if it was an American curio worth studying. He didn't take anything from it, though, but simply placed it on the ground, beside Kenshin's pad, and retrieved some small object from his own pocket that he put down with the other two. Then he stood and contemplated the scene as if it were a painting he'd just finished, or more exactly, something he wanted to have a certain effect on those who saw it next. Just as if he wanted them to reach an immediate conclusion, to know what it all meant with just one look. And it didn't take a genius to understand what he'd left lying there on the ground, especially not when Kinosuke was carrying an exact replica in his pocket.

When the man moved to grab Kenshin's ankles, Kinosuke knew it was the right moment to stop it all. It was only one man, and now his hands were busy. Yet he hesitated. He didn't really care what happened to the gaijin—he'd been about to slice his throat open, hadn't he?—but if something went wrong and the man escaped, Kinosuke wouldn't know who was behind the attacks on the Shinagawa. And that was the only important thing in the whole business. Let Kenshin take a little mauling, it wouldn't be less than he deserved.

So Kinosuke didn't move when the man pulled at Kenshin's ankles to drag his body out of the playground and to a car nearby. But no matter how many times he repeated to himself that he didn't care about the gaijin, Kinosuke couldn't help cringing at the way the blond head bumped against the concrete as Kenshin was being dragged over the hard surface.

While the man struggled to lift the limp body into the trunk, Kinosuke slipped out of his hiding place and rushed to his own car, ready to follow the guy, see where he took the American. Maybe then the gaijin would be finally useful for the Shinagawa.

CHAPTER 21

SHIGURE put down the receiver. It was dark outside, but Kenshin still wasn't home, or knowing him, he was too focused on some drawing to even hear the phone. He felt the smile tugging at his lips. He loved that about Kenshin, the way he'd put his whole self in what he did, be it drawing, or fighting, or—

"Boss?"

Tachibana stood at the door, holding a small envelope between his thumb and forefinger as if it might self-destruct.

"A messenger brought this, and Atsushi had already left for the evening."

Shigure extended his hand, trying not to roll his eyes.

"Thank you, Tachibana."

The door slammed closed after Tachibana, and he wondered how Atsushi managed to avoid making any noise when he was around. That's what came from growing up as a rich kid, he supposed. If your background had been constantly filled with the noise of pachinko parlors for all of your teenage years, you wouldn't really pay attention to slamming doors or stomping feet.

Shigure lifted the small envelope. It must be from their sōkaiya expert. He had so many people hacking into the companies' systems and listening to their phone conversations that he didn't trust anything but traditional mail to render important messages. And even then, he was as cryptic as he could get away with. "Them too, no favorites" was the only thing written across the white card in boldface.

Shigure smiled. Short and to the point. Pity it was bad news, as he'd very much expected. Ever since Uehara had warned him about the rumors going on in the streets against both them and the Daitō-kai, he'd suspected the rival gang was having the same exact problems as the Shinagawa. And there it was. Some companies had stopped paying the Daitō-kai sōkaiya as well, as if they weren't afraid of the gang's retribution anymore. It could only mean that the analysts of those companies had somehow learned that the two most powerful gangs would soon stop being so, and only a war between them could manage that result. Still, they could be betting on one of the two sides to come out the winner, and to test that, Shigure had asked his man to try to replace the Daitō-kai sōkaiya, make the firms pay the Shinagawa instead—with no luck, it seemed.

So there really was a third party trying to pit the two gangs against each other, waiting for them to be destroyed so that a new power could fill the huge void left by them. But which among the tiny gangs scattered all over Tokyo would be so greedy? And, most importantly, who inside the Daitō-kai—or the Shinagawa—was helping them? Because any way one looked at it, no other gang had the resources to access the information they'd need to start a war, the kind of detailed information that would tell them exactly when a mere apprentice from a gang would cross into enemy territory to fix the scabbard of a Korean sword.

KEN opened his eyes and panicked. He couldn't see a single thing. It wasn't only that the room was dark; there was always something to be seen even in the murkiest of spaces, some hint of light, some hue, some shape better and better outlined as the eyes got used to the dim. But here the darkness was a solid block against his eyes, something so thick he found it difficult to breathe.

He tried to open his mouth to let in more air, and when he felt the hard object pressing his tongue down, he thought he'd go crazy, a muffled cry leaving his throat as his arms flailed about in terror, or tried to, for as soon as his muscles flexed, they were met with the resistance of rope against his wrists and ankles. And then it was all too much to take in, and he simply lost it, struggling madly against his bonds, screaming into the gag filling his mouth, shaking his head from side to side like a mindless beast trying to bite off the restraints it couldn't reach.

DAMN traffic. Kinosuke banged his hand against the wheel. All night waiting for the man to leave, only to lose him in the morning rush hour.

Fuck. He needed to know who he was going to report to, find out who his boss was.

The license number he'd gotten was of no use, since he figured no hit man would be fool enough to use his own car for a job. Shit. Now he'd have to go back to where Kenshin was being held and wait for the man to come back, if he ever did.

He had no way of knowing whether the man had finished the gaijin off, the place he'd taken Kenshin to being a well-protected construction site, or rather would be. Now it was only a decaying house about to be demolished, but already surrounded by a chain-link fence with the company logo on it and cameras everywhere.

Kinosuke'd had to wait the night out in his car, without daring to jump the fence lest he trigger some alarm, so he didn't really know what the man had been up to until he emerged in the morning with the same cap on his head and one of those masks people wore against pollution and whatnot.

It didn't make much sense to go to so much trouble just to kill Kenshin, though, so Kinosuke guessed he still had a chance to see the kidnapper and follow him back to his boss. He debated for all of two seconds whether to call for help, but he knew any of the men would tell Matsunaga straight away, and the boss would rush to free Kenshin as soon as he learned where he was, spoiling any chance at discovering who was fucking with the Shinagawa. That wouldn't do. He was alone in this.

As soon as the traffic light changed, Kinosuke made a U-turn and headed back to the construction site.

HE MIGHT have blacked out for a while, Ken couldn't really tell the difference. He was calmer now, anyway, or finally so exhausted that he didn't feel the urge to move.

It hadn't gone very well before, moving. The more he moved, the more he discovered new, disquieting details, like the way his wrists were tied, his arms stretched along his sides to get to some kind of bar that he could touch, since the ropes only wrapped around his wrists. The problem was his ankles were tied to that bar, too, as he'd discovered when the bamboo—by the sound of it—hit the floor, preventing him from rolling to either of his sides, or from sitting up, since he could get no leverage to push forward.

He didn't know when the panic had hit the worst, when he'd understood how he was tied—his legs up in the air, folded at the knees so that the ankles could be bound to the bamboo rod next to his wrists—or when he'd felt the bamboo press against the back of his thighs and graze the sensitive skin behind his balls, and learned by that less than subtle caress that he was naked.

He must have thrashed about for a while, because now he felt dizzy, parched, and nauseated, his head throbbing with a kind of pain that made him see flashes of light behind his closed lids. It was just an illusion, the light. The darkness was as solid as before, but he knew it was mostly because there was a blindfold covering his eyes. Yeah. Another wonderful discovery, the fact that he was wearing a first-class, perfectly fitting, supple leather, fucking blindfold.

Shit. He didn't know what was worse, the sheer terror he'd just been through or the anger that was filling him now. Anger at the man who had grabbed him and tied him like a hog, anger at his helplessness, anger at his own stupidity, wandering the streets at night even if the country was as safe as they said, going out to draw just because he'd had a stupid nightmare and was too fucking proud to call Shigure for a little bit of comfort, just to hear his voice, just to know he was there for him. Oh fuck. He couldn't go there, not now.

Ken growled into the gag as he felt the tears filling his eyes. No way. No way in hell. He wasn't going to fucking break down and cry. For one thing, he couldn't afford a clogged-up nose when he wasn't able to use his mouth to get in more air. Besides, who knew what a leather blindfold felt like when wet?

The noise that came from his throat sounded very much like hysterical laughter to him, but as he drifted off into restless sleep, he told himself it was much better than crying. He might make a happy corpse after all.

THE clear early-morning sky had clouded over. The monsoon season was upon them, and in Shigure's experience, it always brought rough times. Could be that the hot, humid weather made people edgy, he didn't quite know the reasons, but it was the time of year when he usually had to visit the morgue to identify someone, or, to be more precise, some body. Now it was Harada standing beside him, looking down at the sheet-covered form, his face as white as the fabric delaying the inevitable for yet another heartbeat.

"Shall we?" Sergeant Uehara asked—always the polite, old-fashioned cop.

Harada just nodded, his eyes still on the sheet as the coroner's assistant pulled it back. The face was bloated, but Shigure had no trouble recognizing the receptionist of the Haihīru, Harada's club.

"Is he Ikegami Gōichi?"

"Yes, Sergeant," Harada said, his voice barely a whisper in the cold room. "How did he…?"

"See this mark here?" Uehara pointed to a thin, red furrow running around the neck. "He was strangled with a rope, by the look of it."

"What if he hanged himself?" Shigure said. "Wouldn't it look about the same?"

"Not exactly. Hanging tends to leave a diagonal furrow, and this one is perfectly horizontal, as if someone had pulled at the rope from behind him."

At least it wasn't the typical yakuza hit. No self-respecting gang member would use anything other than guns, swords, or knifes. Who in the hell walked around with a length of rope in his pocket? Probably just someone who didn't have access to any other weapon, and that ruled out most of the underworld.

"Does it take a lot of strength, to, uh, pull the rope?"

Uehara studied him for a moment. "A woman could do it, if that's what you're thinking."

Shigure nodded. The sergeant had a quick intelligence, so you didn't really need to spell out things for him, but rather watch out for what you let slip.

"Why would you think it might have been a woman, Matsunaga-san?"

Shigure shrugged. "He worked the front desk at a soapland. That might not agree with the wife too much."

Uehara turned to look at the body, probably to check the ring finger, see whether the flesh looked paler there, whether Shigure was making it up as he went. Sharp guy. And that was exactly why they couldn't afford the sergeant making the connection to the incident with that girl Kei.

She was now the only person left who could recognize the guy who had started all the trouble with the Daitō-kai, and if she'd felt threatened enough to kill the other person who'd seen the man, it could only mean it wasn't the casual mishap that it'd appeared then. She might have been in on it from the start, and the receptionist had somehow learned about it and tried to blackmail her.

The other possible scenario wasn't any more reassuring, either. The killer might be cleaning up after himself, and then Kei would be in even more serious danger.

Either way, Shigure didn't want the police sniffing about and scaring off their only possible source of information.

"Did he have any other problems that you know of? Drugs, debt, anything like that?"

Harada looked at the sergeant. "I don't hire obvious junkies, gamblers, or sickos, but beyond that, I don't have any reason to go looking into my employees' lives. He did his job fine, and that was all that mattered to me."

"How long had he been working for you?"

"About a year."

"Hmm. Fairly long it seems, for that kind of job. I should have thought your business had a high turnover of staff."

"It's mostly the girls who come and go, not so much the other staff."

"So I suppose you get to know them pretty well, the other staff, I mean."

"Look, Uehara-junsa-buchō, it's not Toyota that I'm running. We don't hold company parties at the Haihīru, or outdoor seminars, or collective workouts. I just make sure my employees have the right qualifications and do their jobs well. In return, they get a fair pay and respectful personnel management. That's all there is to it. I won't pretend we are a family, or even friends."

There was an awkward silence as the coroner's assistant pushed the sheet-covered gurney out of the room. Shigure felt suddenly too old, too wearied by the familiarity with death, too used to the out-of-date conviction that there's safety in numbers to understand Harada's little speech. Of course in times like these no small business owner could afford to look after his employees the way it was done in the buoyant economy of years past, but Shigure felt out of place in a world ruled by efficiency alone, a world where you would strangle someone from behind because it saved you the inconvenience of looking into the victim's eyes. It didn't feel like Japan anymore.

"When did he die?" Harada asked, all the hostility gone from his voice as if he'd only just remembered what he was there for.

"When did you first notice he was missing?" Uehara asked in turn.

"I didn't."

At the sergeant's raised brow, Harada went on. "He asked for some days off. I wouldn't have noticed until Friday."

"Did he explain why he needed those days?"

"No. He just said he had some personal matters to look into." Harada shrugged. "It was his due, and I didn't need to know anything else."

Uehara nodded his understanding. "And I suppose if he hadn't showed up on Friday, you wouldn't have reported it anyway."

"Report him? To the police? I thought we were in Japan, sergeant. Just because my establishment is a nightclub, I don't have to assume all my absent employees will end up in the morgue. I would have phoned his contact number and replaced him when he didn't answer, just like any other manager would have."

The sergeant bowed in apology. "I meant no offense, Harada-san. I was just stating a fact. He didn't have any close relatives in Tokyo, and since you wouldn't have reported him missing, we might have never known he'd been murdered, never found his body."

"Why? Where did you find him?" Shigure asked.

"He was dumped in the bay, with a heavy stone tied to his feet. We'd never have found him if a drain nearby hadn't needed some repairs after yesterday's downpour."

"So when do you think he died?"

"The corpse had already lost his fingernails, so we are guessing eight to ten days ago."

"What about the stone?"

"What about it?"

Shigure made an impatient gesture. "Have you studied it? Found out what kind of stone it is, where it comes from?"

If the sergeant hadn't been so well-mannered, Shigure had the impression he would have been laughing in his face. "You know Japanese police is very traditional, Matsunaga-wakagashira. We stick to people in our investigations. We don't keep track of stones."

CHAPTER 22

"MOSHI moshi."

"Nishimura-san? This is Matsunaga Shigure."

"Oh. Matsunaga-san. What can I do for you?"

It might have been his imagination, but Shigure would have sworn Ryū Nishimura sounded surprised to hear from him, and not in the good sense. They didn't talk that often, but he had never appeared this reserved, almost wary, to Shigure before.

"I hope I'm not bothering you. I was just wondering if Kenshin-san was with you."

"With me?"

Now that was definitely weird, when Nishimura was Kenshin's best friend and up until a few weeks ago, Kenshin had been a guest in his house. Wouldn't it be logical to assume Kenshin would hang out with him sometime?

"Uh, I'm afraid I haven't seen him in a while."

Shigure felt his cheeks flush. He hadn't realized he'd been monopolizing Kenshin that way. A sigh from the other side of the receiver startled him out of his thoughts.

"He never told you anything, did he?"

"Told me what?"

"Do you remember that day you and I bumped into each other in Kenshin's hallway?"

"Yeah."

"I haven't seen Kenshin since that day."

Shigure mulled over those words and what they meant. "You argued over something."

"Uh-huh."

"You argued over me."

The silence on the other end told Shigure he had guessed right. He had done that to Kenshin—made him break up with his childhood friend—and he had never even known. Kenshin didn't have to tell him anything. He should've seen the signs. But no, when it came to his gaijin, all Shigure did was take what he wanted, never mind the consequences.

"I don't have anything personal against you, Matsunaga-san, but—"

"But I'm a yakuza, and he's your friend."

"I don't want him hurt."

Neither do I, he thought, *but it doesn't seem I've been doing such a good job of it.* So he changed the subject instead, tried to at least fix what he still could, and find out where Kenshin might have gone.

"Nishimura-san, I know Kenshin can get distracted easily—"

"That's the understatement of the century."

He chuckled. "Yeah, maybe. But he wouldn't forget to go home for the night, I mean, he wouldn't stay out drawing or something like that, would he?"

"You mean he hasn't spent the night at home?"

The note of concern in Nishimura's voice made his hackles rise. "No, and he isn't answering his cell, either. Does he have any other friends here?"

"Not really." Nishimura seemed to hesitate before he went on. "I suppose he could have, uh, met someone, and you know, gone home with him?"

"No." The word sounded so much like a growl that Shigure thought he could hear Nishimura jerk away from the receiver. He tried to speak calmly, but he was too indignant to control his tone. "Kenshin would never do that. He is with me now. And I very much doubt he'd go to bed with some stranger he'd just met even if we hadn't been together."

The awkward silence that followed was seriously starting to piss Shigure off. This was Kenshin's best friend? The one suggesting the American was more or less a slut?

"He said the same about you." Nishimura's voice was so low that Shigure didn't quite understand him.

"What?"

"Kenshin. He defended you too."

Oh, this was getting better by the moment. "And what did you accuse me of, Nishimura-san? Trafficking in children, drug dealing, or plain murder?"

If Nishimura kept silent one more second, Shigure swore he'd go and show him personally what murder looked like.

"I told him you were a burakumin."

All the air went out of Shigure's lungs.

He didn't care if they said it behind his back, if it was rumored in the streets, or if an enemy tried to throw it in his face. He would have laughed at that. But the stupid fucker had gone and told Kenshin. Kenshin. The only person in this world whose judgment mattered to Shigure.

"I'm sorry, Matsunaga-san."

"Sure you are. It's been a pleasure talking to you, Nishimura-san."

"Wait! Don't—"

But he had already hung up. He wasn't in the mood for half-assed apologies. He knew by heart what people like Nishimura thought about the burakumin. He just hadn't imagined it would hurt that badly, after all this time.

KINOSUKE was getting bored, watching the same fence for hours on end. The neighborhood was too quiet. There was only a park in front of the construction site, and an unremarkable temple on the other side, so very few people walked by in the busy hours of the day.

Since the night before, he hadn't seen anyone enter the property, and he was beginning to wonder who was watching Kenshin. There must be someone keeping an eye on him, someone managing the security cameras along the fence. And yet, nobody had crossed the gates, not even now that it was nearing lunchtime.

Kinosuke waited one more hour, until he couldn't delay a visit to the men's room any longer. In a record time of twelve minutes, he was back at watching the gates, sitting on a park bench and eating from the bento box he'd bought.

As he munched on the spicy onigiri, he realized there was something odd about the cameras on the fence. There were two that he could see, and both were targeting the gate. Why would you need two cameras to cover the same, small area? Wouldn't it be better to have them targeting different parts of the fence, or at least program them to swing about and cover more angles?

He waited a few more hours, still not seeing movement in or out of the site, the cameras sitting atop the gate like two fat cats. Then he finally decided to follow his hunch and strolled leisurely to the fence, approaching one of the cameras from behind. He feigned interest in the plate with the construction company logo and slowly, very slowly, lifted his head pretending to watch the sky to check for rain.

"Fuck me sideways," he said under his breath when he saw the darkened indicator light on the camera. He walked to the other camera without taking any further precaution, only to find it wasn't running either. "What the hell?"

He would have checked the lock next if a group of kids hadn't walked by right that moment. He went back to his car instead, waiting, going through the options he now had.

The way Kenshin had been drugged, it wouldn't have been difficult for the kidnapper to simply tie the gaijin and leave him in the abandoned house without anyone else to keep watch. If it was so, Kinosuke could just walk in and free the American. The problem was he'd never learn who the man was working for that way, and even if Kinosuke waited long enough to spring a trap on him, he might never talk after being captured.

Then again, if this was a one-man operation, it was far more likely to be a kidnapping—without any connection to the Shinagawa— and then Kinosuke might just be wasting his time, for he couldn't care less if Kenshin had to spend some days tied to a wall until his family or his rich friends paid his ransom.

The afternoon brought heavy rain, the sky darkening long before sunset, the heat unbearable in spite of the air conditioner Kinosuke kept cranking up. He was getting a little stir-crazy, so he wiped at the steam clouding the windshield, riffled through the glove compartment, checked his hair in the sun visor mirror, turned the radio on, turned it off again, drummed his fingers on the steering wheel, and finally pushed the door open and got out of the car.

He told himself he'd check the lock just because he was bored, just to see if his fingers still had the knack of it. But when the padlock clicked open, he couldn't resist crossing the gates to take a look.

The moment Kinosuke stepped inside the abandoned property, he heard a car turning the corner onto the street. He'd been parked on that street all day long, and he knew pretty well what the chances were of a car just passing by the construction site, so he pushed the gates closed, secured the padlock, and ran toward the bushes growing wildly around the house. He barely managed to hide before he heard the gates swinging open.

CHAPTER 23

AFTER all that heavy silence, the sound of a door opening was like an explosion in his ears, so much so that Ken forgot he was tied and tried to scramble to his feet, only managing to tilt his body to one side and bang the bamboo rod against the floor with a loud noise. Then he kept as still as he could, his heart beating fast, as he strained to hear any new sound and understand what was happening.

For a moment, there was nothing, but then he heard the unmistakable sound of feet descending stairs. So it was a basement, after all. He hadn't thought it was because most Japanese houses didn't have one—and because any other kind of structure, any kind of industrial building or storage facility would mean more isolation and less hope of ever being found alive.

As the footsteps approached, Ken fought the urge to move. He knew it was useless, the way he was tied, but it was very difficult to restrain the impulse to cover his naked body somehow. He felt exposed and vulnerable, especially when he stopped hearing footsteps and knew the man was standing there, just looking down at him.

It probably lasted only a few seconds, but Ken hated how terrifying it felt, not being able to see or speak, to judge the situation, just waiting in the dark for some stranger to decide what he wanted to do with him. Of course he knew it was deliberate, being made to feel helpless, and that angered him enough to believe the tremors that started shaking his body came from rage and not fear. He had to hold on to that belief if he wanted to keep his pride intact, for he had the impression he was going to need it whole in the next few minutes.

When something touched him behind his ear, the contact was so unexpected that he couldn't help ducking his head, only to have his face slapped so hard his whole body tilted to the other side with the force of it, the bar he was tied to slamming against the floor again as he let out a muffled cry.

"Keep still!"

Ken froze, his muscles going tight at the sound of a human voice so close to him.

"That's better. I know you like having cocks in your mouth, but you might want it removed to take a sip of water."

It was only when his addled brain processed the Japanese words that he actually noticed the shape of the gag lodged in his mouth. And then he almost choked on it, unable to control the distressed sound that escaped his throat. *Oh God. A penis gag.* Someone had tied him naked and thrust a penis gag in his mouth, and Ken couldn't for the life of him deal with what it all meant for his immediate future.

IT WAS raining hard as Shigure walked across the hospital parking lot. Kotarō was getting better. He should be glad about it, and forget about everything else. But he couldn't.

He'd resisted the urge to call Kenshin every five minutes, and he called every other hour instead, always getting voice mail. Knowing that the American hadn't been to visit Kotarō didn't help, either, especially when he'd learned that nobody had seen Kinosuke since the day before.

Shinya ran to him with an open umbrella.

"Thank you—" Damn. He almost called his man "Scar-face." What was wrong with him? Of course he knew what was wrong, but he couldn't admit it right away. No matter how much he tried to convince himself that Kenshin had finally dumped him, every single thought Shigure had concerned the gaijin—what he'd said, the way he'd looked at Shigure when they made love, his silences, his gestures, his voice, his hands.

If he managed to let go of his wounded pride, Shigure found it hard to believe that Kenshin would simply leave when he learned that his lover was a burakumin on top of a yakuza. According to that rat Nishimura, Kenshin had known it for some time, too, and it wasn't like the gaijin to keep his thoughts to himself. Kenshin wasn't afraid of

Shigure—that was for sure—and if he'd decided to leave the yakuza, Shigure would have no doubt heard it straight from those sexy lips.

Still, the other possibilities were too frightening to consider.

Shinya closed the car door after him and rounded the hood to get to the driver's seat.

"Where to, boss?"

He looked up into serious black eyes and almost smiled. Any other time Shinya would have driven him home without asking, but in his own quiet way, his man noticed everything, and he'd obviously sensed there was some trouble between Shigure and Kenshin.

"You heard Kinosuke when Kotarō was brought to the hospital, the way he spoke about Kenshin-san?"

Shinya nodded.

"You think he might go as far as to—"

Shinya didn't even let him finish. "He's just jealous. He wouldn't hurt Kenshin-san."

"Jealous?"

"Yeah. You know how Kotarō worshipped him—he was always going about aniki doing this or aniki saying that—but since Kenshin-san arrived, the kid has been all starry-eyed about him. And Kinosuke can't help resenting the gaijin for that."

Shit. He hadn't even noticed. Of course he'd been too dazzled himself to see anything that wasn't Kenshin, but that only meant he'd been neglecting his most important responsibility—his men. If he'd spoken with Kinosuke earlier, he would've found a way to reassure the young man of his place in the Shinagawa.

"So you think Kinosuke's just avoiding me for a few days?"

Shinya shrugged. "That or he's trying to show Kotarō how it feels when his aniki isn't around to look after him."

Could Kenshin be doing the same? Trying to teach Shigure what losing him would feel like? Proving that he had better things to do than waiting in a tiny, one-window apartment for a burakumin to show?

"Take me to Kenshin's place."

Shinya nodded and turned to start the car.

No. It might be Kinosuke's way, but it sure wasn't like Kenshin at all, quietly hinting at a problem when he could be shouting it in Shigure's face. The more he thought about it as they crossed the darkening streets, the more Shigure worried he might have wasted precious hours feeling sorry for himself when he should have been searching for the American all over the city. Hadn't he been to the morgue already? What if he had to go back there to identify someone he really cared about? What if it was Kenshin's face under the white sheet next time, just because he'd been too busy getting offended at being called a burakumin? *Damn fucking pride.*

He didn't wait for Shinya to open the door for him. He jumped out of the car and took the stairs two at a time, the key already in his hand even before he reached the door.

"Shit."

The apartment was in complete disarray, as if Kenshin had hosted a well-attended party—or someone had conducted a thorough search.

"What the hell?" Shinya mumbled dragging his index finger over the table and lifting it covered in some kind of whitish powder.

"*Kuso,*" he swore again as he started pacing like a caged bear. If the police had been there, it might already be too late. At least there was no chalk outline on the floor. That was something.

His phone sounded outrageously loud in the empty apartment.

"What?" he barked into the receiver.

"Uh, boss?"

Shigure closed his eyes and tried to calm himself. Yelling at his men wouldn't help Kenshin.

"What is it, Tachibana?"

"Sergeant Uehara is here with two gaijin. I didn't know what to do, boss. Atsushi-san had already left, and the sergeant said—"

"It's all right. Show them to the tatami room and have some tea brought to them. I'll be there in ten minutes."

Shinya was already out the door, Shigure on his heels as they trundled down the stairs and got the car moving in record time. With the heavy rain slowing the traffic, it almost took them twenty minutes to reach their destination, and Shigure had to use all his willpower to stop from running into the house as soon as they arrived. He hadn't been so anxious to see the police in his whole life.

KINOSUKE approached the ramshackle outbuilding with care. It intrigued him that the man had chosen it over the more solid main building, but it was probably easier to control by a single person. It must have been a garage, the wooden panels of the walls a little slanted now, the sliding front door permanently open since it wouldn't fit into the rails anymore.

He peered inside cautiously, the empty space illuminated by the light coming from an open trap door in the concrete floor. Was it a basement? Kinosuke had never seen one, but he'd heard some rich houses had them for storing wine. Perfect to keep a prisoner, too, especially in an abandoned house with no close neighbors but a temple and a park.

Having seen what he wanted to see, Kinosuke was turning to go back to his car when he heard the man speak. He froze in place. There was too much distance to the gate to make it without being discovered if the man chose to leave now, so Kinosuke hid beside the building door.

The man kept on talking, but he could only hear a few, unconnected words. Was he actually talking about tattoos? Whatever it was he was talking about, he seemed to be enjoying the sound of his own voice, so Kinosuke felt it was safe to go. Until he heard the first scream.

Oh shit. And the sick motherfucker was laughing, speaking so loud now that Kinosuke could hear him clearly.

"So sorry," the wacko was saying, "but it's an art that takes time to learn. I'll do better now, you'll see."

And there came the second scream, and then the third, and no matter how hard Kinosuke tried to cover his ears, still they kept coming, over and over again, weaker every time but still there, until they turned into a low keening and then nothing, the silence suddenly so overpowering that Kinosuke could hear every individual drop of rain as it hit the dirt around him. Somehow he had slid along the wall behind him, his knees too weak to hold him upright, his hands shaking like *momiji* leaves.

He would have laughed if he hadn't been about to empty his stomach. Shit. He thought he hated the gaijin so much that it would have been easy to kill him, but hearing those agonized cries had been the worst experience in his whole fucking life. Some yakuza he'd turned out to be.

The sound of footsteps took too much to register in his addled brain, so much so that Kinosuke barely had time to drag his uncooperative body farther back along the wall of the outbuilding before the man stepped out the door. He plastered himself against the wooden panels and prayed that it was already too dark to notice him, even if the man turned back to check the place.

The minutes ticked away, and Kinosuke resisted the urge to risk a look. What on earth was the fucker doing now? Did he intend to stay there all night, lounging by the garage door? Only when he heard the scraping noise of a match against its box did he understand what was going on. The damn sicko had the fucking nerve to stop and smoke a cigarette, just relaxing after whatever it was he'd done to Kenshin. And he was taking his sweet time about it.

Finally, the butt was tossed away, and the man started walking. Kinosuke pressed himself flat against the wall, counting the steps with his eyes closed, just like a kid counting sheep to forget about the monster under the bed.

The gate squeaked open and then closed, footsteps fading into the night until there was nothing else to be heard. Yet Kinosuke didn't move, waiting for the sound of a car engine to confirm that the man had left for sure. And then he cursed a blue streak. He'd lost another chance to follow the bastard to whoever it was that was paying him. Just because he'd been too fucking impatient to stay put. He might have saved himself from hearing Kenshin, too, if he'd stayed in his car.

Shit. What was he supposed to do now? He wouldn't have had any problem opening the gate and getting the hell out of there, but he still got goose bumps remembering those screams. He was probably going to have nightmares for a week, and the worst of it was not knowing what had happened, if the gaijin was just a crybaby who would yell at being backhanded, or if the man had really hurt him—even killed him, by the way it sounded. Being practical, Kinosuke thought he'd better check, anyway, mostly because, if Kenshin were dead, there would be no reason for the man to come back anytime soon.

He stood and followed the wall to its front opening. His eyes had gotten used to the semi-darkness around the abandoned house, the city lights reflecting on the cloud-covered sky and giving back a soft ambiance light enough to go by. Inside the garage, it was quite a different thing, but Kinosuke remembered the place was empty, so he didn't have to worry about any obstacles until he found the cellar door.

It was a simple trap door, easy to lift, with no lock, and he opened it without much fuss. The problem was finding the light switch inside that pitch-black hole. He wouldn't much like to break a leg and have to stay down there keeping the gaijin company.

It didn't take too much fumbling about, though, the switch pretty obvious on the wall as soon as he took the first three steps down, and then the rest of the staircase was easy to descend in the stark light of a high-wattage bulb. Somebody had wanted to avoid tripping with an expensive bottle in hand—he guessed—or rather had made the decision after one mishap or two, the way those stains on the floor looked just like…. *Oh fuck.*

His heart hammering in his chest, Kinosuke followed the trail of blood to the farthest wall of the room, his eyes unable to see anything that wasn't Kenshin. It was impossible not to see him, the way the sick bastard had carefully set the gaijin's body on display as if one of those photographers from an artsy *shibari* magazine was coming next to get some shots.

The problem was those cool photos didn't usually have blood in them, just naked bodies and enough rope to supply a hardware store. Not that Kinosuke had ever understood what was so exciting about tying all those knots around one chick, but at least he could tell the result looked wickedly sexy sometimes. What he had right in front of him was simply sick.

A horizontal bamboo rod hung from the ceiling, Kenshin's arms wrapped around it and tied at both elbows with the same hemp rope that crisscrossed his whole body in a weirdly symmetric pattern that looked like the shell of a turtle. But it was just rope and pale skin that made the pattern, skin so fragile that the bastard had seemed to delight in breaking it open, letting the blood run down and soak the hemp to make a new pattern of its own. And it still hadn't been enough. The man hadn't just cut the skin to write his message in big, bloody kanji, he'd gone and filled the cuts with ink, creating his own personal style of savage tattoo all over Kenshin's body.

Kinosuke had heard many times how they used to mark criminals that way, tattoo some circles, or bars, or the kanji for dog on their arms and faces, so that everybody'd recognize them for what they were, and he knew that to be the origin of the yakuza fondness for tattoos—the need to cover those marks bringing them right to the door of the tattoo artists that would ink away to hide the old marks.

The man had obviously got his history right, for he'd tattooed the word "dog" all over Kenshin, the slim kanji traced in the messy calligraphy of a child—or an adult trying to carve the character into a living body. Shit. There were big, bloodied blue kanji on both hips, around the navel, on both forearms, and a prominent one tearing open Kenshin's left nipple. Fuck. Small wonder the gaijin had screamed his head off. Kinosuke couldn't begin to imagine how that must have hurt. But what in all hell had the animal used to make those cuts? No way were those needle marks. Kinosuke knew what a proper tattoo looked like.

When his searching eyes found the bloodied ice pick, bile rose in his throat, and he had to reach out for the nearest shelf to keep his balance. Shit. A fucking ice pick. The raving lunatic had dipped an ice pick in blue ink and stabbed Kenshin with it, as if it hadn't seemed enough to leave big, kanji-shaped scars all over him. Just in case some of them healed, the inked word would forever remind the gaijin that he was no more than a dog. Supposing he was still alive to be reminded of it, that is.

Kinosuke turned back to Kenshin. The blond head hung limply forward, wet spots staining the edges of the leather blindfold that covered his eyes—sweat and tears, was Kinosuke's guess. But if he didn't focus too much on the torn nipple, he could see that the thin chest was rising and falling with shallow breaths, and strangely enough, it made Kinosuke's own breathing easier. No matter how much he'd thought he hated the gaijin, he hadn't that much hatred in him to think Kenshin deserved that kind of suffering. It was a terrifying way to die, being rendered helpless, at the mercy of a man who considered you no better than an animal.

Kinosuke searched his pockets for the tantō knife he always carried with him. Now that he'd seen Kenshin, he couldn't just climb the stairs and sit out there to wait for the man. There'd be enough time to take the gaijin to the ER and come back with some of his brothers to catch the fucker. Yeah. The boss might even thank him for saving Kenshin, and the foolish gaijin would surely think twice before meddling with the yakuza again, because no way on earth had this been a simple kidnapping. It had only happened because someone knew who was fucking Kenshin, because it was an easy way to get to the Shinagawa by pretending it'd all been done by the Daitō-kai.

As Kinosuke pulled the tantō out of its sheath, he thought the man would have sent Kenshin's dead body to the boss after he'd tired of playing with the gaijin. Or worse still, perhaps he'd been hired to make it look like a passionate crime and send Matsunaga to jail, hitting much harder on the Shinagawa that way.

Well, none of that would happen now, and Kinosuke was glad he'd been there to stop the whole fucking mess. The boss would forgive him when he understood he'd never meant to disrespect him, that he had only been worried about the clan's future when he'd said those harsh words to him.

Kinosuke studied the rope carefully, trying to decide which thread to cut first to avoid having Kenshin suddenly crumple in a heap to the cement floor. Maybe it was better to leave on the fancy knots that wrapped around the body and go for the bamboo rod that held Kenshin's weight. That way he could use the knots as handles to avoid dropping the gaijin.

He reached out for one of the ropes hanging from eyebolts in the ceiling and braced his free hand on the bamboo rod. Rope that thick wasn't easy to cut, so Kinosuke went at it slowly, kind of sawing through the hemp instead of actually cutting it. He was so focused on his task that he barely heard the small noise before pain exploded in the back of his head, and he felt himself slide along Kenshin's body. Then there was nothing but blackness.

CHAPTER 24

"WHEN was the last time you saw Mr. Harris?"

Shigure frowned at the big gaijin. It was difficult enough to understand his stilted Japanese, but every time he called Kenshin "Mr. Harris" he thought the man was talking about somebody else Shigure didn't actually know.

"Tuesday."

"You sure?"

He just looked at the man, not bothering to repeat himself. What were the Americans thinking, sending a pair of brutes who hadn't the slightest idea how to behave or even speak properly? Was it because he was a yakuza, or were all American cops this rude?

Of course Sergeant Uehara noticed his mounting irritation and tried to smooth things out.

"I'm sorry, Matsunaga-wakagashira, but it would help if we could establish a date for the kidnapping."

"Sergeant!"

Shigure ignored the gaijin's protest. "So you do know it's a kidnap. Has there been word of a ransom yet?"

The Americans were falling all over themselves to stop Uehara from answering, but the good old sergeant wasn't easily intimidated.

"As a friend of Mr. Harris, Matsunaga-san has a right to know what this is all about, gentlemen, so you either tell him or I will."

"This is not right, Sergeant. Matsunaga is a—"

"It is standard procedure in Japan to show respect to the people you're interviewing, especially when you are a guest in their house."

Shigure nodded his thanks to Uehara. He'd had the decency to use the verb "interview" instead of "question," though Shigure very much doubted the gaijin understood the difference. They hadn't bothered to conceal the fact that they considered Shigure a clear suspect, hadn't learned that aggressive questioning in Japan was the fastest way to get uncooperative witnesses and offenders, especially when you were dealing with the yakuza. Did they actually teach the agents anything about the country before they sent them all the way here? Or did they pick them fresh out of the academy just because they looked American enough to appear threatening? Those two certainly looked typical, the big, blue-eyed blond and the broad-shouldered black. They might stop terrorists by sheer intimidation.

"The ransom?" Shigure said as if nothing had happened, making the blond guy sigh impatiently. Somewhere in the middle of his unintelligible speech, Uehara started translating.

"Senator Harris received a phone call early this morning warning him they had his son."

Senator Harris. Kenshin's father was a senator, and he'd never told him. Well, Shigure hadn't told Kenshin his father was a burakumin, so he guessed they were even. But it still hurt.

"Have they given any proof he is alive?"

The big blond lifted his hands as if he was holding a piece of paper.

"Picture, with newspaper," he said.

"May I see it?"

The two gaijin exchanged a look, and Shigure started counting in his head. If they told him they weren't carrying the photo on them or any other excuse, he was going to kick their American asses out of his house, FBI legal attachés or no.

"Uh, I would advise that you show it to Matsunaga-san, gentlemen," Uehara said softly. "He has a deep knowledge of this city, and might be able to see something we haven't."

To his surprise, the black guy extracted a folded paper out of his suit pocket. Was he actually carrying the photo on him? And what was he hoping to do with it, go asking around? In his extraordinarily fluent Japanese? With his looks? Nobody—except maybe giggling high-school girls—would tell him the time of day.

Shigure studied the printout carefully. It took him some time to understand why Kenshin didn't look like himself at all, and then he had to fight hard to school his face. The photo appeared lifeless not because of its bad quality, but because someone had stripped Kenshin of the whirl of blinding colors that were his clothes, and his usual spiky hair was now a matted heap of straw around his gaunt face. Still those eyes were unmistakable, as the kidnapper must have known.

"It's not a private house," he said, keeping his voice steady.

The gaijin gave him matching uncomprehending stares.

"Unless you are a fancy architect, you don't build a home with bare concrete slabs," he explained.

"A warehouse, maybe?" Uehara suggested.

"The docks?" asked the black American.

Shigure studied the photo once again, trying to look at everything but Kenshin.

"There seems to be some kind of shelves here. It must be a smaller place. They don't keep this type of shelves where they use pallets and forklifts."

"Basement?" said the other American. At least they tried. Shigure had to give them that.

"Except for high-rises, we don't excavate deep foundations here in Japan, because of the earthquakes. Our houses are pretty light, with no basements."

There was an awkward silence, and the blond gaijin gave Uehara a look he might have thought to be discreet. The sergeant kept his face blank, but he turned to the extremely formal speech he used when he expected his words to offend.

"Uh, Matsunaga-wakagashira, we have been talking with Nishimura Ryū-san, and he implied that you and Mr. Harris had become very close... uh... friends."

Shigure clenched his teeth. So that was the reason the Americans thought he had something to do with Kenshin's disappearance. He could very well imagine what else the little rat must have implied.

"Do you think someone else might be aware of that fact?"

He stared blankly at Uehara for a heartbeat and then blanched.

"You found one of those damn badges, didn't you?" He didn't wait for the sergeant to confirm it. "Where?"

"In a small park two blocks away from Mr. Harris's apartment."

Shit. He knew that park. It was more of a playground, really, but swings seemed to be one of the silly little things that fascinated Kenshin, in addition to koi, streetlamps, roof ornaments, and ugly buttons.

"How did you know?"

Shigure turned to look at the blond American. He couldn't for the life of him remember the guy's name, so he was deliberately rude. "What do you mean, deka-san?"

He'd more or less called him "Mr. Cop," but the gaijin took it in stride, probably considering it another quaint Japanese mannerism. "The badge. How did you know?"

"I didn't know. But what better way to drive the police off the kidnapper's trail than planting a Daitō-kai badge near Kenshin-san's belongings?" Shigure stopped. "What was it that you found, his watch, his wallet, what?"

The blond guy was narrowing his eyes at him. "I didn't mention the Daitō-kai."

Shigure resisted the urge to roll his eyes. Maybe Japanese was a difficult language to learn for Americans, and Kenshin was as exceptional in that as he was in many other areas. And maybe these agents were good at what they did and could help Kenshin in their own way.

"We've been having problems with the Daitō-kai lately—or someone is trying to make us believe we do, probably to start a war between our two groups. If the kidnappers knew this and knew Kenshin-san was friends with a Shinagawa underboss, it's only logical that they might have used it to their advantage."

"You and Mr. Harris, were you—?"

Here it came. "Yes, as I'm sure Nishimura has already told you, Kenshin and I are lovers. What does it have to do with anything?"

"The Daitō-kai, they know?"

"It's no secret, so they probably do. But I don't see them running off to tell the press."

"Uh, Matsunaga-wakagashira," Uehara said. "What Campbell-san is trying to ask is whether the Daitō-kai would hurt Kenshin-san to make you start a war."

"Why would they bother to disguise it as a kidnapping, then?"

"To distract the gaijin cops?"

Oh shit. They weren't that dumb, after all, the gaijin cops. But that was the only scenario Shigure couldn't allow himself to consider, because if it had been the Daitō-kai all along, they wouldn't give a damn about the ransom. They would kill Kenshin and deliver his corpse to Shigure's door. And then a terrible notion came unbridled to his mind.

"The kidnappers haven't called back with their conditions yet?"

"No."

"So you believe this is no kidnapping at all."

"It's still early to think so. It could be because of the time difference with the States, but we have to consider other possibilities."

Yeah, there were two other possibilities the gaijin might be considering. If they were stupid, they'd think his jealous yakuza lover had gone at Kenshin with a katana, or if they were smart, they'd think the same person who had been trying to push the Shinagawa and the Daitō-kai into a turf war was getting frustrated by his lack of success and was going for desperate measures. Either way, Kenshin would be dead.

CHAPTER 25

HIS name. Someone was calling his name. Shigure, most probably, but he still wanted to sleep some more.

"Kenshin-san."

His eyes flickered open, and he saw nothing. Still dreaming, then, dreaming that he was awake.

"Kenshin-san!"

He tried to turn away from the voice, and everything came back to him in a rush. First was the burning pain, then the numbness in his fingers, and then all the memories that explained why he couldn't see, why he was tied to a bamboo rod, why he hurt.

"Kenshin-san?"

He tilted his head to one side, trying to listen, but all he managed was to make his temples throb, nausea roiling in his stomach, making him shut his sightless eyes.

"Can you hear me, Kenshin-san?"

What game was the guy playing now? His voice sounded different, almost eager, as if he really wanted Ken to hear him. Was he tired of waiting for him to wake? He supposed it wasn't that much fun if he couldn't scream.

He'd promised himself he wouldn't give his captor the satisfaction of hearing him scream, but his resolution had lasted for all of ten seconds. He never imagined a blindfold could make things feel that intense. Pity he'd never used it while having sex.

"Please, Kenshin-san, talk to me. That man will be here in no time."

What? The voice sounded familiar now, not muffled like before, but his brain felt like mush, and he couldn't make any sense of it. Was there someone else with him? Why wasn't he at least trying to untie Ken?

"Who…?" he managed to croak.

"It's Kinosuke. I… followed the man here."

Kinosuke. Of course he wasn't untying Ken. The guy hated his guts. But what did he want from Ken now?

"Kenshin-san." Kinosuke sounded frustrated, as if he were reining in his temper. "One of the ropes is almost broken. If you pull forward with all your weight, you might get one arm free."

Why would one of the ropes be broken? And why wouldn't Kinosuke—oh. He was stupid.

"He's tied you."

Kinosuke didn't answer immediately, his silence charged with something Ken supposed was shame at being caught. "I didn't hear him come back."

There was some nagging thought trying to push its way to the front of his consciousness, but Ken was too tired, too sore to think any further, and so he tried to focus his attention on the rope.

"Which side did you cut?" he asked.

"Uh… the left one, I think. I mean right, your right."

"You are blindfolded?"

He almost laughed at the huff Kinosuke let out. Yeah, he was probably rolling his eyes at the stupid gaijin, but Ken was relieved that the man had gone to all that trouble to prevent them from seeing his face. It meant they might still make it out of there alive, especially if Ken managed to break the rope. Okay. He could do this.

Ken's ankles were tied together, but the rope that crisscrossed the rest of his body left some room for movement, so he guessed he could try to bend his right knee so that it supported most of his weight and pulled at the weak rope.

"Son of a bitch!"

"*Nani?*"

He panted, unable to answer Kinosuke's worried question. The theory had been great, but he hadn't counted on the rope sliding as he moved and sinking into his open cuts. He'd straightened back up so fast that he might have gotten rope burn.

"I'll keep trying," he said in Japanese for Kinosuke's benefit, but he just stood there, thinking about how to avoid the pain, until he felt like a coward. Would he rather the man came back to play some more? At least this pain he could control, and it might bring him a reward in the end. So the choice was not that difficult.

He took a deep breath and decided to go for all. He needed all his weight hanging from the rope, so he bent both knees until his arms got enough purchase on the bamboo rod to allow him to lift his feet off the floor. But as soon as he did, his whole body tilted forward, the pull on his elbows so hard he thought his arms would break, the rope sliding further up and right into the grooves carved in his skin, rough hemp pressing so deep into the open wounds that he couldn't stop the scream that tore out of his throat.

"Kenshin-san?"

He vaguely heard Kinosuke's voice in the background of his pain, and it somehow brought everything into perspective. He wasn't alone anymore. If he failed, someone else might die because of him, and the fact that it was Kinosuke sharing his fate made Ken want to fight even more, show the guy you didn't have to be a yakuza to have endurance.

He took deep, shuddering breaths, trying to calm himself. The pain was still unbearable, especially where the rope sank into his left nipple, but his legs had stopped jerking wildly, and he was recovering his balance. It gave him hope to feel that his body was slightly bent to his right, because it meant that the rope was giving way where Kinosuke had cut it. He just needed to pull harder in that direction.

He almost laughed hysterically when he thought he wished he were fat. His scrawny body weighed less than a wet chicken, and he'd have to thrash around a lot to bring the rope down. The only problem with that was the other fucking rope, how it was going to hurt to have it slide in and out of his cuts with every movement he made.

"Here we go," he panted, trying to spur himself into action, his knees folding as if he were on a swing, making his body tilt forward to get momentum and then straightening his legs to reverse the movement. "Fuck!"

It was the most God-awful swing he'd ever ridden, curses pouring out of his mouth along with yells, groans, and outright whimpers, but he kept pushing and pulling, sweat and probably blood running down his body and smoothing the way for the rope to rub every inch of his skin.

He was making so much noise that he couldn't hear whether the rope sounded about to break or not, but he knew if he stopped to assess the situation, he would never find the strength to start again, so he just hollered every four-letter word he could think of until his voice became hoarse and his legs started to falter. In the end he just hung there, not feeling anything in his arms from his elbows down, his body swinging like a pendulum in an almost dead grandfather clock, his limbs growing numb, as if the excruciating pain was something he could settle into.

And then, all of a sudden, he was falling to one side, his feet slamming against a cement wall as his full weight came to hang from his left arm, where it was tied to the bamboo rod near the elbow. The pain was so sharp that he was sure he wailed before he felt the dizziness that usually precedes total blackness. No. Not now. He couldn't faint now. He gulped air desperately, trying to push oxygen into his fading mind.

"Gambare, Kenshin!"

It was lame, but Kinosuke was actually cheering him on, and it made all the difference in the world that it was Kinosuke who thought Ken could pull it off, for if there was someone in Japan who wouldn't give him empty praise if his life depended on it, it was the young yakuza. And his life sure as hell depended on it.

He took another deep breath and stretched his right arm over his head until he felt the tingle of his numb fingers touching the rope hanging from the ceiling. Then he grabbed it and pulled his body upward to get some weight off his mauled left arm. It was a relief to do so, but he wasn't in any shape to hold on like that much longer, so he got a little momentum to make his bound legs swing again, trying to find a surface where he could rest them.

When his arm was already shaking, his toes hit what appeared to be a metal shelf right behind him. Oh yes, he remembered it. The man had untied Ken to take a picture of him holding the *Asahi Shimbun*, his back to that very shelf. And Ken had been naïve enough to expect he wouldn't tie him again to that damn bamboo rod.

Now if he could get his feet to stay on the shelf, he'd have leverage enough to untie the remaining rope. Shit. How he wished he had prehensile toes like a regular chimp. He groaned with the effort to hold himself more or less upright so that he could swing back his legs in the same exact direction.

It took him four tries, but finally his feet found purchase, and he stopped moving about like the planchette on an Ouija board.

"Yes!"

"Kenshin-san?"

He almost laughed at the concern in Kinosuke's voice. The poor guy must be desperate to see how things were going, how close to freedom they were.

"Almost there, Kinosuke-san," he panted. "I just need to—"

"You need to cut this rope, I believe."

The sound of that hideously muffled voice came to him just a moment before the tension in his arms disappeared and his body started tilting forward. In those few seconds, he had time to experience the full terror of falling in complete darkness, with his hands and feet tied, unable to at least protect his head, unable to see what he would hit or when the floor would rise up to receive his dead weight. And when it did, when his face lay twisted to one side on the cement, his brain functions about to shut down to block the intolerable pain, he thought in an oddly dispassionate way how weird it was to not hear any other sound but the words of that ugly voice.

"I see you didn't find that harness to your liking. I agree. It didn't do your best qualities justice. Let's see if we can manage something that makes you more readily available."

SILVANO'S looked quite different today, the dark mood of the meeting wafting from their table like the garlicky smells from the kitchen. It was raining outside, too, and the fake Italian décor appeared even more garish in the artificial overhead lighting.

Onga had agreed to meet Shigure alone, both his men and Shigure's waiting in the cars outside. The Korean underboss was wearing a bottle-green suit, of all things, but the shirt with it was in an unusually subdued shade of yellow, making him look almost decent.

"What is this about, Matsunaga-san? Are you still smarting over that sword? You know there was no other way to go about it."

"I know. It was one of my men who started the trouble, so the sword is your due. I didn't call you here to talk about that."

Onga sipped his coffee, waiting. They hadn't ordered any food, and Shigure was grateful for that, since he didn't have the stomach for pasta right now, not when he had to either start the war they'd been skirting or beg his enemy for help. It had to be done bluntly, without the usual tiptoeing both captains did around each other, because this time Shigure needed answers, and he would risk anything to get them.

He held Onga's eyes, ready to catch any reaction to his next words.

"Where is Kenshin-san?"

They kept silent, studying each other for a long, uncertain second. In spite of his boisterous behavior—or maybe because of it—the Korean was a good player, quite proficient at hiding his true intentions, but he was also a forthright man, and Shigure was counting on that, since not a single muscle on his face had moved at Shigure's question. Finally, Onga blinked, and Shigure held his breath.

"Who?"

The bafflement in those usually crafty eyes was so comical that Shigure would have laughed if Onga hadn't just cut his chances of finding Kenshin in half. It would have been awful if the Daitō-kai were the ones keeping the American, but at least Shigure would have known what he was fighting against.

"Harisu Ken," he said wearily, and Onga's face reflected even more confusion at the foreign name. "The gaijin I've been... uh... seeing."

"Ah, that gaijin. What, you've lost him in a *matsuri* crowd?"

"He's been kidnapped. And guess what they found beside his wallet."

Onga's smirk froze. "A Daitō-kai badge."

Shigure nodded, and the Korean's curses were so heartfelt he either had to be sincere or had to be a damn good actor.

"This is becoming a true pain in the ass. Who on earth would be stupid enough to try to play us against each other?"

"Don't know, but he's almost succeeded twice. It's only logical for him to keep raising the stakes."

"Yeah, it's logical if he wants to go honor his ancestors in person."

"Oh, don't worry. I'll make sure he pays a visit to hell even if he hasn't any ancestor there. But I have to catch the bastard first."

Onga nodded solemnly. "I'll keep my eyes open and let you know if I find anything."

Shigure clenched his teeth. Any other time he'd have been happy with that promise of cooperation from the Daitō-kai, but now it wasn't enough. Yet any step he took from there would be dangerous, and they both knew it, the way Onga's eyes kept searching the place for a waiter to bring them the check and put an end to their meeting on a good note.

"Onga-san, I need you to tell me who warned you about the sword."

As he expected, the Korean's expression turned hard, a clear warning in his curt answer. "You know I can't do that."

"I guarantee there will be no consequences for him, whoever it is."

"Who do you think you are to guarantee that? Of course there'd be consequences, maybe not from you, maybe not today, but there sure would be. And you damn well know it. What's the matter with you?"

Shigure lowered his eyes, his voice a mere whisper. "Please, Onga-san, I beg you."

In the silence that followed, Shigure felt Onga's searching stare on him. "Tell me one thing, Matsunaga-san, so that we're clear on this. Is the gaijin that important to you, or is it a question of wounded pride at someone taking what's yours?"

And for the first time, Shigure really thought about it. He couldn't deny that the outrage he felt at the kidnapping sprang from the notion that someone had dared snatch Kenshin from right under the nose of a Shinagawa captain, that and the guilt about not being able to protect his own lover from his enemies. But wasn't there more to it? Didn't he care about Kenshin enough to risk his position and even his life, or would he go to those extremes just to prove nobody toyed with him and got away with it? Was this again just a question of his usual stubborn pride? To his surprise, he found he couldn't answer with absolute certainty.

"I suggest you make up your mind about it soon, Matsunaga-san, because this looks as if it's going to get very ugly very fast, and you need to be sure where you stand."

He watched Onga strut out of the restaurant in his tacky outfit, and for the first time since he'd met the Daitō-kai captain, he felt the Korean had always been the real thing, while Shigure kept blundering about like a poser.

CHAPTER 26

KINOSUKE was so glad the man had gagged him after he started hurling insults at the bastard, because it was a damn good incentive not to throw up as he might have many times over the last few hours, or what felt like hours, anyway.

And he had thought the man was a sicko before. Fuck. That didn't even begin to describe him. He was more what the tengu mask he had chosen to wear now suggested, some monster only half-human, and not especially human in the most human features, the bird's head looking as sinister as it was befitting.

What kind of man would do what the bastard had been doing to Kenshin-san? For hours on end? Taking off Kinosuke's blindfold so that he had an audience? It had started mildly enough, the guy just tying and untying around the heap on the floor that was the gaijin's body after the fall he'd taken. Shit. That must have hurt like hell. And after Kenshin-san had gone to all that trouble trying to get free for both of them.

Then the fucker had looped another rope through the hook in the ceiling and lifted the gaijin so that he hung in midair, but this time he had used the bamboo rod for another purpose. The hemp rope—he must have purchased it wholesale he had so much of it—was now tying Kenshin-san's bent legs, thigh to shin, the rod put through the crook of his knees with more rope securing it so as to keep the thin legs spread and show everything in between.

When Kenshin-san had been naked before, Kinosuke had thought it was just so the bastard could have a ball carving his tattoos all over the gaijin's skin, but now he knew better. The guy was a fucking pervert, so much so that if Kinosuke hadn't seen the man leave a yakuza badge beside Kenshin-san's wallet, he'd have thought the gaijin had just been kidnapped because, in his own foreign way, he was a looker. Yeah, even Kinosuke could see how the boss might find that smooth skin attractive, or that pretty face, or that… yeah, well, he could damn well see the attraction, but not like this, not like Kenshin-san had to be punished for it.

And Kinosuke just wished he wasn't there to see the motherfucker go about it as if he were smiling under the tengu mask. Shit. The bastard had as many toys as he had rope, and he was using every one of them on Kenshin-san.

He had started with a cock ring that had a wide, rubber strap attached to it, so that when the man was finished, the base of the gaijin's cock was trapped in the ring and his balls were stretched forward and away from his body. It didn't look very comfortable to Kinosuke, apart from not making sense at all—weren't contraptions like that used to prevent someone from coming too soon? If the guy expected Kenshin-san to even get hard in this situation, he was far more cracked than he appeared.

But soon Kinosuke understood the man had a completely different goal in mind. He tied a thin rope around Kenshin-san's cock and pulled the remainder of the rope up till it reached the gaijin's mouth. Then he forced it between his teeth and tied it behind his head, so that his cock was fully stretched in the opposite direction from his balls.

Shit. And Kenshin-san was so out of it because of the blow he'd received that he didn't make a sound or resist in any way. Not that he would have been able to do much, but he was just hanging there, and it was making Kinosuke's stomach clench for him, dreading what the bastard might do next.

When the guy clamped Kenshin-san's right nipple, the thin body shuddered in surprised pain, and jerked the rope attached to his cock, making him groan. Oh fuck. Kinosuke could quite see where this was going, and yanked at his own bonds in rage. If the bastard so much as grazed Kenshin-san's torn nipple, Kinosuke was going to fucking kill him.

As if reading his mind, the tengu mask contemplated Kinosuke in mockery for a heartbeat and then turned to secure another clamp to Kenshin-san's left nipple. It was a difficult task, the way the gaijin kept jerking about, blood making everything slippery until the vise was in place, the muffled screams nonstop since the bastard went on working at tying another rope to the clamps and then up into Kenshin's mouth around the other rope already there. So every time the gaijin's body jerked, he himself yanked both ropes, pulling hard at his cock and his injured nipple, which again made him jerk in agony. It was a fucking loop of pain.

Kinosuke was breathing so hard his throat burned. He thought he'd never felt so much hatred, so much impotence in his whole life, but the man soon proved him wrong, because in the next few minutes, he felt there was no way he could keep watching without going crazy.

IT LOOKED like an early meeting of night revelers, the way everybody appeared tired and bleary-eyed after long hours of combing the city for clues. Even Atsushi looked exhausted, though Shigure had only called him to go bring Kotarō home from the hospital. He guessed the kid had been babbling all the way, distressed as he must be from both Kenshin and Kinosuke disappearing on him.

"How is Kotarō?"

Atsushi seemed to flinch at the question, but Shigure understood everyone was so wrought up in the house, it was as catching as a bad cold.

"He's still bruised and sore, but much better," Atsushi said.

Shigure nodded and looked at the men sitting on the tatami in a loose circle around him. He hadn't had to order any of them to search for Kenshin. They'd all jumped to the task because they felt it like a personal affront, that someone had gone and snatched their pet gaijin.

It was obvious they'd have answered Onga's question without doubt, the way the room bristled with wounded pride. After the incident with Kotarō, most of them believed the Daitō-kai were behind everything that happened, especially since nobody had been able to locate Kinosuke in the first thirty hours after Kenshin's disappearance, and they needed to feel sure the culprit wasn't one of their own.

Shigure was not so sure. He'd heard Kinosuke's sentiments about Kenshin, and his sudden disappearance didn't throw a good light on him. Sooner or later they'd have to admit the possibility that he was involved and plan their next steps accordingly, as they were running out of leads to follow.

Before Shigure could address his men, the door slid open, and a flustered Tachibana poked his head in.

"Sorry, boss, but the two gaijin cops are here with Kotarō."

"What do you mean with Kotarō?"

Tachibana shrugged. "They showed at the gate together."

"And what was Kotarō doing outside the gate? Wasn't he supposed to be—" He turned to Atsushi as realization dawned on him. "You never went to pick him up."

Now it was Atsushi's turn to look flustered.

"I'm sorry. I phoned the hospital to check on him, and they told me he was sleeping, so I thought—"

"Boss! Have you found Kenshin-san? Is aniki here? Are the gaijin omawari-san going to help?"

Great. Hurricane Kotarō had finally arrived, his face looking as if one of those makeup artists had been practicing new shades on him.

"Mr. Matsunaga, sorry to intrude, but we need your help."

And of course the FBI clones weren't there to help but to be helped. Shigure felt the beginnings of a headache pressing against his temples.

"Come in and take a seat, gentlemen. And Kotarō, do me a favor and go straight to bed right now. We'll talk later."

"No."

He turned his most dangerous glare on Kotarō and saw the kid blush and lower his eyes.

"Sorry, boss, I just want to help. Please?"

Damn. The poor kid looked so earnest, so ready to cry. Shigure could only imagine how guilty he felt, how useless.

"All right. Stay, but keep quiet."

"Hai!"

He suppressed a grin at Kotarō's enthusiasm and turned to consider the gaijin. Shigure's men had moved to make room for them, and now they sat on their heels awkwardly, their bodies too big and unyielding to be comfortable in that position. As the day before, they appeared to be in a hurry, without any time to address anyone properly, or wait to be addressed first, as even a schoolkid would know to do. What did they think, that Shigure wasn't in a hurry to find Kenshin too? That he didn't know the more hours that went by, the less hope there was of finding him alive?

"Mr. Matsunaga, Senator Harris has been contacted by the kidnappers."

Shigure's heart started racing. Maybe it was a kidnapping after all, and the yakuza connection was just a diversion. He somehow doubted it, but clinging to that hope was easy, though he didn't want to dwell on the fact that it was probably easy because it would mean what happened wasn't Shigure's fault.

"Why do you speak of kidnappers, Mr. Campbell? You know there's more than one?"

"I'm Bradley, sir. He is Campbell," the black agent said. Shigure damn well knew who was who, but if they insisted in calling him Mr. Matsunaga, he'd call them what he wished to. "Our technicians have deduced the second and the first caller might be different persons."

"Might?"

"Uh... the voices were very distorted, so we don't really know for sure."

So Japanese technology has proven its superiority once again, Shigure thought, but kept it to himself. He knew if it had been the other way around, Japanese police wouldn't have bothered to use the nation's renowned technology to record the calls, dismissing it as yet another fancy, Western-police-procedural technique.

"The ransom?"

"We are not allowed to discuss that."

Shigure snorted. "How can you expect me to help if you don't share your information with me?"

Now it was Campbell—the blond legal attaché—who spoke, his accent so thick Shigure could almost hear the words hit the tatami mat as they fell from the man's lips. "I'm sorry, but all we can tell you is that we have less than forty-eight hours to find Mr. Harris."

He tried to rein in his anger. They still thought Shigure might have Kenshin hidden or had dumped his body somewhere, but at the same time, they'd been told enough about Japan's underworld to know they wouldn't get very far without the yakuza. So he guessed they were both investigating him as a suspect and trying to benefit from the human resources he had at his disposal as a Shinagawa underboss.

"Did they let the senator talk to his son?" he asked.

"No. But they sent this," Campbell said, pulling a photo from his jacket pocket and handing it to Shigure.

He felt it like a punch to the gut, the way those glazed eyes looked back at him, lifeless and indifferent, as if all the ebullient emotions they usually held when they looked at Shigure had been drained from him, slowly oozing out of the cuts that marred Kenshin's beautiful skin.

"Kuso," someone muttered to his right, and Shigure passed the photo to the man closest to him in that direction. He knew if he held it for a moment longer, his fingers would start shaking with the rage he felt boiling inside.

"Mr. Matsunaga, according to the information we've gathered on other yakuza-related kidnappings, that level of cruelty is not common, is it?"

"That's because you've been considering kidnaps perpetrated by yakuza, not directed against them," Shigure spat, anger barely suppressed as he glared at the gaijin.

"You mean—"

"I mean the senator can rest assured he won't lose any money over this. Those bastards don't give a damn about the ransom. They're just doing it to score one on the Shinagawa."

"Excuse me if I don't get it, but Mr. Harris being a foreigner, why would the Shinagawa see his kidnapping as a blow to the organization?"

"I believe what you're trying to ask is why would the Shinagawa care for the gaijin boy toy of one of its bosses, isn't it?"

"I didn't—"

"I'll tell you why, Mr. Campbell. Unlike the FBI, the Shinagawa is a family, not an organization. We care about our own, no matter who their ancestors were or whom they choose to bed. Of course, you may say that being the casual fuck of a yakuza doesn't make Kenshin-san one, and if he had been just beaten or cut in a random way, I'd agree with you in this not being yakuza related. But that picture says differently."

"How so?"

"*Katagi no shū*," Shinya said.

"The people who walk under the sun," Shigure explained, "are those who know nothing of the yakuza shadow world, and the yakuza has a time-honored tradition to avoid hurting them. So unless I'd made it clear that Kenshin-san is my family, no gang would touch him except to gain some easy money out of his father, and then they wouldn't torture him. But whoever has done this has used the kanji for 'dog' to mark him, and if you'd done your homework, you would have learned that was one of the ways the law marked criminals in ancient times."

"So his captors are marking him as yakuza."

"Exactly."

"Do you think the Daitō-kai badge was meant as a signature and not a false clue for us?"

"After seeing that picture, my first reaction would be to think the Daitō-kai had been behind this from the beginning."

Bradley studied him for a moment. "And you believe that was the only purpose of the photo, to make you blame them."

Shigure nodded. "The Daitō-kai is almost as old as the Shinagawa-gumi, and our ways are much the same. If they wanted a war, they wouldn't go about it in such a twisted way. It's both too subtle and too blunt for them. But of course, that'd come in pretty handy if they wanted to accuse us of starting a war without justification."

The gaijin looked overwhelmed, and Campbell shook his head sadly. "Mr. Matsunaga, I don't need to tell you how beyond our experience this goes. As foreign legal attachés, there's really not much we can do except collaborate with the local police, either."

"To be honest," Bradley added, "you're our best hope of finding Mr. Harris. So if you can use our help in any way, please let us know."

They both handed their cards to Shigure, and he took them respectfully because, for the first time, they'd done something to deserve it. He wasn't naïve, though, and he knew that, even if the FBI agents managed to be of any use, their superiors wouldn't be very keen on allowing them to work side by side with the yakuza. But at least it was obvious their concern for Kenshin was sincere, so much so that they were ready to go beyond their strict duty and risk their bosses' wrath. And then a terrifying notion crossed Shigure's mind.

"It'd help if you would answer a question honestly," he said.

"We'll do our best," Campbell said, raising both palms as if to mean they weren't exactly free to do so.

"Has the senator any intention of paying the ransom?"

"We are not—" Campbell started, but Bradley cut him short.

"No, sir. As a US senator he feels he has to follow our government policy of never negotiating with terrorists or gangsters."

"Especially if it concerns a son who is not only queer but also involved with a yakuza. I guess that's why you're not supposed to discuss the ransom, because the good senator doesn't want the media sniffing about as they'd surely do if they knew there'd been a kidnapping in his family."

The agents seemed angered by his words, but since they didn't deny them, Shigure understood they were angry because they couldn't be denied, and not the other way around.

"Thank you for your honesty, gentlemen. I'll keep you informed."

"Thanks, we'll do the same."

"Atsushi, please show these gentlemen the way out."

As the door slid closed, Shigure felt the oppressive silence in the room as the men mulled over what had been said. And because it was so quiet, he could hear the sobs coming from behind him.

He turned to see Kotarō holding Kenshin's photo, and almost swore before he realized it was time for the kid to grow up and face life, since life wouldn't wait for him to grow up.

Sensing he was being watched, Kotarō pawed at his tears and looked up angrily, lifting the photo in front of him. "Tell me we're not letting this go unpunished," he said, holding Shigure's gaze without wavering. "Tell me we're not letting one of our family die."

Shigure turned to look at the men around him. It was only logical for Kotarō to react when he'd learned Kenshin's father wouldn't move a finger to help him. Kotarō had joined the yakuza because his own family didn't want him around, so it was easy for him to relate. But it was different for the other men. They might be mad at someone snatching a gaijin they had befriended, but they wouldn't go as far as to consider their boss's lover part of the Shinagawa family, even if Shigure had implied that to rile the Americans.

As Shigure studied each man's expression, he thought that maybe that had been his mistake from the start, thinking his own shame would be reflected in the eyes of his men, because, in thinking so, Shigure himself had seen them as his subordinates, not his family. And it was only Shigure's insecurities that had fueled the rage in Kinosuke's heart and made it grow into hatred.

Onga had been right. He was a fool, and that might cost the man he loved his life. It was time to put his pride and his heart where they should be: in the same fucking place.

"No, Kotarō. The Shinagawa is not letting one of their own die," he said.

The kid nodded solemnly. "Good. How do I find Kenshin-san?"

The men chuckled all around, and Shinya patted Kotarō's head. "Kid, if we knew that, you'd be the first the boss would send to spread terror among our enemies."

Kotarō grinned from ear to ear. "And to rescue Kenshin-san."

"Yeah, and to rescue our gaijin."

Shinya turned to look at Shigure, and he saw the challenge in his man's eye, daring him to deny Kenshin was theirs as much as he was Shigure's. And he finally understood that Kenshin was not just their boss's lover, but also a man they'd come to know and respect for his own merits. And that was the crux of it all. He had only judged Kenshin as he would reflect on himself, on his position as a yakuza captain. It was Shigure who had considered Kenshin the boy toy of a yakuza underboss.

CHAPTER 27

KINOSUKE lunged forward with all his might, not caring if he dislocated his shackled ankle in his effort to reach the damn shock box and unplug it. When the buzzing sound finally stopped, he just stood there panting, shaking like an infant, as ready to cry as a child would be, watching as Kenshin's body convulsed for the last time and then went limp on the ropes holding him upright.

He was going to kill the motherfucker if it was the last thing he ever did. But not now. The lousy son of a bitch had left in a hurry after someone called him. Well, not exactly in a hurry. The bastard had taken his time to untie Kinosuke's arms and leave him to attend to the gaijin, securing his right ankle to the wall so that he couldn't escape. And all the while, Kenshin-san had been receiving electric shocks through the straps attached to his cock and balls, and through the ridged dildo the perv had stuck up his ass.

He needed to kill that sicko. Even the ringtone coming off his cell was creepy, one of those opera stunts that sounded like a woman being slaughtered to furious music. He knew what it was because he'd heard it on another phone or something, he couldn't quite remember, but someone told him it was from an opera written by an Italian about an American in Japan. He could only imagine what a complete fuck-up the whole thing must be.

Kinosuke huffed. He knew he was only delaying approaching Kenshin-san because the closer he'd get, the more he'd have to fight the urge to either throw up or cry. Shit. He was such a coward, and the bastard hadn't even touched him. If he'd been in the gaijin's place, he would have started begging hours ago. He supposed that was why every time he thought about the American's name now, he always added the honorific in his mind.

He shuffled forward, testing the length of his chain. Long enough to reach Kenshin-san, though not very comfortably, as the fucker had probably intended. Never mind that. He was not going to leave the gaijin trussed up.

As he approached Kenshin-san, he hesitated. He really didn't know where to start. Maybe he should first take care of the things that looked as if they hurt, even though the gaijin seemed to be unconscious now. Better this way—it would also hurt to remove all those contraptions.

Closing his eyes for a second to brace himself, Kinosuke finally reached out and released the clamp on Kenshin-san's right nipple. When there was no reaction from the limp body, he let out the breath he'd been holding and went for the other clamp. As soon as he released it, though, blood started oozing from the wounded nipple.

"Fuck!"

He looked around desperately, but the bastard had only left bottled water and some food on a shelf, nothing to staunch the bleeding or clean the cut, so he yanked his shirt off and tore it into long rags. He was going to need every inch of it the way things were.

When he already had one of the rags pressing against the wound, Kinosuke stretched to reach the knots behind Kenshin-san's head with his free hand. It took him a bit to untie them, but first one and then the other rope fell, one to the floor, and the other to hang loose from where it was still wrapped around the gaijin's cock.

Without stopping to think, Kinosuke uncoiled the rope and studied the cock ring and ball strap until he found the way to remove both of them. Only then did he notice how red and swollen the whole area was, small burns from the electric currents marking the spots where the conductive tape had touched skin.

He forced himself to keep going before Kenshin-san would wake, and reached behind the gaijin's balls until he could grab the base of the dildo and pull. He clenched his teeth at the resistance he felt, trying his best not to imagine what it'd be like to feel the ridges of the damn thing scraping all along an already sensitized passage. When he finally got the full length of it out, blood started dripping onto the floor.

"*Ano yarō!*" Kinosuke yelled as he sent the dildo crashing against the cement wall.

He was going to kill the motherfucking bastard, and he repeated it again and again in his head until it became a calming mantra that helped him slow his breathing and go back to his gruesome task.

The rag he'd pressed against the bleeding nipple was already soaked through, so Kinosuke left it on the nearest shelf and used both his hands to untie the ropes around the gaijin's legs and remove the bamboo rod keeping them spread. Then he went to the hook on the wall where the rope bearing Kenshin-san's weight was attached and very carefully untied it, holding on with all his might as he brought the limp body down by small increments.

When the gaijin finally lay on the cement floor, Kinosuke breathed his relief, right until he heard a small pained moan and saw Kenshin-san stir. Fuck. He shouldn't wake now. The more time he spent conscious, the more he would hurt. And there was nothing Kinosuke could give him to dull the pain. He rushed to the gaijin's side.

"Shigu... re." It was barely a whisper, but those cracked lips were calling the boss's name, and Kinosuke felt his stomach clench in a tight knot. He crouched beside the mauled body and reached out without thinking, his fingers resting lightly on the sweat-matted hair. Of course the gaijin flinched at his touch, making rage boil inside Kinosuke once again, forcing him to close his eyes to stop from yelling that he was going to kill that man for the hundredth time. He tried to make his voice come out reassuring instead.

"It's all right, Kenshin-san. You're safe," he said, his hand moving in a soft caress until he felt the gaijin calm and actually lean into the touch. Shit. It made him feel as if someone was squeezing his lungs so tight he couldn't get enough air in him. "I'm taking the blindfold off now, okay? It's gonna hurt a little, all this light, but it'll be okay. We're alone now."

Kinosuke untied the leather blindfold and saw the gaijin blink and close his eyes back with a groan. "Yeah, that damn bulb sucks. The clever clogs who invented them forgot to tell people it's bad manners to use bulbs without a shade. Those things are naked, man, showing all their bits, and—"

He felt two-colored eyes on him and shut his trap abruptly. The usually bright irises were dull now, but there was a slight quirk in those lips that made Kinosuke smile with relief. "Hey, gaijin-san."

"Kino… suke-san," it was barely a whisper, but at least Kenshin-san recognized him. "Are we…?"

Oh fuck. The gaijin thought they were free now, and Kinosuke had to crush his hopes, on top of everything else. He busied himself with the knots still tying the skinny arms behind Kenshin-san's back, to gain some time before he answered.

Those thin fingers were ice cold, circulation cut off by the hours he'd spent bound, and Kinosuke massaged the gaijin's arms briskly as soon as he untied them. It must hurt, getting blood to circulate again, but Kenshin-san only made a small hoarse sound. That throat had been screaming for too long, and it was no surprise everything coming from it sounded raw.

"You must be parched. I'll get you some water."

Sure enough, the bastard had placed the water bottle and the food on a shelf that Kinosuke could barely reach the way he was chained. It took three tries, some acrobatics, and a lot of cursing, but he finally managed to grab the bottle with one hand and the bento box with the other. The problem was Kenshin-san had been following his every move, and now Kinosuke didn't need to tell him they were still trapped at the mercy of that sicko son of a bitch.

Neither of them said a word as Kinosuke helped the gaijin drink, but then Kenshin-san reached out for him.

"Help me sit."

"No, Kenshin-san, you must rest."

"I can't eat lying down."

Kinosuke couldn't keep the surprise from his voice. "You're hungry?"

The eye roll he got in response almost made him laugh, until Kenshin spoke. "I'll need all the strength I can get to climb those stairs." Then Kinosuke couldn't wrap his mind around the obvious. The gaijin intended to go out to find help. He'd taken one look at Kinosuke's predicament, and decided it was he who had to do the rescue thing, since he was the only one free now—he, who couldn't even lift his own head to take a sip of water.

"Kinosuke-san?"

Kinosuke realized he was crying, huge tears rolling down his cheeks as if all the time he'd spent in his life holding them back had fattened the small drops into the behemoths he could almost hear now splashing against the floor. It was a disgrace for a yakuza to be seen crying, but Kinosuke felt well beyond infra dig at the moment, the failure that he was highlighted even more by the man lying naked on the cement beside him. Of course he once thought he hated this man, because that's what you did when you were the lowest of the low, convince yourself you hated everything you wished you had.

"I'm sorry, Kenshin-san, I really am."

"This is not your fault. You're chained to that wall only because you tried to rescue me."

Kinosuke shook his head angrily. "You don't understand. I could have stopped all this before—"

"I understand how you feel, but the fact that you tried is the only important thing to me."

"No! You don't understand a fucking thing! I was following you. I saw the man take you and did nothing. You get it now? I could have stopped him from kidnapping you in the first place, and I did nothing. Not a fucking single thing!"

The gaijin was frowning now. "You were following me?" Oh yeah, Kinosuke could almost see the gears in that pretty head working to reach the obvious conclusion. "You wanted to—"

"Hai. I was there to kill you. And then I just followed the man to see who was trying to score one on the boss. I didn't give a rat's ass what happened to you."

Kenshin-san held his eyes steadily. "Where did he catch you, that man?"

"Down here."

"And what were you doing down here?"

He blushed. "I was... uh... trying to untie you after—"

"So, you were trying to rescue me. Weren't you?"

"Yeah, but—"

"But nothing. You were trying to rescue me and ended up chained to a wall for your trouble. That's all that matters to me."

Kinosuke studied the bruised face looking up at him with a determined glare matching any oyabun's he'd ever known, and felt new tears filling his eyes.

"Stupid gaijin," he mumbled.

"Hare-brained *chinpira*."

Shit. The gaijin calling him a lowlife so seriously was more than he could take. They cracked up at the same time, their laughter probably the weirdest thing that had happened so far in that ugly basement.

SHIGURE toed off his shoes and contemplated the slippers lined on the rack. Almost everybody else was out there looking for Kenshin in one way or another, even Kotarō. They'd found the perfect task for the kid. The girls of Kei's age might find Kotarō harmless—or most probably, cute—and they might talk, help them find the girl who'd worked at the Haihīru.

Harada had come up with a photo, one of those sloppy shots taken with a cell phone, but it would do, or so Shigure would be thinking if he hadn't the gut feeling Kei had already left, and not merely the city, or even the country. The next time they'd see her, it'd probably be at the morgue.

It was already their third day without any useful leads and, as the hours went by, they were running into more and more dead ends. Up until then, the Shinagawa could brag that nothing happened in Tokyo without their knowledge, but Kenshin's captors seemed to come from nowhere and had no apparent relation with anyone in the underworld.

The Chinese triads swore they had nothing to do with it and had not heard the slightest rumor about it, and so did the other foreign groups working their streets. Shigure was sure they weren't lying since they were only allowed to carry on their businesses because the Shinagawa granted them some leeway. They wouldn't be so stupid as to anger the Shinagawa, even those who worked in the Daitō-kai turf, or especially not them.

It wasn't the right time for a war between the two larger gangs. Their leadership was so solid that even if two local captains went down—namely Shigure and Onga—both groups would stand firm at the top of the food chain. And every single one of the smaller gangs in Tokyo knew that. So the blow had to come from someone outside those circles, either someone not yet connected to the underworld—some bunch of greener-than-green kidnappers—or someone connected to higher circles and able to smooth their way with serious money. The first would have made waves in the streets, and the second would have left a trail of political connections the American agents would know how to follow. So far, none of it had come to pass.

What was left, then, but a personal vendetta? Shigure had sent Shinya after Kinosuke with the sinking feeling that it would only serve to bring closure, because the kind of rage the young man harbored was an immediate thing. If Kinosuke had gone after Kenshin, it could only be to kill him. And so the kidnap masquerade confused Shigure to no end. He couldn't imagine someone as hotheaded as Kinosuke carefully planning it as a simple diversion.

It was all a quagmire Shigure found almost impossible to navigate, so much so that he was trying even the unlikely. He had come back to the house to retrieve the address of a Russian mafia underboss he had once befriended in Sakhalin. Not that he believed the Russians were interested anymore in messing with the Americans as they once used to, but they would know if anything moved on the European side or—more importantly—in the Islamic arena. He couldn't quite ignore the fact that Kenshin's father was a US senator.

He snorted as his eyes rested on Atsushi's dress shoes. How could a pair of shoes manage to look prim? These did, even though they now had a slight coat of dust on the usually shiny surface, which spoke volumes about the general state the house was in if even Mr. Perfect forgot to clean his shoes.

The truth was Shigure had been noticing Atsushi too much lately because he made too many mistakes. As any good secretary, he was usually invisible, but the atmosphere these days was too charged for anyone to escape its influence. And it must be driving Atsushi mad, failing so miserably. Yet the man didn't let it show, and Shigure wondered how it was that after so many years among boisterous yakuza, he hadn't taken on their expansive moods. He guessed growing up as a rich kid had left its indelible mark on him, just the same as Shigure growing up in a burakumin household had.

What would it be like to grow up as a senator's son? Not that good, it seemed, judging by the way Kenshin had avoided talking about his family. Shigure's own insecurities had made him see it differently, but now he understood Kenshin must be ashamed of his father. The man acted like a regular jerk, like every politician Shigure had known—and being the only other power that mattered in the local district, he'd had to deal with quite a few.

The senator didn't deserve a son like Kenshin. Nobody deserved him. And especially not Shigure, who was just standing in the genkan, looking at a bunch of slippers as if they could tell him where Kenshin was.

He shook himself out of his trance and left the shoes untouched. As tired as he was, if he put on a pair of slippers, he might be tempted to stay in and surrender to the feeling of hopelessness that was numbing him more and more as the hours went by. It was as if he had already resigned himself to losing Kenshin, and he didn't want to dwell too closely on what it said about him.

The door to his office slid open, and Atsushi nearly jumped out of his skin when he saw Shigure.

"Any calls?" he asked to allow his secretary to slip back into his professional, cool self.

"Nishimura Ryū-san called, sir."

Shigure only raised an eyebrow.

"He said to tell you that he would like to help in any way you find suitable."

"Yeah, right. Anything else?"

"No, sir. The mail is on your desk."

"Thank you, Atsushi."

The man bowed as stiffly as ever and left. It was a relief to see his secretary acting normal—stick-up-his-ass normal—and Shigure entered his office to get the address he'd come to look up. He had a tendency to jot down anything interesting on whatever piece of paper was available and then throw all the little bits in his desk drawers, relying on Atsushi to sort them the way he sorted the mail in small, separate piles according to importance.

Now, there were three of those piles on the desk that Shigure had pretty much intended to ignore, until he saw the small package standing apart. It wasn't the time of year to receive presents, and people usually delivered those in person, anyway, carefully wrapped up in something quite different from the coarse brown wrapping paper and hemp rope that sat on his desk now. Not big enough to be anything dangerous, either, though these days you could make a bomb the size of a cell phone. Whatever this was, it could fit into a very small rectangular box.

Shigure weighed it as he studied the handwriting. It was so light that it must have been quite cheap to have it delivered. The handwriting appeared shaky, his name misspelled, almost like the handiwork of a child—or a school dropout—which would point too obviously to the yakuza rank and file to be anything other than a setup. He bet there'd be a Daitō-kai badge among the contents too.

The knots came off easily, and Shigure set aside the wrapping paper carefully. His and Atsushi's prints would be everywhere, but he knew Uehara would be interested in offering it to the Americans as a show of good faith, if nothing else.

There was a Styrofoam container on the desk now, and Shigure tried to ignore the feeling of dread that was chasing his rational thoughts away. For a heartbeat or two, he held on to the silly notion that maybe if he didn't lift the white lid, there'd still be hope, there'd still be something he could do to save Kenshin, but then he felt the dread change into that numbness that kept hovering over him like a crow over a Dumpster, and anger filled him. He was so afraid of losing Kenshin that he was already preparing himself for it, he was already learning to accept it because, even more than losing Kenshin, he feared showing the world how much he cared, how much a gaijin could bring a yakuza captain to his knees.

He reached out with trembling fingers and yanked open the container. And then his knees did bend, a strangled cry leaving his throat as he crumpled to the floor holding the small alcohol bottle.

He didn't need to look too closely to know to whom that finger belonged. It was only the first knuckle of a little finger, but he had kissed that ridged nail too many times, had seen that little finger curl under a *bokken* too many times not to know whose left hand was missing a knuckle, the most important knuckle to control the range of movement of a Japanese sword.

CHAPTER 28

HE WAS going to kill that bastard. Kinosuke rocked back and forth as far as the rope allowed, repeating the same sentence over and over in his head. It was safer this way. If he started thinking anything else, he would go crazy.

The chain had been removed, his ankles tied loosely together, his arms behind his back, tied to another rope that hung from a hook in the ceiling. He was fucking comfortable, nothing too tight, his remaining clothes keeping the ropes from his skin, a gag in his mouth to prevent him from having to apologize to death.

It was as if the motherfucker wanted to do right by him, as if he thought Kinosuke would understand the need to act as he was acting. And Kinosuke only wanted to scream, because he knew some hours ago he might as well have.

But not now. Not after what he'd seen. Not after he'd helped Kenshin-san reach the stairs and watched as he crawled up, one step at a time, leaving blood stains on the wall, dragging his uncooperative body up by sheer willpower, skinny legs shaking so badly Kinosuke thought the gaijin would roll down the steps any moment. And yet he didn't. He was like one of those clockwork toys that would keep trudging blindly about even when they met an obstacle or fell. He knew the man would crawl all the way to the street and manage to keep standing until he made sure someone came back for Kinosuke.

That short, scrawny gaijin was so fucking focused that he didn't even faint when a vicious kick to the side of his head sent him crashing against the cement wall and trundling down the stairs. He lay there in a heap of long limbs, still trying to reach out and stop the bastard until he had a knife to his throat. And damn if it hadn't made the sicko mad with rage.

It was a sight to see, or rather hear, because the fucker was still wearing that bird mask, but curses spilled from under its beak like water from a running tap—a tap that had almost gone rusty with disuse, by the sound of it. Funny that. Up until now, Kinosuke would have thought a beast like the one holding them must be someone with a very short fuse, but he understood now it took a lot of control to go about torture the way the bastard did, slow and easy, as if it weren't so much a thing of anger but some kind of fucked-up craftsmanship.

Now, though, Kenshin-san had made the bastard lose his cool, and Kinosuke had no way of knowing whether it was a good thing, not until the man dragged the gaijin to his usual spot, tied him with the sloppiest knots Kinosuke had seen so far, and turned menacingly to his other prisoner.

It could have been his chance to do something, since he was only chained to the wall by an ankle, but even mad as he was, the bastard was clever enough to move out of Kinosuke's reach. He'd been shouting his head off, trying to rile the fucker even more to push him off balance, and finally he could almost see the waves of hatred puffing out from under the tengu mask.

A fine picture the creep made, all proper from the waist down—in slacks and dress shoes—and half-naked from there up, his white undershirt stained with Kenshin-san's blood, a butcher knife in one hand, and a silly mask on his face. Almost like a salaryman after a company party, drunk enough to fool around and sing karaoke.

But then the hatred seemed to congeal into something solid, the eyes in the mask holes smiling to Kinosuke in a manner that shut him up faster than any blow. And then the bastard walked back to Kenshin-san, ignoring the desperate taunts Kinosuke sent his way, the chain rattling as he tried to stretch it as far as it could go, knowing full well the gaijin was going to pay for whatever the sicko thought the world owed him.

Kenshin-san should have been a chickenshit, girly-weak fucking gaijin. By rights, he should have been, what with that pretty face and those dainty hands of his. The little twink was a faggot, for crying out loud. He should have fainted the first time the sicko laid a hand on him, and stay out of it from there on. But no, the damn gaijin had to keep those scary eyes open and fixed on the bastard, glaring murder at him with his pretty lips fucking sealed like one of those actors playing the tough ronin on the screen, keeping so damn quiet that Kinosuke had been able to hear the sound a knife made when it met bone.

He knew he was going to remember it for as long as he lived, the silence. It made every single noise so loud he would have known what happened even if he'd been blindfolded. Even with his eyes closed, he could have heard blood gushing out of the wound, the clatter of the knife as it hit the floor, the grinding of teeth under the mask, the angry panting behind the tengu face as it stood looking down on Kenshin-san's little knowing smile.

Because the crazy gaijin was smiling. Fucking smiling with those *oni* eyes all lit up like festival decorations as he managed to stare the bastard down even when he had to look up to meet the man's eyes.

For the first time since he'd been captured, Kinosuke understood they weren't going to make it out of there alive. And for the first time, he felt he didn't care.

It was a screwed-up way to get to it, in the only damn basement that existed in the whole city, with a fucking gaijin calling the tune and a sicko salaryman playing the bad guy, but he was right center stage of one of those scenarios he'd dreamed of as a boy, the kind of epic battle where you could die honorably and be forever remembered as a man of worth.

And wasn't it fitting that the hero in this fucked-up play should have bloody tattoos all over his body and was now missing a pinkie like a damn yakuza?

THE men behind the cameras must have been stunned out of their wits to see him there, because Shigure was halfway up the stairs to Onga's office before anyone tried to stop him, *try* being the key word.

He knew the staircase to be narrow—as it should be to prevent the full swing of a sword—but the advantage of a *bokken* was that you could grab it anywhere along its polished surface and use it as a baton instead, especially if the goons facing you had only been trained in the fine art of flower arrangement.

It spoke volumes about the generation gap that the first automatic gun that was finally aimed at him was Onga's. The Daitō-kai captain held his eyes while waving his free hand at his men, the hand that was missing two knuckles from the little finger.

"Shut the fucking door, and watch out for Matsunaga's men," he yelled before sitting behind his desk and mumbling, "fucking idiots."

Shigure didn't say anything, just made a show of putting two of his fingers inside his jacket pocket to extract the badge he then placed carefully on the desk between them.

Onga groaned. "Here we go again. Where was it this time?"

"Next to this," Shigure said, placing the alcohol vial beside the badge.

"*Chikushō*," Onga cursed under his breath. "Is it his?"

At Shigure's nod, Onga lowered his gun and fumbled with his already wide-open shirt collar until Shigure could see hints of a hairy chest and the charm the underboss wore on a chain.

"I hope you don't think me that stupid," Onga finally said, pointing at the vial with the knuckle in it. "And what is your gaijin supposed to be apologizing for, anyway?"

"You tell me."

Onga huffed. "Oh, come on. You know you can get one of those badges anywhere. Any schoolkid could have one."

"A schoolkid wouldn't know how to chop off a pinkie."

"You would be surprised what kids know these days. They read all kind of shit in the Wikipedia and then sure as hell get it all wrong. Cutting your own finger is supposed to send a clear message: you're trying to show someone you're so sorry for your mistakes that you've given up something vital to you—the finger you most need to control your katana—something that would actually weaken you, make you dependent on the wronged person's goodwill to forgive you when he could easily finish you, now that you can't use your weapon properly. So what yakuza worth his salt would chop off another man's pinkie? He'll be the laughingstock of all the gangs in the country, for the rest of his sorry life."

"But what if it was intended as a message? A hint for a true yakuza to do what he should?"

"Is that why you are here, Matsunaga-wakagashira? Out of duty?"

This time, Shigure didn't have to think it over. "I'm here to retrieve Kenshin-san."

Onga cocked his head to look at him. "Because he's yours?"

"I don't own him, same as I don't own the Shinagawa. But the Shinagawa are my duty. Kenshin is both my duty and my will."

The Daitō-kai captain held his eyes for a moment longer and then sighed loudly.

"You know I don't have him, don't you?" When Shigure nodded, Onga went on with a resigned expression. "But you still want to know who told us about the sword."

"Hai."

"And of course you know I can't tell you that."

"Hai."

"Damn it, Matsunaga. You don't stand a chance against my automatic with that toothpick of yours."

Shigure grinned. "It depends on how fast I can kill you with this toothpick," he said, moving into a defensive stance, the *bokken* poised to strike.

Onga shook his head, mirroring Shigure's grin. Among the new generations of white-collar yakuza, they were both old war dogs, big ugly animals who didn't fit well in the new corporate environment, but who could still be trusted to enjoy a good fight without the least concern for their lives.

Their eyes were the only things moving in the now-silent room. Onga hadn't raised the gun from the desk, probably thinking he needed to give Shigure a head start if he wanted the fight to keep any semblance of fairness, though he surely believed fifteen rounds of ammunition made fairness a moot point right from the start. He was probably correct, but Shigure knew there was a small chance if he managed to cross the distance between them before the second bullet struck home. That of course meant that Onga had to miss Shigure with the first, or at least miss his most vital organs.

When Onga finally started to move his hand, he appeared to be doing it in incredibly slow motion, but Shigure knew his own body appeared the same as it seemed poised in midair instead of rushing forward at his target. And it was in that strange moment of suspended time that the music came crashing in from behind the closed door, a screeching tune that almost made Shigure lose his balance and startled Onga's hand on the gun into shooting wide, allowing Shigure to thrust the *bokken* against Onga's throat.

The door banged open, armed Daitō-kai men pouring into the room and stopping at the sight in front of them, at the improbable sight of Shigure standing behind their captain and holding a *bokken* against his throat in a choking hold, while their boss grabbed the piece of wood with his two hands, the gun all but forgotten on the desk.

And then there came Sergeant Uehara, strolling into the room as if he owned the place, his wizened hand shoving gun barrels aside casually, a flushed Atsushi following on his heel and making a show of shutting down his cell phone.

"The American attachés are at the front door, sir," Atsushi said, and Shigure understood the awful music had come from his assistant's phone.

Shigure heard Onga chuckle. "Saved by *Madame Butterfly*," he mumbled. And Shigure could only chuckle in turn. Trust Onga to recognize an Italian opera on a cell phone ringtone while fighting for his life.

"Now gentlemen, if you would be so kind as to give me your weapons, I'm sure we can end this misunderstanding peacefully," Uehara said, with a clear emphasis on the word misunderstanding.

Shigure pitched his voice to be only heard by Onga. "Will you consider this a misunderstanding? No reprisals?"

"I will if you forget about the informant."

Shigure weighed his options. He knew Onga would never tell him who had warned them about Kotarō entering their territory, and killing the Daitō-kai captain would only start the war they'd managed to avoid so far. It would get Shigure killed too. Storming the place and surprising them all was one thing, but leaving it unharmed would require a miracle now that he had all the guns in the place trained on him. And he needed to be alive if he was ever to rescue Kenshin.

"Thank you, Matsunaga-wakagashira," Uehara said as he took the *bokken* from him. Then he retrieved the gun from the desk and nodded at Onga. "Thank you, Onga-wakagashira."

They both bowed to the old policeman like reprimanded schoolkids, matching smirks on their faces.

Onga fingered his bruised throat, thick fingers travelling down to touch the charm on its chain as if grateful for its timely intervention. "Next time you visit, Matsunaga-san, be sure to phone first. My men are a little loose on the trigger these days."

"I'll keep it in mind," Shigure said as he took the small vial from the desk and followed Uehara to the door, with Atsushi close on his heels. He was almost outside when he remembered. "Onga-san?"

"Hmm?"

"Where did you get that charm?"

Onga laughed. "Lucky, isn't it? A friend brought it from Jōkyō-ji temple. It's said to guarantee a long life."

"Yeah, I can see that."

As he turned to leave, he noticed Atsushi looking sick. He guessed entering a rival gang's headquarters wasn't supposed to be among a personal assistant's tasks, and it must be quite a shock to see his employer handle alcohol-preserved fingers with ease. But that was the state of things. His employer was a yakuza who knew when the time came to use a weapon and fight, and that little vial was all the hope he had left. He knew what the fingers on a corpse looked like, and this knuckle he now held had been torn from a living, suffering body. And he couldn't wait to put his own hands on the man who'd wielded the knife.

CHAPTER 29

HE WAS so cold. Pain should be hot, but it wasn't, or at least not the pain in his hand, freezing and pointed like a sharp icicle. Maybe it was because the man had tied his left wrist to the wall high above his head—to stop the bleeding, he supposed.

The cement walls and floor didn't feel so cold, though. Their porous surface was rather welcoming, if it weren't for the cuts on his skin. Ken smiled to himself. Now that he had tattoos and was missing a pinkie, he could be apprenticed to the Shinagawa like Kotarō, and even call someone like Shinya aniki. Yeah, that scary gangster would probably be a better big brother than his own brothers were.

He looked up to meet Kinosuke's eyes, and the concern he saw in them made Ken laugh aloud. There. Another big brother to worry about him. And by the look in his eyes, now he probably thought the gaijin had gone bat-shit crazy.

"I'm all right, Kinosuke-san," he said. "Just seeing the irony in all this."

He received a blank stare. Damn their captor for keeping Kinosuke gagged, though he could understand why the man would want to go without the yells. The Japanese language was not very rich in insults, but Kinosuke seemed to know them all and invent new ones as he went.

"I was thinking I look like a proper yakuza now," he tried to explain. "I mean, with these sort of tattoos and the—"

The way Kinosuke closed his eyes made Ken hurry to add, "I'm not trying to mock you or your people, I just—" And now Kinosuke was shaking his head furiously.

"I suppose that means you're not offended."

One nod.

"Okay. That's good. I have offended enough people as it is."

Kinosuke raised his brows in question.

"Well, I take it the man with the ice pick is not just some body-art aficionado, for one."

Eye roll.

"Yeah. Bad joke. But jokes aside, this seems quite personal to me. He hates me for some reason. Same as you did, though your reasons I can understand easily."

Ken waved a dismissive hand at Kinosuke's sheepish look.

"Don't worry, I know you don't hate me anymore. But the fact that you did makes me wonder if others in the Shinagawa consider me a stain on Shigure's reputation. I think Shigure himself sees me like that sometimes. He doesn't say a word, but I can feel he's ashamed of being seen with a gaijin, and a male gaijin to boot."

Ken snorted. "It only goes well because I'm short and skinny. I'll always look like a boy to Shigure's badass manly man. And as long as I look the part of Shigure's boy, it'll be all right. I can be ignored as some kind of fetish that only adds variety to Shigure's sex life. Nothing to worry about. Funny that my best friend Ryū would see it just the other way round, as if Shigure was my fetish, my own depraved way of taking a walk on the wild side. Christ. I'm babbling. I must be feverish."

Kinosuke frowned at him, and Ken couldn't resist teasing him. "Has anyone ever told you that you're a good listener?"

The eye roll he got in response made him chuckle. "Yeah, stupid gaijin, I know."

He sobered, feeling suddenly exhausted. "I hope you don't take it the wrong way, but I'm glad you are here with me." He paused, the seriousness in Kinosuke's eyes encouraging him to go on. "When I draw all those monsters for children's books, I find that scary things look much more interesting than the plain beautiful ones. But I guess I never knew what the real scary looked like. It's... ugly. And I don't like the way it makes me feel."

He let out a humorless laugh. "Yeah, I know, that's the point of it all. But I meant scary things should scare you, not make you feel...

dirty. And I cannot stop wondering if there's a reason why I should be made to feel like that, kind of ashamed too, you know?"

He closed his eyes, dreading what he would find in Kinosuke's expression if he looked now. Why in all hell had he gone and said that? He didn't even know he thought it until it poured out of his mouth like something foul he'd just eaten. It must be the weakened state he was in or the closeness to death. Yeah, that would do the trick nicely, realizing he'd die the kind of freakish death everyone expected from a freak like him.

He was startled out of his thoughts by the loud noises coming from Kinosuke's direction. Damn. He looked furious. Small wonder, after Ken had told him he was glad the man would die in this basement with him, with the gaijin everyone was ashamed to be associated with.

"I'm sorry, Kinosuke-san. I didn't mean... Shit, I just wish you didn't have to go through this, but—"

Kinosuke shook his head so hard Ken knew it must hurt.

"You're not sorry?"

Nod.

"You're not sorry to be here with me?"

Nod.

"You know we are going to die here, don't you?"

Nod.

He searched Kinosuke's eyes and saw no hint of fear in them. It made him remember what Shigure had told him about carps, about the calm, resigned way they faced death. "I'm honored I'll be dying with you, Kinosuke-san. You're a brave man."

Kinosuke acknowledged his words with a nod, but then his chin lifted slightly, pointing, and Ken had to fight the urge to look behind him, because he knew damn well they were alone in that basement.

"THERE'S no trace of him," Shinya was saying. "His old cronies haven't seen Kinosuke since he joined the Shinagawa, he hasn't been to his usual haunts lately, and he hasn't visited his family since last *Obon*. I informed all our affiliates that we're looking for his car, made them believe we didn't want it to be known that some petty thief had stolen a yakuza car, but that's all I could do short of telling them we're hunting Kinosuke down."

"Maybe we should. Tell them, I mean."

Shinya's eyes widened. "But, boss, that'd be a death sentence for Kinosuke. If we're after him, it'd only be because he's run afoul of the Shinagawa, and the smaller gangs would be falling all over themselves to bring us his head."

Shigure crossed the room in two steps to face Shinya. "So what? Do you think I care after what he's done to Kenshin? Do you think *I* won't take his head if I see him first?"

His man didn't step back, didn't look down. "Kinosuke would never cut another man's finger. No true yakuza would do it."

"What if he forced Kenshin to do it himself?"

Shinya shook his head stubbornly. "It would lose all its meaning. Giving up something irreplaceable only makes sense when you know why you're doing it, when you're willing to do it in atonement for something you did wrong."

"Maybe Kinosuke doesn't give a damn about yakuza traditions. Why would he, when he's willing to go against his leader over some stupid jealousy?"

"He has a quick temper, but that doesn't mean he's not a true yakuza at heart. You know he's only young and misguided, but he's not devious, and that"—Shinya pointed to the vial on Shigure's desk—"is beyond devious. That's fucking sick."

Shigure sighed. "Yeah. No matter how mad he makes me, I can't imagine Kinosuke grabbing Kenshin's hand and cutting off his finger." He rounded the desk and sat heavily on his chair. "And more than that, I'm sure he wouldn't have told Onga about the sword. He might have done it to punish me, but he knew Kotarō'd be hurt, and he would have never allowed that."

Shinya nodded. "He cares about the kid."

"I know. The problem is that without Kinosuke we have nothing, nowhere else to look. I believe Onga when he says the Daitō-kai are not involved, and if it had been a kidnapping, and they were trying to disguise it as a yakuza hit, they wouldn't have sent the finger to me, but to Kenshin's father, to force him to pay. So what have we left?"

Dejected, he covered his face with his hands. It was maddening, having proof that Kenshin was still alive and not being able to do anything. And maybe that was the true intention behind the sending of the vial, to mock Shigure's attempts, to prove the Shinagawa were powerless to protect their own.

"Have you heard of Jōkyō-ji temple?"

The astonished silence he received made Shigure lift his head to look at Shinya. The scarred man was blinking at his unexpected change of subject, and he himself wasn't very sure why he'd remembered Onga's charm right now—most probably because he could certainly use a little luck.

"You know where it is?"

"Yeah, why?" Shinya asked, as if he expected Shigure's to be a trick question.

"The charm Kotarō found at the Haihīru came from that temple. Whose territory is that?"

"A minor gang's, the Terada-kai. We have some kind of agreement with them."

"Hmm. The charm could belong to that girl, Kei, but I very much doubt it would be considered fashionable by a woman her age."

Shinya snorted. "Naw. Charms are for old geezers and uncool thugs."

"That's what I thought. So we can assume it belonged to the man who beat Kei." Shigure's face fell. "Even that doesn't mean the guy was one of the Terada. Onga was wearing one of those charms, too, and anyone can get a charm from that temple, yakuza or no."

Atsushi's loud voice came to them from the other side of the door.

"You can't enter there, Nishimura-san. I have to—"

An angry voice answered right before the door slid open none too gently.

"Like hell I can't." And then the owner of the voice was bowing respectfully to Shigure like someone with a personality disorder. "Pardon the intrusion, Matsunaga-san."

"Nishimura Ryū-san. I don't remember inviting you to my home."

"I'm sorry if you think I've offended you, but we must put our differences aside. Kenshin is in danger."

"Is he now."

"Please, Matsunaga-san. Let me help."

"You can leave your card with my assistant on your way out. He'll let you know if we find something for you to do."

Nishimura seemed to hesitate between begging and cursing, and Shigure was about to sign for Shinya to kick him out when he remembered something.

"The credit card they used in the Haihīru, wasn't it stolen in the Terada-kai's turf?"

Shinya's eyes widened. "You're right. It's too much of a coincidence."

"That's what I think," Shigure said, pushing the chair back and standing. "Let's pay a visit to the Terada oyabun."

"Are you going to see Shinozaki-san?"

They both turned to look at Nishimura in astonishment. "You know the man?"

"Yeah, I play golf with him, why?"

Shigure exchanged a knowing look with Shinya before patting Nishimura's back with a smile on his lips. "Well, Nishimura-san. It seems there's something you can do, after all."

CHAPTER 30

"Kenshin-san."

He didn't want to open his eyes. It hurt. Everywhere.

"Kenshin-san!"

Christ. Why was Kinosuke yelling? His head hurt. And everything else from the head down. Wait. Wasn't Kinosuke gagged? Ken opened his eyes, and the world exploded in a sharp white pain that kept pulsing in his temples even when he lowered his lids to shut it out.

"Please, Kenshin-san. You need to stay awake."

"*Itai*," he mumbled, as if Kinosuke couldn't see that he hurt.

"I know. That motherfucker should have given you another shot."

Now he did open his eyes, trying to focus the blur in front of him that should be Kinosuke. "Another?" he only managed to say, his tongue feeling three sizes too big to fit inside his mouth.

"Yeah. He gave you something right after he… after the… you know."

"The *yubitsume*," he supplied. Yeah. He knew the fucking name. He was stupid enough to believe he'd felt perfectly fine after having one of his knuckles hacked off, but hey, he knew how to give the whole mess a Japanese name. Go him.

"Here, have some water."

He reached for the bottle with his left hand and found it shackled to the wall behind him. Kinosuke's arm was stretched as far as it could go, but Ken still had to use his other hand to grab it.

"He's chained you again," he said before drinking from the bottle as if he could get drunk on mineral water.

"Yeah. The bastard has a thing for ropes and chains."

For that and for other, less normal things, but Ken didn't want to talk about those. Whatever the man had given him had made him babble like a parrot before, but now that the high was long gone, he felt broken, and so tired he only wanted to close his eyes and never open them again. What was there to look forward to, anyway?

"Don't fall asleep."

He tried to glare at Kinosuke, and found that he couldn't, not after seeing those black eyes look at him in desperation, begging him to stay. Damn. He wished he was alone, wished he could just die.

"He kicked you in the head. You're not supposed to sleep when your head is hurt."

Bet Kinosuke had experience with that. He must have spent every day at school with scratches and bruises of every kind. And after he left school, it probably only kept escalating into knife, sword, or even bullet wounds.

"Sit."

"What?"

Ken patted the cement floor. He didn't want to have to crane his neck to look at Kinosuke, and the man had better start talking if he wanted to keep him awake.

"Oh, right. Sit."

Kinosuke sat with his legs crossed, the chain rattling as he moved, but then he simply watched Ken, as if waiting for him to say something. Ken fought the urge to roll his eyes only because he knew it would hurt.

"How did he chain you?" he asked. "Don't look at me as if I were daft. He only shackles your ankle, so how does he prevent you from attacking him?"

"He uses another rope and takes the end with him when he finishes chaining me. Then he just pulls, and the knots go loose, and he's too far away for me to reach him."

"Shit."

"Yeah. The bastard knows the ropes."

Ken looked up. Had Kinosuke just made a joke?

"Not funny, I know."

Ken smiled. "It wasn't bad—for a first joke."

Kinosuke let out a surprised laugh. "You're mean, Kenshin-san."

"Yeah, bad gaijin." And maybe that was why he always ended up being the one who was punished. The man handled Kinosuke with care, with respect, almost. He had even let him keep his clothes, though Kinosuke didn't seem to realize how humiliating it was for Ken to be naked. It was a true Japanese thing, having no problem with nudity, but somehow the man had guessed it wouldn't be like that for Ken.

"Kenshin-san?"

God. He was so tired. "I'm fine. Just thinking."

Kinosuke gave him a sheepish look. "If you're thinking how the fucker manages to tie me in the first place, well, he just puts a knife to your throat."

He had to close his eyes. He didn't want to hear any more, didn't need to have someone else's death on his conscience, even if Kinosuke had wanted him dead what seemed like ages ago.

"Don't feel guilty. You were trying to get us out of here," Kinosuke said, and it took Ken a moment to understand what he meant.

"Oh, yeah. That was when he caught me climbing the stairs." He frowned. "And you couldn't get to him because he got to me first."

"You were injured, and weak, and he had a knife. You couldn't possibly—"

"I know," Ken interrupted, feeling a hint of hope, "but look at me now, Kinosuke-san."

He moved the shackled wrist to make Kinosuke see his point.

"You're chained."

"Exactly. To *this* wall."

And then Kinosuke realized what he was trying to say. "There's no way he can reach you without getting near me first." Now there was a big feral grin on Kinosuke's lips. "I'm gonna give that bastard a piece of my mind. You're not daft at all, Kenshin-san."

He chuckled. "Thank you—I suppose."

They smiled at each other for a moment and then seemed to sober at the same time. Ken finally had to say what they were both thinking. "He will expect us to try something like this."

"No, he thinks he's already broken us." But Kinosuke sounded as if he were trying to convince himself.

Ken shook his head. "He only left you that much leeway so that you could take care of me while he's out, but he'll have anticipated your attacking him."

"Yeah? And what's he gonna do to stop me?"

"Pull a gun on you?"

All the defiance left Kinosuke in a rush, but he still tried to argue some more. "He's never used a gun before."

"He didn't need it to deal with a stupid gaijin."

They were silent long enough for Ken to remember how much in pain he was, how tiring and hopeless everything was. Maybe it was true his head was badly hurt, and if he were lucky, he would close his eyes and fall into a coma, go from nothing to nothing in a pleasant, dreamless sleep.

"Kenshin-san?"

"Hmm?"

"Don't fall asleep, damn it!"

He opened his eyes, startled by the note of panic in Kinosuke's voice.

"Just don't, okay?" Kinosuke was trying to sound firm, but there was fear in his eyes. In a way, it was reassuring to know someone dreaded losing him, but right now Ken could have done without the responsibility it implied. He was too exhausted, too hurt to be strong for anyone else's sake.

"Let me sleep a few minutes." He forced himself to smile convincingly. "I promise I'll wake up when you call me."

Kinosuke took a deep breath. "Okay. Sleep. I'll keep watch."

Ken nodded as he closed his eyes. Yeah. He could pretend he was gathering his strength to keep fighting, and Kinosuke could pretend he'd be able to do something to help him.

"OHAYŌ gozaim... I'm Nishimura R... yu... expecting me."

There was so much static that Shigure had to guess half the words Nishimura was saying. Blue eyes met his. "It'll sound better soon."

Shigure nodded to the blond legal attaché. Even if the reception didn't improve, he couldn't complain. The Americans had gone out of their way to help, provided all the equipment and stayed in the van to record the conversation, illegal though it may be. They weren't planning on using whatever was said in court. It was just meant to lure the enemy out of his lair, make him show his true colors. And Shigure didn't want to think it'd be their last chance at finding Kenshin.

"It's good to see you, Shinozaki-san. How are you these days?"

"I'm fine, Nishimura. Come sit down."

It didn't escape Shigure the different way they addressed each other, the Terada oyabun clearly establishing his rank by adding a more familiar suffix to Nishimura's name than the polite "san," and ordering him about without regard to his position of heir to one of the major construction corporations.

Now there was a lot of noise, people entering the room, the clink and splash of something being served to the two men—most likely sake—and then the door sliding closed. Soon enough, Nishimura embarked in the right amount of pleasantries—about golf, the oyabun's family, and even the weather—required to show respect.

"We'll run out of tape if he keeps that up," Campbell whined.

Shigure tried not to sound patronizing. "He's speaking with the equivalent of a company's president. If he cuts short on the good manners, Shinozaki'll find him unusually eager and suspect something."

"No offense intended, but I expected you people to be less exquisite in your manners."

"You mean we being gangsters and all."

Campbell shrugged and his partner swatted the back of his head, to Shigure's amusement.

"You'll have to forgive him," Bradley said. "He grew up in a foster home and never got to watch *The Godfather*."

Shigure laughed. "Well, we're slightly different from the Sicilian Mafia—no matter what Onga thinks—but I get your point. Every organization has its own protocol to keep order within its ranks."

"And how is your family's business going, Nishimura?"

"There," Shigure said, "he's giving Nishimura an opening."

"Not so well. We try the best we can, but the times are bad for everyone."

"Isn't that too blatant a lie? Nishimura's company is pretty far from red numbers," Bradley said.

"You don't go bragging about your own success in any negotiation here," Shigure explained. "Both parties know exactly the other's worth, but it's customary to pretend neither of them is doing too well."

"Yeah, these times are making it hard to make ends meet for my people too."

"See what I mean? The Terada-kai is a small gang, but their businesses are quite lucrative. They're not exactly going through a bad patch."

"I get it."

"It's sad. I see the big companies leaving behind their old suppliers to make alliances with other big companies, just looking to assure their margins."

"I hear you, Nishimura. There's no loyalty left."

"Exactly. My father is always repeating that in hard times is when the small businesses show their mettle, when loyalty produces its best returns."

"Your father is a wise man. It'll do you good to follow his advice."

"I agree. You know, I look at the biggest companies and see that no matter how many deals they make, they always seem to be on the brink of war."

"Hmm. I don't think that'll happen anytime soon. A united front gives them a solid advantage."

"They've lost me," Bradley said.

"Yeah, what on earth are they talking about?" Campbell asked, throwing his hands in the air in frustration. "They sound like the *Financial Times*."

"The Terada-kai is affiliated to the Shinagawa-gumi," Shigure explained. "They're the small suppliers to one of the two biggest conglomerates, the Shinagawa and the Daitō-kai. Since Nishimura is trying to tempt the oyabun into an underhand business, he has to make a show of applauding the loyalty between small parties—Terada and Nishimura—when the big companies—Shinagawa and Daitō-kai—are about to fight for their profits and abandon the smaller allies to their fate."

"Jesus. We're so out of our league here."

"Well, I've heard a lot of rumors, Shinozaki-san. According to them, the two biggest players are just about to part company. There seems to be growing bad blood between them."

"The street is always brimming with rumors. You shouldn't believe all you hear."

"I don't usually, but I know there have been some incidents that might escalate into something bigger."

"Bah. Just scuffles. It'll only make their ties more solid."

"He doesn't seem to be taking the bait," Bradley said.

Shigure frowned. "It's true. He should at least let Nishimura go on, see where he's leading."

"You must be right. It's just the first time I've heard people talk about the way those companies keep Koreans and burakumin in executive posts."

"Yeah, I've heard that too, Nishimura. It's really bad."

"Here we go."

Shigure didn't want to feel relieved that the leader of a supposedly traditional yakuza gang had forgotten their time-honored open-mindedness about their recruits' ancestry. It was another sign of the times they were living in, but if it meant that Shinozaki was the man they were after, the *oyabun* could spit on Shigure's ancestors for all he cared.

Nishimura sounded relieved too. *"That's what I thought, and what brought me here to talk to you in the first place. I knew you'd understand."*

"I see your point. It might be a good time for the small suppliers to make some alliances."

"My sentiments exactly."

"Yeah, if rumors of that sort are so widespread, it can only mean that someone outside our circles is pulling the strings."

"That's not what he should be saying, is it?"

Shigure started pacing in the small space. "No, it isn't, and if Nishimura doesn't get his meaning and opens his mouth to say what he really thinks about burakumin and Koreans, we'll need to pull him out of there fast."

"Shit."

"Outside our circles." Nishimura repeated it without intonation, as if reflecting on what Shinozaki had said. It would gain him time, as long as the oyabun felt like explaining.

"Hai, outside."

No such luck. Nishimura was silent now, probably bobbing his head in agreement and wondering what the hell he should say next. There was the sound of a liquid being poured and more silence.

"God. Why doesn't he say anything? Shinozaki is going to smell something's wrong."

"It's better this way. He might think Nishimura is just waiting for him to go on, showing deference."

Campbell didn't look convinced, but finally Shinozaki's voice came through the speakers. *"I've been wondering, Nishimura."*

"Hai?"

"You know, all these international police conferences that have been taking place here...."

"Uh-huh."

"They must be making Japanese cops lose face, all those gaijin experts telling them how big a problem organized crime is and thinking our people are the same rabble as the riffraff they have back home."

"Very true."

"So I believe they're the ones spreading those rumors, shaking some trees to get the ripe fruit to fall."

"Shit."

"Fuck, he's not our man."

Shigure slumped against the van's side. He should have known even the greediest yakuza oyabun wouldn't have handled the whole business like that. They did things in a certain way, and any gang with aspirations would have challenged its rivals openly, not try to pit them against each other in what would appear to everyone as the coward's way.

"Should we get Nishimura out of there?"

Shigure didn't even move. "It's okay. He's not in danger."

"But he'll have to go through with his offer."

He shrugged. "Yeah, well, he might make some money out of it yet."

The two agents looked at him dubiously, but Shigure couldn't find it in him to care. He just pushed himself off the metal wall and climbed out of the van, closing the door quietly behind him. There was nothing left for him to do here—or anywhere else, for that matter.

He thought he had already resigned himself to losing Kenshin, but found he couldn't just let go. It felt as if some vital organ had been removed from his body, something that he had taken for granted all this time, and now the rest of the pieces didn't fit together quite right. All the normal functions and movements of his body were awkward, rough, every small muscle and ligament requiring his conscious effort to keep working, even breathing turned into a voluntary act that needed his full attention.

He felt like an invalid, his feet barely managing to take him two blocks before they made him stumble, his knees hitting the pavement hard. And then he just stayed there, kneeling in the deserted street, the pain crawling up his body until it reached his throat and exploded in a mad howl, something that sounded like rage and hurt squeezed into the two syllables of a name.

CHAPTER 31

HE WOULD have thought no sound could reach the basement, but maybe because he'd been waiting for it, Ken could clearly hear the slam of a car door and, after a few moments, the other, more distinctive sound of the trap door to the basement.

He turned to Kinosuke, his heart racing in his chest. The yakuza looked like a big hungry cat about to jump a mouse, and it made Ken feel like throwing his head back and laughing, but he was too frightened for even that small movement, only his lips coming up in what must look like a deranged smile.

Kinosuke responded in kind, a feral grin turning his features into something scarier than his usual murderous glare. Yeah, that was the difference between them. Ken would have pissed his pants if he still had them on, because he knew his death would not be an easy one if they failed to stop the man, while Kinosuke was just jonesing for a little action, his mind completely focused on the task at hand, the idea of what might come afterward never even grazing his thoughts.

As the bird head appeared in the crude light of the basement, Ken couldn't help thinking the man with the tengu mask looked like every illustration of death he'd seen over the years, something vaguely resembling humanity in a way that made humanity impossible, the mighty reaper looking always evil because its very existence mocked any pretense at human worth.

When the man reached the bottom of the stairs, Ken made a show of trying to stand, and Kinosuke hurried to help him. The tengu mask turned from one to the other, and the man shouted.

"Stay where you are! And you, stay down!"

Both he and Kinosuke spoke at the same time, their voices loud as they kept moving to increase the confusion.

"He's gonna die if you don't do something!"

"You can't keep me here!"

The bird head swung crazily to keep them in sight, and the man took some angry steps forward, but he still wasn't where they wanted him, so Ken pushed himself up, ignoring the pain, letting all his fears come out to make his begging even more believable.

"Please, you have to let me go. I have money, and I can get more from my father. He's a senator, and he can—"

The man's hollow laughter threw Ken off kilter. Had he seen through their awkward scheme?

"Your father? He won't give a dime for a piece of shit like you."

Ken blanched, his fear turning into a different kind of dread.

"What? You truly expected your father to pay a ransom for you?"

He found it difficult to breathe. He wasn't his father's favorite son, but he'd never defied him openly, never stood in his way, never even used his money or his name from the moment he'd been able to make a living for himself. There wasn't much love lost between them, but it would have never occurred to Ken that his father would not hesitate in sentencing him to a sure death.

"Poor kid. You thought your father loved you." The man clicked his tongue in disapproval. "And what did you do to earn his love, huh? Should have thought about that before you started whoring for the yakuza, should have thought a man can bring his whole family down in one single careless move."

Ken was so blinded by the contempt in that muffled voice that he didn't realize the man had moved so close that he could see the angry glitter in the eyes behind the mask. And then he didn't have to think about what they'd planned, hurt and betrayal fueling the rage that exploded out of him in a roar as his free hand shot forward and hit the man square on the jaw.

He stood there trembling, watching the man stumble, the mask slanted over his face and letting show the thin line of a bitter mouth that screamed in surprise as a strong arm pressed against his windpipe.

Ken lunged forward to help Kinosuke, but the two struggling men had moved out of his reach, and he cursed loudly, fear and pain drowned in the anger that made him pace about like a caged lion, just waiting for his chance to jump at his captor.

The man was obviously trying to roll them over so that Kinosuke had to fight the pull of his chain, but Kinosuke shoved his shackled ankle between the man's legs, using the chain to anchor himself while he kept the pressure on the man's throat.

The man's movements were growing desperate, his breath coming out in frantic pants as Kinosuke's chokehold tightened even more. And just when it all seemed about to be over, the string holding the mask in place snapped, and the plastic tengu face hit the cement floor with a clatter.

Ken's eyes widened, a name frozen on his lips. It couldn't be. This couldn't be the man who had tied and tortured him, the man who hated him as if Ken had only been born to ruin his life. It couldn't possibly be.

He shook his head at the incongruity, expecting reality to change somehow, but it was only solidifying into the fate they'd tried to escape, all their chances lost the moment Kinosuke caught a glimpse of the now-bared face and his hold wavered, just an instant, just an inch, but just enough for an arm to move, the elbow thrown back into Kinosuke's ribs.

From then on, everything went down fast. Kinosuke let go even more, groaning in pain, and there was a glint of steel, Ken's warning ignored because there was no time left, no room for Kinosuke to move away. The yakuza didn't cry out. He only grunted as he curled up protectively on himself, a knife sticking out of his right shoulder, kicks and curses raining down on him until all was silent, the three of them frozen in a tableau vivant featuring the ill-fated yakuza, the despised gaijin, and the vengeful spirit of ancient wrongs.

SHIGURE stood in front of the door to his den, watching the slippers on his feet and trying to remember when he had changed into them. Or gotten back to the house, for that matter.

It was morning all right, but he couldn't say what time. He'd spent the night drifting from back street to back street, searching for places with storage rooms, wine cellars, broom closets, anything with four concrete walls and metal shelves along them.

Sometime around dawn his phone had run out of battery, and he'd decided to go home, check on his men, charge the damn thing, and go back out to keep searching in that completely absurd way. It was all he could do now, and he wasn't going to stop until he visited every single sample of bare concrete architecture in Tokyo.

"Matsunaga-sama?"

He turned his head to see Atsushi standing beside him, his arms full of envelopes of every size and color. No small packages, though.

"What happened to your face?"

Atsushi ducked his head in embarrassment. "I cut myself shaving."

"People use a single Band-Aid for that purpose, you know," Shigure said, almost managing to feel amusement at the sight of the three adhesive bands that piled on top of each other on one side of Atsushi's face.

"It wouldn't stop bleeding."

He could imagine it perfectly, his prim assistant cursing like a fiend in front of his mirror as blood came out of a minute cut and threatened to mar his proper attire or make him—God forbid—late for work. He actually looked a little harried, though Shigure guessed he himself didn't look much better after a night wandering the streets.

As Atsushi pushed the door open for him, Shigure noticed his assistant's slacks had too many wrinkles, the hems in need of a good brushing. Hadn't he been to his place at all? He was one of the few men who didn't live in the house—since he wasn't a yakuza—and Shigure always sent him home early for the same reason. Loyalty to the Shinagawa couldn't be reduced to a few extra hours of a salaryman's time. It was a life commitment that Atsushi had not shown any interest in making, and so his presence outside of his working hours would have felt like an intrusion.

"Where did you spend the night?" he asked casually as he walked over to his desk.

Atsushi flinched as if Shigure had slapped him, gripping the envelopes he was carrying as a shield. "I... I was at home, sir."

If he hadn't been so bone-tired, Shigure might have found the situation funny. His prissy assistant was probably having an affair of some kind, something so utterly adventurous that his staid façade was beginning to crack. And maybe he'd thought it'd go unnoticed in the hectic atmosphere of the house.

Shigure opened the first drawer of his desk, the one he used to store all the gadgets he rarely wore on him, including his phone charger and his semiautomatic. The clatter of envelopes hitting the floor made him look up sharply.

"When did you find out?"

Shigure blinked at his assistant's harsh tone, at the way he was looking warily from him to the gun in the drawer, all his formality left behind as he addressed Shigure with something akin to resentment.

"You haven't been exactly careful lately," he said, trying to bait Atsushi into telling him what it was that Shigure had found out. Maybe the man had been stealing from them. That would surely explain the Porsche he drove and the quality of his clothes.

Now his assistant was looking at him with clear disdain, his usual respectful attitude dropped as easily as the envelopes he'd been carrying. "You seemed too busy looking for your precious gaijin." He shrugged. "Not that anyone in this house pays any attention to me. You're too full of your own importance to notice those outside the yakuza—unless they fall prey to your games, that is."

"And who is it that fell prey to our games, someone close to you?"

By the way Atsushi stepped back, Shigure knew he'd hit some nerve. Whatever this was, it wasn't about money, but revenge.

"You never even asked, damn you," Atsushi said. "You and all the other brainless thugs just took me in because the oyabun said I was to work for you. And you never even wondered why a man like me had to work as an underpaid assistant."

A man like me. The little shit thought himself so interesting, so above the men around him, the men who had never had any other chance in life but to join the yakuza to become someone respected, even if that respect came mostly from fear. And this spoiled brat had the nerve to complain about having to work in an office to pay his debts when he could have been sent to one of their construction or waste-disposal companies? Would he have found a job on his own? Did he even have the qualifications to work in something that wasn't a convenience store?

"You were in the oyabun's debt, so I never asked what for out of politeness to you. Besides, you think I'd be interested in your dirty little secrets? I've never cared what stupid rich kids like you do to enjoy your worthless selves."

"It wasn't me who owed your fucking boss!" Atsushi yelled. "And do you know what I did to enjoy my worthless self? I studied for the university entrance exams, every moment of the day and a good part of the night. Because my future was settled. I was to succeed my father at the head of the family business. I was to inherit the house, the company, the family properties in and outside the city. I was going to be the head of the clan, and I wanted to make my family proud."

"Until your father started gambling your future away," Shigure said. "Is that your sob story? You grew up rich until your father ruined your family, and then you had to work to pay his debts? Excuse me if I don't cry for you."

Shigure had never seen the man so angry. In fact, he'd never seen him show any kind of emotion except barely suppressed contempt. It figured. He must have felt that he'd been robbed of his brilliant prospects in life, resentment eating at him every time he used the honorific to address his boss—his yakuza boss—working for a meager salary in a disreputable business, being called Atsushi when he should have received all the honors of a company's president.

"You can't imagine what it was like," Atsushi said, his hands clenched into fists, his face flushed with anger. "How could you? You grew up in the mud, and you probably don't even know who your father was, but I do. My father was a respected man, my family one whose descent could be traced back to the days of Emperor Kimmei. We had a responsibility to our country and the means to assume it, and year after year we proved the strength of our bloodline with our full commitment to Japan's prosperity. But then my father made a mistake, just one single misstep, and your people fell on him like vultures, pinning him down where he lay, making sure he would never stand on his own two feet again."

Shigure reined in his anger because he'd heard it so many times in so many different versions that it mostly left him indifferent, the way people reverted to blaming others for their own mistakes. He wasn't interested in victims and their grand justifications, but if his personal assistant had felt wronged all this time, he might have been using his position to enact his petty revenge against the Shinagawa. And what better way to do it than slipping information to the Daitō-kai? That would explain why Onga knew about the sword, and that would certainly explain why the Korean had been so reluctant to reveal the identity of his informant.

"And what mistake did your eminent father make?" Shigure said, letting all the contempt he felt weigh his words to force a reaction from Atsushi. "Did he use our sōkaiya experts to bring down the competition? Or was it more personal? Did he want someone dealt with discreetly?"

"My father was an honest man!"

"Was he, now? So he needed the yakuza services for what exactly?"

Atsushi hesitated. "He... he hadn't been himself for some time after my mother died."

"Uh-huh. Let me guess, he took to drinking and lost control of his finances."

"It wasn't like that. He could always hold his liquor. He was used to long nights out with his business associates—"

"But he started drinking on his own, didn't he?"

Atsushi glared at him, his lips compressed in a thin white line. "It would have been all right. He would have moved on easily if he hadn't met that woman, that damn gaijin whore."

Shigure froze, the memory of Kenshin spitting those very words to Shigure's face suddenly filling his mind and shutting out everything else. It was like removing the bottom card from a card house, the whole flimsy building falling down with such a deafening sound that Shigure stopped listening to Atsushi's pitiful story to pay attention to what really mattered. There was more than resentment in that strained voice. There was pure and simple hatred—the kind of emotion that would drive a man to risk everything just to get rid of the nagging feeling of injustice that would only keep growing day after day, year after year, until there was no room for anything else, no thought, no other emotion to keep blood pumping to the center of a lifeless heart.

For the first time since Atsushi had come to work for him, Shigure really looked at his assistant and wondered how had he possibly ignored what was so plainly reflected in the man's eyes, how could he have mistaken contempt for good manners, how hadn't he seen the hard edge to those narrowed pupils.

Here was a man whose single goal in life was to get even, a man whose manicured fingers would kill without a second thought, a man who had nothing to lose, and Shigure knew exactly how to deal with that kind of man, just as he knew there was no reasoning with a rabid dog. But he still needed to get the man to talk, to tell him where Kenshin was.

Careful to keep his face blank and his gaze on Atsushi, he inched closer to the open drawer. For once, he was glad he kept his gun loaded in anticipation of a less-than-likely attack to the house, but it wouldn't do to threaten his assistant with it. Atsushi didn't fear death, but he would dread failure, so Shigure hoped his laughter sounded convincing.

"Oh please, don't tell me you went to all that trouble just because your father was about to give you a gaijin stepmother. What are you, Cinderella?"

"Shut up."

He laughed harder, watching Atsushi's knuckles turn white, his jaw so tightly closed that Shigure could see his veins throbbing. "That's why you beat the girl at the Haihīru? Yeah, I bet that's what happened. You probably planned a minor theft to blame it on the Daitō-kai, but you couldn't resist hitting the woman because she made you feel as weak as your father. Or was it because you couldn't fuck her? Did she pity you because you couldn't act like a man with a simple whore?"

"Shut up!"

Shigure slammed the drawer shut and saw Atsushi's eyes widen. He hoped that sent the clear message that he didn't consider his assistant a threat, that now that he knew it was him behind all the trouble, Shigure found his little schemes inconsequential.

"Yeah. That must have been it. You hadn't the balls to speak up to our oyabun, so when the whore took pity on you, it was easy to act like a girl and slap her face." He smirked with all the contempt he could muster. "Is that why you kidnapped Kenshin? Because you wanted to know how it feels to be fucked by a gaijin?"

That seemed to do the trick, Atsushi stepping forward, his face contorted with the urge to strike back at Shigure. "I'm not a dirty little fag like your gaijin boy! You should have heard him moan when I clamped his tits and shoved a dildo up his ass, should have seen him come again and again in spite of the cock ring."

To laugh then was the most difficult thing Shigure had ever done, but he did it, shoved the anger down, made his voice even sound amused, forced himself to leer. "Yeah. That one has always been a slut."

And for the first time, he saw Atsushi hesitate, doubt flashing in his eyes for a second before he tried to regain his balance. "Don't pretend you don't care. I was there when you got his finger in the mail."

"Well, I must admit you got me frightened there. It was one thing to enjoy myself with a good fuck, but man, I was not prepared to be extradited to an American jail for a gaijin, tight ass or no. The little shit should have told me he was the son of a senator. I would have kept my paws off him."

Atsushi was looking at him in something close to shock, so he decided to push a little further. "And why did you chop his finger, anyway?" Shigure said it grinning, as if he found it the funniest thing he'd been told in a long time. "He must have given you a hard time cleaning the mess. I bet he soiled himself, and your neighbors must have come knocking down your door about the racket."

"I'm not that stupid. There are no neighbors around the—" Atsushi stopped, a smile lifting the corners of his thin lips. "Is that what you were trying to do, pretending you didn't care to get me to talk? You're not as dumb as you look, I have to give you that."

Shigure didn't bother hiding his rage anymore. Atsushi hadn't fallen for his little game, and there was nothing left to do but to force the confession out of him in whatever way he could manage. As if he was reading his mind, Atsushi asked, "So what are you going to do now? You know you can't kill me if you want to find your gaijin."

Shigure let his grin show teeth. "Oh, I'll be very careful not to kill you. You know how many bones a human body has?" He started to walk around the desk, his assistant retreating with every step he took. "And you know how many you can break before the person dies?"

Atsushi looked from him to the door, and Shigure prayed there was someone in the house who hadn't gone out to look for Kenshin, someone at least manning the outer gate in case his assistant outran him. If Atsushi made it to the street, everything would be lost.

Shigure took a cautious step forward, watching for the exact moment when Atsushi would turn to run for the door, both of them measuring the distance, time frozen as they weighed their chances. And just when Shigure was about to move, the door slid open, and Kotarō stepped in, his voice ringing too loudly in the charged silence inside the office.

"I found her, boss!"

Atsushi turned sharply, his face the picture of outrage until his gaze traveled behind Kotarō and his eyes widened almost comically.

"That's him!" a woman's voice cried from the door. And then all was chaos.

Atsushi shoved his hand into the inner pocket of his jacket as if searching for a gun, and Shigure lunged for his own gun in the desk drawer, but before he could even pull it out, the sound of a shot echoed through the room. He turned in time to see Atsushi's body crumpling to the floor in a heap.

"Are you all right, boss?" Tachibana stood by the door, his semiautomatic still trained on Atsushi.

Shigure cursed, ignoring his man, his attention completely focused on Atsushi's lying form, on the slight rise and fall of his chest. He walked over to his assistant's side, crouching beside him.

There was a ruckus at the door, more people coming in at the sound of the gun, but Shigure ignored every other voice except Atsushi's.

"Just… like my father," he was muttering. "Felled by… a whore."

Shigure saw the blood spreading over the white shirt and knew there was no time left. "Where's Kenshin?"

Atsushi stared blankly at him.

"Where is Kenshin?" he yelled, shaking Atsushi's arm. But his assistant only looked up at him, a hateful smirk turning his already pale face into a mask of contempt.

"You'll never… find them."

Atsushi's eyes glazed over, his pupils dilated to absorb the light they'd never see, his lips fixed in a rictus that would forever mock Shigure's attempts at finding the only thing he cared about.

CHAPTER 32

KINOSUKE'S gaze traveled one more time from the key at his feet, to the katana a few steps away, to Kenshin-san's lying form. It was all he could do, move his eyes in that maddening circle and breathe through his nose, careful not to move any other part of his body.

Atsushi. That fucking prissy son of a bitch. The boss should have never brought a piece of shit like him to work for the Shinagawa, whatever the oyabun said. But no, he always obeyed the supreme leader, always bowed his head and submitted.

Kinosuke closed his eyes. That was how things worked. That was what made the Shinagawa so powerful. Matsunaga had never liked Atsushi to begin with—he hadn't even allowed the fucker to bunk in the house with the men—but the boss had done what he had to do, like he always did. And Kinosuke wouldn't have found himself in this situation if he'd listened to his boss. He wouldn't be about to die in a filthy basement if he had.

One of the ropes tugged at his neck, and he opened his eyes in panic. Shit. He must stop thinking crazy stuff, or he would hang himself. Fucking Atsushi. People thought yakuza were an evil bunch, but it was always the uptight, quiet sort who had the most twisted minds. You fucked with a yakuza, and you were dead, but with bastards like Atsushi, you'd wish you'd never been born.

Kinosuke could tell the sicko had been enjoying himself. Even as screwed as he'd been after Atsushi beat the shit out of him, he could still see that disgusting little smirk while the fucker tied him, and heard Atsushi laugh when he wrapped the rope around Kinosuke's neck. Shit. He could even smell the man's arousal, and he was sure Atsushi didn't even go for men.

The way the bastard had tied Kinosuke could have been great for sex, his right leg bent backwards and held up in the air by a rope tied to a hook on the ceiling. The position would have exposed his endowments if he'd been naked, but Atsushi wasn't interested in that. He'd only done it to force Kinosuke to stand on one leg, his body tilting forward to compensate and forcing most of his weight to lie on the two ropes on his upper body. Except those two ropes weren't tied around Kinosuke's chest, as they should've been if this was a normal *shibari* pose.

The two final ropes went around his neck like a fucking cozy muffler, and then up to different hooks on the ceiling. If he so much as sneezed, he would hang himself, though he couldn't quite work out how he was going to sneeze with a gag in his mouth.

"Shit."

Kinosuke had to smile around the gag. That was Kenshin-san waking up. The crazy gaijin cursed as much as a yakuza. And the way he'd hurled insults at Atsushi after Atsushi had stabbed Kinosuke and started raining kicks on him.... That had been incredible. Where on earth had he learned to speak like a Japanese trucker?

"Oh fuck, Kinosuke."

Yeah. The guy was smart too. He'd taken in the situation in a second, those funny eyes going from Kinosuke's neck to his leg and then right down to the key and the katana on the floor. And now of course, he was getting up to test the length of the chain shackling his ankle.

He swayed a little, cursing a bit more under his breath. That coward Atsushi had had to threaten to kill Kinosuke if Kenshin-san didn't keep still, just to be able to give the angry gaijin the shot that put him out. He bet the fucker's jaw was now a brilliant purple from the American's fist.

The chain was long enough to pick up the katana, but not the key that would have set Kenshin-san free. The gaijin studied the blade carefully, wincing as his injured left hand closed around the handle.

"At least it's a good sword, and well kept too. The motherfucker must have stolen it from Shigure," he said, his expression turning a bit wistful, as if he knew he'd never see the boss again, but it was gone when he lifted his head, his face the picture of concentration as he studied the three ropes that hung from the ceiling.

"Shit. I can't reach your leg."

Yeah. It'd be the easiest solution. If Kinosuke could stand on his two feet, there'd be no problem with his balance, and Kenshin-san could cut one rope after another without any risk.

As things were, the only way out of it was cutting the ropes over his head in one single blow. If Kenshin-san only managed to cut one of the ropes that coiled around his neck, Kinosuke would overbalance and hang himself on the other.

He knew the gaijin was good with a sword, but it was one thing to play around with a *bokken* and another to deliver a live-blade strike that would need both precision and strength to work. After the battering Kenshin-san had taken, there couldn't be much strength left in that skinny body. They hadn't eaten much for what seemed to be a few days, either, and he didn't know what Atsushi had given the gaijin in that shot.

"Fucking Atsushi."

He smiled. Yeah. His sentiments exactly.

Kenshin-san smiled back at him. "You and I, Kinosuke-san, we're gonna rearrange that dickhead's face as soon as we're out of here."

Crazy gaijin. He just wished he'd gotten to know him, really know him, before this shit. He would have loved to have had a friend like him, fearless, funny, smart. But now it was too late, and what pained him the most was to understand that Kenshin-san would bleed or starve to death, chained to the wall by Kinosuke's corpse, his last hours filled with the guilt of having failed to save the yakuza.

"This won't do," Kenshin-san said, watching his bandaged hand as it curled around the sword handle. Even if the whole hand didn't hurt like Kinosuke imagined it did, the knuckle Atsushi had chopped off was vital to controlling the katana's motion, and control was badly needed in this case.

Kinosuke stared. *What the hell?* Kenshin-san was changing hands, making the right one grip the bottom of the handle. What was he thinking? That only worked for left-handed people, which he knew for sure the gaijin wasn't. He couldn't help making a disgruntled sound through the gag.

"Don't worry. I know what I'm doing."

Oh shit. He knew he was going to die anyway, but this was lame, this was—

"Look at me, Kinosuke."

He opened his eyes, startled by the authority in that voice. Kenshin-san had moved as far back as the room allowed, his feet slightly wider apart than shoulder width, the katana held in front of him at the exact upward angle, long fingers keeping a grip that managed to appear both firm and relaxed at the same time.

He looked focused, determined, the savage tattoos covering his naked body giving him the frightening appearance of a demon, the blade glinting in the crude light of the basement and making his strange eyes look fierce.

"I'm getting you out of those ropes, but I need you to keep perfectly still."

No goodbyes, no apologies. Those *oni* eyes looked straight into Kinosuke's eyes, and there was no room for failure in them. He was just giving Kinosuke something to focus on, offering him the illusion that he could help somehow.

And for the first time, Kinosuke regretted the gag in his mouth. He needed to tell the man in front of him that it had been worth it, meeting someone like Kenshin-san. He just hoped his eyes would convey his feelings, and he forced himself to keep them open as Kenshin-san gained momentum and lunged forward, bare feet slapping the concrete floor, his slender body flowing like water from one movement to the next, the katana tracing a beautiful arc as it rose and glided over his head.

It had been worth it, living so far, just to see that beautiful dance, just to hear the slicing sound of a katana, just to feel Kenshin-san's *kiai* reverberate in every fiber of his being.

CHAPTER 33

THE apartment wasn't exactly cluttered, but every surface was covered with knick-knacks, petty reminders of a luxurious life that must have fueled Atsushi's resentment every time he looked at them, but nothing that could tell Shigure where Kenshin and Kinosuke might be.

It hadn't taken him long to understand Kinosuke hadn't really run away. Atsushi had told him that he'd never find *them*—not *him*, not Kenshin. He should have figured it out much earlier, but he'd been too disappointed in Kinosuke to see clearly. His anger had made him want to blame the young man when he should have been blaming himself, his own blindness, for everything that had happened.

"There's more rope in here," Kotarō said, showing him a box full of coiled ropes of different colors and textures, from flashy red cotton to plain, undyed hemp. "What are they for? Does he... did he climb or something?"

Shigure studied the kid's face. He didn't look troubled. The correction seemed to have come automatically to him. It was true that he'd been a little shocked after the fact—it was the first death he'd witnessed, after all—but he'd searched Atsushi's clothes for his keys without prompting, more anxious to start looking for Kinosuke and Kenshin than affected by the presence of a corpse in their house.

The events of the last months had made Kotarō grow up fast, it seemed. He'd shown initiative and perseverance in finding Kei, and even though he could have died in a hospital bed, he'd never wanted to quit the Shinagawa after the beating. It was about time to end his apprenticeship, and there was no point in hiding any of life's realities from him.

"He used the ropes to tie people, Kotarō," he explained, waiting for the questions.

"You mean he's kidnapped more people before this?"

"No. What Atsushi did is called shibari, rope bondage. It's the art of making a naked body look beautiful as it's bound into certain positions. Some people like it because it looks good, like a flower arrangement, and some people find it arousing."

Kotarō's eyes widened. "You mean—"

"Yeah, kid. They use it for sex," Shinya said from where he crouched in front of the sink. "But that chickenshit used it for other stuff as well. The guy was a fucking handyman."

Kotarō looked really troubled now, and it wasn't very difficult to understand why. Shigure couldn't stop hearing Atsushi's words in his mind, praying every time that his assistant had only said them to hurt Shigure and not because he'd actually done all those things to Kenshin.

"Atsushi strangled a man with that rope, Kotarō," he said. "You remember the receptionist of the Haihīru? He was the only one apart from Kei-san who'd seen his face, so Atsushi killed him when it was obvious we didn't believe it had been one of Onga's men."

"That's why he was carrying that rope with him? As a weapon?"

"Yeah. He would have tried to kill Kei-san with it if Tachibana hadn't shot him."

That's what he'd told Sergeant Uehara, and he really hoped Tachibana didn't have to pay for killing a rat like Atsushi, even though his bullet had cut their chances of finding Kenshin and Kinosuke alive.

"You did a great job finding Kei-san," Shigure said, patting Kotarō's shoulder. "But now we must hurry to find your aniki and Kenshin-san. You know Kenshin-san is hurt, and they probably haven't any food or water."

"*Hai*, boss."

Kotarō was a good kid, always eager to help. Shinya hadn't even stopped rummaging about as they talked, and there had almost been a fight at the house when it was obvious none of his men wanted to stay behind guarding the gates when they could be out looking for their two missing brothers.

"Boss?"

He looked down and saw the pair of bolt cutters Shinya held. "What did he need these for if he used rope?"

"To break into someone else's property."

Shinya nodded. "That's why that key looked so new."

They only found one key in Atsushi's key ring whose lock was not accounted for, and no records showing that he had bought or leased anything resembling a storage room. "He must have bought a new padlock to keep the place closed."

"I can't quite see that jerk as a cat burglar, so it must be somewhere deserted, no people about to catch him fumbling with the lock."

"He told me there were no neighbors," Shigure said, "and his shoes were dusty. Shit. You know how many parks there are in this city? Or construction sites? Or—"

Shinya stood facing him, his face stern. "We'll search every fucking dusty place in Tokyo if we have to, but it won't help anyone if you lose it now, boss."

Shigure bowed his head, ashamed that his man had to give him lessons on bearing up. He felt Shinya's hand touch his arm lightly. "We'll find them, boss. That gaijin is tough, and he's not alone."

He nodded. After all he'd suspected Kinosuke of, it was a relief to know he was with Kenshin. Shigure knew the young man would do his best to protect Kenshin, probably had already, if the bruise hidden under the Band-Aids on Atsushi's jaw and the finger marks under his shirt collar were any sign.

"You're right," he said, giving Shinya's forearm a squeeze. "Let's tear this place apart, see if that bastard left some other clue."

As he let go of Shinya's arm, he noticed something glittering on the man's thick wrist. "What's that you're wearing?"

He'd have sworn his unflappable man was blushing as he showed some sort of garish bracelet to Shigure. "It's from my silly niece. She said it'd bring me luck."

Shigure was about to laugh when the images flashed through his mind: the cheerful pattern on the charm Kotarō had found in the Haihīru, the old picture of Atsushi in formal attire standing with his parents in front of his family home, Onga's face as he showed Shigure the charm he wore around his neck.

"Where did Atsushi's family live?" he asked.

Shinya shrugged. "I don't know for sure. Somewhere around Takanawa district."

"Kotarō!" Shigure called. "Turn on Atsushi's laptop and Google Jōkyō-ji temple. Search for any large property on sale close to it, or a project for a new building there."

"*Hai*, boss," Kotarō said, his fingers already flying over the keypad. "Want me to check it on Google Earth, see if we get any images of construction sites there?"

Shigure wanted to kiss the boy. "Good idea, kid. Do that, and watch out for vacant lots too."

When the fence with a construction company sign on it filled the screen, they were out of the door and in the car in five seconds flat, Kotarō guiding Shinya as he sped through busy intersections, honks blaring everywhere and making Shigure shout to be heard as he phoned everyone he could think of, his men, Uehara, the gaijin cops, anyone who could get to the location before them, though he doubted anything other than a helicopter would cut through the streets faster than the Mercedes in Shinya's reckless hands.

He could hear the wail of sirens even as their car turned into the street with the wire fence, and Shinya's eyes met his in the rearview mirror.

"Boss?"

The car wasn't slowing down, and Shigure understood. "Keep going!" he yelled.

He was flung against the door as the car swerved violently to charge headlong into the gate. There was a deafening screech of metal against metal, sparks flying everywhere as the Mercedes broke through the gates and sped onto a dirt road that soon had the windshield covered in a cloud of dust.

When the cloud dissipated enough to see ahead, he heard Kotarō's warning cry the very moment his eyes took in the figures standing right in their path.

"Abunai!"

Shinya hit the brakes so hard that the Mercedes fishtailed, and all Shigure could see were those big hands gripping the wheel before his body was flung forward, his mind crying out *I can't die now, not now*, his whole world disappearing in a cloud of white as the car hit a solid wall.

CHAPTER 34

A FUCKING airbag. Shigure paced up and down the narrow hallway, glaring evenly at the nurses, his men, Sergeant Uehara, and any patient who dared cross his path. He'd almost choked on the fumes of a fucking airbag—potassium chloride, the doctor said, as if it were the most common thing in the world—and the paramedics that arrived on the scene had had a hard time deciding which bunch of crazy people to tend to first, the three yakuza inside the crashed Mercedes or the two bleeding, half-naked young men they'd almost run over.

Fuck. Even with a knife wound, three broken ribs, and one eye swelled shut, Kinosuke had been about to punch Shigure as soon as he recovered consciousness, people walking by probably wondering what mental hospital the ambulance was rushing to, the way the patients inside were shouting their heads off.

He glared at Campbell, too, but the man simply ignored him, the BlackBerry still glued to his gaijin ear. It seemed Shigure couldn't manage to get anything right since the fucked-up rescue. He hadn't even gotten to hear Kinosuke's tale in private, the two FBI legal attachés and Uehara insisting this was police business and parking their asses around Kinosuke's bed as he spoke about Kenshin being tortured. Fuck. He wished Atsushi were alive to kill him all over again.

"Who's here for Harisu-san?"

Under different circumstances, Shigure would have laughed at the doctor's expression when he saw about ten people answer his call. The poor man looked at the least scary face amongst the crowd in front of him and spoke directly to Uehara.

"He is out of danger now, but we'll keep him under observation tonight."

"When will it be possible to move him?"

Shigure whipped around to stare at Bradley, but the doctor anticipated his question.

"Move him? You mean to a room?"

"No," Bradley said. "His family wants him in an American hospital as soon as possible."

His family. Shigure clenched his teeth. The same family who hadn't wanted to pay a ransom for him. Not that it would have mattered, but they had no way of knowing that until the very end. They'd simply abandoned their son to his luck, and now all they probably wanted was to shut him away from any contact with the Japanese press.

"You won't be able to transfer him to another hospital until at least the day after tomorrow. He's too weak, and there's still a high risk of infection. He might lose his finger completely if we're not careful."

"What about the...?" Kotarō waved a hand in the air, his gaze searching Shigure's for help. He nodded to the kid.

"His other wounds, doctor. Will they leave permanent scars?" Shigure asked.

"I'm afraid so. His kind of skin scars easily, and there's also ink under the tissue in most of the wounds, so there'll be marks one way or the other."

Shigure saw Kotarō's jaw clench, and he had to suppress the urge to touch him. He wasn't a kid anymore, and he wouldn't appreciate being treated as one in front of his Shinagawa brothers.

"Uh... is there anyone called Shigure here?"

He turned to face the doctor, his heart suddenly in his throat. "I'm Matsunaga Shigure."

The doctor nodded at him. "Harisu-san has been asking for you. Follow me, please. I'll take you to his bed."

As soon as they crossed the doors into ICU, the quality of the silence around them changed, the noise of people walking about all but disappearing in favor of the small sounds of pain, bodies moving restlessly under the white sheets, someone crying quietly, all sorts of medical equipment beeping away in each curtained cubicle they passed.

"Doctor," Shigure whispered.

"Hai?"

"Kensh... Harisu-san was also...."

The doctor nodded his understanding. "I didn't think it appropriate to talk about it in front of so many people."

"Thank you, Doctor." He took a deep breath. "How bad was it?"

"To tell you the truth, from a strictly medical point of view, it wasn't really bad—some minor burns in the genital area and a few tears that'll heal fine without suture. There weren't traces of semen, and his blood tests came out all right. Still, I don't need to tell you that kind of injury usually leaves permanent psychological scars. I'd suggest a good therapist, but I suppose his family would want an American professional in this area too."

He couldn't blame the doctor for sounding bitter, and the doctor didn't even know Senator Harris wasn't so much making an informed choice about his son's medical care as sweeping embarrassing facts under the carpet. He very much doubted the senator would even consider paying for a therapist, unless it was one of those who had the latest definitive cure for homosexuality.

When Shigure didn't say anything, the doctor kept walking until they reached one of the cubicles and then told him the usual litany about not staying long lest he tire the patient. Shigure nodded and bowed as required, but his mind barely registered anything the man said. He was too busy trying to control his heartbeat, trying to squash the anger that was making his fingers itch.

It was no use, though. As soon as he stepped into the area enclosed by the curtain, his rage grew until it reached the peak that would have triggered every alarm in the machines all over the place if he'd been connected to them.

Damn. Kenshin looked even younger than Kotarō as he lay sleeping in that hospital bed, his foreign features relaxed, purple circles under his eyes highlighting his paleness as if he had been carefully made up for one of his gothic attires, but the blood staining the gauze wrapped around his chest was too real for cosplay, and any amount of scrubbing wouldn't manage to erase the sloppy kanji carved into his skin and repeating the word "dog" to anyone who could read.

Shigure counted the beeps of the heart monitor and forced his fists to unclench. Anger was the last thing Kenshin needed to see in his expression when he woke, and he sure as hell should be grateful his gaijin was willing to see him after all that had happened.

His gaijin. Had he ever let Kenshin know that was the only way Shigure thought about him? Did Shigure himself even understand what it meant exactly?

He took Kenshin's left hand in his, careful not to jostle the IV tubing or touch the bandaged finger. It must have hurt so badly, having the knuckle cut off by someone who didn't know or even cared about doing it right. And yet Kenshin had managed to use both his hands to wield a sword and save Kinosuke from a sure death.

He was tough, his gaijin, no matter how fragile he looked with that skinny body and those round childish eyes. He could still see Kinosuke's awed expression as he told them about Kenshin mastering that katana left-handed and cutting both ropes over his head in one mighty strike. Shigure had kept to himself the fact that Kenshin had trained for years to be able to use both his hands with such ease. He'd enjoyed letting them wonder, his chest swelling with pride as they started to see why a yakuza underboss like him might be interested in a scrawny gaijin like Kenshin.

"Shi… gure."

He looked up and met bloodshot eyes that had lost their shine, but that still managed to look strikingly different in the stark hospital light, one clearly dark brown, the other green.

"*Okaerinasai*, Kenshin."

"Sorry. I don't believe… this qualifies as a… *tadaima* kind of place."

Shigure smiled in spite of himself, the urge to kiss those cracked lips overwhelming. He settled for kissing the pale fingers he was holding instead.

"Is everyone…?"

He sighed. Kenshin had seen their stunt with the Mercedes, so there was no point in hiding it.

"Yeah. The rescue party from hell is perfectly fine. I was only at risk of being beaten by Kinosuke, anyway."

It was so good to see that little smile that Shigure couldn't help reaching out to touch that blond head he'd missed so much.

"I'm sorry, Kenshin," he whispered, the contact between them barely enough to transmit the whole amount of emotion constricting his throat. But Kenshin must have felt it anyway—all his frustration, his regret, his anger, his guilt, his pain—because he closed his eyes, the heart monitor beeping faster as the thin, bandaged chest rose and fell quickly.

"It wasn't... your fault."

Yes, it was. He might not be responsible for Atsushi's actions, but he had failed to protect Kenshin, had kept him apart like a dirty secret, and made him a target, a weapon to be used against the Shinagawa.

He let his fingers stroke Kenshin's hair. This was not about Shigure anymore. He had the rest of his life to apologize properly. This now was Kenshin's time, and Shigure had to focus on Kenshin's needs.

"You have to rest."

Bicolored eyes gave him a frightened look. "Please don't go."

It hurt, that fear. He could only imagine how many times Kenshin had prayed for Shigure to be there, to help him, to save him—enough times that now Kenshin didn't take his presence for granted.

He bent to kiss Kenshin's forehead. It felt clammy, but that only made Shigure want to kiss every inch of battered skin to make the pain and the fear go away.

"I'll stay till the nurses kick me out, and then sneak back in while Kotarō distracts them."

There. That was the smile he wanted to see, or not quite, but close enough for now. He wasn't taking his eyes off his gaijin ever again.

CHAPTER 35

EVERY time the tengu mask got close enough for him to see the hatred in Atsushi's eyes, he screamed, pain radiating from his torn nipple to the missing tip of his finger and back up from his groin to the cluster of wounds on his chest and arms. And every time he screamed and thought he would die, big hands shook him awake, and Shigure's face hovered over him, his voice whispering reassurances until Ken closed his eyes again.

It lasted a whole night, or probably more, he couldn't tell for sure, but when he opened his eyes next, he was in a private room, cheerful daylight landing squarely on a bunch of flowers, fruit baskets, and other small gifts cloth-wrapped and ribbon-decorated to death.

He groaned and tried to pull the sheet over his head, but only one of his hands cooperated, the other feeling like a swollen piece of dead meat that someone had bandaged to his bones.

"Kenshin? Are you cold?"

Oh shit. He kept his eyes tightly shut, his hands doing their best to shred the bed linen.

"Kenshin, what...?"

Big sure hands enfolded his, and he actually whimpered, too weak to fight them, too ashamed to accept their comfort. The hurt he felt in his chest now had nothing to do with his stupid kanji-shaped wounds. It was angry, and it burned; it spread its rage all over, scorching his insides until he shook with the urge to scream or kill something. And then those hands hauled him upright and pressed him against a broad chest, thick arms locking him in a suffocating prison he had no strength to escape.

He screamed like he had all night, his ineffectual fists banging against an unmovable wall of muscle, his anger unending, limitless, feeding itself with all the shame he couldn't contend with, all the guilt that piled like sewage in the bottom of his mind, deep down where everything was filthy and dark, in the place where he kept all the horrors he couldn't draw out into harmless bedtime stories, because they were all his, all that made him what he was, the disgusting slime that he was.

SHIGURE stepped out into the hallway, closing the door behind him. He didn't want to go very far in case the nightmares started all over again, but he couldn't stay in the room one second longer, or he'd send all those thoughtful get-well presents flying against the wall.

It was hard, hearing Kenshin scream in his sleep, but it was harder still when he rejected any comfort Shigure might offer, fighting him with surprising strength until he exhausted himself into fretful sleep.

The doctor had told him to expect that, both anxiety and anger, but also detachment. Post-traumatic stress disorder, he'd called it, and though he said it responded well to antidepressants, the only signs of detachment Shigure had seen in Kenshin had come right after the prescriptions kicked in. So no, it wasn't any fancy disorder, what Kenshin was going through. He'd just been robbed of his chance to get even, since Atsushi had conveniently died before the American could have at least given him a piece of his mind, or seen him go to jail in his expensive dress shoes.

Uehara had confirmed that Atsushi's family were old money, up until the moment the head of the clan started seeking comfort after his wife's death in alcohol and pretty hostesses. It seemed he had a penchant for choosing foreign women, Europeans mostly, and that one of them had even taken up residence in the family house, much to the chagrin of the remaining clan members.

Atsushi's father never married the gaijin woman, but he spent a fortune in clothes and jewelry for her, and stopped taking care of the family business, a lucrative waste-disposal company. Since construction and industrial waste disposal were both sectors with a high presence of yakuza-related businesses, it wasn't difficult to imagine that Atsushi's father had some kind of agreement with the Shinagawa, and so they were the first he resorted to when his company sank into debt.

He kept spending money on parties and expensive gifts for his gaijin woman, and the debt with the Shinagawa increased accordingly, until visits from burly crew-cut men to the family house were an everyday occurrence. And then the man had the brilliant idea to pull what was called a *yonige*—a "midnight escape"—and he simply vanished, leaving behind an eighteen-year-old Atsushi to fend for himself in dealing with the Shinagawa.

The oyabun didn't offer Atsushi a job as Shigure's assistant out of kindness. He was kept as a hostage for years to warrant that the debt was paid, and that Atsushi himself didn't *jōhatsu*, or "evaporate," like those people who ran from loan harvesters were said to do .

If Kenshin hadn't been a gaijin, Atsushi would have never even looked at him twice, since he wasn't too useful in his big revenge scheme against the Shinagawa. But his presence had hit too close to home, and Shigure had failed to see the hatred in his assistant's eyes every time he'd had to deal with Kenshin. He had simply assumed it was yet another side to Atsushi's arrogant behavior, to the way he used to look down his aristocratic nose at everyone around him.

"Matsunaga-san?"

Speaking of arrogant bastards. "Nishimura."

"How is Kenshin?"

"As well as can be expected."

Nishimura nodded and held his eyes, waiting, but Shigure didn't add anything or move aside to let him enter Kenshin's room. He wasn't going to make it easy for the man who'd tried to stop his gaijin from seeing him.

The silence stretched for more seconds than was proper, and Shigure understood Nishimura was smart enough to keep his mouth closed—he wouldn't ask for permission to see his friend.

"I'll be in the cafeteria. Please let me know if there's any change or anything I can do."

Shigure gave him a curt nod and was about to turn when Nishimura added, "I trust you to take good care of him."

He couldn't hide his surprise, especially because Nishimura seemed to mean it.

"I know I have been...," Nishimura said, fumbling for the right word.

"An arrogant prick?"

Nishimura laughed. "I was going to say 'reluctant', but I guess I deserve that." He sobered and looked at Shigure frankly. "I'm not trying to excuse my behavior, but you must understand where I was coming from, Matsunaga-san. I didn't want my friend to get hurt."

And when his friend had indeed gotten hurt, Nishimura had done his best to help. Trying to expose the oyabun of the Terada-kai might have been risky if things had turned out differently—Shigure had to admit that—and, to be fair, he could see that Nishimura cared about Kenshin the only way he knew how.

"Look," Shigure finally said, "I'm not trying to keep you from seeing Kenshin, but this is not the best moment. He's facing a lot of demons right now, and visitors only distress him."

Nishimura looked both relieved and sad to hear it, and Shigure was about to add something when he caught sight of Shinya hurrying toward them.

"What's wrong?"

"It's those gaijin cops, boss. They're moving a lot of paperwork down at the reception desk."

"Shit."

"Matsunaga-san?" Nishimura asked.

"Kenshin's family," he explained. "They're trying to move him to an American hospital. And I imagine it's not because of better facilities."

Shigure debated what to do, anger and helplessness fighting in his conflicted brain. He couldn't let them take Kenshin away to some institution where Shigure wouldn't be able to watch over him and keep an eye open for the senator's scheming, but if Shigure caused a scandal in a public hospital involving an American citizen, even the Japanese police would be after him.

"How many men do you have here?"

He eyed Nishimura warily. "Three, not counting the one who's lying in another bed two doors down there. Why?"

"If you can stop the FBI agents for some time, I can move Kenshin out of here before they arrive."

Shigure didn't have to consider it. "I won't have him go through another kidnapping, not even a friendly one."

"Oh, come on. Who do you take me for? I have connections in this hospital. I can have him officially transferred to any other hospital or clinic—hell, even a spa if I try hard—with an ambulance, flashing lights, sirens, and the whole fucking deal. But I need some time to do it through the proper channels, or those gaijin won't stop until they get Kenshin where his family want him, and that, Matsunaga-san, will be a proper kidnapping, believe me. So, can you delay the Americans or not?"

He had to smile in spite of himself. "You should have been a lawyer, Nishimura-san. How long do you need?"

Nishimura was already flipping his phone open, a wild grin on his mouth. The little shit was enjoying himself. "As long as you can give me without a fight. The last thing Kenshin needs is you going to jail for this," he said as he turned away, already speaking with someone at the other end of the line, and Shigure didn't even want to imagine what it would be like to have Nishimura as an enemy.

CHAPTER 36

THERE were two elevators at the end of the hallway, but one of them was marked as hospital personnel only, so it seemed safe to guess the FBI agents would use the other, unless they rode with the orderly who had to wheel Kenshin out, but somehow Shigure doubted it. They weren't Nishimura, after all. They had no connections to smooth hospital proceedings for them, and they were gaijin, which meant the staff would be in no hurry to help them.

"Kotarō, stand behind me."

Kotarō pouted as he moved to comply, shuffling his feet all the way. It was difficult to restrain the long-suffering sigh that wanted to come out, but Shigure managed to throw the pup a bone instead. "Cover my back. If any of the gaijin get past me, do whatever it takes to stop them. I'm counting on you to protect Kenshin-san."

Kotarō's grin almost split his face. "*Hai*, boss." Then he must have realized the situation didn't exactly call for smiles and forced an even more comical frown on his slightly bruised face. Shit. They made quite a picture, the four of them.

Tachibana and Shinya flanked the elevator doors, looking like the two sides of the proverbial yakuza image. Where Tachibana wore his hair rather long and combed back with industrial amounts of gel, Shinya's was shorn close to his scalp, making the long scar on his face stand out. That, plus the hard edge to his eyes and the dark suit, gave him a forbidding appearance, while Tachibana looked boastfully dangerous in his sunglasses and the most eye-jarring combination of black and green shirt under a brown jacket two sizes too big for him.

Shigure stood some paces behind them, right in front of the elevator, his hair short, his charcoal pinstriped suit carefully chosen to show his rank. Oyone had taught him that while people would always cower from the hard angles of his face, an expensive suit would make them respect him, too, so he'd become adept at dressing in style, his silk ties a perfect match, his dress shoes glinting under any light. There was no way to mistake him for a business executive, but he sure hoped he was giving an impression of power, especially now that he wasn't carrying a weapon.

Standing farther down the hallway, Kotarō looked like a goaltender ready to jump and intercept any ball coming his way. He still hadn't developed a style of his own, his thick black hair neither too long nor too short—though his bangs had a boyish tendency to fall over his eyes—his only suit a conservative navy blue that he wore most of the time without a tie, looking very much like a schoolkid at his midmorning recess.

When the elevator finally dinged, the doors slid open to show the American agents, but they hadn't come alone this time. There were two beefy gaijin escorting them, and even though they wore no uniform, the way they held themselves screamed military from miles away.

"Matsunaga-wakagashira," Bradley said. "We don't want any trouble."

Interesting, how the gaijin remembered to address him properly now. The pinstriped suit must be doing wonders. "Neither do I, Bradley-san. My men and I are just visiting one of our own."

The doors closed behind the four men who now stood surrounded by yakuza, the Marines—or whatever they were—eyeing their aggressive stances warily. Shigure almost smiled to himself. The gaijin had probably heard a lot of rumors about the yakuza, and with any luck, they probably expected him and his men to be packing, or at least to be proficient in some martial art or another.

Bradley and Campbell didn't look too confident, either, but the black agent was doing his best to sound nonchalant as he nodded at Shigure's words. "We have no business with the Shinagawa. We are here to take Kenneth Harris to an American hospital, that's all."

Shigure nodded amicably too. "I'm afraid that's Shinagawa business, Bradley-san."

A muscle in Campbell's jaw twitched. "He's an American citizen. You have no business with him."

"Sure I do. He's family."

The disbelieving looks he got from the Americans were priceless, and Shigure didn't know whether to laugh or let his fist fly. It was beginning to grate on his nerves, the way everybody assumed Kenshin was just his boy toy.

"*Kyōdai da ze, Kenshin-san wa.*"

Now it was his turn to stare at Shinya in disbelief. The man had just said that Kenshin was his brother, and he was giving the gaijin his best challenging look, which coming from Shinya was more than a little scary. The Marines shifted uneasily where they stood.

Tachibana nodded sagely at that. "*Sō, sō. Kyodai da na.*"

Shit. It was getting better and better. Shigure felt a smile tugging at his lips at the way Tachibana said the same as Shinya in his own casual style: "Our brother, ain't that the truth?"

And then Kotarō spoke from behind him, and Shigure almost cracked up, his men ducking their heads to hide their grins.

"*Ore wa otōto da ze.*" The kid stated most seriously that he was Kenshin's little brother.

"There you go, gentlemen," Shigure said before he lost it. "Harisu-san is family, so it's our business to look after his interests."

"If that's so, Matsunaga-san, I'm sure you'll want him to have the best medical care available."

"Are you saying Japanese doctors are worse than American ones as a whole, or are you just comparing them with the few American doctors working in Japan?"

Campbell clenched his jaw. Of the two agents, he was obviously the less adept at playing good cop—he was too impatient for that, maybe even too impatient for the way things worked in this country.

"Look, Mr. Matsunaga." So he was back to being a mister. It seemed even Bradley was losing his patience. "I have no doubt this hospital is great, but you have to understand that his family back in the States would want him to be in a place they know the workings of. They'll be less worried that way."

"And why the fuck didn't they worry when Kenshin-san was chained to a wall, huh? He wasn't family then?"

Oh shit. He didn't need to turn around to know that Kinosuke was standing in the hallway, striped pajamas, pressure bandages, and all. He wasn't exactly whispering, either, so they'd soon have a bunch of nurses around, and that just supposing they were lucky enough someone didn't think to call the cops. Shit. He had to give Nishimura more time.

"Bradley-san, you live in this country, you know hospitals here are very good, and they're not the impersonal medical facilities American ones can get to be. We have a tradition of letting the family take care of their own, of making the sick feel as much at home as possible, and I don't need to tell you how important that is when someone has suffered as much as Kenshin has."

"I can see your point, but he'll be well looked after, and surrounded by his own countrymen."

"Is any member of his American family coming?"

"Like hell they are!"

He ignored Kinosuke's outburst and locked eyes with Bradley until the gaijin averted his gaze.

"Senator Harris can't abandon his responsibilities," Campbell said as if reciting a well-rehearsed text.

"So he just sends the cavalry to take care of things," Kinosuke said. "You can tell the scumbag that Kenshin-san manages quite well without his gorillas."

The Marines bristled, and one of them mumbled something in English that sounded too close to "fucking yakuza" for them not to understand.

There was a moment of perfect silence, the air around them feeling so stretched that everybody seemed reluctant to breathe it lest it shattered and stopped sustaining the roof over their heads. But then someone said the magic words, someone murmured, "Kuso gaijin," and started a chain reaction as impossible to stop as a grenade without the safety pin.

Tachibana's fist landed squarely on a big gaijin nose, the cracking sound unmistakable as the Marine covered his bloodied face with his hands. To his right, Shinya ducked to avoid a punch from the other Marine and wheeled to send a vicious kick that the soldier barely managed to parry, just as Kotarō ran past Shigure to throw himself on top of Campbell as the agent tried to help the Marine facing Tachibana. Bradley turned to aid the other soldier as best he could against the blows Shinya kept delivering without pause, and all Shigure could do at that point was grab Kinosuke's arms to keep the struggling youngster from jumping into the fray as well, broken ribs or no.

When the elevator doors opened to let out what appeared to be the whole contents of a police station, Shigure lifted his eyes to the big clock on the wall. Twelve minutes. Considering how expedient Japanese police were in their dealings with the yakuza, especially if there were gaijin witnesses about, the arrests wouldn't take more than five minutes. So seventeen minutes, give or take.

Shigure could only pray it'd be enough for Nishimura to get Kenshin to safety.

CHAPTER 37

HIS mouth felt dry, and he thought he might need help to open his eyes, his lids were so heavy. He could ask Shigure, reach out and tug at the sleeve of that strong arm, hear the yakuza move closer and bend to study him as he'd been doing every time Ken came awake.

But he couldn't bear it, that look. He hated it, and yet he dreaded waking up to find it gone. And the more he needed it, the more it angered him, because if he'd ever been proud of anything, it was of standing on his own two feet, of never depending on anyone.

He guessed those days were over. The wreck that he now was would forever depend on medication, forever look over his shoulder to see if he was being followed, forever have nightmares without gentle hands shaking him awake and stroking his hair to calm him down.

He took a deep breath and forced his eyes to open, but the second the blurry room came into focus, he knew something was wrong. The door was not where it should have been, he was wired to a heart monitor again, and there was no chair in the place where Shigure had been sitting every time Ken looked.

It took his addled brain two more seconds to piece it all together, but it wasn't until his eyes checked the new room for windows and found none that he started shaking, panic clawing at his chest so viciously that he had to let it out, his scream so high-pitched that he couldn't quite tell it from the alarm of the monitor until the room filled with people in masks, and he knew this was no nightmare, this was real life pushing his head underwater and trying to drown what was left of him. And maybe if he'd had time to think, he would have chosen to lie back and let it happen, but his survival instinct had kicked in too fast, and his body fought for all it was worth until the room got first blurry and then completely black, like another basement, or a new grave.

THE yukata was not long enough to cover Kenshin's ankles, the fresh marks an angry red that felt raw to the touch as Shigure let his fingers trail them.

He could have killed those stupid doctors who had strapped his gaijin to a gurney as soon as he opened his eyes. And still they tried to give him some lame justifications about panic attacks and who knew what else, but of course all of them had fallen immediately silent when Shigure'd asked how they would feel if they'd woken in a windowless room after been tied and chained and tortured for days in a fucking basement.

It seemed every time he tried to save Kenshin from something, he ended up hurting him further. He was only glad Nishimura's machinations had worked amazingly well, the head doctor of the psychiatric ward deciding on the spot that their American patient needed to be transferred urgently to a private clinic, with all the paperwork—that surely had taken the FBI legal attachés at least a day to get moving—ready in five minutes, an ambulance at the door in another five, and Kenshin conveniently doped and carefully wheeled out in the next five. Fifteen minutes, all in all. Pretty impressive.

The part the Shinagawa had played in the whole scheme hadn't gone so smoothly, though.

"Mmmhmm."

Kenshin shifted against him, frowning as he let out a small pained sound. Shigure stroked the soft hair and started murmuring nonsense, his tone even and—he hoped—reassuring.

"*Shizuka ni shiro, Ken-chan*," he crooned, rocking a little with Kenshin's back pressed to his chest, the movement seemingly quieting the American until he opened his eyes. Then his gaijin went all tense, ready to fight his way out of Shigure's arms.

"Shhh. You're safe, Kenshin," he said, tightening his hold on the thin body. He wasn't letting go, even though he knew he was pressing on some of Kenshin's wounds. His gaijin started breathing fast, his head moving as he scanned the room, every muscle taut until he saw the *yukimi* shoji, the papered sliding doors with a glass cutout in the middle that gave the room a nice view into the garden. Only then did he relax, his weight slumping back against Shigure.

"It's over now. You're safe."

Kenshin was silent for a while, and Shigure moved his hands, slowly petting the flat belly over the bamboo pattern of the yukata.

"Did you just call me Ken-chan?"

"I was trying to avoid the Shin-chan part, you know."

He could almost hear Kenshin smile, but he resisted the urge to lift his fingers and touch those pretty lips. His gaijin was doing fine so far, and he didn't want to act too fast too soon, didn't want to overwhelm him.

"Is this your room?"

"This is my favorite room at Oyone's place."

"Oh."

Oh indeed. Shigure closed his eyes as he felt the amount of disappointment weighing that single word. Kenshin started to shift, too, trying to move away from him.

"I should be home," he said.

He couldn't agree more. "Yeah. I'll take you there as soon as possible."

The muscles under Shigure's hands tensed, and Kenshin's voice sounded hard, anger barely contained. "No. You take me right now. And I sure hope you still have the one key I gave you, because I don't want to break into my own apartment."

Shit. He'd screwed up again. "You can't go there."

"Why the fuck not?"

"Because I told the landlord you wouldn't be needing it anymore."

Kenshin turned around to face him, wincing as the movement pulled on his wounds.

"You did what?"

Fiery eyes glared at him, one dark brown, the other light green, anger giving the pale skin around them a furious blush, a vein throbbing in the long white neck, the light summer robe opening to reveal a stretch of creamy skin before the bandages began, long limbs pushing up to help the lithe body lunge if necessary. Damn. His gaijin was the most beautiful creature he'd ever seen.

"I got rid of your apartment because you're coming home with me."

Kenshin blinked. "What do you mean?"

Shigure was sure Kenshin knew perfectly well what he meant, but he guessed his gaijin needed to hear the words. "I'm taking you home to the clan house."

"I can't go there."

"Why not?"

"Atsushi—"

"Atsushi is dead, Kenshin."

Troubled eyes looked away, and Kenshin turned, legs shifting to get him off of the futon they were sharing.

"Stop," Shigure said, wrapping his arm around the thin waist. "Come back here, and tell me why you can't go back to my house."

Kenshin fought the pressure of his arm, keeping the distance between them, his voice angry. "That's not your house. It's the whole damn Shinagawa-gumi's house."

"Only my men share it with me," he answered calmly. "And it never used to bother you before."

"You're fucking right. A lot of things never used to bother me, before. But this is now, and *everything* bothers me. *You* bother me," he spat, grabbing Shigure's arm and trying to pry free from its hold.

"Why?" Kenshin kept fighting him, and Shigure kept pushing. "Why do I bother you?"

"Let go."

"Tell me why."

"Let go!"

Kenshin let out something that sounded like a snarl, trying to use both his hands, even the bandaged one, to claw at Shigure's arm.

"Stop it. You're gonna hurt yourself."

His gaijin snorted. "I'm already hurt, you dimwit, and you have no say in what I choose to do or stop doing. I'm not one of your fucking soldiers to order about!"

"You sure as hell aren't, because I don't fucking screw my soldiers."

As soon as the words left his mouth, he wished he could take them back. There was a world of hurt in those big weird eyes, and the anger turned into something different, something flat and defeated that had nothing to do with the short-fused emotional firecracker that Kenshin was.

"Stop it."

The American wasn't even pushing at his arm anymore. He just sat there, unmoving, unmoved, waiting for him to tire. And Shigure hated it.

"Kenshin, stop it!"

He shook the skinny body, not caring whether his fingers dug into the tattooed kanji.

"What else do you want from me, Shigure?"

It was the "what else" that made the hair on the back of his neck bristle. It was nothing but the truth that for a long time Kenshin had given him anything Shigure wanted, taken any of his challenges, accepted any of his rules, his lifestyle, his men, and then he'd given even more, his life, almost, for Shigure, because of Shigure.

"I want you to let me take care of you."

"Why? Because you failed to take care of me before? Because it's your fucking duty to provide redress?"

At least the anger was back. That was something Shigure could deal with.

"Yes, I failed to protect you, and not a single minute goes by that I don't regret it. And yes, it's my duty to right any wrong caused by people in my employment. But I'd want it anyway, want you anyway, even if nothing had happened."

The furious sparks in those eyes could turn Oyone's wood-and-paper ryokan into smoldering ashes in no time at all. And maybe spread the fire over the whole city after that, a spectacular brown and green fire of rage.

"If nothing had happened, you'd still be trying to figure out whether you wanted to play some more with the freakish gaijin or drop him right away before your badass yakuza reputation started to suffer."

"I'm sorry I gave you that impression, Kenshin, but I never played with you."

Kenshin snorted as he moved away from him, his bare feet already on the tatami mat, his good hand pressing against the futon to help him stand. "Don't get all contrite on me now, Shigure. We both knew what we were getting into, or rather I should've known if I weren't a fucking airhead. And it sure isn't your fault that I'm stupid, so spare me the apologies already. I'm gonna puke if I have to put up with another second of Japanese properness."

He didn't even have to think before his body shot forward, his arms lifting Kenshin forcefully and throwing him onto the middle of the mattress, his legs straddling the slim waist and pinning Kenshin's arms to his sides, Shigure's hands landing hard on the bony shoulders, their faces inches apart.

"Listen to me, you little shit. I've never been a proper Japanese in my whole fucking life. I was born improper. I grew up as an outcast, spent my youth in and out of jail, and became a fucking yakuza underboss, so don't you dare assume I do anything out of politeness."

There was no trace of fear in the blazing eyes that held his defiantly. "Oh, excuse me for insulting your burakumin sensibilities, Matsunaga-wakagashira. I do know you can be a rude son of a bitch when you want to, but you're still the most righteous bastard I've ever met. You're always honor-bound to this or honor-bound to that. You can't take a fucking step without checking the Bushidō code first."

"So what? You have a problem with honor now?"

Unable to move any other part of his body, Kenshin still lifted his head off the mattress, their faces so close now that Shigure could feel the warmth of his gaijin's breath, almost touch the sharp angles of the words he spat next.

"No, I have a fucking problem with being some motherfucker samurai's duty, you asshole!"

They stayed like that for a long second, the air between them crackling with electricity, the anger in their eyes so violent that their gazes could have drilled holes in concrete had they looked away for even a moment, but they were too busy challenging each other, drinking in each other's tense features as if they were meeting for the first time on opposing sides of a battlefield.

And then, in the next second, their mouths clashed together of their own accord, teeth clicking as their tongues lashed at each other like live blades, Shigure's hands shooting up to grab that wild fury between his fingers and hold him there, stealing the breath from his lungs, biting at his lips and tongue, even as Kenshin tried to devour him in turn, the coppery taste of blood mixing with the sweet flavor of his gaijin until he thought he would drown in the sensations that flowed over him.

When their lips parted, they made a wet sound as if they'd been glued together, and their eyes still locked as they panted for breath.

"Kenshin," he just said, wanting it to mean everything he never managed to put into words, watching in awe as the flames in those weird eyes quivered and turned into something else, black pupils dilating and eating away at the rings of color but still burning, the heat coming off that thin body enough to bring Shigure's blood to boiling temperature.

"Let me...," Kenshin mumbled, his voice rough and urgent. "I need to...."

He reached down, loosening the pressure of his thighs and grabbing Kenshin's wrists to push them up and away over the blond head, the movement stretching his gaijin's body until he was all exposed before him, the yukata enticingly open to show the play of muscles as Kenshin tried to free his hands.

"I'm not letting you go."

"Fine. Just stop talking and do something productive."

He would have laughed, but Kenshin was looking at him too seriously, the intensity in those eyes scorching, anger and need mixed together into something that seemed too desperate for Shigure to even smile.

He bent forward to take those swollen lips in his mouth, tasting fear, frustration, and anxiety all bundled up in layer after layer of want, wide eyes watching him as if he would disappear if Kenshin so much as blinked, and the lithe body under him arching up to meet him.

Shigure let go of the thin wrists, and Kenshin immediately wrapped his arms around his neck and pulled him down for more kisses, more pressure, more friction—as much of him as he could get.

He groaned, trying to keep his weight from pressing against the bandaged chest, but Kenshin would have none of it. "If you stop now, I swear I'll kill you."

"I don't want to hurt you."

"They're just some fucking tattoos, for Christ's sake. It's not like I'm gonna—"

He swallowed Kenshin's cry into his mouth as he covered him, the slender body disappearing under his bulk, bony hips jabbing at him, bandages scratching his chest and making his nipples harden, his cock twitching as he felt Kenshin's arousal pressing against his lower belly.

It wasn't the perfect fit yet, so Shigure shifted, his lips never leaving Kenshin's as he pressed his hands against the futon and pulled his body just a little higher, right where his shaft slid along Kenshin's length through the cotton fabric of their yukatas, his gaijin's moan vibrating in his mouth and making him shudder.

He lifted his head to put some distance between them and watched the man beneath him. He wanted to get an impression of him from every one of his senses, carve that beautiful image into his retina, burn his sweet taste into his taste buds, fix the soft scent of that skin into every one of his cells, stop hearing anything that wasn't Kenshin's moans of pleasure, his fingers unable to feel anything beyond the velvety touch of his gaijin's fine hair.

And yet, as much as he wanted that, he understood he was trying to make a memory, his mind working to prevent the sense of loss of having Kenshin taken away from him. He was trying to protect himself by remembering as much as he could for the time when he had nothing. And that wouldn't do. Because he would never be ready to lose Kenshin again.

"Shigure, please."

Kenshin's good hand pressed against his nape, trying to pull him back down and hide under the cover of Shigure's body. It made his chest ache to know there was more than shyness in that defensive gesture, made him both want to break something and hold onto his gaijin so tightly that not even air would graze that marred skin ever again.

"Let me look at you, Kenshin."

His lover made a pained sound, almost a whimper, still trying to pull Shigure to him.

"Please don't hide from me. I want to see you, want to learn you again."

Kenshin's arms let go of his neck, those fiery eyes narrowing as they glared at him.

"You want to learn what Atsushi turned me into? Want to count how many times he wrote 'dog' on me? Want to see where his little toys burned me, where the bigger ones tore me? Want to see if you still fit inside me, if the scars will stretch enough? Is that what you want?"

Shigure recoiled from the venom in Kenshin's words, but he realized how much of it was self-directed, how much of the anger came from helplessness and shame. And he knew Kenshin would hate it if he made the mistake of showing compassion, so he gave his own anger free rein.

"Yes, I want to see what damage that bastard caused, want to see every single mark he left on my personal property, want to measure how long it will take for me to erase any trace of him from what's only mine, and yes, I want to leave my scent all over your skin and my seed inside you so that every other fucking animal that dares look at you will know that you're taken."

Kenshin looked away, trying uselessly to shift to his side. Shigure's fingers reached out to turn the pale face to him.

"Let me see you, Kenshin," he said softly.

"I don't want you to," Kenshin muttered, his eyes tightly shut as if he could fight Shigure that way. "I'm just…. It's…."

He let his fingers trace the creased brow and kept his voice soft, almost a whisper. "It's what?"

Kenshin just shook his head.

"I'm not going anywhere till you say it, Kenshin."

"No, you're a fucking pigheaded yakuza son of a bitch."

There they were, those fiery eyes, wide and gorgeously blazing, trying to drill a hole into his skull, and Shigure couldn't stop the smile that pulled at the corners of his mouth. "That's me, the fucking yakuza SOB. Now tell me why you don't want me to look at you."

Kenshin huffed. "Shit. You're insufferable."

"Yeah, we've already established that. Now tell me."

His gaijin tried to keep glaring at him, but it came out more like a pout, swollen lips pushing forward in a totally kissable gesture of annoyance.

"Stop mocking me."

"I'm not mocking you, Kenshin," he said, though he knew he didn't sound too convincing, the way his smile kept creeping back.

"Yes, you are."

"Am not."

"Are too."

"I'm not mocking you," he said in his most serious face. "I swear it on the Bushidō code."

Kenshin swatted his arm, hard, but Shigure saw that his lips were twitching. "You bastard. I was trying to insult you here."

"Yeah, I'm sure you were trying." Shigure laughed at Kenshin's chagrined expression, his fingers automatically reaching out to stroke the lovely face. His gaijin leaned into the caress, his eyes fluttering closed, and Shigure took the chance to push himself up and move to kneel beside Kenshin on the futon. The American gave him a frightened look, his slender hand immediately grabbing at Shigure's yukata.

"Shhh. I'm not going anywhere."

"What are you...?"

Instead of answering, Shigure pulled at one end of the *koshihimo* sash that held Kenshin's robe in place and untied the simple knot. The long fingers on his own yukata tightened even more, round eyes looking up at him, wide and scared.

"Please don't."

It was hard to ignore Kenshin's plea, but he knew he had to do this. They both needed to come to terms with what had happened, stop ignoring that things had inevitably changed, that they had both changed in ways they hadn't yet acknowledged.

"Please."

He stroked Kenshin's face once, and then slid his hands inside the yukata and pushed the cotton fabric to the sides, exposing the thin, bandaged body. Kenshin whimpered like a battered puppy, the knuckles of his right hand white where they clutched at Shigure's robe.

"Shhhh. Just let me look at you."

"No, please. It's—"

He calmly pried open Kenshin's hand, one finger at a time, and brought it to his lips. "It's what?"

Kenshin moaned as Shigure gave his hand openmouthed kisses, his tongue darting out to taste the salty skin. "Tell me."

"It's... it's ugly."

When he looked up from his finger-worshipping task, he saw the fear and shame in those amazing eyes, and guilt hit him so hard that he almost flinched. It was no one's fault but his own that this brave gaijin would now be reduced to a trembling mess for fear of being rejected, being found disgusting because of the very injures that one of Shigure's men had inflicted on him.

Nothing he could say now would convince Kenshin that he didn't find him ugly, so Shigure forced himself to really look at the body displayed before him on the futon.

Bandages covered him down past his waist, and it was obvious that he'd lost weight, the bones in his hips protruding sharply as the usually flat belly now curved inward. He looked like a starved kid, the boyish image accentuated by the absence of hair where the doctors had shaved him to treat the burns that had left raw patches of skin everywhere Shigure looked, even along his shaft and on the most sensitive areas around it.

The long legs appeared unmarked except for the ankles with their overlapping red lines, the different patterns signaling the places where Kenshin had been tied, shackled, and finally strapped to a hospital bed.

Shigure tried to breathe steadily, to keep calm. His anger was useless now. He forced himself to reach out and tear off the strip of tape that secured the loose end of the bandage.

"What are you doing?"

"I want to see you."

Kenshin groaned. "What for? You already know how to write dog."

Shigure gave him a proud smile. He knew his gaijin was terrified, could see it in the way his eyes shifted anxiously, but still he was trying to make light of it, trying to act as if he couldn't care less.

"It's all right, Kenshin," he said, stroking the clenched jaw, the tips of his fingers sliding softly to touch the full lips. "Just let me look at you. There's nothing to be ashamed of."

His gaijin looked away, a pained expression on his face. It was not the time to search for the right words, so Shigure simply started pulling the bandage off, little by little, making sure he touched the skin under it as soon as it came into view, flawless skin giving way to the brutally carved blue and red lines of the crude kanji.

There were two matching ones above Kenshin's hip bones. Shigure bared the characters and forced himself to study them in a detached manner, as if he were grading a kid's calligraphy exercise. They didn't look much better than that, actually, the slipshod lines appearing hesitant, too thin where they should have been broad, the fourth stroke added as an afterthought, ink blotted haphazardly where the skin had soaked it up and leaving the deepest incisions untouched, the result a sloppy red-and-blue draft that looked more like a removable sticker than a permanent tattoo.

Time would change the red lines into white scar tissue, probably making the outline less apparent—less readable as an actual word—but still too obvious on that beautifully pale skin.

He traced the contours of the kanji with the tip of his fingers, avoiding the open cuts, watching as his gaijin squirmed under his touch.

"Does it still hurt?" he said to distract Kenshin from the movements of his fingers as he went on uncovering the mauled skin.

"No. It just burns a little when I move."

Shigure raised his eyebrows. "A little?"

"Yeah. A little in each of the fucking dogs in the pack. Happy now?"

He chuckled. "Yeah, happy to have my grouchy gaijin back."

"I'm not grouchy."

"Ill-tempered?"

"No!"

"Feisty, then."

Kenshin made a rude noise, and Shigure laughed, leaning forward to get a taste of that sulky mouth. His lover didn't waste a second to wrap his arms around Shigure's neck to pull him closer, hungry lips latching onto his, needy moans filling his mouth and almost making him forget what he'd been trying to do.

But he didn't allow Kenshin to distract him from the task at hand, one of his arms circling the trim waist to lift his gaijin off the futon. Kenshin clung to his neck, never stopping the ravenous kisses, and he had a hard time unlatching the tight grip of one of the slender arms and shoving the yukata sleeve down.

It was somehow easier with the other arm, but now he had a fully naked gaijin trying to climb up him, long legs folded under the lithe body to push him up to Shigure's level. Soon they were both kneeling face to face, and Kenshin's fingers went for the sash of his yukata.

"Stop, Kenshin."

His gaijin blinked, so many emotions playing on his face that Shigure didn't know where to start.

"Bear with me a little longer, Kenshin. Let me do this first."

"Why? It's the same all over. You don't need to—"

He took a gentle, lingering kiss, drowning the last objections, swallowing Kenshin's whimpers of fear.

"Just these last bandages," Shigure said, his fingers already working on the white strips around Kenshin's left arm. "We'll make love afterwards, I promise."

Kenshin ducked his head, mumbling something he couldn't hear.

"What's that?"

Shit. The look in those eyes. The anger in them was so painful that Shigure almost expected to see blood flowing freely from every single cut on Kenshin's body.

"Make love? You call it that now because I'm wounded? Well, I'm sorry to inform you that not even a pity fuck will do in this case. I'm too damaged to take your cock up my skinny gaijin ass."

"I don't need to put my cock in you to make love to you, you intractable son of a bitch. And I call it making love because that's what you do when you love someone, even if he's one stubborn, foul-mouthed gaijin."

Kenshin blinked and looked away. "You can't—"

"Oh, sure I can. Same as you do."

Confused eyes met his.

"Yeah, I might be a stupid yakuza, but I'm not blind. I know I'm more to you than an occasional fuck buddy."

Kenshin looked away again, but now he tried to put distance between them, his good hand reaching out for the discarded yukata.

"Oh no, you're not going anywhere. I'm not done with you yet."

"What if I am?"

He shrugged. "I don't care. I'm getting to see you—all of you—even if I have to tie you with these bandages."

Kenshin gave him a defiant look for a second, but then he seemed suddenly tired of fighting him, his head lowering in defeated silence as he lay back down on the mattress, his whole body going limp as his eyes closed.

CHAPTER 38

KEN waited for Shigure to say something, but he didn't, sure fingers returning to the bandages still left on his arms and removing them purposefully.

Fine. It'd soon be over. Shigure would look his fill of tattooed kanji and leave him alone at long last. Because that was what the yakuza would do when it finally got into his thick head that Ken was disfigured for life.

Something in the back of his mind kept trying to repeat Shigure's words about making love, but he silenced that voice harshly. Sure the tough guy hadn't spoken the actual three words, had he now?

"Hmm."

His curiosity was stronger than his pride, and Ken opened his eyes to see what Shigure was doing. The yakuza was looking down at him, appraising his upper body as if it were an oil painting about to be auctioned.

Strangely enough, there wasn't any sign of disgust, concern, or pity in those sharp slanted eyes, but simple, almost distant contemplation, and Ken couldn't help squirming a little under that focused glance.

Shigure gave him a small smile and returned to his silent study, black eyes traveling slowly over his skin. Then it seemed looking wasn't enough, and the yakuza leaned forward to touch, the pressure of his fingers almost nonexistent but still there, following the carved lines of the kanji without touching the wounds, measuring the patches of unmarked skin, the look in his eyes one of intense concentration.

It was driving Ken crazy, not knowing what Shigure thought, unable to gauge the feelings behind that excruciatingly gentle touch, just lying there waiting for a verdict. And as much as he tried to repeat in his mind that he wanted it over with, wanted Shigure to finally let him be, he had never been this afraid in his whole life, not even when he was in that basement, waiting for Atsushi to find new ways to hurt him. That had been primal, instinctual fear, but this was much worse, because there was no risk to his life and so there was no survival instinct kicking in.

He felt the tremors start in his legs, and hated himself for being this weak. Shigure didn't seem to notice, though, and Ken prayed he was too absorbed in whatever it was that he was doing to see the way Ken was trembling.

"I think Maedasaki-sensei would get it right."

"What?" It came out as a squeak, but he couldn't help it.

"The tattoo," Shigure said, as if it were the most obvious thing in the world. "Maedasaki-sensei did mine and most of my men's. He's very good. I think he could use the scar lines as part of the white he sometimes uses for waves or kanji, maybe the Lotus prayer running down from this nipple"—he grazed the torn nipple and drew a diagonal line across Ken's chest—"to end covering this kanji here. The ones on your arms are ideal for something scaly, maybe snakes, or dragons." His fingers kept drawing on Ken's skin as if he could see the actual tattoo taking shape in his mind. "Mostly blue, I think, to cover those irregular blots you already have, with some of their limbs touching your back, though I must warn you that the sensei's favorite parts are the buttocks, so I don't think he's gonna let you walk out of his studio with those untouched...."

The tears were running freely down his cheeks, and he hadn't the strength to wipe them away. It was silly, and he damn well knew it, but it was the way Shigure spoke—his enthusiasm at imagining Ken with the kind of tattoos he and his men wore—and the way he touched him, as if his damaged body were something familiar, something that was his to decorate, to cherish, like some old heirloom he wanted to restore to its ancient splendor, something the yakuza would never even consider getting rid of because it was simply his right to keep.

"Kenshin? Why are you...?"

As vexing as it was, still he couldn't stop or even answer Shigure's concerned question. He just clenched his fist and cried for all he was worth until big hands lifted him and pressed his naked body against a broad chest.

He couldn't help hissing when Shigure's yukata rubbed against his exposed wounds, but it was beyond humiliating that even his bandaged hand tried to hold on to the yakuza when Shigure began to pull away.

"It's all right, Kenshin. Just let me take this off. I don't want to hurt you."

"*Gomen... nasai,*" he mumbled.

Shigure shoved his own yukata down and grabbed him fiercely, strong tattooed arms wrapping around him and holding him tight.

"Don't you dare apologize to me, you silly gaijin."

"I—" His voice broke into a sob, and he hid his face in the crook of Shigure's neck.

"Shhh. Let it all out, Kenshin. You're safe now."

It was all the prompting he needed to bawl like a baby, Shigure's hands petting him as if he really were an overgrown child, gently rearranging them so that Ken sat in his lap, and he could shower his face with small tender kisses, but the more tender the fearsome yakuza got, the more Ken felt like crying and burrowing a hole in that warm chest to stay there hidden forever.

Only when he heard Shigure call him Ken-chan did he allow himself to smile a little.

"Mmmm. I love that smile."

He looked up to search the surprisingly soft black eyes. "Glad you do, Shigure-chan."

It was the best sound in the whole world, that laughter.

"Don't call me that in front of the men, or they'll stop respecting me."

"I very much doubt it, but I'll call you whatever you want me to, Matsunaga-san."

"Shigure will do fine, thank you."

When those eyes had gone from tender to hungry he couldn't tell, but Ken's mouth went immediately dry under the heated stare.

"Shigure—"

The kisses began again, but not so soft this time, Shigure's tongue coming out to lick at the salty trail of his tears while sure hands explored Ken's thighs, his back, his arms, his chest.

He shuddered, his breath coming out in short pants. Long-denied need pulsed in his veins, warmed his skin, made this strange sound push out of his throat to call his lover to him. As an answer, Shigure's mouth crashed on his, and Ken opened himself to the assault, moaning at the taste, his tongue dancing with the invading one, his good hand reaching out to hold on to Shigure's neck.

Eager for more contact, he moved to straddle Shigure's thighs, but the yakuza grabbed his buttocks to stop him and forced him to lie back on the futon. He let out a frustrated whimper, and Shigure was on him in a heartbeat, the hard body pressing against his from toes to hip, the yakuza's taut arms holding his torso away from Ken's chest to avoid his open cuts.

He stared at that gorgeously tattooed body, his mind divided between the need to watch in awed reverence and the more pressing need to touch, taste, lick, and lave that whole expanse of tempting flesh that rippled for him and made the stormy ocean on Shigure's skin come alive with all the creatures that dwelled in its deep blue waters.

Unable to help himself, Ken reached out to trace the contours of the peony around Shigure's left nipple, almost expecting to feel the silky touch of the actual petals, the tattoo was so vibrantly red and alive. It reacted to the contact, too, the brown nub in its center hardening as if to call his attention.

He obliged, lifting his head to better reach it, his tongue coming out to get a taste. Shigure hissed in response, the muscles in his arms trembling slightly as he fought to keep himself upright. It was a heady feeling, knowing that he could get such a strong reaction from the smallest swipe of his tongue, and Ken felt himself smile in anticipation, his whole mouth—teeth and all—closing on the helpless bud without warning.

"Kuso," Shigure cursed, a shudder traveling along his broad frame.

Ken looked up without letting go, just easing the pressure of his teeth and sucking softly instead, smiling around the hard flesh as the big man squirmed, watching him as if he were this close from lunging at Ken to eat him alive.

"You little shit," Shigure said when he caught Ken smiling, but his voice was so husky that it sounded more like an endearment.

"I'm not little," Ken answered, rubbing his arousal against Shigure's ridged belly. It stung a bit where the skin had been burned, but he craved the contact too much to care.

"Kuso gaijin."

Ken chuckled at Shigure's feeble attempt to curse him. The sound suddenly turning into a surprised yelp when the yakuza rolled onto his back, groaning mightily as he dragged Ken on top of him.

"Much better," the big man said with a wicked smile of his own. "I can use my hands now."

And boy, did he use them. He cupped Ken's buttocks and kneaded them, the movement pressing their erections together, the burn so painfully good that Ken arched, his own hands seeking leverage on the tattooed skin beneath him, a grunt escaping his throat as his injured finger pressed against hard pectoral muscles.

"Careful there, Kenshin, you are—"

He silenced Shigure with a searing kiss, his chest resting fully against Shigure's as he bent to devour that tasty mouth, sensation threatening to overwhelm him as his nerve endings received a million different signals. His open cuts stung fiercely where they pressed against Shigure's unyielding flesh, and his nipples hardened at the contact, the torn one screaming in pain at the involuntary contraction. Shigure's fingers sank into his scalp, holding his head in place as the kiss became a battle over territory, tongues thrusting and retreating, teeth nipping, no space left for breathing air that didn't come from one another's lungs.

They were both moving now, unconsciously grinding their hips to get more friction, Shigure's pubes rubbing painfully against Ken's newly shaved skin, the drag of their shafts bringing such excruciating agony that Ken's cry filled Shigure's mouth with a choking sound.

Shigure immediately broke the kiss, searching his eyes.

"Please," Ken croaked, reaching out a trembling hand to Shigure's concerned face.

"Shit, Kenshin. You make me want so much."

He couldn't control the whine that pushed out of him. "Please, I need you. I'm not gonna break."

Shigure studied him with his jaw clenched, fighting to control his emotions.

"Please, Shigure. I need to...." He felt color rising in his cheeks, but he had to say it, had to trust that the man who looked at him as if he were something precious, would understand what he felt. "I need to be sure this is real, need to feel you, need to know you're not going to... disappear on me."

When the yakuza swore loudly and shut his eyes, Ken felt his whole body start to shake. He couldn't for the life of him find the strength to move away from Shigure even though he knew he should, so he just closed his eyes to stop seeing that angry expression on the sharp Japanese features, his trembling body submitting entirely to the pressure of Shigure's hands as the yakuza grabbed Ken to shove him away.

It was even worse that Shigure would still be gentle as he deposited Ken onto the futon, the rustle of the fine sheets telling him exactly when the yakuza retreated, readying himself to step onto the tatami floor. So it came as a surprise when he felt Shigure's weight closer to his legs, and a startled cry left his mouth when strong hands pushed at his thighs to get them to spread.

Ken looked up to meet pitch-black eyes fixed on him, a thunderous expression making the man kneeling between his legs look like a kabuki demon ready to snatch his soul.

The trembling got so bad that Ken believed he'd fall apart under that frightening stare, but he couldn't take his eyes from those blazing coals, not even when Shigure's hands landed on his hipbones and started dragging their way up Ken's body, the pressure constant even when they reached the carved tattoos, all the air in his lungs leaving him in a rush as pain stabbed him, his cry ringing loud in the room when a sword-calloused palm dragged over his torn nipple. He didn't have time to recover before wet heat replaced the hand on his nipple, his back arching off the futon as pain and pleasure became unbearable together.

Shigure's mouth followed the same path down that his hands had taken on their way up, his tongue probing mercilessly into and around the open cuts, Ken squirming wildly under the torture, noises pouring out of him without control. He tried to grab Shigure's head—he wasn't sure whether to shove him away or keep him in place—but the yakuza caught both his wrists easily in one of his big paws and kept going down, his mouth now reaching the shaved patch of skin.

Only Shigure's hand kept him from jerking off of the futon as soon as those lips sucked hard on the sensitive skin. At his cry, Shigure straightened and sat back on his heels, both his hands grabbing Ken's hips and dragging him until his ass rested on the yakuza's powerful thighs.

Ken looked up, panting, exhausted, his whole body tingling with sensation as sweat beaded his skin in spite of the air conditioning.

"I love you, Kenshin. I'm never going to disappear on you again."

Before he could even process the words, Shigure's hands slid under his buttocks and lifted his hips, pushing forward until Ken's body bent over on itself, his raised knees almost touching his shoulders. It was still comfortable, since part of his back rested on the futon and part against Shigure's thighs, and the yakuza's strong hands held him without any effort, but it was a little confusing as to what Shigure intended to do. At least until those fingers spread his cheeks and the flat of Shigure's tongue dragged across his hole in a playful swipe.

Ken let out a surprised yelp, his body trying to move away from the intense sensation only to have Shigure's fingers dig into his flesh to keep him at his mercy, the warm tongue lapping at his entrance with broad strokes and then circling it slowly, again and again, the pressure soft and maddening over naturally sensitive areas made more so by the small burns and tears he'd suffered at Atsushi's hands. It should have been scary, even painful, to be touched there, to be reminded what he'd been through, but all he had to do was look up to meet Shigure's eyes intent on him, gauging his every reaction, care and need so obvious in them, so openly offered that Ken felt his whole body melting under the heat of Shigure's emotions.

The wet caress reached farther with each stroke, his sensitive perineum receiving the same attention, the intensity of the sensations making it difficult to breathe, his hands itching to grab something solid.

When Shigure's mouth sucked hard on his hole, Ken cried out, the fingers he could move immediately curling around Shigure's wrists and holding tight while the ring of muscle around his entrance started contracting and relaxing on its own, as if anticipating penetration.

The yakuza didn't seem to care about the bruising grip of Ken's fingers, and he soon forgot he even had hands, the way Shigure's tongue suddenly pushed into his hole, stretching the muscle just enough to make him feel the invasion without pulling at the tears Atsushi's toys had caused in his passage.

It made his attention shift to focus on that small area of his body, the contact more intimate than any other they'd shared before, Shigure and him. It was, in fact, the first time that someone had been willing to do it, not just to slick his hole with a quick swipe of a wet tongue, but to really explore, to taste those areas of him that seemed darker, filthier, more private.

Kenshin looked up, a little unnerved. Shigure's black eyes were watching him, too, but there was no doubt in them. He was just trying to deepen the connection between them by any means he could use, all his senses trained on Ken as if he were the only thing that really mattered to Shigure, him and his needs, his feelings, his pleasure.

Ken moaned low and closed his eyes, unable to watch anymore. It wasn't much different, though, because somehow he could still feel the intensity of that look on him, and the sensations increased tenfold in the dark: the way Shigure's tongue kept probing his hole and then retreating to make him tingle all over, the wet sounds, the feel of Shigure's hands on his upturned ass, the way his own fingers felt on Shigure's heated flesh, his back on the yakuza's muscled thighs, the drops of pre-come that kept falling on his chest from his neglected cock.

He was being possessed, gently but unmistakably, and his chest started aching as if something were growing in the space between his ribs, something so huge that his skinny body would never be able to contain it, the need to let it all out so strong that he began making small pained noises, little whimpers that begged for some kind of release, some way to push the enormity of his feelings out of him.

Shigure's tongue disappeared suddenly, a shiver running along Ken's frame as cool air grazed his wet skin. It made the yakuza groan appreciatively, and his big hands slid softly on Ken's ass, allowing his back to rest more fully on Shigure's thighs.

Ken opened his eyes and got a little distracted by the way his flushed cock looked from that angle as the tilt of his body turned everything upside down, his balls standing out prominently, the skin of his now tight sac almost purple with blood, glistening with sweat, while his shaft hung for once below his scrotum, slowly dripping on Ken's chest like a tap in need of fixing.

He caught a glimpse of Shigure's smile at his distraction before that wicked mouth closed around one of his shamelessly displayed balls, the world going red with sensation, his own mouth now busy letting out a string of curses.

Shigure made an odd sound that Ken would have sworn was a chuckle, and he made a feeble attempt at swatting the big dork's head, but his fingers seemed to have an altogether different intention, immediately curling around the short strands of black hair, needing more contact, so much so that his other hand reached out to do the same, even if his bandaged fingers could only press against Shigure's scalp like an inanimate lump of white fabric.

"Shigure—" he called, not quite sure if he needed the yakuza to stop or to increase the pace.

Shigure's mouth let go to shush him, strong hands caressing the back of his thighs.

"I'm here, Kenshin, relax."

"Oh, I know you're there, you goof," he panted, the heat in his body turning to almost unbearably sweet warmth as he heard Shigure's laughter. It was a little silly that in spite of his flippancy, he just couldn't stop his hands from holding on to Shigure's head as if he needed to make sure the yakuza wasn't going anywhere soon, and Shigure seemed to know exactly what he was feeling, his eyes going all soft even as he tried to make light of it.

"Glad you noticed. Wouldn't like all this hard work to go to waste."

He grumbled and pulled at Shigure's short hair, but the yakuza flashed him a wicked smile and bent to run a wet tongue along the underside of his shaft.

"Fuck," he swore, the position of his body making it impossible to find relief in the small movements, forcing him to just lie down and take it, let the pleasure run through him as it would.

It was both exhilarating and unnerving, and Shigure damn well knew it, his smile now smug as he kept raising the stakes, nibbling at the wrinkly skin of his balls and then tonguing the tip of his cock, his hands stroking Ken's ass and thighs all the time, a stray finger coming at intervals to draw light circles around his hole.

As the heat ratcheted up once again, Ken felt that familiar oppression in his chest, and the noises he made started sounding desperate. It was more than the simple need for release. He knew something was going to give if Shigure kept pushing, and he was scared to let it happen, terrified that it was infected tissue Shigure was prodding at, and the result would only be more pain and an ugly eruption of thick greenish pus.

"Shigure—" he called again feebly, lost and frightened, his fingers clenching into fists on Shigure's black hair.

"Shhh. Let it go, Kenshin. I'm here for you."

There was no time for anything else, his whimper turning into a sharp cry when Shigure's mouth engulfed his cock completely, and one finger slid into his hole. He came so hard that his whole body shook, his seed bursting into Shigure's mouth, his movements as the yakuza swallowed around his shaft only increasing Ken's pleasure, the burn of that one single knuckle inside him strangely comforting as he rode the waves of aftershocks.

And then it seemed as if his own shudders were infectious, and Shigure had no way to escape contagion, his body shaking even with Ken's shaft still in his mouth, a tale-telling wetness spreading against the small of Ken's back.

It registered somewhere in his addled mind that Shigure had enjoyed giving him his undivided attention as much as Ken's selfish body had. It had not been an act of pity, or some task the dutiful yakuza felt compelled to carry out. It had been exciting to him, to taste Ken where nobody else had ever wanted to.

"Shigure," he whispered, watching intently as the yakuza slid his lips down his shaft for the last time, gently letting go with a kiss to the wet crown. "I...."

Dark eyes met his, careful hands supporting his back as Shigure slowly made him rest completely on the strong thighs, Ken's legs flopping down onto the mattress with an ungainly thud. Then those hands took Ken's fingers to disentangle them from Shigure's hair, but he couldn't summon the strength to be embarrassed about his desperate clinging.

"Tell me," Shigure said softly, kissing the fingers of his bandaged hand.

Ken took a deep breath. There was nowhere to hide, nowhere to run to. Shigure had seen all that he was, and wanted him anyway.

"I love you," he said, keeping his gaze steady on those black, slanted eyes.

Shigure's jaw clenched for a moment, and then he was moving from under Ken to have him lie on the futon and wrapping around him like a warm blanket, holding him tight.

"I know, Kenshin. I know," he whispered in his ear, his voice strained with emotion, and Ken finally let go in those strong arms. He was safe, at last.

CHAPTER 39

SHIGURE followed Oyone down the hallway, their tabi socks padding softly on the tatami mats. She looked older in her gray tsukesage kimono, a sprinkle of delicately embroidered white blossoms the only detail that lightened its formal sobriety, the pattern flowing up from the hem like it was carried on a gentle breeze that came to a sudden halt at the obi belt around her waist, the capricious gust of wind blowing again on her right sleeve to splatter more of the little white flowers all over the sleeve and up to her shoulder.

Looking at her, Shigure had trouble reconciling the elegant matron walking daintily in front of him with his memories of the wild, often dirty tomboy who used to play in the streets no one but them acknowledged as a burakumin ghetto.

"He looks harried," she said without turning to face him.

"Harried? Are we talking about the same Uehara here?"

Now she did turn, her hands landing on her hips in the most unladylike manner, her glare much more intimidating than the Shinagawa oyabun's. Yeah, that was the Oyone he knew and loved.

"Are you going deaf with age? That wisp of a man has only two different faces to wear—the constipated samurai's and the smart-ass sleuth's—and I'm telling you he's wearing neither today."

He tried hard to suppress a smile. "So what face is he wearing now?"

"The harassed underdog's, that's what face."

Shigure's laughter resonated in the quiet hallway, and Oyone rolled her eyes at him.

"Chinpira," she mumbled before turning away.

It was always refreshing to be called a punk again, since nobody but Oyone dared to call him names so openly anymore. And nobody did it as affectionately as his childhood friend, except, perhaps, Kenshin. He had a foul mouth, too, that one.

Shigure couldn't help smiling at the thought of Kenshin. He'd left the American sleeping like a baby, sprawled naked across the futon, for once careless about his exposed wounds. They would take some time to heal, those and the less visible ones, but Shigure was confident that Kenshin would now seek his help when he needed it.

"Oh, stop smiling like a sap," Oyone hissed. They had already reached the shoji doors to the room where Uehara waited. "This can be the right time to squeeze one or two favors from that uptight bastard, but you have to get your head out of your ass for that—or out of your gaijin's ass, that is."

"Oyone!"

"Shut up and do your best imperturbable yakuza impersonation."

He opened his mouth to protest that he didn't have to pretend to be what he actually was, but Oyone was already sliding the doors open and bowing meekly to the man inside the tasteful tatami room.

It was a surprise to find Uehara already standing, as if he'd been pacing the room instead of sitting patiently as he usually did. To someone who didn't know the old cop, he would have appeared composed, almost indifferent, but Shigure could tell that his inquisitive eyes looked a little harried today, just as Oyone had hinted.

"Uehara-junsa-buchō."

"Matsunaga-wakagashira."

They bowed to each other, and Shigure waved his hand in silent invitation for the sergeant to sit. Oyone had left without a sound, but they both knew that she would soon be back to offer them sake, and so they only exchanged the obligatory pleasantries about one another's health, the weather, and the like.

Oyone appeared on cue with a small tray of lacquered wood, and deposited two white-and-blue *ochoko* cups on the low table between the two men. The sake flask followed, decorated with deceptively simple calligraphic motifs in matching hues.

When she left, Shigure served Uehara the milky white *nigorizake* from the chilled flask, making a mental note to praise Oyone for her choice. Her establishment always served the best sake, refined or no, and she never had the need to warm it to mask its taste, unless some uncouth client asked for it.

"To what do I owe the pleasure of your visit, Sergeant?"

He only understood why Uehara seemed to cringe at his question when the proud cop moved a little away from the table and bowed to the ground in front of him.

"I've come to ask you a favor, Matsunaga-wakagashira."

"Please stand, Sergeant. You know I will always help you to the best of my ability."

Uehara rose from his bow and sat back on his heels, the posture far from relaxed, his eyes never meeting Shigure's. It must have been hard for the old man, to have to ask a yakuza for favors.

"In the incident concerning your assistant," he began, and Shigure nodded, understanding that by "incident" Uehara meant Atsushi's death. "I took depositions from all the witnesses."

"Yes. I remember that."

"Well, there seems to be a problem with those depositions."

Shigure kept nodding and waited for the sergeant to make his point.

"The sequence of events is rather clear. You had confronted your assistant about Harisu-san's kidnapping when some of your men entered the room. Feeling cornered, your assistant tried to attack them, and Tachibana-san had to shoot him to defend himself and the others."

"Uh-huh." Shigure was starting to see where the problem was— somehow Kei hadn't made it into the picture. The emphasis on Tachibana having to defend himself was reassuring, though.

"All of those present agreed about the events happening the way I just described, but they seemed to be under the impression that there was someone else in the room."

"I was under that impression too, Sergeant."

Uehara nodded. "As I said, all the statements were in accordance—too much in accordance, if you get my meaning."

So it was going to be that way. The old cop might have come to ask a favor, but he'd be sure to first negotiate the amount of the debt he'd be getting into.

"I hope you remember it wasn't a neighbor who called the police," Shigure said.

"Of course. I'm well aware that nobody would have heard the shot, given the location of your house. You could have simply tried to dispose of the body."

"But we did call the police, because we had nothing to hide. So what would be the point in purposefully changing our statements after the fact?"

"Well, I imagine the first thing you did was search your assistant for a gun and, when you found nothing but some length of rope, I suppose you thought it might not look too good for Tachibana-san and his semiautomatic—which, by the way, he doesn't have a license for."

"Atsushi had killed with that rope before. I had no doubt it would've been a lethal weapon in his hands," Shigure countered.

Uehara made a dismissive gesture. "Of course. You and I know that, but maybe you thought a judge might have his doubts, seeing that your men are all trained in the martial arts and could have easily stopped an unarmed man without having to kill him."

"Unless there was some defenseless woman in the room, you mean."

"Exactly."

They kept silent for a moment, until Shigure was sure Uehara was not yet ready to lay all his cards on the table.

"It makes sense, Sergeant, but the truth is Kotarō had actually been trying to locate a woman."

Uehara nodded. "The girl who worked for Harada-san."

"Yeah. So what makes you think he hadn't found her and brought her to the house?"

"He couldn't possibly have, because I happen to know where the girl was when your assistant was killed."

"And where was that?"

"She was attending her father's retirement party."

Shigure didn't have a hard time connecting all the dots. "A colleague of yours, I suppose," he said, more than asked.

"Hai."

No wonder Uehara was trying to bargain his way through it all. Now all Shigure had to do was tread carefully to get the upper hand without making the sergeant lose face.

"He must have been very upset when he learned what his daughter had been doing behind his back," he offered, and he could tell Uehara liked the turn of the conversation.

"He was devastated. And now that he's just beginning to enjoy his retirement after an honorable career, I wouldn't want him to have to deal with this misunderstanding."

"Of course. I wouldn't want to further upset your friend, either, but you must understand my concern. You said it yourself, that it might not look good in court—Tachibana shooting an unarmed Atsushi—and I'm worried that the judge will only see a trigger-happy yakuza with an illegal gun."

"I can assure you it won't come to that. Your assistant's crimes are proven beyond doubt, and Tachibana-san offered his full cooperation to the officers at the scene, surrendering his gun voluntarily. With the favorable report of the officers considered, myself among them, I'm sure the state won't press charges, and I very much doubt the remaining members of your assistant's family will."

"I'm relieved to hear that, but Tachibana is not exactly a first-time offender," Shigure insisted. "In fact, he's in custody as we speak."

Uehara looked positively smug now. "He and Nakatani Shinya-san have already been released with no charges. It was obvious to everyone that the disturbances at Okusawa Hospital had been due to a cultural misunderstanding."

"Indeed." Shigure had a hard time reining in his smile. "And about the illegal gun?"

"Considering all the mitigating circumstances, I'm sure Tachibana-san will only be charged with a fine."

"Then I will give a new deposition, and so will my men."

"I've taken the liberty to write them down. You'll only have to sign them."

"Good. I'm glad that we straightened out this misunderstanding, Uehara-junsa-buchō."

The sergeant bowed deeply again. "I'm in your debt, Matsunaga-wakagashira."

"Don't mention it."

Having said what needed to be said, both men stood. Shigure saw Uehara to the door, and the sergeant walked away with his usual brisk step, wearing what Oyone would no doubt call his constipated samurai's face. It was all right by Shigure, since he'd got a pretty good deal out of it. His men were already back on the streets, Tachibana's case wouldn't even be seen in court, and Uehara would still owe him big time for saving his friend's daughter's reputation. That was why he always encouraged his men to fully cooperate with the local police.

CHAPTER 40

KEN lifted his pen. Oyone's ryokan was a pretty little jewel of traditional architecture blossoming right in the middle of the concrete wasteland. It had been built in the late twenties, ravaged by the incendiary bombs dropped on Tokyo during World War II, and miraculously restored in the fifties when the rest of the city was trying to get rid of the symbols of what was considered its backward past.

If it hadn't been a yakuza favorite since it opened its doors as a traditional inn and restaurant, Ken suspected all those luscious cedar planks would have ended warming someone's winter nights. He was glad they hadn't, especially since it prevented him from having to look inside his mind for inspiration. He wasn't too keen on visiting the usual places his monsters dwelt in now that they'd been fed raw, bleeding meat.

This small garden, though, had nothing scary lurking behind the azalea bushes around the bench where he sat, but still had so many beautiful corners, so many details he wanted to capture, that he'd been drawing it for almost a month and still could find precious views to capture his attention for hours on end.

But not today, it seemed. He was too distracted, too worried to focus on anything that wasn't Shigure and all the yakuza was trying to hide from him.

He closed the sketchbook with a loud thwack.

"Chotto, chotto, nande sonnani urusai no."

Ken nearly jumped out of his skin. Jesus, that fine lady could sneak up on you like a Navy SEAL. Talked like a gunnery sergeant too.

"Sorry, Oyone-san. I didn't mean to be so noisy."

She made a noncommittal sound and pulled a pack of cigarettes and a slim lighter out of her kimono sleeve. "Don't give me that look.

It's either a cigarette or plain murder, and I can't kill my clients if I want to keep this place running, can I now?"

He smiled. "I always forget people in Asia still smoke a lot."

"Honey, never say this is Asia to any Japanese. We don't live on islands for nothing."

Ken had to laugh at that. Yeah, the Japanese were different, or so they wanted to believe even when all their culture had sprung from the continent they despised—maybe for that very reason.

"So, what's got you so bothered?"

He shrugged. "I suppose I have too much time to think, that's all."

"Huh. I thought you Americans had less fear of speaking your minds than, say, certain tattooed thugs over here."

"Yeah, but we can hardly speak our minds without an audience, and certain tattooed thugs are making themselves scarce as of late."

"That's right. Seems to me he's up to something, that one."

Ken perked up. "You think so too?"

Oyone watched him for a moment before turning her head to exhale smoke through perfectly made-up red lips. "He might just be trying to protect you from what he does, you know."

He made a frustrated sound. "It should be clear by now that I don't care what he does, what he is. And I'm not a child for him to protect."

"You aren't, but you can't blame him for worrying after what happened to you."

"It wasn't his fault. Could have happened to anyone."

Oyone raised an eyebrow at him.

"Okay. Not to anyone. But it still wasn't his fault."

"You should see his face, every time he comes back here. He doesn't really start breathing right until I tell him where you are."

Shit. That silly man.

"I've known him since we were kids," Oyone went on, "and I can tell you I've never seen him this far gone before. You're it for him, Ken-chan."

He smiled at her use of the diminutive both she and Shigure had taken to calling him.

"*Hai, Onēsan,*" he said, raising his arms to prevent his "big sister" from whacking his head.

"Don't mock me, you gaijin runt. You've been head over heels for that big lug for as long as I've known you."

He sobered quickly. "Yeah. Took Shigure long enough to notice, though."

"Bah, men can be as dense as miso paste in matters of the heart. And they can be even thicker when it comes to everyday logistics."

"Logistics?"

"Yes, logistics. Have you two given any thought to how you're going to live from now on? Are you staying in Japan for good? Are you moving in with Shigure? Is Shigure's oyabun all right with you living in one of the Shinagawa houses? Or is Shigure moving out to some other place with you? Are you ready to be a yakuza's spouse?"

Ken just stared at her, speechless.

"That's what I thought."

"I'm sorry, Oyone-san. I hadn't realized how long I've been staying here. You must be sick of us already."

Oyone waved the cigarette dismissively at him. "Bullshit. I like you far more than I like most of my guests—especially since I can give you a piece of my mind whenever I want. But I can see Shigure is trying to make things work out in his usual masterless-ronin fashion, and I can't begin to tell you how bad it can get if you leave that foolish man to his own devices."

"What man? Do I have to beat the shit out of someone?"

They both turned to find Shigure frowning at them, though the overall forbidding image was somehow spoiled by the way his lips twitched.

"Don't drop your job to pursue an acting career, Gure-chan," Oyone said, leaning on Shigure's arm to lift one of her delicate feet and stub her cigarette out against the wooden sole of her geta sandal.

Shigure laughed. "You're a cruel woman, always crushing my dreams."

"*Hai, hai,*" she agreed, waving them away as she left the garden.

Shigure moved closer to where Ken sat on the wooden bench.

"Hey there," the yakuza said softly.

Ken tugged at the sleeve of Shigure's dark suit. He was impeccably dressed, as always, even in the still clammy weather of late September. "Hey. Sit with me?"

The yakuza obliged, sitting down with a sigh, his leg immediately pressing against Ken's. They were in the part of the garden that could be seen from the guests' windows, so neither of them made any further move to close the distance between them, though Ken was dying to loop his arms around Shigure's neck and kiss the spiffy yakuza senseless.

"Have I told you how hot you look in that suit?" he whispered.

"Yeah, I'm hot all right. This weather's killing me."

Ken must have pouted because Shigure chuckled and bumped him with his knee. "I know what you meant, you little gaijin devil, but I don't want Oyone to kick us to the curb anytime soon."

He looked away, remembering what Oyone had told him. It was true that he hadn't given any thought to the future, but it was mostly because he had been doing his best to avoid thinking—about anything and everything—until it stopped hurting so much. Then again, maybe it was better to jump straight into it while the wounds were still tender, much like he'd been doing with his tattoos, drowning them in new ink before he could develop one of those post-traumatic phobias about the whole body-art thing.

"Kenshin?"

He looked up into concerned black eyes. This man had told him that he loved him, so what was he afraid of?

"How long am I going to stay at Oyone's place?" he blurted out, searching Shigure's eyes for any reaction. And he did get a reaction, but not quite the one he expected.

The yakuza averted his gaze so quickly that Ken barely had time to catch the guilty look in those eyes. "You know it's just a temporary arrangement."

Still Shigure wouldn't look at him, and Ken felt a flutter in his stomach that had nothing to do with excitement. "You are ashamed of me. You don't want me to live with you," he said, hating the way his voice sounded weak and scared.

"No."

Oh God. The only time a Japanese said a straight no to his face had to be this one time, when it hurt like a punch to the gut. He bolted off of the bench, only to have two strong arms wrap around him and stop his mad flight.

"Shit, Kenshin, I meant no, I'm not ashamed of you."

All the fear turned into anger he didn't know how to handle. "You fucking idiot."

Shigure's arms tightened around him, solid warmth enveloping him as his back pressed against the broad chest. "I love you, Ken-chan, and I'm more than proud of you. Of course I want to live with you."

"Don't 'Ken-chan' me."

He could almost hear Shigure smile, feel those lips curve up as they kissed the sensitive skin behind his ear.

"Don't try to get me sidetracked either. This is serious."

"I know." Those arms squeezed him tighter and then let go. "Come sit. Let me explain."

He followed Shigure back to their bench and sat with his arms crossed. The yakuza reached out to run gentle fingers along his cheek. "I'm sorry, Kenshin. I would have wanted to take you home with me, but I didn't want the American attachés to know where you were, at least for a time."

Ken frowned. "What do the legal attachés have to do with anything?"

"Uh…. The truth is we sort of snuck you out of the hospital."

"You what?"

"They wanted—your family wanted—to move you to an American hospital, so your friend Nishimura got some doctor to sign the papers to have you transferred to a private clinic while we distracted the gaijin cops."

He couldn't believe what he was hearing. "How come nobody has told me a fucking thing? Jesus. Even Ryū… And what do you mean by distracting the attachés? What did you do?"

Shigure gave him a sheepish look. "The idea was just to keep them talking while Nishimura worked his magic, but it got a little out of control."

He rubbed a hand over his face.

"Don't worry. Shinya and Tachibana were released straight away."

"Released? They were arrested?" He let out what could have only passed for laughter in a mental facility, and Shigure's hands took his immediately, thumbs moving in soothing circles over his skin.

"They wouldn't have allowed us to see you, Kenshin, and none of us was ready to accept that." Shigure snorted. "You should have seen Kinosuke coming out of his room to shout at the poor bastards."

"Shit. I'm sorry. I never—"

"Shhh. It's all right. I'm only telling you this to explain why I brought you here instead of my house."

Ken looked down. "So my father wanted me contained lest some of my filth spatter him."

Shigure didn't say anything, but tightened his hold on Ken's hands, and Ken forced himself to look up again to search Shigure's eyes.

"You're not telling me everything."

Shigure sighed. "I can deal with it, Kenshin, trust me. You're still healing."

He shook his hands free from Shigure's hold and stood, barely remembering to keep his voice down. "How can I trust you when you keep things from me? This is my life, too, and I won't have you dealing with it. And I'm not on a fucking vacation here, for Christ's sake. What kind of wuss do you think I am? You expect me to be healing for the rest of my life? From some fucking knife wounds?"

Shigure shot off of the bench and stood looming over him, fury burning in his eyes, hands clenched into fists as if ready to strike, but Ken refused to move, the more intimidating Shigure looked, the angrier it made him that the yakuza would be trying to browbeat him into silence. So when Shigure opened his mouth, Ken didn't even let him begin to speak, his loud voice shattering the Zen-like peace of the garden.

"Don't you dare mention PTSD to me, or I swear I'll make you eat every fucking syllable of the whole claptrap and shove the chopsticks down your throat afterward. You hear me, you big bird-brained *gokutsubushi*?"

The silence was so thick now that Ken could clearly hear every drop that fell onto the water basin on the other side of the garden. He forced himself to hold Shigure's blazing glare, and when the yakuza moved, he fought the urge to flinch with all his might. He would be damned if he let the big bully see how intimidating he truly was.

To his surprise, Shigure turned and walked two steps away from him, his hands still clenched at his sides, his shoulders shaking with anger. His own anger left him in a rush as he watched the yakuza fight to control his rage. The Japanese were proud people by themselves, but a yakuza had a reputation to keep, too, and a burakumin had everything to prove. The three things together would make it almost impossible for Shigure to take an insult without answering, especially since they were more or less in public and someone must have heard his harsh words.

Ken felt awful watching Shigure struggle against his pride just for his sake. He was about to apologize when he heard a muffled sound. Was that...?

"Are you fucking laughing?"

"I'm... not... laughing," Shigure wheezed in the most unconvincing way.

"You bastard," Ken spat, his legs taking him to Shigure in two huge steps, his hands moving on their own to grab one thick arm and make the yakuza turn to face him. And there it was, that barely restrained smile that made Shigure's eyes glint.

It weakened his knees, that smile, and Ken tried to cover it by banging his fists ineffectually against the broad chest in front of him. Big hands wrapped around his wrists and held them without apparent effort.

"Shit, Kenshin, you're a firebrand."

"Yeah, right. And I inspire holy terror in you."

Shigure had the nerve to laugh openly at him now. "Sorry, but you just sounded like my mother. She used to call me a good-for-nothing loafer too."

"And I bet she threatened to feed you your chopsticks too, right?"

"That was a distinctive Kenshin original," Shigure said, immediately cracking up.

"You're a doofus," Ken said, trying uselessly to stay mad. He'd always loved Shigure's laughter, and he hadn't heard it in a long time.

The yakuza let go of Ken's wrists and pulled him to his chest. Ken went easily, his arms wrapping around the trim waist, his head leaning against a strong shoulder.

"Someone might see us," he said without moving.

"Yeah. We boorish yakuza are always putting on shows."

Ken looked up into still smiling black eyes. "I was serious, you know."

"About the chopsticks?"

Ken rolled his eyes, and Shigure laughed. "I know, I know, Ken-chan. I promise we'll discuss this soon enough, but now there are some pressing matters that need our full attention." As he spoke, Shigure's hands slid down Ken's back to his ass and squeezed.

Ken made an appreciative sound as Shigure's erection pressed against his belly, his own cock straining against the zipper of his light cotton pants.

"Inside?"

"Uh-huh."

But neither of them moved, except to laugh at each other.

"Come on, you shameless gaijin. Get that tight little ass moving for me."

And Ken did, because he'd do anything that man wanted him to do. Anything.

CHAPTER 41

HE LET Kenshin undress him. No one had ever looked at him the way his gaijin did, a rapt expression on that gorgeous face, those incredible eyes full of desire and something else that was quite difficult for him to understand.

That mixture of curiosity and awe in Kenshin's eyes got to him every time. He'd had enough lovers in his life to know he had a certain dose of rough appeal, his fit body his best feature, considerably helped by Maedasaki-sensei's tattoo art, and the thrill some people got out of his being a yakuza. Yet it wasn't until Kenshin looked at him for the first time that he'd felt truly naked in front of a lover.

It might be because his gaijin was an artist, but he never seemed to take the most obvious appearances for granted, and he looked at things as if he'd never seen them before, dissecting every detail, every hue, every texture to recreate an image in his mind that had nothing to do with the generic, everyday, name-tagging view everyone else would get from watching the same object. It was a little scary, that look, the knowledge that you were the absolute center of someone's attention, but when those fascinating eyes would meet his after the thorough inspection, what he saw in the twin mirrors left him breathless all the time.

Kenshin's eyes were looking at him that way now, making him preen and ache all over, a smile curving his lips when he thought he had just discovered how those eyes worked. Easy enough, those contrasting irises had to be like the bicolored lens on 3-D glasses, his gaijin's eyes the only ones prepared to give a truly three-dimensional image of Shigure, the closest to reality and, at the same time, the most beautifully false one.

"What?" Kenshin said, smiling, too, long fingers touching Shigure's lips as if to trace the contours of his smile. He tried to speak through those fingers, making his gaijin laugh at the mumbled nonsense. "Tickles."

"*This* tickles," he said, guiding his own fingers to the places along Kenshin's ribs he knew would make the slender body squirm. He got a squeak in response, Kenshin trying to dance away from him. "Oh no, you're not going anywhere with all these clothes on."

"Is that a new kind of toll? As in, leave an article of clothing and you can ride the full distance of the Shuto Expressway?"

Shigure laughed. "Yeah. But you know how expensive Japanese highways are, so I'm afraid a single article of clothing won't be enough."

He pulled at the hem of Kenshin's electric blue T-shirt, and his gaijin took it off, his eyes immediately returning to Shigure's. Maedasaki-sensei had started working on the kanji, the shoddy lines beginning to disappear under the waves of a new, masterfully applied tattoo, but still Kenshin didn't find it easy to look at his own body.

"Hmmm. That'll only cover the first two miles, I think."

Shigure, though, loved watching that body change as it healed, raw cuts turning into thin white scars, bones fleshing out with Oyone's cooking, muscles recovering with Kenshin's regular visits to the nearby dojo.

"Will this be enough?" Kenshin said, white cotton pants dangling from his fingers in front of Shigure.

"Let's see," he croaked, taking the pants and throwing them on top of the discarded T-shirt. His eyes went straight to Kenshin's groin, and he would have laughed if his throat hadn't gone completely dry. Damn. Where on earth did he find that crazy underwear?

He was wearing a pair of tight low-riding trunks with huge momiji leaves printed on a deep blue background, the almost childish cuteness of the pattern all but disappearing because of the fabric used to make them. Mesh underwear. And the big Japanese maple leaf on the front pouch was doing a poor job at hiding the contours of the bulge under it.

"What now? I think I've paid more than my fair share already," Kenshin said, affecting innocence, the little shit.

"That you have," Shigure said, his eyes never leaving the maple leaf, "if you were driving a light car. But I'm afraid that there is a small-sized truck, mister. I'll have to charge you double."

Kenshin's eyes twinkled, and the maple leaf seemed to expand under Shigure's unwavering attention. "Jesus. This is pure highway robbery. Strip me of my last coin, will you?"

Shigure's chuckle turned into a moan when Kenshin shoved his fingers under the waistband and started pushing the translucent fabric down. His blond curls had already grown back, but Kenshin stopped right there, suddenly turning around to give Shigure a full view of that incredible ass.

"Kuso."

"Like what you see?" Kenshin said, wiggling as he bent to slip out of the exotic underwear.

Instead of answering, Shigure moved closer to those beckoning globes, his fingers reaching out to stroke and knead the tight muscle under the smooth skin. Kenshin gasped and pushed back into the touch, his body still bent in silent offering. It was the perfect position for Shigure to simply inch a little closer and sink easily into the tight heat he so longed to possess, but they'd waited all this time for Kenshin to heal, and Shigure would go on waiting for as long as it took.

"Come up here," he said, letting his hands slide to the flat belly and pushing a little for Kenshin to straighten. He heard a muffled protest, but soon he had his arms full of naked gaijin, his cock nestling comfortably between the round cheeks. "Hmmm, nice."

Kenshin moaned and leaned against him. "Please, Shigure. I want you."

"Want you too," he whispered, sucking on the sensitive skin behind Kenshin's ear, the shudder he got in response making his cock jump and start leaking along Kenshin's crease. "How do you want me?"

Kenshin tilted his hips back, pressing harder against Shigure. "In me, please?"

The way the plea came out as a question gave Shigure pause. Maybe waiting hadn't been such a great idea if it had made Kenshin feel this unsure. Or worse still, maybe he was asking just because he thought that was what Shigure wanted.

He took hold of the thin shoulders and made his gaijin face him. He needed to see those eyes.

"Are you sure, Kenshin?"

The pretty face was flushed, pupils huge inside bright circles of green and brown, lips parted to let out one single desperate sound. "Please."

"Bed, now," Shigure almost growled, his cock so hard he feared he might come just from watching Kenshin walk to the futon. A hand reached out for his, the missing tip of one finger evident, and Shigure made a show of taking it into his mouth and sucking lightly on the scarred pinkie, his eyes never leaving Kenshin's.

"Weirdo," his gaijin teased, though he couldn't hide how much his cock liked the attention. Shigure smiled around the bumpy surface, nibbling and licking, getting Kenshin so distracted that when he pushed him just a little, he fell back onto the futon with a startled cry.

He chuckled, but his gaijin took his sweet revenge, long legs spreading enticingly, one hand wrapping around a flushed cock and tugging, sultry eyes raking over Shigure's body, the rosy tip of a tongue coming out to wet full lips the very moment those eyes zeroed in on Shigure's leaking shaft.

"Kuso gaijin," he cursed, grabbing the base of his cock and squeezing.

Kenshin tried to laugh at his predicament, but the sound came out a little choked, both his hands reaching out to Shigure impatiently. "Come down here and fuck me."

"Shit. You gaijin have no manners."

Slender fingers grabbed at him with surprising force and pulled him down, Shigure barely managing to keep his full weight from landing on top of Kenshin. "No manners at all."

"You'll have to teach me those," Kenshin said, pulling him down for a kiss even before he finished the sentence.

"Yeah. I have to teach you the basics, like never speak with your mouth full," he said when they came up for air.

Kenshin's smile was a sight to see, affection and mischief lighting up his whole features as he lifted his head to recapture Shigure's lips. "You mean like th—"

"Mmhmmm. Exactly like that. Now the second most important thing is to never let your guests do all the work."

"I can do that."

"Show me," he said, rolling to his side and bringing Kenshin with him to reverse their positions. Now his gaijin was stretched on top of him, the weight of his lean body a welcome pressure, warm and solid against his own heated skin.

"I like this," Kenshin said, resting his head on Shigure's chest. "You make a great pillow."

He swatted a round ass cheek with a loud thwack and got a cry and a wide-eyed stare in response, the way Kenshin's body squirmed against his making his voice come out hoarse. "Don't sleep on your guest, you rude gaijin."

One single slap and Kenshin's cheek had gone all rosy, goose bumps rising all over his thighs and buttocks. Shit. His lover was so responsive, so sensual. How could anyone want to harm this incredible creature?

His hand followed the curve of Kenshin's ass, soothing the burn. If Shigure had his way, he'd never even let clothes cover that delicate skin, and only his hands and lips would be allowed to worship the wild grace of that slender body.

Some of his feelings must have shown on his face because Kenshin was searching his eyes and frowning.

"You didn't hurt me, you know."

Maybe not now, but he knew he had, and he'd never forgive himself for the damage he'd caused. The smile he used to dispel the somber mood wasn't very convincing, it seemed, since Kenshin's lips closed in a tight, sour line. There went his chances to make this a playful experience.

His gaijin pressed his hands against Shigure's chest for leverage and pushed back until he was straddling Shigure's hips.

"Lube," Kenshin ordered, unique eyes fixing Shigure with a blazing stare. He obeyed without thinking, mesmerized by the fire in those eyes, his hand reaching under the pillow to retrieve a familiar tube and offering it to Kenshin.

The tube was uncapped, the following spurt loud in the tense silence of the room. Then Kenshin reached back and thrust two slicked fingers inside himself. Shit. That was not the way it should be. Kenshin was out to prove something, hiding his wince as best he could, turning what should have been a sweet reacquaintance into a test of bravery.

"Stop, Kenshin."

His gaijin ignored him, fiery eyes glaring down at him.

"Please, Kenshin," he said softly, his hand wrapping around a thin wrist to still its movements.

"I won't break," Kenshin said, trying to sound harsh and only managing to make it into a plea, his eyes a little lost now, as if he feared Shigure might not want him anymore.

Shigure took a deep breath, afraid his own heart would break at Kenshin's insecurity, his free hand reaching out to stroke the beautiful face. "I know you're strong, Kenshin. You don't have to prove it to me."

His lover frowned, but allowed him to gently remove his fingers. "Let me?" he asked.

Shigure didn't wait for an answer, but took the lube and slicked his own fingers, giving Kenshin time to stop him. When he didn't, Shigure rubbed the cool gel over Kenshin's hole, pressing softly without pushing in.

His gaijin made a small sound and leaned back, trying to get more friction, but Shigure grabbed a bony hip to keep him still. "Easy, Ken-chan."

Kenshin rolled his eyes at the diminutive, but he let Shigure set the pace, his fingers rubbing in small circles until he felt the muscles spasm in anticipation. Only then did he push one of his knuckles in, stopping when he heard his lover gasp.

He looked up to find Kenshin's eyes focused intently on him, and realized Kenshin needed to make sure it was Shigure trying to breach into his body. He bit back a curse and forced his voice to sound as reassuring as he could.

"Shhhh, Kenshin, relax. Let me in, let me touch you inside."

His gaijin shuddered at his words, and the pressure around his finger eased enough for him to push deeper past the ring of muscle.

"That's it. Relax. I'm going to move now," he crooned, flexing his finger so that it could explore the heated flesh engulfing it. "Hmmm. You're so hot."

Kenshin moaned and rocked a little into his touch. Shigure kept talking as he pushed a second finger into the tight opening, eyes locked with his lover's, letting him know it was Shigure touching him deep and not some alien object tearing its way forward.

"So good, Kenshin," he said, fighting back the rush of anger when his fingers touched the unyielding surface of scar tissue. "You'll soon be ready for my cock."

When his gaijin whimpered for him, he started moving his fingers in and out, slowly, seeking Kenshin's gland on the way in. Kenshin's soft cry told him exactly when he'd pegged it, his neglected cock jumping at the sweet sound, eager to fill the space his fingers occupied.

"Shigure, please," his lover panted. "I need you now."

He nodded, scissoring his fingers a little before pulling them out of their cozy nest. Kenshin immediately wrapped his fingers around Shigure's shaft, the touch, the sight of his lover guiding his cock to his hole almost enough to push him over the edge.

He forced his hands to grab the sheets to let Kenshin feel he had total control, even if the excruciatingly slow pace was driving Shigure crazy, a delicious ache spreading from the head of his cock to his balls and from them to his belly, a deep, guttural sound escaping his throat when he looked down to see his shaft suddenly disappear into his lover's body.

"Shigure...."

Kenshin's eyes were shut, a bead of sweat trickling down the soft skin of his neck, his long rosy shaft only half-erect now, the burn, the unwanted memories warring with his obvious arousal.

"My brave gaijin," Shigure said, his voice laced with all the pride, all the love that threatened to burst out of him without further stimulation. He reached out to pet the strong thighs, his fingers moving up over the hipbones, stroking the tight belly, dancing over the new tattoos, grazing nipples that were as mismatched as the eyes that now looked down at him with a love so fierce that he knew he'd never be a match for the wild being he once thought he could possess. He was only prey to the much stronger predator, and so eager to be devoured that he himself pulled down that mouth to him and opened wide to its assault.

They both grunted into the toothy kiss when the position of Kenshin's body made Shigure's shaft slide out a little. They were too far gone to laugh, and the noises that poured out of them grew feral and disgruntled, hunger too strong to be anything but painful when Kenshin broke the kiss and started moving on Shigure's shaft, pushing himself up from his knees to quickly sink back down, taking Shigure to the root every time.

Shigure held onto the lean hips, his eyes fixed on the most beautiful work of art he'd ever contemplated, a landscape of love and strength, stunning in its powerful movement, perfect in its rough asymmetry, the hands of nature and man giving shape to a beauty that was only fragile in that it was irreplaceable, unique.

"Kenshin—"

He barely managed a name before pleasure exploded out of him, the intensity of his orgasm blinding him for a second and only bringing him back in time to watch Kenshin's expression as he came, enigmatic eyes on his as if capturing Shigure in a soul-bonding spell.

Shigure pulled the lean body to him while they were both still shaking and held on, Kenshin's seed gluing their skins together, their sweat mingling into a new compound that smelled like sex and love and promises to be made.

"Stay with me, Kenshin," he whispered, not meaning now, or in this bed.

"Yes," his lover answered softly, and Shigure knew he meant forever.

CHAPTER 42

HE WAITED for his men's reaction to the bomb he'd dropped on them. Only his most trusted soldiers were sitting around him now. The rest would learn the news in due time, but these were his friends, the ones who cared about Kenshin enough to understand what Shigure was doing.

The tatami room was so quiet that nobody would have guessed it was occupied. His men sat in *seiza*, their faces somber, mulling Shigure's words over, trying hard to contain their first impulsive reactions.

"You can't quit, boss!" Well, some of them were trying, anyway.

"I have to, Kotarō."

"But there must be another way—"

"As long as I'm recognized as a yakuza, Kenshin's father won't stop until he gets a judge to declare his son incapacitated and appoint him as Kenshin's guardian. And if that man starts making decisions for Kenshin, the least that'd happen to him would be to be forced to return to America. I wouldn't put it past the good senator to throw his son into a mental institution."

"The bastard," Kinosuke mumbled.

"What if you left the country?" Tachibana asked.

"There'd always be an American embassy, and I won't spend the rest of my life hiding."

"If Kenshin-san wasn't an American citizen—" Tachibana insisted.

Shigure shook his head firmly. "He's offered to renounce his citizenship, but he's already lost enough because of me. It's my turn to make some sacrifice."

Silence grew heavy in the room. These men had the right to be angry since their leader was abandoning his duty to them, and yet, none of them had suggested the most obvious solution. Everything would be fine if Shigure left Kenshin.

Of course the oyabun had done more than suggest it, but the old boss had never been Shigure's friend, never even tried to understand why Shigure might feel more honor-bound to a skinny gaijin than to the Shinagawa-gumi, the organization that had given a burakumin outcast power and wealth.

"There's one thing I don't get, boss," Kotarō said.

"Only one?" Kinosuke teased.

Shigure couldn't help admiring Kotarō's newfound confidence as he watched the young man ignore the chuckles around him, the way he still called Shigure boss warming him deep inside.

"You said Kenshin-san's father is only worried that the press might find out that his son has yakuza connections," Kotarō went on, "but if you're not a yakuza anymore, won't he leave Kenshin alone? I mean, quitting the Shinagawa is not enough? Do you and Kenshin still have to go to America?"

"Kenshin is a foreigner, Kotarō. As an artist, he'd be allowed to stay in Japan for three years, but if he wanted to stay longer after that, he'd have to apply for naturalization, which means he'd have to give up US citizenship—supposing he'd be granted Japanese nationality in the end."

"And you can't trust the fucking senator to keep from trying to screw Kenshin-san anyway," Kinosuke added, "yakuza connections or no."

"Yeah. You know how the saying goes: 'keep your friends close, and your enemies closer.' I can't anticipate the man's moves from here, and Kenshin'll have more resources in America if he is to fight back."

"Won't you become the foreigner in America, boss?" Shinya asked.

He shrugged. "Better me than Kenshin. I don't mind if I have to rough it for some time."

"But how will you manage to get in there?"

cared about Shigure's long years of unwavering loyalty, hadn't even cared about having to replace him in the trusted position he'd occupied as an underboss. All he'd cared about was the money he could get when he sold Shigure's valuables.

The integrity the gaijin cops had shown, though, had been a surprise. They had contacted Shigure to warn him about the intentions of Kenshin's father, putting their careers on the line for what they thought was the right thing to do.

There were still people who lived by honor, it seemed, and Shigure hoped he himself was one of those few. That was why he now sat formally on the thick towels, in front of the low table with all the items he would need.

He hadn't told anyone about this. The house was empty, in fact, his men believing he wanted a chance to say goodbye to the place that had been his true home for years. His pride wouldn't allow witnesses to watch his penance. It was a private matter between him and the man whose name had been carefully written on the padded envelope.

Pride had blinded him before, made him turn his head and ignore what had been right in front of him, and the harm that followed could never be undone. Now it was time to pay for his mistakes, and pride would keep his hand steady.

He pulled the tantō out of its plain scabbard and laid it on the towel that covered part of the table. He smiled to himself. This was not done for show, so he wasn't going to pull a stunt like those guys in *jitsuroku* movies who acted like trained sushi chefs with their chopping boards.

He held the leather-bound handle with his right hand, keeping the spine of the blade pressed against the towel. Then he carefully placed the first knuckle of his left little finger on the sharp edge and inhaled deeply.

He closed his eyes to focus on his breathing, keeping it deep, the muscles on his stomach expanding and contracting, slowly changing his awareness of time. When an image of Kenshin's face filled his mind, he let those captivating eyes guide his vision and simply bent over, his own body weight pressing his finger against the blade.

It made no sound as it fell on the towel, that small piece of flesh and bone, and everything else became a noiseless explosion of two colors, the dazzling white of sharp pain and the furious red of fresh blood as it splattered onto the white towels.

So much blood, Shigure thought distantly when the pain began to ebb. He reached out for the gauze and pressed it against the open wound, wondering how long Kenshin had been forced to watch blood oozing from his injuries, probably wishing he'd been left to die that way, painlessly bleeding onto the cement floor.

"I hope you will forgive me someday, Kenshin, because my life belongs to you now."

There'd be time to pick up the mess before he left to pay a visit to a trusted doctor. He'd have to remember to open all the doors, all the windows, so that not even the smell of blood remained. Nobody but those closest to him would know about this. But he still had to let one person know.

He pressed fresh gauze onto the wound and taped it. The small knuckle was covered in blood, so he took his time cleaning it before uncapping the bottle with alcohol and placing it inside. He then replaced the seal and studied the kanji depicting his full name on the small label.

"Should've written it in romaji," he said aloud, chuckling.

Or maybe not. He guessed Senator Harris had enough money to pay for a translation.

EPILOGUE

"HEY Ed, here comes a plane from Tokyo."

US Customs and Border Protection Officer Edward Rowling shifted nervously, making his brand-new shoes creak. He actually felt his whole uniform might creak, too, alerting every passenger arriving at Honolulu International Airport of his rookie status.

"Yakuza screening?" he asked his supervisor, Officer John Kimber.

"You know it, kid."

He forced himself not to roll his eyes at being called a kid. If he ignored the ribbing, he might learn something from his "ancient" supervisor.

"Should we look for missing pinkies and full body tattoos?"

"Nah. Those times are long gone. Crooks these days don't have the balls it takes to cut off your own finger or spend years being jabbed at with handmade bamboo needles."

"So, what are we looking for?"

"Guys in Armani suits."

He counted to five before Kimber cracked up. That little trick had saved him a lot of embarrassment over the previous days. "Stop teasing me, will you?"

"Okay, kid. But, so you know, some of those guys do wear Armani."

He finally had to roll his eyes, and his partner chuckled.

"Okay, okay. Now, the way to spot a bunch of yakuza is this— you watch the passengers walk."

Ed raised an eyebrow.

"I'm serious, kid. Japanese tourists, they walk sort of respectfully, you know? As if they were being polite about the whole walking thing."

"And yakuza don't?"

"Nope. They swagger."

"Uh-huh."

There was no time for more expert opinion as passengers started trickling through the gate. He studied the way they walked. He would never say it out loud, but he loved watching the light-framed, fine-boned Japanese, especially the men—though he really hoped his colleagues wouldn't notice, since he wasn't out to them. He had a good excuse, after all. It'd be a waste of time to look for yakuza among the women.

Japanese men dressed in style, their lean bodies making the most of the expensive casual gear they wore with the confidence of runway models. They didn't walk like models, though. His partner was right in this. They walked kind of humbly, trying to disappear into the crowd, most probably intimidated by the fact that they were entering a different country with a whole new set of rules—and a lot of rude gaijin to boot.

"Holy shit."

He turned to follow the direction of his partner's gaze and had to fight very hard to keep his mouth from hanging open.

The sea of passengers parted easily to make way for a group of six men who marched determinedly forward. Ed didn't know where to look first, his eyes shifting from the two shorter guys—one Japanese, the other Caucasian—in gothic outfits, to the four men in suits walking—swaggering—behind them. Jesus. He couldn't tell an Armani from a Hugo Boss, but those weren't your everyday salarymen for sure.

"Fuck me sideways. Would you look at those tattoos?"

Tattoos? Ed looked at the gothic boys, since they were the only ones wearing sleeveless clothes—sort of. His eyes were drawn to the Caucasian guy, who appeared gorgeously freakish with his hair and eyebrows bleached white, contacts in two different colors, knee-high black leather buckle boots, skinny leather pants, and a tight leather vest over some kind of mesh fabric that, rather than conceal, made the tattoos on his arms stand out even more.

Damn. He'd seen dragon tattoos before, but those flat, comic-like monsters had nothing to do with the live beast that crawled up one slender arm, every feature delicately shaded, bright red fire coming from its open mouth, billowing clouds of white and blue partly hiding the long tail that ended down the other arm.

"If I didn't know better, I'd swear there's a candid camera somewhere close. Tattoos and missing pinkies. Fucking unbelievable."

Oh Christ. The sexy freak was reaching out with his left hand to take what looked like a passport from the imposing guy right behind him, the tip of the little finger conspicuously missing from both their hands.

Ed looked at the guy acting like top boss and met black murderous eyes head-on. Shit. He was the authority here, and he shouldn't feel like a rabbit in front of a salivating wolf, for Christ's sake. But the guy seemed to emanate power in waves. He wasn't tall, but broad, his compact body filling an elegant dark suit, rough features giving him a dangerous allure.

He told himself he wasn't looking away but merely checking the threat the other guys posed, though it might have been a big mistake. He didn't really know where to look to keep his composure.

"This looks like the cast for the Japanese *Godfather*," Kimber said.

He couldn't agree more. There was a guy with a scar running along the left side of his face, another wearing enough shoulder padding to play for the Hawaii Warriors, and walking—no, that was pure strutting, all right—beside the alpha male was another fine example of Japanese gorgeousness, of the cockiest variety: thick black hair falling over scowling eyes, collar buttons undone, loose tie, and pointy shoes.

Then again, what were the two goths doing with a bunch of yakuza-looking toughs?

"Couldn't they be a couple of singers with their bodyguards?" Ed asked.

Bleach Hair sure was drop-dead stunning. And the other one was cute too—a little too much on the young side for Ed's taste, but he looked like one of those teen celebrities the Japanese were so crazy about.

"We'll find out soon enough. Here comes the freak show."

Ed moved in sync with his partner to block the group's advance.

"Passports, please." Kimber didn't bother with the few Japanese words they'd been taught as a polite greeting, and Ed tried to mimic his partner's authoritative stance. The way the group reacted, subtly rearranging itself into a defensive formation around the two goths, seemed to confirm his bodyguard theory.

"Here's mine," Bleach Hair said, handing over a US passport and turning to Big Bad Wolf. "And you have the rest, Shigure, don't you?"

"Yeah."

Well, at least the guy seemed to understand English. It might have been Ed's imagination, too, but he'd have sworn the odd couple had exchanged a significant glance. Yeah, right, as if. It must be one of those days his gaydar chose to go into overdrive.

Kimber took the offered documents and started inspecting them. Japanese passports were so nice to look at, with all those flowery symbols and weird letters, that Ed glanced down at them for a second, taking his eyes off the group.

"Shit, Kenshin, I told you they'd figure you out."

There was a moment of panic when everybody tensed, Kimber reaching for his holster and sending a warning glance in Ed's direction, while the young punk in the pointy shoes went on in the same nonchalant drawl. "Shouldn't have bothered with the fucking contacts. You can't hide what planet you come from."

A hand shot out to whack at the punk's head. "Shut up, Kinosuke."

"*Hai*, boss."

Ed couldn't stop staring. Jesus. These guys were something—joking in front of two armed cops. They were either too brash for their own good or too used to traveling abroad to fret about customs procedures.

"Sorry, officers. My friend was just kidding," Bleach Hair said, and added in a stage whisper, "I can't tell you which is worse, dealing with the members of a teenage boy band or with their bodyguards. Can't decide who's more brattish of the two."

"Boy band?" Kimber asked, but Ed was too busy trying to rein in his smile. He'd guessed right. His partner might be the veteran, but Ed had good instincts for a rookie, even if he said so himself.

"Yeah. *Heru*—as in the Japanized English for 'hell.' Kotarō here is their singer," Bleach Hair said, pointing to the cute Japanese goth. "They're the latest hit in Japanese charts, so much so that we've had to book a recording studio in Maui to be able to work in peace. And of course send each band member on a different plane to avoid the fans. 'Hell' might just be the right word for them, if you know what I mean."

Even his dour partner smiled at that, and Ed all but beamed at the gorgeous Bleach Hair. He still couldn't work out what the missing pinkie thing was about, but show-business people were said to lead wild lives, weren't they?

"Everything's fine. Welcome to Hawaii, gentlemen," Kimber said, handing back the passports to the bodyguard team leader.

Big Wolf nodded to them like one of those samurais in Kurosawa's movies, managing to appear both respectful and forbidding in the same gesture. Then, without even looking down, he laid the hand with the missing pinkie on the small of Bleach Hair's back and gently steered him away, the other guys moving to cover the young singer's back like a well-trained army unit.

"Fuck," Kimber said in an amused tone, and Ed simply nodded, grinning, his eyes still glued to that big hand where it rested possessively on the smaller man's back as the group slowly disappeared from view. It seemed his gaydar was working just fine, after all.

H.J. BRUES lives in Spain, enjoying the hot weather, the brisk language, the warm-hearted people, and the thousands of books of the library she works in. She has a degree in medieval history and loves castles, knights in shining armor, and barbarian warriors with no armor at all. She practiced fencing till her knees started complaining, took archery till her elbow almost fell off, and then, wisely, switched to the less martial of the martial arts, tai chi.

You can contact H.J. Brues at hjbrues@gmail.com.

Also by H.J. Brues

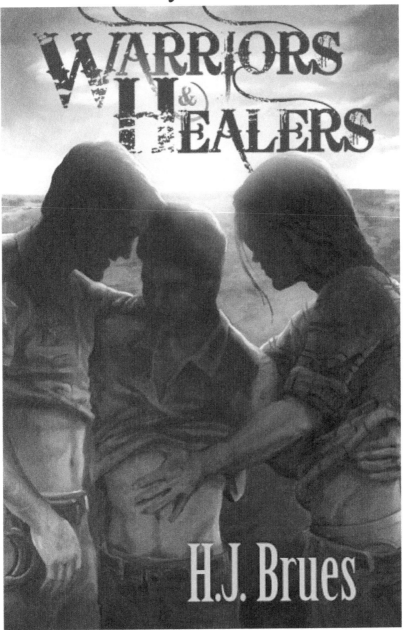

From DREAMSPINNER PRESS

Lightning Source UK Ltd.
Milton Keynes UK
UKOW06f1954210715

255602UK00018B/488/P